An Amish Heirloom

Other Books by the Authors

Amy Clipston

The Amish Homestead Series
A Place at Our Table
Room on the Porch Swing
(available April 2018)

The Amish Heirloom Series
The Forgotten Recipe
The Courtship Basket
The Cherished Quilt
The Beloved Hope Chest

The Hearts of the Lancaster Grand Hotel Series
A Hopeful Heart
A Mother's Secret
A Dream of Home
A Simple Prayer

The Kauffman Amish Bakery Series
A Gift of Grace
A Promise of Hope
A Place of Peace
A Life of Joy
A Season of Love

Young Adult
Roadside Assistance
Reckless Heart
Destination Unknown
Miles from Nowhere

Novellas
A Plain and Simple Christmas
Naomi's Gift included in *An Amish Christmas Gift*
A Spoonful of Love included in *An Amish Kitchen*
A Son for Always included in *An Amish Cradle*

Love Birds included in *An Amish Market*
Love and Buggy Rides included in *An Amish Harvest*
Home Sweet Home included in *An Amish Home*
Summer Storms included in *An Amish Summer*
The Christmas Cat included in *An Amish Christmas Love*

Non-fiction
A Gift of Love

Beth Wiseman

The Amish Secrets Novels
Her Brother's Keeper
Love Bears All Things
Home All Along

The Daughters of the Promise Novels
Plain Perfect
Plain Pursuit
Plain Promise
Plain Paradise
Plain Proposal
Plain Peace

The Land of Canaan Novels
Seek Me with All Your Heart
The Wonder of Your Love
His Love Endures Forever

Other Novels
Need You Now
The House that Love Built
The Promise

Novellas
A Choice to Forgive included in *An Amish Christmas*

An Amish Heirloom

Amy Clipston,
Beth Wiseman,
Kathleen Fuller,
Kelly Irvin

ZONDERVAN®

ZONDERVAN

Amish Heirloom

Copyright© 2018 by Amy Clipston, Beth Wiseman, Kathleen Fuller, and Kelly Irvin

This title is also available as a Zondervan e-book.

Requests for information should be addressed to:

Zondervan, *3900 Sparks Dr. SE, Grand Rapids, Michigan 49546*

Library of Congress Cataloging-in-Publication

Names: Clipston, Amy, author. | Wiseman, Beth, 1962- author. | Fuller,
  Kathleen, author. | Irvin, Kelly, author.
Title: An Amish heirloom : a legacy of love, the cedar chest, the treasured
  book, a midwife's dream / Amy Clipston, Beth Wiseman, Kathleen Fuller, and
  Kelly Irvin.
Description: Nashville : Zondervan, 2018.
Identifiers: LCCN 2017048417 | ISBN 9780310351887 (paperback)
Subjects: LCSH: Amish--Fiction. | GSAFD: Love stories. | Christian fiction.
Classification: LCC PS3603.L58 A45 2018 | DDC 813/.6--dc23 LC record available at
  https://lccn.loc.gov/2017048417

Printed in the United States of America

18 19 20 21 22 / LSC / 5 4 3 2 1

Contents

Glossary

ach: oh
aenti: aunt
appeditlich: delicious
bedauerlich: sad
bopli/boppli: baby
boplin: babies
bruder: brother
bruders: brothers
bu: boy
buwe: boys
daadi: grandfather
daed: father
danki: thank you
dat: dad
dawdy/daadi haus: grandparents' house
Dietsch: Pennsylvania Dutch, the Amish language (German dialect)
dochder: daughter
Englisch/Englischer: English or Non-Amish
fraa: wife
freind: friend

freinden: friends

froh: happy

gegisch: silly

geh: go

gelassenheit: fundamental Amish belief in yielding fully to God's will and forsaking all selfishness

gern gschehne: you're welcome

Gmay: Church District

Gott: God

granddaadi/groossdaadi: grandpa

grandmammi/groossmammi: grandma

gut: good

Gut nacht: Good night

haus: house

Ich liebe dich: I love you

jah: yes

kaffee/kaffi: coffee

kapp: prayer covering or cap

kichli: cookie

kichlin: cookies

kinner: children

lieb: love

liewe: love, a term of endearment

maed: young women, girls

maedel: young woman

mamm: mom

mammi: grandmother

mann: man

mei: my

mudder: mother

naerfich: nervous

narrisch: crazy

nee: no

Ordnung: the oral tradition of practices required and forbidden in
the Amish faith

rumspringa: running-around period when a teenager turns
sixteen years old

schee: pretty

schtupp: family room

schweschder: sister

schweschdere/schweschders: sisters

sohn/suh: son

Was iss letz?: What's wrong?

Wie bischt?: How's it going?

Wie geht's: How do you do? or Good day!

wunderbaar/wunderbarr: wonderful

ya: yes

yer: your

yerself: yourself

yung: young

*The German dialect spoken by the Amish is not a written language and varies depending on the location and origin of the settlement. These spellings are approximations. Most Amish children learn English after they start school. They also learn high German, which is used in their Sunday services.

Legacy of Love

AMY CLIPSTON

In loving memory of my grandparents,
Emilie and Emil Goebelbecker

Featured Amish Homestead Series Characters

Frieda m. Menno King
Benuel ("Ben")
Leon

Orpha m. Phares Bontrager
Susie
Betty

Marilyn m. Willie Dienner
Simeon (deceased)
Kayla
Nathan

Eva m. Simeon (deceased) Dienner
Simeon Jr. ("Junior")

Dorothy (deceased) m. Vernon Riehl
James ("Jamie")
Mark (Laura's twin)
Laura (Mark's twin)
Cindy

Elsie m. Noah Zook
Christian

CHAPTER 1

Leon King swallowed the swelling lump of emotion that threatened to choke him as he stood in a cemetery, surrounded by a multitude of community members. He was vaguely aware that the warm September sun was beating down on his shoulders and black hat, but he didn't care. He was staring at the moist earth covering the grave of his friend Charlie Glick.

As the minister began reciting a closing prayer, Leon lifted his head to observe Minerva Yoder, Charlie's fiancée. Tears poured down her cheeks, and she gripped her father's arm as if it were a lifeline.

Leon had seen Charlie only a couple of weeks ago. Their volunteer fire companies both responded to a call, a traffic accident on Lincoln Highway in Paradise. The two men worked together to free the passengers from a car pummeled by a tractor trailer, and once the injured were loaded into ambulances, they chatted as they cleared the scene. Charlie talked about his upcoming wedding and moving into the house he'd built on his father's farm.

But now Charlie was dead. Two days earlier he'd been hit by lightning while repairing shingles on his father's dairy barn. He was gone in an instant. And he was only twenty-five years old, the same age as Leon.

Leon looked to his right. His friend and fellow volunteer firefighter Jamie Riehl stood with his girlfriend, Kayla Dienner. Kayla sniffed and wiped her eyes, and Jamie released her hand and put one arm around her shoulders. She leaned against him. Like Minerva, Kayla seemed to rely on someone else to hold her upright.

The affection between Jamie and Kayla touched Leon deep in his soul, surprising him. And then an unexpected thought overwhelmed him.

He was alone.

He hadn't had a serious girlfriend in nearly four years. He had no one to comfort, no one special to encourage him after a tough day at the fire station or working at his father's furniture store.

A nagging hollowness filled his gut as his gaze moved back to the grave. He couldn't allow himself to waste another day. He was ready to find someone special and settle down.

He looked again at Charlie's grave, and a chill moved down his spine at another gripping thought. *I don't want to die alone.*

When the minister's prayer ended, a murmur of conversations spread throughout the crowd, and community members slowly and quietly began to make their way to the buggies that lined the long street.

Leon turned to Jamie and Kayla.

"I can't believe he's gone." Jamie spoke in a low voice and shook his head. "We just saw him at that traffic accident a few weeks ago."

Leon sighed. *"Ya."*

"We never know God's plan for us," Kayla nearly whispered, and her shoulders shuddered slightly, as though she was still trying to regain her composure.

Jamie nodded. "We have to appreciate every day the Lord gives us."

Leon cleared his throat against another knot of emotion as his friends studied each other for a moment. What was wrong with him? Why was he so sensitive today? It wasn't as though he hadn't seen grief before—or two people in love.

He needed to change the subject before his emotions got the better of him in public.

"Are you volunteering this week, Jamie?"

"*Ya.* I'm on for Friday."

"I am too." Leon folded his arms over his chest. He looked past Jamie, and his breath stalled in his lungs as his gaze landed on Susie Bontrager, his ex-girlfriend. They worshiped in different church districts, and he hadn't seen her for a couple of years. Her eyes met his, and a smile tugged at the corners of her lips. She gave him a little wave. He returned the gesture.

Susie was standing with her fiancé, Joshua Chupp. She looked up at him and said something, and then they both started walking toward Leon. The muscles in Leon's shoulders tightened. Susie's face was radiant with a bright smile, and she was as pretty as ever.

"I'm going to take Kayla back to her family's restaurant," Jamie said, yanking Leon from his thoughts. "I'll see you at the station on Friday."

"*Ya.*" Leon nodded at Kayla. "Take care."

"I'm sure I'll see you at the restaurant soon." Kayla gave him a shy smile before taking Jamie's hand and leaving with him through the crowd.

"Leon." As Susie came close, her blue-green eyes sparkled in the midmorning sunlight. "How are you?"

"I'm *gut.*" He smiled at her and then nodded at Josh, who returned the greeting.

"You know Josh, right?" Susie touched Josh's arm.

"Of course I do." Leon swallowed a chuckle. "We were all in the same combined youth group when we were teenagers."

"Right. I forgot that." Susie's cheeks blushed, a pretty complement to the bright-red hair peeking out from under her prayer covering. "We're getting married in November."

Josh nodded. "I'd heard that. Congratulations."

A man appeared beside Josh and touched his shoulder. Josh looked at Leon and then at Susie, as though he might be reluctant to leave them alone. "Excuse me," he said before stepping away.

As Leon was drawn to Susie's gorgeous eyes, regret slammed through him. Why had he let her slip through his fingers four years ago? "You look *gut*."

"You do too." She smiled up at him, but then her smile faded. "I was sorry to hear about Charlie. He was one of Josh's cousins."

Leon grimaced. "I didn't know that. I'm sorry for Josh and his family."

"*Danki*. It was a shock. Charlie's *dat* said it wasn't even raining when it happened. The storm popped out of nowhere, completely unexpected." She clasped her hands together. "Are you still volunteering with the fire department?"

"*Ya*. I volunteer one or two days every week."

"I remember how much you loved it. Is that how you met Charlie?"

"*Ya*. We saw each other on quite a few calls. I just saw him at the scene of an accident a couple of weeks ago."

"Josh and I saw him at church on Sunday. I didn't imagine we'd bury him today. You see someone one day, and then the Lord calls him home the next. Change can come in an instant."

"*Ya*."

And then only silence passed between them as they stared at each other for a moment. He longed to know what she was thinking. Was she remembering their time together as boyfriend and girlfriend? Did she ever miss him? Why, after all these years, did he suddenly feel this rush of attraction toward his ex-girlfriend— especially when she was engaged to someone else?

"I was wondering if I could ask you a favor. I've been planning to get in touch with you." Susie's words crashed through his thoughts.

"Sure." He folded his arms over his black vest and white shirt. "What do you need?"

"*Mei mammi* left me two rocking chairs. Do you remember them? They were always in our *schtupp*."

"*Ya*, I remember them. I sat in them quite a few times." Susie had been so close to her grandmother. Leon knew those chairs meant a great deal to her.

"Right. I was wondering if you could repair them for me."

"I'd be *froh* to. What's wrong with them?"

"The pieces of wood that make up the back." She pointed toward her spine. "You know, where you rest your back?"

He tried in vain to fight a grin. "You mean the spindles?"

"Right." She gave a little laugh, and she looked adorable. "They're loose on both chairs. The arms are loose as well. Come to think of it, the legs and rockers are too. *Mei dat* says they can be repaired, but he's not a furniture expert. I also think they need to be restained. It's been a long time since anyone cleaned them up."

"I can sand them down and restain them for you, as well as make the repairs. Just bring them by the store."

"*Wunderbaar*," she said with a wide smile. "I'll pay you, of course."

He shrugged. "All right. I can fit them in between projects I'm doing for *mei dat*. How soon do you need them back?"

"Not until the end of November. I want to put them in our new *haus*. Josh is building it on his *dat*'s farm, and he says I can decorate and furnish it any way I want. I always dreamt of putting the chairs in *mei haus. Mammi* left *mei schweschder* her hope chest, but she knew how much the rockers meant to me." She blushed. "I'm sorry. I'm babbling."

"It's fine. It's *gut* to talk to you. It's been a long time."

"*Ya.*" She nodded. "I haven't seen you since last year, right? When some of our *freinden* went to the lake. Or was that two summers ago?"

"I think so. You weren't dating Josh then, were you?"

She shook her head. "No. We've been together only a year."

"Oh." Once again he took in her beautiful face. How did Josh convince Susie to marry him in a year? Of course, marriage was what Susie had wanted.

Why did he care? It was none of his business. Not now.

"I'll bring those chairs to the store tomorrow."

"That would be perfect," he told her.

Josh returned and touched Susie's arm. "I'm ready to go now," he said.

Leon said good-bye to the couple and then made his way to his buggy through the thinning crowd of mourners. He was sad about losing Charlie, but at the same time seeing Susie lifted his spirits—even though she was engaged to another man.

Leon's Sunday best now hung on a peg in the restroom, where he'd changed into his work clothes before stepping into the workroom at Lancaster Furniture Sales and Repair. His older brother, Ben, was working on a wingchair. "How was the funeral?"

"*Bedauerlich.*" Leon took a bottle of water from the propane refrigerator at the back of the room, and then he went to his work area and hopped up on a stool. "Minerva Yoder is his fiancée, and she sobbed through most it. His *mamm* did too."

Ben blanched and sat down on a stool beside the chair he'd been repairing. "*Ach*, that had to be tough to see."

"It was." Leon opened the bottle and took a long drink as his thoughts turned to Susie. She was still so stunning. Her red hair and striking eyes had made her the most alluring young woman in his youth group. It took him a year to work up the courage to ask her to be his girlfriend. He'd convinced himself she would say no, but she'd responded with an excited yes. In fact, she said she'd hoped he would ask her.

Then after two years everything fell apart when she told him she wanted more out of their relationship. She wanted marriage, and he'd had no choice but to admit he wasn't ready to take that step. He was only twenty-one. Almost before he knew it, they'd broken up.

"Leon?"

"Huh?" Leon's gaze snapped to his brother.

"Where did you go just now?"

"Go?" Leon lifted an eyebrow.

Ben laughed as he pointed at him. "You were lost in thought. What's on your mind?"

As he debated how much to share with his brother, Leon squeezed the bottle of water, which crinkled in protest.

"You don't have to tell me, little *bruder*." Ben stood and returned to repairing a leg on the wingchair.

Leon usually didn't appreciate Ben's little reminders that he was two years older. Strangers would have no idea which brother, both with the dark eyes and dark hair inherited from their father, was the eldest. But today he'd ignore his comment.

"I'll tell you." Leon pushed off the stool. "I saw Susie at the cemetery."

"Susie?" Ben turned toward him. "Susie Bontrager?"

"*Ya.*" Leon finished his water and tossed the bottle into the nearby trash can. "Josh Chupp was there too. They're getting married in November, and they were at the funeral because Charlie was Josh's cousin. Susie asked if she could bring her grandmother's rocking chairs here for me to restain and repair, and I assured her she could. She wants to put them in her new *haus.*"

He paused. "She looked really *gut.*"

"Okay." Ben sank down onto his stool. "Susie is getting married?"

"Right."

"Then why are we even talking about her?"

"We're not. I'm just telling you she's bringing in her rocking chairs." Leon turned toward his work area and studied the bureau he'd started to sand before heading to the funeral. He pulled on his face mask, retrieved his sanding block, and set to work trying to erase Susie's attractive smile from his mind.

Then Ben appeared beside him, and Leon jumped with a start.

"What?" Leon pulled off his mask and glared up at his brother.

"Forget the rocking chairs. Do you still have feelings for Susie?"

Leon frowned. Why had he told Ben anything?

Ben lightly punched his arm. "You do! Leon, you need to let that go if she's getting married. Besides, you two broke up . . . what? Four years ago? Why would you even consider—"

"Leon!" *Dat* had appeared in the doorway, and Leon blew out a sigh of relief.

"I didn't even know you were back. You must've slipped in the back door. How was the funeral?"

"It was really *bedauerlich.*" As Leon recounted some details about the funeral, he was thankful his father had interrupted Ben's interrogation. He didn't want to discuss his confusing feelings about Susie with his brother.

But he had to admit the truth to himself. He was looking forward to seeing her again.

CHAPTER 2

Susie Bontrager stared up at the Lancaster Furniture Sales and Repair sign. It seemed like only yesterday she was visiting Leon in his father's store after shopping at the market. They'd been dating then.

Betty, her younger sister, tapped her shoulder. "Suze? Are you going to get out of the truck? Or are you going to stare at that sign all afternoon?"

"Oh, right." Susie pushed open the passenger door of her driver's four-door pickup truck and climbed down as her sister exited from the backseat. "I'll go see if Leon and Ben will carry the chairs inside for us."

"I can take one of them."

Susie spun and then swallowed a gasp. Leon stood grinning at her from the sidewalk in front of the store. "You startled me." Had he been standing at the window, watching her stare at the store's sign like a dope?

"I'm sorry. I thought you saw me come out. I was working the front of the store when I saw the truck pull up." Leon stepped off the sidewalk and moved to the bed of the truck where Grayson, her driver, stood waiting. "I've been watching for you."

"You have?" Susie blinked.

"*Ya.*" Leon's smile seemed . . . sheepish. "Is that bad?"

"No." Susie shook her head. *But it's surprising.*

Grayson dropped the tailgate and picked up *Mammi*'s chair. Leon grabbed *Daadi*'s.

"I'll get the door." Susie jogged over and pulled it open.

Leon and Grayson carried the rocking chairs through the showroom and toward the workroom as Susie and Betty entered the store.

"Susie! Betty!" Leon's father came around the front counter and shook Susie's hand. *"Wie geht's?"*

"Hi, Menno. We're well. How are you?" Susie always found herself marveling at how similar Leon's eyes were to his father's and brother's. They reminded her of melted chocolate.

Betty sidled up to Susie and extended her hand as well. "It's nice to see you, Menno."

"Leon told me you were going to bring your grandparents' rocking chairs in for repair." He leaned back against the counter. "He's excited to work on them."

"He is?" Susie asked.

"*Ya*, he is." Menno touched his graying brown beard. "How are your parents doing?"

"They're well," Betty chimed in. "The farm keeps us all busy. *Dat* hired a couple of *buwe* from my youth group to help him. Susie and I are still helping *Mamm* with all the household chores and quilting."

"I haven't seen your *dat* in a while. Tell him to stop in the store sometime. Or I suppose I can go to see him."

"Susie."

Susie turned toward the doorway that led to the workroom. Leon was beckoning her.

"Could you come here for a moment?" he asked.

"*Ya.*" Susie looked at his father. "Excuse me." As she approached Leon, she took in his face. She'd forgotten how handsome he was with his intelligent dark eyes, dark-brown hair, strong jaw, broad shoulders, and wide chest. He was muscular too, as though he spent hours every day working on a farm, not making and repairing furniture.

She bit back another gasp. How dare she contemplate how attractive she found her ex-boyfriend? She was engaged! Josh would be hurt if he could read her mind.

Leon raised his eyebrows as she came closer, and she shook off her inappropriate thoughts. The sweet scents of wood and stain filled her senses as she stepped into the workroom.

"What do you need?" She hoped her cheeks didn't radiate embarrassment as she went to stand beside him.

"I'm sorry to interrupt you." Leon gestured toward the rocking chairs sitting in the middle of the workshop as Grayson and Ben inspected them. "Ben asked me how old the chairs are, and I don't know. Do you?"

"*Mei daadi* made them for *mei mammi* as a wedding gift. They have to be at least sixty years old."

"Really?" Ben's face lit up. "I can't get over the intricate carvings." He ran his fingers over the top of one chair. "I suppose this one with the carved flowers was for your *mammi?*"

"*Ya.*" Susie walked over to the other chair. "The one with flowers was for *Mammi* and the one with the more masculine-looking carvings was for *Daadi.*"

"They're stunning. And I love that your *daadi* used hickory," Grayson said. "You must cherish these."

"I do." Susie's chest swelled with gratitude mixed with bereavement as she thought of her grandparents. "I'm so thankful *mei mammi* gave them to me."

"And you're going to let *mei bruder* work on them?" Ben said, clearly teasing. "Maybe you should take them to a professional."

Susie clicked her tongue and looked at Leon. "That's not nice, and it's not true."

"He's got a point." Leon flinched and then jammed his thumb toward the doorway. "You might want to ask *mei dat* to work on them. In fact, let me go get him. He can look at them right now."

"No." Susie shook her head. "I want you to rebuild them. I've seen your work. I still have the nightstand you gave me for Christmas."

"You do?" Something unreadable flashed across his face. Was it shock? Or maybe appreciation?

"Of course I do." She looked at Ben. "I'm sure Leon will do a great job on the chairs for me."

"All right." Ben shrugged as a smile curved his lips. "They're your chairs." He looked over at Grayson. "Do you still want to look at our buffets? We have one or two in oak."

"Yes, that would be great." Grayson turned to Susie. "I'm going to go look at some furniture. I want to surprise my wife with something nice for our anniversary. I won't be long."

"Take your time," Susie said.

After Grayson and Ben left the workroom, Susie fingered her apron as she looked at Leon. "I know Ben was teasing you, but you'll do a great job with the chairs. When *mei dat* suggested I have them repaired, I immediately thought of you."

The strange expression that had flickered over his face earlier returned for a fraction of a second, and then it disappeared. "You thought of me?"

"*Ya.*" She shrugged. "Why wouldn't I? I know how talented you are."

He crossed the room and came to stand beside her. "I'll take *gut* care of the chairs."

She looked up at him and silently marveled at how he towered over her by several inches. She'd forgotten how tall he was. He stood just over six feet, a couple of inches taller than Josh.

He touched the spindles on *Daadi*'s chair. "I always marveled at your *daadi*'s talent when I sat in this chair." Then he nodded toward his work area. "I have to finish staining that bureau this afternoon, but I can get started on these on Saturday."

"Are you volunteering tomorrow?"

"*Ya*, I am." He pointed toward the refrigerator at the back of the shop. "Would you like a bottle of water? I think Grayson is going to be awhile looking at our buffets."

She hesitated, but then she nodded as the thought of getting caught up with Leon warmed her heart. And since Betty hadn't appeared, she suspected she was content talking with Menno out in the showroom. "*Ya. Danki.*"

He took out two bottles of water and handed one to her. "Have a seat." He gestured to the stool in Ben's work area, and then he sat down across from her on the stool in his. She hopped onto the stool, opened the bottle of water, and took a drink.

"How is Charlie's family doing?" Leon asked.

"We visited with his parents last night, and they're having a tough time." She took a deep breath as tears stung her eyes. "Minerva is absolutely broken. I can't imagine losing my fiancé like that. Charlie was supposed to visit her that night, and when he didn't show up, she assumed he'd been called to the firehouse. But then his *bruder* arrived with the news." She took another deep breath in hopes of keeping her tears at bay.

"I'm so sorry to hear that. When Simeon Dienner died last

year while on a fire call, he left a *fraa*. And she was expecting a *boppli*. Loss is difficult."

"It is, but we must put our faith and trust in the Lord. He'll get us through it."

"That's right." He took a long draw from his bottle.

She fingered the label of her bottle as she studied him. "How are you doing?"

He shrugged. "I'm fine. I'm just busy with work here and at the firehouse."

"Are you seeing anyone?" The question surprised her. She hadn't planned on getting too personal, but curiosity overtook her shyness. She wanted to know who had Leon's heart.

"No." He shook his head and then took another drink.

"You're not?" She'd responded with yet another gasp and then longed to take back her reaction.

He raised his eyebrows. "Why is that so unbelievable?"

"I just assumed you would be. You're twenty-five, and you're, well, um . . ." Hot humiliation crawled up her neck to her cheeks. How could she tell him she'd thought he might even be married by now because he was handsome? That she'd been surprised to see him clean-shaven at the funeral, without a beard to signal he was a married man? Not only was it shallow to base her assumption on his looks, but it was also an inappropriate thing to tell her ex-boyfriend.

"I'm what?" He pinned her with a curious stare.

She quickly drank more than half her water, desperately trying to come up with an answer. Fortunately, she thought of one.

"Well, you're outgoing, and you have a lot of *freinden* in the community. I thought you might be getting married this fall too." When his smile returned, she swallowed a sigh of relief.

He shrugged. "I guess I just haven't found the right *maedel.*"

"I'm sure you will soon." She searched her mind for something safe to discuss. "How's your *mamm* doing?"

"She's fine." He rested his bottle on his knee as the conversation turned to mutual friends in the community.

"Susie?" Betty stood in the doorway. She gave Leon a smile and then turned back to Susie. "Grayson and Ben are loading up the buffet Grayson purchased for his *fraa.* We need to get going to the grocery store and then home to start supper. Josh is supposed to be out at our *haus* at five, and it's almost three."

"Oh my goodness! I didn't realize how long we'd been talking." Susie hopped down from the stool. "*Danki* for the water, Leon." She took a last sip and then tossed the empty bottle in a nearby trash can.

"*Gern gschehne.*" Leon followed them into the showroom. "I'll write up a ticket for the chairs."

"Let me know what I owe you," she said as they stopped at the counter.

He waved off the comment. "Don't worry about that now."

"Okay. Be careful tomorrow while you're on duty."

He raised an eyebrow. "I will."

"I think I'll come back and check on my chairs in a few days when I'm in town."

"You do that. You can make sure I haven't ruined them." He grinned and then looked past her. "Take care, Betty."

"'Bye, Leon!" Betty replied, and then she grabbed her sister's arm. "We need to go. You want to have supper ready when Josh arrives."

"It was *gut* seeing you," Susie told him before allowing Betty to steer her out of the store.

After saying good-bye to Ben and Menno, she climbed into

the truck. As they drove toward the market, she realized she was glad she'd see Leon again soon.

She wasn't quite sure what to do with that.

"Supper was *appeditlich*," Josh said later that evening as he sat beside Susie on her back porch. He stretched his arm out on the back of the swing, brushing it against her shoulders. "*Danki* for inviting me over tonight."

"*Gern gschehne.*" She smiled up at him, taking in his ice-blue eyes and warm smile. "I'm *froh* you could come."

"Well, it's not like it's a very long walk." He pointed toward the pasture fence that separated their two farms.

She laughed. "That's true."

"The sheetrock is almost all up in our *haus*. I should be painting early next week." He rubbed her shoulder, as if to emphasize the good news.

"That's *wunderbaar.*" She looked toward the house that stood at the back of his father's property and smiled. She couldn't wait to live there, and it was within walking distance. She could visit her parents' home as often as she wanted.

"I'm hoping to have the interior finished by the middle of October. Once that's done, I'll start moving in."

"Oh, that reminds me." She angled herself to face him. "I took my rocking chairs to Leon's store today. He's going to refurbish them for me."

"Oh." His smile dissolved. "Leon King?"

"*Ya.*" She nodded.

"Your ex-boyfriend."

"Right. You know he's a carpenter, like his *dat* and *bruder.*"

She studied the lines that popped up in his forehead. "Are you upset?"

"No, I'm not upset. I'm just a little surprised."

"Leon and I are still *freinden*. Our breakup was sort of a mutual thing. There's no animosity between us."

"I know." Josh looked toward her father's pasture.

"Josh, please look at me." Sudden worry had twisted her stomach into a knot.

"*Ya?*" He turned toward her.

"I'm marrying you, but Leon is still *mei freind*. You have nothing to worry about. Okay?"

Leon nodded, but his expression told her he wasn't convinced. "It's getting late." He removed his arm from her shoulders and stood. "I should get back home. I need to be up by five to start my chores."

"Okay." She stood as well and looked up at him. Josh was attractive, but in an ordinary sort of way, with his light-brown hair and kind face.

Why was she thinking about that now?

"Tell your parents I said hello, Josh."

"I will." Leaning down, he brushed his lips over her cheek.

She closed her eyes, but her body didn't react to his touch. Had she imagined the butterflies in her stomach when Leon used to kiss her cheek and hold her hand? She swallowed a groan. She had to stop these random musings about Leon.

"Susie?" Josh's eyes searched hers.

"*Ya?*" She froze, hoping she hadn't said her thoughts aloud.

"What are you thinking about?"

She shook her head. "Nothing, really."

"Oh. Okay." Josh looked out toward the pasture again.

A long silence followed their exchange, and Susie wished it wasn't always up to her to start a conversation.

She cleared her throat while racking her brain for something to say. "Josh, I was wondering if I'll see you tomorrow. Do you think you'll have time?"

"Oh." His expression relaxed. "I can come by around lunchtime."

"Perfect. I'll make you something special to eat." She squeezed his hand. "Sleep well tonight."

"You too." He touched her cheek. *"Gut nacht."*

"Gut nacht." She leaned against a porch post as Josh headed down the steps and strode toward the path that led to his father's farm. As she watched him, she wondered if someday they would easily chat back and forth about their day the way her parents did. Surely all married couples fell into that comfortable relationship eventually.

Didn't they?

CHAPTER 3

Thunder from the earlier storm still rumbled in the distance as Leon pulled off his helmet and set it on the bumper of the fire engine. He pushed his hand through his thick, sweaty hair. The air around him was heavy with a combination of smoke and humidity.

He turned to Jamie beside him and blew out a deep sigh. "It's a *gut* thing we got that brush fire out before it reached the barn. As dry as it's been, that barn could've gone up in smoke."

"That's the truth." Jamie lowered himself onto the bumper.

Leon's eyes moved to the two-story, white farmhouse across the street from the pasture where the brush fire had started. His chest constricted as his gaze focused on the second-story window on the right side of the house. That was Susie's window, and light was coming from there as well as from downstairs. Surely she and her family had been asleep when they arrived about an hour ago. The sirens and rattle of the diesel engine would have wakened them, but now it was probably close to midnight and they'd be going back to bed soon.

"Want some water?"

Leon turned to Noah Zook, who held up a bottle dripping with condensation.

"*Danki*. That would be great." Leon grabbed the bottle and opened it before taking a long drink. The cool liquid soothed his parched throat.

"We should be loading soon. Brody is finishing up." Noah nodded toward where their chief stood talking with the home-owner and the chief from the fire station in Ronks. That unit had also responded to the call.

Leon nodded and then took another long draw.

"Isn't that Susie's *haus*?" Jamie pointed his empty bottle toward the house across the street.

Leon choked. Taking deep gulps of air, he tried to stop the coughing fit that overtook him. He placed the bottle of water on the bumper and bent at the waist. When the coughing subsided, he looked up at Jamie, who raised an eyebrow.

"I didn't mean to get you all choked up about it." Jamie grinned.

Leon glowered as he picked up the half-empty bottle. He was in trouble now. The teasing and jabbing would begin, and most likely last throughout the rest of the night.

"I guess the answer is *ya*, huh?" Noah leaned against the truck.

Leon nodded as he cleared his throat.

"Who's Susie?" Noah asked.

"His ex." Jamie turned toward the house and his grin wid-ened. "Well now. Speaking of Susie . . ."

Leon turned toward the direction of Jamie's gaze, and then he swallowed. Susie, Betty, and their parents were all walking toward the fire engine. They each held a Coleman lantern, and the soft, yellow glow lit Susie's beautiful face.

"*Was iss letz*, Leon?" Noah nudged him with his shoulder. "Do you still have feelings for your ex?"

"No. I'm over her." Leon tried to wave off the comment, but he wasn't being truthful. "Besides, she's engaged."

"And you need to *remember* that," Jamie quipped.

Noah turned to Jamie. "Let's go see if we can help with cleanup. That way I can get back home, and you two can get back to the station and get some rest."

"*Gut* idea," Jamie said before he and Noah started for the other station's fire engine.

"Leon!" Susie's father called out as he approached the truck with his family in tow. "It's *gut* to see you."

"You too, Phares." Leon shook his hand and then nodded at the women.

"What happened?" Phares asked. "We waited to come until we thought we wouldn't be in the way."

"The pasture caught on fire." Leon pointed behind them. "It was lightning."

"Was anyone hurt?" Orpha asked, and he saw Susie place a comforting hand on her mother's arm.

"No." Leon pointed to the homeowner, who was talking to Brody, the fire chief. "Mose saw the strike and called right away. We got it before it spread to the barn or the *haus*."

"Oh, praise God," Phares said. "I'm going to check on Mose and see if he and his family need anything." He walked past Leon and headed for the house. "Mose! I'm so glad you're all right."

When Orpha and Betty followed Phares, Susie lingered behind. She was wearing a blue dress with a matching headscarf that complemented the errant fiery-colored wisps of hair that framed her face. Her blue-green eyes shimmered in the warm glow of the lantern.

She grinned up at him. "It's been a long time since I've seen you wearing your uniform."

"*Ya*, I suppose it has been awhile." He leaned back against the bumper. "How do I look?"

She scrunched her nose as if contemplating the question. She was adorable. "Old."

"Old?" He guffawed. "I'm only twenty-five."

"I meant to say older." She giggled, and he relished the sound. "It's been four years. You've changed a lot."

"I couldn't have changed too much."

"*Ya*, you have." She patted her chin as though trying to decide just how he'd changed. "You seem more mature."

He considered that. "I *am* more mature."

"I should hope so." Her grin was back. "I'm twenty-four now. Do I seem more mature?"

"You're still the sweet Susie I remember."

She stilled at the comment, and then she looked toward the truck. "When I heard the diesel engine and saw the lights reflecting off my bedroom wall, I hoped you were here."

"Really?" His insides warmed at her admission, and he worked to keep his expression nonchalant. *She's engaged! She's only* mei freind*!*

"*Ya*. I woke up my parents and Betty, and then we decided to come as soon as we could to make sure Mose and his family were okay." She looked toward her house and then back at him. "Was it difficult to douse the fire?"

"No. We got here before it spread too far. We quickly deployed hoses and put it out."

"I'm glad it was easy. Have you had any other calls tonight?"

"*Ya*." He lowered himself onto the bumper. "We had a car accident earlier in the evening."

Her eyes widened. "*Ach*, no. Was anyone hurt?"

"*Ya*." He rubbed his clean-shaven chin as the accident scene filled his mind. "An SUV ran a red light and a van hit it broadside. The SUV was flipped onto its roof." He went on to describe the scene as Susie listened, still wide-eyed. "The driver was banged up pretty badly, but he'll be fine. The driver of the van was stunned. She was going into shock when the ambulance took her."

"How *bedauerlich*. I'll pray for them."

"*Ya*, I will too." He nodded in the direction of her house. "You should probably get some sleep. It has to be close to midnight now."

"I'm not in a hurry. I'll wait for my family." She set the lantern on the bumper next to him. "You must be tired. Have you had any sleep tonight at all?"

"Very little." He swallowed a yawn. "I had just fallen asleep when the alarm went off. Jamie had to yell at me to get up."

She laughed. "You once told me you used to sleep through the alarm on your clock."

"*Ya, mei bruder* still has to wake me up sometimes." He rested his hands on his lap. "I bet you get up before the alarm even goes off."

She lifted her chin. "How did you know?"

"Because I know you better than you think."

They chuckled as Josh walked up behind Susie. Leon's back went rigid as Josh met his stare.

"Leon," Josh said with a curt nod before turning to Susie. "What are you doing out here so late?"

Her smiled faded as she looked up at him. "The same thing that probably brought you over from your *haus*. My family and I wanted to make sure Mose and his family are okay."

"What happened?" Josh asked.

"It was a brush fire." Leon stood up straight. "We got it out before it spread to the barn or *haus*."

"Oh." Josh studied Leon for a moment before turning his attention to the activity all around them.

Leon hoped Josh wasn't angry that he was talking to Susie. He hadn't seen Josh for a long time, but he'd hate to lose his friendship. Not only had they been members of the same youth group when they were teenagers, but they had talked occasionally since then.

Jamie came up behind Leon. "We're heading out. Hi, Susie."

"Hi, Jamie. It's been a long time." She gestured between Josh and Jamie. "This is my fiancé, Josh Chupp."

"I'm Jamie Riehl." Jamie shook Josh's hand.

"Nice to meet you," Josh said.

Jamie turned to Leon. "Brody is finishing up, and Noah is heading home. Maybe we can catch some sleep before the next call."

"We can hope, right?" Leon grinned.

"I'll walk you home, Susie," Josh told her. "It's late."

"I'll wait for my family." She pointed to where her father was still speaking with Mose.

Leon folded his arms over his turnout coat, and he took in Josh's pained expression as he looked toward Mose and Susie's family. Once again he hoped Josh wasn't upset because Susie was talking to him. Leon might regret letting Susie go, but he would never try to steal her from the man she loved.

Brody arrived and greeted Susie and Josh before beckoning to Leon and Jamie. "All right. Let's load up." He climbed into the driver's seat of the fire engine.

Jamie said good-bye to Susie and Josh and then climbed into the passenger seat.

"I'll see you soon." Leon gave Susie and Josh a wave, then went to the back door of the engine and wrenched it open as the diesel engine rattled to life.

"Wait." Susie jogged after him.

He held on to the door as he turned toward her.

She smiled up at him. "When I'm in town next week, I'll stop by to see how you're doing on the rocking chairs."

He looked past her to where Josh stood watching them, a little too intensely. But he looked down at Susie and smiled back. He couldn't be rude. "I don't know how far I'll get with the chairs, but you're always welcome to stop by."

"Great. *Gut nacht.*" She waved and then turned to rejoin Josh.

Leon climbed into the truck and slammed the door before buckling his seat belt.

As Brody steered the engine toward the main road, Jamie leaned into the backseat. "What was that about?"

"What do you mean?"

"You and Susie."

"I'm repairing two antique chairs that belonged to her grandparents. She wants to put them in her new *haus*." Leon shrugged. "No big deal."

"Really?" Jamie raised his dark eyebrows. "It looked like a big deal. She was awfully eager to talk to you."

"We're *freinden*. That's it."

Jamie's brow furrowed, and Leon felt compelled to say more.

"She and I dated a long time ago, and we ended it on *gut* terms." *Unfortunately. Not that we dated, but that it ended.*

Jamie turned toward the windshield.

"How are things with you and Kayla?"

Jamie grinned. "They're great. We've worked out all our issues."

"That's *wunderbaar*. I'm *froh* for you."

"*Danki.*" Jamie turned toward him again. "Now we need to find a *maedel* for you."

"Ya." Leon swallowed a sigh. If only he could find someone with whom he could build a future.

"Don't look so glum. There's someone out there for everyone, right, Brody?" Jamie glanced over at his chief.

"I think so." Brody looked at Leon in the rearview mirror. "My nana used to say every pot has a lid. Now we just need to find your lid."

"If only it were that easy," Leon muttered.

"Don't worry," Jamie said. "If Kayla can put up with me, certainly a *maedel* is out there who can put up with you."

"I hope you're right." Leon gazed out the window as streetlights and farmland whizzed by in a blur. Maybe someday he could be as happy with a special woman as Jamie was with Kayla.

CHAPTER 4

Susie stood in the doorway to Leon's workshop on Tuesday afternoon, watching as he worked on her grandmother's chair. She studied his handsome face, crumpled with a frown as he pulled apart the pieces of wood. His dark eyes were trained on his project as if he were deep in concentration. She leaned against the doorway's wood frame, and the large brown paper shopping bag she held rustled in complaint.

Leon looked up, and his eyes widened. "What are you doing here?"

"What kind of greeting is that?" she teased, stepping into the workshop.

He grinned. "Well, it's not every day that a redhead spies on me while I work."

"Spies on you?" She motioned toward the doorway. "I wouldn't be a very *gut* spy if I just stood right there."

"No, you sure wouldn't." He leaned against his workbench and pointed at her bag. "You've been shopping."

"I have." She set the bag on the floor.

He straightened and walked toward her, a mock-serious look on his face. "Did you buy top-secret items for your spy job?"

A giggle burst from her lips, and she clamped her hand over

her mouth. Why did Leon's silly jokes always tickle her funny bone? He knew how to make her laugh, no matter how dark her mood was.

He raised his eyebrows. "So you *are* hiding super-secret spy things in that bag. What did you buy? Maybe a device to tap into my phone conversations?"

She jammed her hand on her hip. "And what would I hear if I tapped into your phone conversations?"

He cringed. "You wouldn't be very impressed."

"That's doubtful. I imagine I'd hear some classified discussions about staining, sanding, and sawing."

"And those would be rousing conversations," he deadpanned.

Then he laughed, and so did she. His sense of humor was what had first attracted her to him. She'd always loved his electric smile, his loyalty, his sense of adventure, and his outgoing personality.

"So, tell me." He pointed again at the bag. "What's in there?"

"You really want to see?"

"That's why I'm asking."

"All right." She pulled out the hunter-green bolt of material she'd bought. "I bought this to make the dresses Betty and I will wear for my wedding."

"Wow." He smiled. "That's the perfect color."

"You think so?"

"*Ya.*" He rubbed one side of his neck. "You always looked great in green. It complements your hair and brings out the green flecks in your eyes."

She swallowed a deep breath as she stared at him.

"It's none of my business, but aren't you starting the dresses a little late?"

She shook herself. What had he just asked her? Oh, right. The dresses. "No, actually. It won't take me long to make them. We still have two months, and Betty offered to help me with the sewing if I get behind."

"Is she going to be your only attendant?"

"*Ya*. Josh is having his older *bruder* too."

"That will be nice." He paused for a moment and then gestured toward the chair. "I'm sorry I haven't made more progress."

"It's all right. I can tell you've been working."

"Well, I've been taking the chair apart. I was planning on starting earlier in the week, but I got sidetracked with a few other projects. I told *mei dat* to stop giving me other jobs so I can do this for you."

"There's no rush, remember? Sometime in November is fine."

"Can you stay and talk for a while?" His expression seemed hopeful.

She wanted to say yes, as if an invisible magnet had drawn her into the workroom and she couldn't pull away. The truth was, she wasn't ready to leave. What was wrong with her? *"Ya."*

"Great." He pulled over a desk chair with wheels on it and set it in front of her. "Sit."

She sank into the chair. *"Danki."*

"Gern gschehne." He carried over a stool and hopped onto it. "Tell me about your day."

"Well, there isn't much to tell. I came to town to get this material, and then I thought I'd stop in here before I get a ride home. How about you?" She folded her hands in the lap of her cranberry-colored dress.

"I finished up another project and then started on this chair." He rested his feet on the rungs of the stool.

"Are you on duty this week?"

He nodded. "Tomorrow."

"Is it a twenty-four-hour shift?"

"Always."

"And do you still work here after you've been on duty sometimes?"

"*Ya*. It depends on if I get any sleep. If I'm up all night on calls, then I go home and sleep first. If I get some rest, then I just go home to change and then come to work."

"Hm." She chewed on her lower lip as she sized him up. He acted so confident when he talked about firefighting, but was he always so courageous in the line of duty? He must have experienced a lot more danger in the last four years.

He leaned forward. "What's on your mind, Suze?"

She blinked at the sound of her nickname. He hadn't called her that since they were dating.

"Come on. Spit it out. You never could hide your feelings. They were always written all over your face."

"I was wondering if you ever get scared when you're on duty."

Leon blew out a deep breath and fingered a hammer as he stared at the floor for a moment.

"I'm sorry. I shouldn't have asked you that."

"No, it's okay." His expression had warmed. "I've been scared plenty of times. A little over a year ago, I was on the scene of a farmhouse fire. We got the family out, but Simeon Dienner was the last one to head for an exit. He never made it. The floor in the mudroom gave way, and he fell into the basement. As soon as he hit the basement floor, the *haus* collapsed on him. Simeon was crushed and died at the scene. I was terrified that day. All my fears came true."

Susie swallowed a gulp as a chill went through her and Leon went on.

"Simeon was a *gut* man, and a great firefighter. And like I told you before, he left behind a *fraa* and a *boppli* on the way. His *fraa* had a *sohn*."

"*Ach.* No."

Leon had always loved how she genuinely cared for others, even when she didn't know them.

"Another time, Jamie and I were trapped in a big furniture store. It was full of smoke, and we got lost. Normally, we can follow the hose, but we couldn't find it. Two other guys had to come in and lead us out. I was afraid the building was going to come down on us or we were going to run out of oxygen before they found us. Obviously, that didn't happen, but it was a fear." He grinned. "I'm not the brave man you thought I was."

"You are." She nodded. "I honestly wondered if your firefighting was a passing craze, but you've proven me wrong."

He gave a bark of laughter. "Now I know what you really think of me."

"What does that mean?" She sat up straighter.

"You didn't believe my heart was in firefighting, so you didn't think I would stick with it, huh?"

"I didn't say that." She shook her head. "I only meant I thought you'd get tired of it."

"Huh." He tilted his head to the side and his smile dissolved, as though he were contemplating something.

She held her breath while she waited for him to say more.

"Is that what went wrong between us? You thought I couldn't stick with anything, so you didn't think I'd ever marry you?"

She gaped as white-hot fury suddenly surged through her. "That's what you think went wrong between us? Not the fact that you specifically told me you weren't ready to make a commitment to me?"

"Whoa." He held up one hand. "I was just wondering."

She took a deep breath as she tried to calm her temper. "You know that's not what happened. I was ready to make a commitment, but you said you weren't. I told you I couldn't see myself staying with you then. So we agreed to break up and just be *freinden*."

"You're right." His expression had grown somber. "I'm sorry for asking you that. Will you forgive me?"

She nodded. *"Ya."* Why on earth had she overreacted? They'd broken up four years ago. She needed to get a grip. She took another cleansing breath to calm her frayed nerves.

"How are the rest of your wedding plans coming along?"

She swallowed, stalling for time. Why did he want to hear about her wedding? Her own father wasn't interested in the details. "They're coming along fine. Betty has given me some great ideas for table decorations, and we're starting to write out the invitations."

"What do you love about Josh?"

For some reason her answer stuck in her throat for a moment. "He's nice, kind, and thoughtful. We get along well, and we never argue. It's just a *gut*, easy relationship."

Leon nodded as if waiting for her to add more.

"He's also a dairy farmer like *mei dat*, and his farm is next to ours, which is really nice. When we're married, I can still walk over to my parents' *haus* and help *mei mamm* or *mei schweschder* when they need me. And the same is true when I need *mei mamm* or *mei schweschder*. They can walk over to *mei haus*. We can cook and sew together, you know?"

"I suppose that's important."

"It is." Her cheeks flamed with sudden embarrassment.

He raised his palms toward her with his eyebrows careening toward his hairline. "Okay. What else do you love about him?"

Her thoughts spun as she stared at his expectant expression.

The room suddenly felt as if it were closing in on her. She tried to take a deep breath, but her lungs refused to fill. She had to get out of there.

She looked at the clock on the wall and then stood. "I should go. I've kept you from your work long enough." She picked up her bag. "It was nice seeing you."

"Wait." He started after her. "I didn't mean to scare you off."

"You didn't," she called over her shoulder. "I just didn't realize how late it was. I'll see you soon." She waved to his father and brother as she hurried through the showroom, hoping to catch her breath and calm her anxiety once outside.

Why did Leon make her feel so off-balance?

Susie stared out the window of the pickup truck during the ride back to her farm. Her thoughts spun with the memory of her conversation with Leon, and her throat burned as she remembered how angry she got when he asked about what had gone wrong with their relationship.

She swallowed a groan as she rested her head against the cool window. Why was she torturing herself with memories of Leon and their relationship? That was all history. Leon was her past, and Josh was her future. Josh was loyal and kind, and he was reliable. He wouldn't just let her go like Leon had.

She sat up straight as her farm came into view and Grayson turned onto the long rock driveway that led to the back porch.

As the truck came to a stop, a thought grabbed hold of her. If Josh was the one for her, then where was the spark she'd always had with Leon?

Leon kicked the doorway's baseboard as Susie disappeared through the front door of the store. *Great job! You scared her off with your personal questions!*

He scowled as he went back to the rocking chair and continued to take it apart. Their conversation echoed through his mind. He'd never expected Susie to get angry when he asked her about why they broke up. Had the breakup hurt her so deeply that she was still angry four years later? But she'd said they would be friends, and she behaved like a friend. So why was she so irate when he wondered if she had wanted to break up because she didn't think he could follow through with anything—not even their relationship?

If I'd promised to marry her eventually, would we have stayed together?

That notion swirled among his thoughts as additional regret curled low in his gut. And then her words describing Josh echoed through his mind.

He's nice, kind, and thoughtful. We get along well, and we never argue. It's just a gut, easy relationship.

Was Josh everything Leon wasn't—everything she needed and craved in a husband?

But then the rest of what she said about Josh struck him. How he was a dairy farmer like her father, and about how his building a house next door to her parents was handy because she'd be within walking distance of her family.

It sounded as though theirs was going to be a marriage of convenience. Yet it wasn't Leon's place to judge Susie's future marriage. That was her business.

But then why did the idea of her marrying Josh give Leon

heartburn? A new level of regret—sudden, sharp, and stinging—sliced through him.

When he looked back, he saw their relationship with a new perspective. Had Susie been in search of a promise, not a rush into marriage? *I was ready to make a commitment,* she'd said. Would she have agreed to wait for him a couple of years if he'd promised they'd marry after he'd saved some money for their future?

He shoved the thought away and focused on the rocking chair. Memories of time spent in Susie's parents' family room washed over him. He recalled her sitting in her grandmother's chair while he sat in her grandfather's chair after church on Sundays. They'd talk and laugh with her parents and then spend Sunday evening playing board games with friends.

Many of their happiest memories were wrapped up in that antique hickory wood. Would she ever think of Leon while she sat in one of these chairs in her new home with her husband?

"That bad, huh?"

"What?" Leon looked over his shoulder at Ben, who was standing at his workstation with his eyebrows raised and his arms folded over his chest.

"I asked if you still have feelings for Susie."

"Why would you ask me that again?" Leon turned to face him.

"Well, let's see." Ben rubbed his chin. "You've been back here working in a daze ever since she left."

"I've just been busy." Leon shrugged and then turned back to the chair.

"Uh-huh. How long are you going to tell yourself stuff like that?"

For as long as it takes to erase her from my mind. "I'm busy, Ben. You need to get back to work too."

How would he ever get Susie's beautiful face out of his head?

Chapter 5

I love the color!" Betty exclaimed as she ran her fingers over the dress material. "It's perfect." She placed it on the kitchen table and grinned at Susie.

"I agree." *Mamm*'s blue eyes glimmered. "I'm so *froh* you picked green."

"*Danki.*" Susie's smile widened as she recalled Leon's compliment—*You always looked great in green.* She pushed the thought away and crossed to a cabinet. "Would you like me to put on the kettle for tea?"

"*Ya*, that would be nice." *Mamm* opened the cookie jar. "I'll grab some *kichlin.*"

Susie filled the kettle and placed it on a burner before setting three mugs and teabags on the counter. Then she sat down at the table across from her sister and mother.

"You were gone for a while." Betty picked up a chocolate chip cookie from the plate *Mamm* had set in the middle of the table. "Did you go anywhere other than the fabric store?"

Susie plucked a cookie from the plate. "I stopped at the Kings' furniture store." She took a bite and savored the sweet taste.

"You went to see Leon?" *Mamm* asked.

Susie started to nod, but then she said, "Well, I went to see if he'd made any progress on the chairs."

"Had he?" *Mamm* asked.

"Not much. He's been busy with other projects, so he'd just started taking apart *Mammi*'s chair today." She took another bite of the cookie as remembering the discussion about their breakup sent tension through her body. Why did it bother her so much? Pushing away yet another thought, she finished eating the cookie.

"That's nice that he's doing that for you," *Mamm* said, no doubt oblivious to her daughter's inner turmoil.

"How much is he charging you to rebuild and restain each chair?" Betty asked.

"I don't know. We haven't discussed his fee." Susie gathered up crumbs with her fingers and then swept them into a napkin.

"I bet he'll do it for free."

Susie's gaze snapped to her sister's. "Why do you think he would do that?"

Betty gave her a little smile. "Because I think he still cares about you."

"No, he doesn't." Susie's heart thumped, but she ignored it.

"He looked awfully *froh* to see you when we dropped off the chairs."

"You're being *gegisch*. We're just *freinden*. Besides, I don't expect to get anything for free. I'll pay him like any other customer."

"I know you don't expect it, but I'm certain he won't charge you."

"Stop, Betty." Susie's patience was wearing thin. "I'm engaged to Josh, and Leon knows that." She needed to change the subject. "I'm really excited to put the rocking chairs in my new *haus*, *Mamm*. I feel like I'll have a piece of *Mammi* and *Daadi* with me, you know?"

Her mother smiled. "That's why your *mammi* gave them to you, that and because she knew how much you liked them."

The kettle began to whistle, and Susie hopped up from the table. She poured hot water into each of the mugs, added the tea bags, and then carried them to the table on a tray. *"Mamm*, what do you remember most about *Mammi* and *Daadi?"*

"What do you mean?" *Mamm* stirred sugar into her tea.

"What was their relationship like?" Susie wrapped her fingers around her mug, enjoying the warmth of the ceramic. "Since *Daadi* died when I was six, I don't have many memories of them together."

"They had a *wunderbaar* relationship." *Mamm* had a faraway look in her eyes as if she were lost in the memory. "They were very loving to each other. They always held hands, whether they were walking through a store together or walking from the barn to the house.

"They liked to tease each other, and they always laughed. He'd say something to tease her, and she would come right back at him." *Mamm* snickered. "One time they were bickering over something *gegisch*. I can't remember what it was. He said something to her, and she started waving a wooden spoon at him. She accidentally let it go, and it hit the small window over the kitchen sink and cracked it."

Susie and Betty gasped in unison.

"Was he angry?" Susie asked.

"No, no." *Mamm* waved off the idea. "They both laughed about it, and he replaced the window the next day." She ran her fingers around the rim of her mug. "They had a truly loving relationship. Of course they argued sometimes. All couples do. But they were like best *freinden* too. They trusted each other, and in many ways they completed each other."

Susie swallowed as doubt crept into her heart. *Is my relationship with Josh as strong as* Mammi *and* Daadi*'s was? Would* Mammi *approve of Josh?*

"Do you think you and *Dat* have a relationship like your parents had?" Betty asked.

Mamm looked at her. "What do you think?"

Betty nodded. "*Ya*, I do. You and *Dat* like to laugh and tease a lot." She looked at Susie. "Right?"

"*Ya*, right. You do." Susie took another cookie from the plate. "Did you ever question your feelings for *Dat*?"

Mamm's smile faded. "No, never once. Do you have doubts about Josh?"

"No, I don't." Susie forced a smile to calm the concern she felt in her mother's eyes.

"When are you going to start on the dresses?" Betty asked.

"Tomorrow."

"*Gut.*" Betty picked up a cookie. "I can't wait."

Susie was drying washed utensils after supper when a knock sounded on the back door. She turned to her mother. "Who could that be?"

"I don't know." *Mamm* shook her head as she dried her hands on a dish towel. "I'll get it!" Betty rushed to the back door.

"You weren't expecting Josh to visit tonight?" *Mamm* asked.

"No." Susie set some of the utensils in a drawer.

"Susie!" Betty called from the mudroom. "It's for you."

"I'll put those away." *Mamm* took the utensils from her. "Go see who it is."

Susie hurried to the mudroom, where Betty stood talking

with Josh. He had a potted flower in one hand and a lantern in the other.

"See you later." Betty grinned at Susie before going back to the kitchen.

"Hi, Josh," Susie said with a smile. "I didn't expect to see you tonight."

"I have something to give you." He held up a hyacinth plant with leaves a brilliant hue of blue. "I saw this at the farmers market today, and I had to get it for you. I know how much you love hyacinths."

"Oh my goodness." She gaped as she took it from him. *"Danki."* She breathed in the sweet aroma. "It's *schee.*"

"Just like you."

"You're too sweet." She smelled the flowers again and guilt wafted over her. How could she ever doubt her feelings for her thoughtful, generous fiancé?

"Do you have some time to talk, Susie?"

"Ya." She set the flower on the bench in the mudroom. "Would you like to sit outside?"

"That would be nice. It's not too cold."

She grabbed her wrap and then followed him out to the porch swing. As they sat down, Josh set his Coleman lantern on the floor.

"How was your day?" She gave the swing a little push.

"Gut. I got my chores done, and then I took *mei mamm* to the farmers market. How was yours?"

"It was *gut.*" She turned her face toward his. "I bought the material for the wedding dresses today."

"Really." A grin lit his entire face. "That's *wunderbaar!*"

"I'm going to start making Betty's tomorrow. I can't wait." She ran her palm over the smooth arm of the swing as she recalled her other errand. "I stopped by the furniture store before I came home."

"You went to see Leon again?" His head tipped to the side, his brow furrowed.

"I didn't go to see Leon. I just wanted to check on the rocking chairs." She took in his hard expression, but before she could speak, he blew out a deep sigh.

"I don't understand why you need to keep seeing Leon."

"I'm not." She pressed her lips together. "I told you, I just wanted to check on how he's doing with the chairs. You know how important they are to me. But he had just started taking apart *mei mammi*'s chair because of other projects he had to finish first."

He studied her for a moment as his hard expression transformed to a simple frown. "Do you still have feelings for Leon?"

"What?" She'd choked out the question. "No, not at all. He's just a *gut freind* who's restoring the chairs for our *haus*." She shifted so her body was angled toward his. "This is about getting our *haus* ready."

His lips formed a thin line, and an uncomfortable silence stretched between them. She had to redirect the conversation, and the discussion with her mother about her grandparents came to mind.

"What do you remember about your grandparents?"

His confused expression locked with hers. "What?"

"What do you remember about your grandparents?"

"I don't know." He shrugged. "I never knew *mei dat*'s parents, and *mei mamm*'s parents passed away when I was ten."

"What do you remember about your *mamm*'s parents, then?"

He adjusted the straw hat on his head. "Well, they were nice."

She laughed. "Anything more specific?"

"What details are you looking for?"

"How did they act together?"

"Act together?" His brow furrowed again. "What do you mean?"

"With each other." She gestured between them. "Were they loving to each other? Did they tease each other or make each other laugh?"

"I don't know." He frowned as irritation seemed to radiate from him. "They were fine together, I guess."

She swallowed a frustrated sigh. He didn't understand what she was trying to pull from his memories. She stared out at the darkening sky in the direction of their future home.

"Why are you asking me about my grandparents?"

"*Mei mamm* was talking about her parents earlier." She settled back on the swing. "I'd asked her what her parents were like, and she said they were very loving." Susie folded her hands in her lap and kept her gaze trained on the dark pasture in front of her. "They used to tease each other. One time they were acting *gegisch*, and *Mammi* accidentally threw a wooden spoon and cracked the window above the sink." She chuckled.

"Really? Was your *daadi* angry?"

"No. They laughed about it, and he replaced the window the next day."

"Huh. I can't imagine *mei daadi* laughing off a broken window."

She looked over at him. "Would you?"

"I don't know. I guess it depends on the circumstances and whether I had the money to replace it."

Disappointment wiped away Susie's smile. She'd hoped Josh would laugh at the story and tell her he'd forgive her if she cracked a window with a wooden spoon. Suddenly she remembered her mother saying her parents always held hands. She reached for

Josh's hand, but he moved it away, placing it on his knee. The rejection stabbed at her heart, and she swallowed back the disappointment that threatened to rise.

The heavy silence from earlier returned as they both stared out toward the pasture. She bit her lower lip and racked her brain for something to say.

"I didn't get a chance to work on the *haus* today, but I plan to work on it tomorrow," Josh said, finally breaking through the stifling quiet. "*Mei dat* and *bruder* said they'd help me."

"Oh *gut*." She turned to look at him. "What do you want to accomplish tomorrow?"

"We finished putting up the sheetrock, so we'll probably start painting."

"I'm so excited!" She clasped her hands together. "Tell me more about the *haus*."

But then he yawned.

"I should get going." He stood and then took her hand and helped her to her feet. "It's late. *Danki* for sitting outside with me."

"I enjoyed it." She smiled up at him, determined to end the evening on a good note—even though she didn't understand why he wouldn't let her take his hand earlier. Had she made him uncomfortable, talking about her grandparents' affection? "*Danki* for the *schee* flower."

"*Gern gschehne.*" He kissed her cheek. "*Gut nacht.*"

"*Gut nacht.*" She leaned forward against the railing as he descended the steps and started toward the pasture, his lantern guiding the way. Josh kissed her cheek and put his arm around her occasionally, but he rarely hugged her or took her hand. And he'd never kissed her lips.

Why had that never bothered her?

Once he disappeared from sight, Susie stepped into the house and picked up the hyacinth. She breathed in the sweet aroma as she entered the kitchen, where *Mamm* sat at the table making what looked like a shopping list.

Her mother smiled up at her. "Look at that gorgeous flower."

"Josh gave it to me." Susie sank into the chair across from *Mamm* and pushed the flower over to her. "You have to smell it."

Mamm breathed in the scent and grinned. "There's nothing like hyacinth."

"I agree." Susie rested her chin on her palm as she recalled her conversation with Josh, doubt swirling through her mind.

Mamm's smile faded. *"Was iss letz?"*

Susie stared down at the wood grain on the table. With her shoulders hunched, she made lazy circles with her fingertip as she contemplated her confusing feelings. "How did you know *Dat* was the one you were supposed to marry?" When *Mamm* remained silent, she looked up into her blue eyes. She looked concerned. "What?"

"This is the second time tonight you've asked if I ever doubted your *dat* was the one for me. Do you want to share something with me?"

Susie shook her head, even though worry constricted her chest.

"You know I'll listen without judging you." *Mamm* leaned across the table and took Susie's hands in hers. "It's okay to have cold feet before your wedding, but it's not okay if you're wondering if Josh is the wrong person for you. You're not married yet. You can change your mind."

"I don't want to change my mind." Susie sat up straight as a surge of certainty rushed through her. "I just want to know how it felt when you were ready to marry *Dat*."

"Oh." *Mamm* paused for a moment. "Well, I just knew in my

heart." She touched her chest. "I was positive God had chosen your *dat* for me. Do you feel that way about Josh?"

Susie's mouth dried at the question. No, she didn't feel that way at all. But Josh was perfect for her. He lived next door to her parents, and he had a solid work ethic. He was an honest, loyal, and good Christian man. Yes, he was the one she was meant to marry. Wasn't he?

Why didn't she feel certain in her heart?

"*Ya*, I do." Susie's knew her response was quiet and unsure, but she hoped *Mamm* believed her. How could she admit she was no longer convinced she should marry Josh?

"*Gut.*" *Mamm* patted her hand and then stood. "It's late. We should go to bed. Our chores come early in the morning."

"*Ya.*" Susie carried the flower to the counter, set it on the windowsill, and stared at it. How could she doubt her feelings for Josh when he was always so thoughtful and giving to her? She was a rotten fiancée. He was even building her a house, and yet she was allowing apprehension to steal her excitement over their upcoming wedding.

"Susie." *Mamm* touched her shoulder, and Susie jumped with a start. "Why don't you tell me what's troubling you?"

Susie glanced over her shoulder at her mother. "I'm fine. I'm just tired." She forced a smile. "I'll see you in the morning. *Gut nacht.*"

She rushed toward the stairs before her mother could ask her another question. As she got ready for bed, she sent a prayer to God, begging Him to quell the doubt in her heart.

CHAPTER 6

Leon sat at his workbench and sanded a spindle from Susie's grandmother's chair. He had already yawned several times, and now he was yawning again.

"You should've gone home and taken a nap."

Leon spun toward his brother, who'd been working at his station across the room. "Why are you watching me?"

"I just happened to glance over to see you yawn. You should've gone home after your shift." Ben looked down at the hope chest he'd been staining.

"I'm fine." Leon turned back toward the spindle as the flash of a figure appeared in his peripheral vision. He swiveled toward the doorway and blinked at Susie standing there. She wore a pink dress and a bright smile. "Suze."

"Hi," she said before greeting his brother. "Hi, Ben."

"Wie geht's?" Ben raised his sanding block toward her.

"I'm fine. *Danki.*" She looked back at Leon, her expression hard to read. "I was in the area and thought I'd stop by. I haven't seen you for a week."

I know. I've been counting the days. "Has it been that long?" Leon gestured toward the spindles on his workbench. "As you can see, I've been busy. I finished taking your *mammi*'s chair apart, and I'm sanding the pieces. I should be ready to stain them tomorrow or Thursday. I'm making *gut* progress."

"Don't listen to him." Ben frowned. "He should have them all stained by now, but he's slow."

"I'm not slow." Leon glared at his brother. "I take my time and do the job right. There's a difference."

Ben rolled his eyes and turned back to the hope chest. "If you say so."

Leon swallowed the urge to throw his sanding block at the back of his brother's head. When he heard a giggle, his gaze snapped to Susie, who had one hand over her mouth. "What's so funny?" A grin tugged at his lips.

"You and Ben haven't changed a bit." She stepped into the shop.

Ben chuckled and shook his head.

"May I see your work?" She walked over to him and stood close.

Leon swallowed as the scent of her flowery shampoo tickled his senses. Did she have any idea how she affected him? "Sure." He nodded toward the spindles. "It's not very exciting."

She ran her long, slim finger over a spindle. "It's so smooth." Then she gave him an embarrassed smile. "That's the purpose of sanding, right?"

"Right." He grinned. He popped off the stool and pushed it toward her. "Have a seat."

"*Danki.*" She sat down and smoothed her hands over the skirt of her dress as she studied the piece of wood on the workbench. "This is an awful lot of work you're doing. Please let me know how much I owe you."

He hesitated. He'd already considered refurbishing the chairs for free, but *Dat* would never approve. Maybe he'd agree to charging her for only the materials, but he still longed to do the work for free. That was a ridiculous idea, of course. He did that only for family members, and Susie wasn't even his girlfriend. He should charge her, but he couldn't seem to bring himself to name a price.

"Really." She gave him a determined look. "I want to pay you."

"We can talk about it after the chairs are finished."

"At this point it may not be until after your wedding," Ben quipped.

Once again Leon considered sailing his sanding block toward his sibling's big head.

"Your *dat* just told me you were on duty last night." Susie's comment extinguished his frustration with his brother.

"*Ya*, that's right." He leaned back against his workbench.

"How was it?"

"Not very busy. We had only two calls for my whole shift, and they were both medical."

"What kind of medical?" She hugged her arms around her waist.

"One man was standing on a ladder while changing a lightbulb in his foyer, and he lost his footing and fell."

"*Ach*, no!" Susie pressed one hand to her chest.

Ben turned toward them. "You didn't tell me about that. Was he okay?"

"I believe he's going to be okay. I heard from the EMTs that he was in stable condition when they got him to the hospital." Leon ran his finger over the edge of the workbench. "His *sohn* was there when it happened, and he called for help right away. Then he talked to his *dat*, telling him to stay calm and keep breathing. He did a *gut* job."

"That's amazing." Susie leaned forward, her eyes sparkling as the sun's rays came through the skylights above them. "How old was the *sohn*?"

"I think about twelve."

"Wow!" Ben said. "He's mature for his age."

"What a blessing." Susie clicked her tongue. "What was your other call?"

"A man was repairing the roof on his shed, and he fell off."

"Was he okay?" she asked.

Leon winced. "I think he broke his leg and possibly a few ribs. He was conscious but in a lot of pain when the EMTs took him to the hospital."

"That's *bedauerlich*, but praise God he was conscious." She shook her head. "I'll pray for him."

Leon glanced at the clock on the wall. It was almost noon. "Are you hungry?" The question leapt from his lips without any forethought.

"What?" Susie sat up straight, and her red eyebrows tugged together.

"Would you like to join me for lunch?" Leon could tell his voice had filled with conviction as the idea took root in his heart.

"Oh, well . . ." She looked up at the clock.

"Do you like Dienner's Family Restaurant?" he pressed, hoping she'd say yes.

"I do, but I probably should get home." She hopped down from the stool. "I shouldn't take any more of your time, and I don't want you to feel obligated to have lunch with me."

"I don't feel obligated at all. Let me take you to lunch. Please." He heard the plea in his voice. Why was he so desperate to spend more time with her? He was wasting his efforts. She was going to marry someone else. Still, he couldn't stop himself from enjoying every precious moment they spent together.

Susie gave in. "All right. We can go to the restaurant, but I'll pay for my own meal."

Across the room Ben stared at him, a hint of warning in his expression.

Doubt invaded Leon's mind. Susie was engaged, and he didn't want to jeopardize her relationship with her fiancé. "Would Josh be all right with you having lunch with me?"

She seemed to hesitate for a fraction of a second, but then her bright smile returned. "Why would he disapprove? You and I are *freinden*, right?"

"Right." Leon wiped his hands on a red shop rag.

"Then it's fine."

"Let me just wash my hands, and then we'll go." When he stepped away from the shop's sink and followed Susie out of the workshop, Ben shot him another concerned look, mouthing the words, "Be careful."

Leon glared at him and shoved away the uneasiness that curled in his gut.

Leon stood beside Susie inside the front entrance of Dienner's Family Restaurant.

"*Gut* afternoon," Kayla said in greeting as she lifted two menus from a shelf beneath their podium's surface. "How are you, Leon?"

"I'm fine. *Danki*." Leon gestured between them. "Kayla, this is *mei freind* Susie."

"It's nice to meet you." Kayla shook her hand. "Lunch for two?"

"*Ya*, please," Leon said.

"Follow me." Kayla led them toward a table in one corner.

As they passed a table where Jamie sat with his brother, Mark, Jamie raised his eyebrows.

"Hi, Jamie." Susie waved.

"Hi," Jamie said as he grinned at Leon.

Leon nodded and hoped Jamie wouldn't comment later about how wrong he thought it was for him and Susie to have lunch together. They were friends. It wasn't inappropriate.

Then why did a thread of guilt taunt him?

And what made him think Jamie wouldn't have something to say about this?

"How's this?" Kayla made a sweeping gesture at the table.

"Perfect." Susie sank down into a chair and took a menu from Kayla.

"*Danki.*" Leon sat down across from Susie and took the other menu.

"Today's lunch special is a pork barbecue sandwich with French fries." Kayla poised her pen over her notepad. "What can I get you to drink?"

"I'll have water, please," Susie said.

"Okay." Kayla looked at Leon.

"I'll have a Coke."

"All right. I'll be back in a few minutes with your drinks." Kayla strode toward the kitchen. But when she reached Jamie's table, she stopped, her expression bright as they bantered back and forth. Leon's chest squeezed as he watched their interaction. Would he ever find a woman who would care for him the way Kayla cared for Jamie?

"Did you hear what I said?"

"What?" His attention snapped to Susie. She was staring at him. "I'm sorry. I didn't hear you."

"You did seem to be lost in thought." She lifted her chin. "I said I was going to have the special. The barbecue sandwich sounds *appeditlich*. What are you going to have?"

"I was thinking the same thing. I've had the pork barbecue sandwich before, and it's fantastic."

She closed the menu, folded her hands, and laid them on top of it. "You eat here often, don't you?"

"*Ya*, I do." He closed his menu too and then nodded toward Jamie's table. "Since the fire station is right next door, we come here often when we're on duty—especially now that Jamie and Kayla are dating."

Susie smiled toward Jamie's table. Kayla was still there. "They seem to have a *gut* relationship."

"They do. They had some issues to work through in the beginning, but they got through them."

"What kind of issues?" She blushed as she shook her head. "I'm sorry. That was rude. It's none of my business."

"I can tell you." He looked over at Jamie. Kayla had gone on to the kitchen, and Jamie was talking to his brother. "Jamie was dealing with guilt from when his *mamm* unexpectedly passed away after a fall. He was focused on work instead of coming to terms with what happened to her."

Susie frowned. "I'd heard about his *mamm*. I was so sorry his family went through that."

"*Ya*, it was tough." He glanced over his shoulder to make sure Kayla wasn't coming. "Kayla was *naerfich* to date Jamie since she'd lost her *bruder* in an accident while he was a firefighter. You recall when I told you last week about what happened to Simeon?"

Her frown deepened. "*Ya*, I do."

"But they both worked through their fears and their guilt, and now they're doing great." He studied Susie's eyes as she seemed to be concentrating. Was she thinking about Jamie and Kayla? Or was she comparing their relationship to her relationship with Josh? He opened his mouth to ask her, but Kayla interrupted.

"Have you decided what you'd like to eat?" Kayla set a glass of water in front of Susie and a Coke in front of Leon before dropping two straws on the table.

"*Ya*, we'd both like the special." Susie handed Kayla her menu.

"Great." Kayla took Leon's menu too. "I'll bring your food right out."

"*Danki*," Susie said before Kayla headed for the kitchen again.

Leon leaned toward Susie. "You've asked me all about my week, but you haven't told me about yours. How are you?"

"I'm fine." Susie ran one finger over the condensation on her glass. "I've been working on Betty's dress for the wedding. I'm almost finished with it."

"That's great. What brought you to town today?"

"To do a little bit of shopping for *mei mamm*." She pulled a piece of paper out of the pocket of her black sweater. "I need to go to the grocery store when I leave here."

"So you came to see me before you started shopping?"

Her cheeks were bright pink again. Why was she blushing?

"*Ya*." She returned the paper to her pocket, unwrapped one of the straws, and stuck it in her glass. "I just wanted to see if you were actually working on my chairs." Her tone teased him.

"Oh, I see." He smirked. "You really didn't want to see me. You only wanted to make sure I was keeping my promise and working on the chairs."

"Exactly." She laughed and then took a drink of water.

Leon unwrapped the other straw and stuck it in his glass of Coke before taking a long drink. "How's Josh?"

"He's fine. He's painting the interior of our *haus*."

"Did you and Josh have issues to work out before you got engaged?"

Susie froze and stared at him. Regret stiffened his shoulders. He'd crossed a line with her.

"I'm sorry." He held up his hands. "You don't need to answer that. It's none of my business."

"Here's your lunch." Kayla set down their plates. "Do you need anything else?"

Leon looked at Susie, and she shook her head. "No, *danki*."

"Okay. Enjoy." Kayla hurried off to seat some new customers.

After a silent prayer, Leon stared down at his barbecue sandwich and French fries. Guilt sat heavy in his gut, like a rock. He'd been enjoying such an easy conversation with Susie, and then he had to ruin it by asking about her relationship with Josh. He needed a neutral topic to discuss with her, but nothing came to mind.

Keeping his eyes focused on his food, he opened the bottle of ketchup and smothered his fries.

"You still like fries with your ketchup."

He looked up and found Susie grinning. The tension plaguing him eased as he smiled in return.

Susie continued. "I remember one time, when we were eating supper with our youth group, you wound up splattering ketchup on your shirt. You had drowned your fries and were left with a lake of ketchup on your plate."

He laughed. "I remember that too."

She chuckled as she picked up her sandwich and took a bite. He did the same, and they ate in amicable silence for a few minutes.

"Josh and I didn't have any issues to work out," she finally said. "We always got along, so it made sense for us to get engaged."

"Oh." He nodded, grateful that the awkwardness between them had evaporated. "That's great."

"*Danki.*" She picked up a fry. "How is your *mamm?*"

"She's well. She's busy with her quilting group."

They caught up on all their family members as they finished their lunches. When their food was gone, Kayla delivered their bill and took their empty plates. Leon picked up the check and reached for his wallet.

"Let me pay for mine." Susie pulled out her wallet from her small black purse.

"No." He shook his head. "I've got it."

"But I—"

"You can pay next time," he said, even though he'd never allow her to pay.

"Oh. Okay." Her expression brightened as she slipped her wallet back into her purse.

Leon left a couple of bills on the table with the check and then stood. "Are you ready?"

"*Ya.*" Susie rose from her chair. "*Danki* for lunch. It was *wunderbaar.*"

"*Gern gschehne.* Would you like me to walk you to the market?" he offered as they headed out of the restaurant together.

"No, but *danki.*"

"How are you getting home?" Leon held the door open for her, and she stepped outside.

"I'm going to call my driver when I'm done. When are you on duty again?"

"Tomorrow."

"Be careful, okay?"

"I will," he promised.

Susie held out her hand, and he shook it. When their skin touched, a bolt of electricity zipped up Leon's arm, stealing his breath for a moment. Had she felt the attraction too? Or was it all in his mind? Her pleasant expression showed no sign of surprise.

He longed to hold her hand forever. No, he longed to pull her into his arms and ask her to be his girlfriend again. But he couldn't. She belonged to another man.

"I'll see you soon." She released his hand and strolled down the sidewalk, turning once to wave before disappearing around the corner.

Leon hurried back to the store and into the workroom, where Ben was still working. "Didn't you take a break for lunch?"

"*Ya*, I did." Ben stood up and wiped his arm over his forehead. "But my break wasn't as long as yours."

"I wasn't gone that long," Leon muttered as he picked up a piece of sandpaper and went to work on the same spindle.

"What are you thinking?"

"What?" Leon looked over at his brother.

"Don't play dumb with me." Ben gestured toward him. "What do you hope to accomplish with Susie? Do you honestly think Josh would approve of your lunch date?"

"It wasn't a date." Leon ground out the words. "We're *freinden*, and sometimes *freinden* go to lunch."

"Right," Ben deadpanned. "You keep telling yourself that."

"Mind your own business."

They worked in silence for several moments as irritation completely seared his previously good mood. Why *couldn't* his older brother mind his own business?

"Leon, please just listen to me," Ben began, and Leon looked at him. "You're treading on dangerous territory. You're holding on to hope she'll fall back in love with you, but it's not going to happen. She's going to marry someone else, and you're going to wind up with a broken heart."

Leon glared at him.

"I know you're annoyed with me, but I need you to think about what I said." Ben's words were slow and measured. "I'm just worried about you."

"*Danki*, but I'll be fine."

As Leon returned to his work, he tried to shove away his brother's warning. Ben was wrong. He had to be. He didn't think Susie would fall in love with him again. And he could be friends with her even after she was married, right? He had nothing to worry about.

Then why did a fog of foreboding seem to be hanging over his head?

CHAPTER 7

H ow's the sewing going?"

Susie looked up from her machine and found her sister leaning against the door frame, smiling.

"It's going well." She nodded to the dress she was making for Betty. "I'm almost done with the sleeves."

"Great." Betty sat down on the chair beside her. "I heard you telling *Mamm* you went to lunch today while you were out shopping. Where did you go?"

A smile overtook Susie's lips as she recalled her time with Leon. "I went to Dienner's Restaurant."

"Really?" Betty grinned. "I love Dienner's. What did you have?"

"Leon and I both had the barbecue pork sandwich. It was so *gut*."

"Leon? How did you wind up going to lunch with Leon?"

"I stopped by the furniture store to see how he was doing with the chairs. He's completely taken apart *Mammi*'s chair, and he was sanding the spindles. It's going to be so *schee* when it's done. I talked to him and Ben for a while, and then Leon suggested we go to lunch. At first I said no, but he insisted. We had a really nice time. We talked about mutual friends, and then we talked about our families."

Susie frowned. "He's on duty again tomorrow. I hope he's

safe. I was just praying for him while I was sewing. He acts as though volunteering isn't a big deal, but I know he puts his life on the line every time he responds to a dangerous call." When she realized she was droning on about Leon, she swallowed against her suddenly dry throat.

Betty's smile dissolved, and anxiety suddenly occupied Susie's stomach.

"Why are you looking at me like that?" Susie asked.

"Do you still have feelings for Leon?"

"No," Susie replied quickly. "I just enjoy spending time with him."

Betty tilted her head. "I think it's more than that. You light up when you talk about him."

"There's nothing going on between us." Susie hoped she sounded convincing, but she recalled the spark she'd felt when she shook Leon's hand. She never felt that when Josh touched her. The realization sent confusion swirling through her, and her hands trembled.

Was she still attracted to Leon? No. And she would never do anything to deliberately hurt Josh. She was only imagining that there was anything other than friendship between her and Leon now. But why did what she'd felt seem so real?

"I've never seen you light up that way when you talk about Josh."

"Sure I have. I'm always *froh* when I talk about Josh."

Betty shook her head. "Not in the same way."

"That's not true. I'm marrying Josh, not Leon." Susie looked down at the dress. "I should get back to work. I need to finish yours and then we can start on mine."

Betty touched her arm. "You can be honest with me. You can tell me if you're doubting your feelings for Josh."

With her face toward the wall, Susie closed her eyes as more anxiety seized in her chest. "I don't doubt my feelings for Josh." She heard the tremor in her voice, but she forced herself to continue. "Please don't try to convince me I do. I want to marry him. I belong with him, and we'll build a *gut* life together." She turned to her sister and swallowed a sigh of relief when Betty smiled.

"Okay." Betty patted her hand. "I just wanted to be sure you're making the right decision." Then she stood and started for the door. "I need to help *Mamm* with supper."

"Do you need me to come down?"

"No, you keep working." Betty reached the doorway, but then lingered. "The dresses will both be *schee*. I'm really *froh* for you." She tapped the doorframe and then disappeared into the hallway, her footfalls sounding on the stairs.

Susie buried her face in her hands as tears stung her eyes. How did her life become so confusing in only a few weeks? Before she saw Leon at the funeral, she was certain she was making the right decision by agreeing to marry Josh. Now she felt as if she were settling for a marriage without a spark. Without true love.

Love?

"*Ach*, no," she whispered into the palms of her hands. "No, no, no!" She was not falling in love with Leon. That wasn't possible. She belonged with Josh, and she had to convince herself of that.

Shaking off her doubt and worries, she turned her attention back to the dress. She had to focus on her wedding and let go of any thoughts of Leon. He was her past, and Josh was her future.

"Let me get this straight, Leon," Jamie began as he sat across from his friend at the long table in the fire station the next evening. "It's your night to cook, and you ordered a pizza."

"That's right." Leon opened the box with the large extra cheese and pepperoni pie. "If you'd rather have something else, you can check the cabinets and the refrigerator to see what's there." He chose a slice and dropped it onto his paper plate.

Brody chuckled as he took a slice. "I think it was a great idea. We haven't had pizza in a while."

"Right." Jamie frowned. "Not since the last time Leon 'cooked.'" He made air quotes with his fingers.

"I thought you liked pizza." Leon pushed the box toward Jamie.

"I do, but it's the lazy man's way out of cooking." Jamie took two pieces.

"Don't be such a grump." Leon grinned and then bit into his slice, savoring the taste as he chewed. He swallowed and then drank from his cold can of Coke.

"It's good pizza." Brody took a bite. "Thanks, Leon."

"You're welcome."

"So, did you and Susie get back together?" Jamie asked.

Leon stopped chewing and stared at Jamie. He swallowed his last bite and shook his head. "No. Why would you ask me that?" *As if I didn't know. I saw the look on Jamie's face.*

"You two looked cozy at the restaurant yesterday."

"She came by the store to see how her chairs are coming along, and we decided to go to lunch. We ate, and then we both went on our way. That's it." Leon took another bite.

"It looked like more than lunch to me. Kayla even commented about it."

"She did?"

"*Ya*, she did." Jamie lifted his can of Coke.

Leon swallowed a groan.

"What am I missing here?" Brody asked.

"Leon took his ex-girlfriend out to lunch yesterday at Dienner's." Jamie pointed his can at Leon. "We saw them there. They looked like a couple, but he's insisting they aren't together."

"We're not a couple," Leon repeated as he wiped his hands clean with a paper towel. "She's marrying someone else in November."

"So she's getting married, but she was out on a date with you." Brody raised his dark eyebrows.

"It wasn't a date." Leon pinched the bridge of his nose. "Seriously, it wasn't. We were just two friends eating lunch together. We had a nice talk, and that was all."

"But you still care about her." Jamie smirked. "Admit it."

Leon couldn't bring himself to lie since the truth was most likely written all over his face. "*Ya*, I do."

"So you *wanted* it to be a date," Jamie surmised. "You know this isn't going to end well for you."

Leon looked down at his pizza and then back up at Jamie. "Look, you don't need to lecture me. I've heard it all from *mei bruder*."

Jamie's expression grew serious. "What did Ben say?"

"He keeps telling me I'm treading on dangerous territory, and I'm only going to get hurt when she marries Josh."

"He sounds wise," Brody chimed in.

"He might be wise, but Susie is the one who keeps coming to visit me." Leon pointed to his chest. "If she doesn't feel something for me, then why does she keep showing up at my shop? She doesn't have to keep checking up on me to know I'm working on her chairs."

Jamie nodded slowly. "That's a really *gut* point."

"I know." Leon took another bite of pizza, even though his appetite had started to dissolve with the painful conversation.

"But you're leaving out one detail," Brody said. "She may keep coming to visit, but she hasn't broken her engagement. If she were interested in renewing a relationship with you, wouldn't she be letting her fiancé off the hook?"

Leon knew Susie well enough to assume she would. And that didn't make him feel one bit better.

Sunday afternoon Susie sucked in a deep breath as she glanced around the large area that would soon be her very own family room. The walls were a crisp white, and the sweet aroma of fresh paint filled her senses. "Oh, Josh. It's so *schee*."

Josh seemed to stand a little taller as he surveyed the room. "I'm so glad you like it."

"I love it!" She touched one wall. "You, your *dat*, and your *bruder* worked hard."

He walked to the doorway that led to the kitchen. "Now we need to finish up in here and install the appliances. We have a lot of work to do, but at least we're seeing progress."

"And we still have time."

"Not really." He frowned. "Next week is October. November is coming fast."

"It is." Her stomach fluttered, but with what felt more like anxiety than excitement. She suddenly recalled the lunch she'd shared with Leon, as well as the twinkle in his chocolaty eyes as they laughed and talked. Could she live without a daily dose of laughter in her life?

"What's on your mind?" Josh came to her.

"Nothing." She smiled up at him. "I was just thinking about how excited I am to live in this *haus* with you."

"We didn't get to talk much this week." He touched her cheek as he looked down at her. "What did you do?"

"Oh." She gave him a shy smile. "Let's see. I worked on the dresses for the wedding, and I'm almost done with Betty's. I helped *mei mamm* finish up a quilt, and I did some shopping."

She hesitated to say more, but why shouldn't she tell Josh about her visit with Leon? She'd told him there was nothing between them, and she meant to keep it that way. She'd just keep the account of her time with Leon light and easy.

"I went to the furniture store on Tuesday to check on the chairs, and Leon was working hard at *mei mammi*'s chair. Then we went to lunch at Dienner's Restaurant. It was so *appeditlich*. We both had the pork barbecue sandwich with fries. He always drowns his fries in ketchup."

She laughed. "I don't know how he even tastes the fries since he puts so much—" She stopped speaking when she realized Josh's face had clouded. Had she gone too far trying to make the lunch sound like no big deal?

She swallowed her anxiety. "Josh? *Was iss letz?*"

"So you're telling me I haven't seen you since last Sunday, seven days ago, but you went to see Leon and had lunch with him?"

She nodded. "*Ya*, but I only saw him because I wanted to check on the chairs, and I happened to be in town to do some grocery shopping for *mei mamm*."

"You went to see him alone?" His voice echoed in the large, empty room.

"Well, we weren't alone. His *bruder* was in the shop, and we ate in a restaurant."

His expression changed, showing what looked like a mixture of betrayal and anger. "How often do you go to see him?"

"About once a week to check on the chairs. I want to make sure they're ready in time." She pointed to a corner of the room. "I was thinking they could go right there. Wouldn't they be nice by the large picture window?"

Josh gritted his teeth, and a muscle flexed in his strong jaw. "I don't like you going to see him."

Susie blinked. She'd never seen Josh appear so angry. In fact, she'd never seen him so animated or emotional about anything. "But we're just *freinden*—"

"Don't tell me you're only *freinden*. I'm not blind, Susie. I see what's going on here." He scrubbed his hand down his face, and then he pinned her with a hard glare. "I don't want you to see him anymore."

She gaped. "What?"

"I want you to stop seeing him. Can you do that for me?"

Despair and disappointment settled low in her stomach. How could she give up her special friendship with Leon? But she had to. Josh was her fiancé, and he would soon be her husband. She had to be submissive to his wishes.

She nodded slowly. "*Ya*, I can."

His expression relaxed, and then something like fear seemed to flash over his features. "Just tell me the truth, Susie. Do you have feelings for him?"

"No." The word came out a whisper.

"Do you still want to marry me?"

"*Ya*, I do."

He lowered his tensed shoulders and smiled. "*Gut*. That's all I needed to hear. I'm sorry for getting frustrated with you." As he cupped her face with his hands and kissed her cheek, she prayed he couldn't detect her growing confusion about her feelings for him—and for Leon.

"*Mamm?* Could I please talk to you?" Susie stood in the doorway of her parents' bedroom later that evening.

Mamm looked up from the devotional she'd been reading and smiled as she patted the bed beside her. "Of course. Have a seat."

"Where's *Dat?*" Susie sank down onto the bed.

"He went out to check on the animals." *Mamm* touched a few tendrils of Susie's hair that had escaped her headscarf. The rest of her hair fell to her waist in red waves. "You were quiet at supper tonight. What's on your mind?"

"I'm so confused." Susie's voice quaked as tears threatened. "I don't know what to do."

"*Ach, mei liewe.* What happened?"

"I'm certain I have feelings for Leon, but Josh is such a *gut* man. He's kind and loyal. He wants to marry me, and he has a secure future on his *dat*'s farm. If I move into the new *haus*, I'll be so close to you, *Dat*, and Betty."

Susie wiped away a tear and then stared at her mother's quilt. "But there's no spark with Josh. When he touches my hand or kisses my cheek, I feel nothing. When Leon and I shook hands after we had lunch the other day, I felt as if a bolt of lightning had shot up my arm. Leon makes me laugh, and we tease each other. Josh hardly ever jokes, and he rarely makes me laugh.

"I don't know if I can live in a relationship that has no spark and no laughter. But how can I back out on Josh now? He's invested so much in our future." She grabbed a handful of tissues from the box on her mother's end table and dabbed at her eyes. "You must think I'm terrible for saying all these things about Josh. I'm a horrible person for even thinking about Leon now. What's wrong with me?"

"Oh, there's nothing wrong with you." *Mamm* rubbed her shoulder. "You have to follow your heart. What do you think God is telling you to do?"

"I don't know." Even to her own ears, Susie's voice sounded weak. "I feel as if I should be with Josh because he's safe, but I can't stop thinking about Leon." A sob escaped, and *Mamm* pulled her into a warm hug.

"Don't cry," *Mamm* whispered into her headscarf. "You shouldn't punish yourself for the way you feel."

"But I shouldn't feel this way. Josh is a *gut* man."

"*Ya*, he is, but he may not be the right man for you. If you have doubts, then maybe God is trying to show you that you belong with someone else. This might have happened even if you hadn't seen Leon again."

"You think so?" Susie looked up at her mother.

"It's a possibility. Marriage is for life. If you can't see yourself with Josh for the rest of your life, then you shouldn't be with him."

Susie crumpled the wad of tissues in her hand. "What would *Mammi* say if she were here?"

Mamm pushed another tendril away from Susie's face. "Your *mammi* would tell you to pray and listen to what God is telling you." She paused. "Your *mammi* took a risk when she married your *daadi*."

"What do you mean?"

"He didn't have a secure future. He'd had two bad years on his farm, and he owed a lot of money to relatives who had given him loans. But they were madly in love, and she believed God wanted her to marry him. The chairs he made for her as a wedding gift meant a lot because he spent the last of his money on the wood. They're a representation of their love. He was so grateful she married him even though her family warned her not to."

Susie let her mother's words marinate in her mind as she considered Josh. "I don't think I love him enough to marry him." She sniffed as more tears filled her eyes. "But I don't know how to tell him how I feel. How did you feel two months before your wedding?"

"I was elated. I threw myself into the preparations, and I dreamt about how my life would be. Some nights I stared at the ceiling and imagined what your *dat* and I would name our *kinner.*" *Mamm* touched Susie's cheek. "If you have doubts, then you need to sort through them quickly and let Josh know how you feel."

"I don't want to hurt him, but I also don't want to marry him if it's a mistake we'll both regret the rest of our lives. I can't imagine being stuck in a loveless marriage." Susie took a deep breath to try to stop her tears. "What should I do, *Mamm?*"

"You should ask God what the right path is for you."

"Will you be upset with me if I change my mind and don't marry Josh? Will you be disappointed in me?"

"*Ach*, no, *mei liewe.* I will not be upset or disappointed. Neither will your *dat*. You need to do what's right for you and what's right in the eyes of God."

"*Danki.*" As Susie hugged her mother, she closed her eyes and prayed. *Please, God. Guide my heart and show me the right path, the one You have for me. Amen.*

CHAPTER 8

M ay I help you?" Leon asked as the front doorbell dinged the following Wednesday. He looked up from the catalog he'd been perusing as Josh came down the center aisle with a hard glare on his face.

"*Ya*, you can." Josh came to a stop at the sales counter in the center of the showroom.

Leon gritted his teeth and then took a deep breath. *Get hold of yourself. He's Susie's fiancé, the one she chose.* "How may I help you?"

"Could I possibly speak to you in private?" Josh gestured toward the front door. "Maybe outside?"

"*Ya*. Let me just get *mei bruder* to take over the desk. I'll meet you out back in the parking lot."

"*Danki*." Josh gave him a curt nod and turned to leave the way he'd come in.

Leon headed into the back room, where Ben was making an end table. *Dat* was working on the books in his office at the far end of the room. "Ben, could you take over out front for me?"

Ben removed his mask. "Sure. Why?" He closed the can of stain.

"Josh Chupp is here and wants to talk to me. I need to go out to the parking lot to meet him."

"Who's Josh Chupp?"

Leon scowled. "Susie's fiancé."

Ben's eyes widened. "Really?"

"Ya." Leon started for the back door. *"Danki."*

Ben called after him, "Hey, Leon!"

Leon spun to face his older brother, who wagged a finger his way. "I said you were treading on dangerous territory."

"Thanks, *bruder*, for pointing that out," Leon quipped before going outside. He found Josh standing on the gravel lot with his arms folded over his wide chest.

Despite the tension building in his own chest, Leon mustered all the patience he could and tried to adopt a pleasant expression as he walked over to face him. "What's on your mind, Josh?"

Josh stepped close to Leon and scowled. "I'd like to know what your intentions are with my Susie."

"My intentions?" Leon took a step back. "I have none, other than to be her *freind*."

Josh responded with a wry smile. "I find that hard to believe. I think you have romantic feelings for her."

Leon's jaw worked, but no words passed his lips. While he couldn't allow himself to lie, the truth would only incense Josh.

"I thought so." Josh poked Leon in the chest. "You need to stay away from her. She's my fiancée."

"I know that, and I respect that." Leon ground out the words as anger boiled through his veins. "But she keeps coming to see me."

"You have no right to take her out to lunch or talk to her even if she does." Josh's eyes smoldered. "You're confusing her."

"Confusing her?" White-hot rage seemed to burn through

Leon's every muscle. "How am I confusing her if she's engaged to you?"

"You're too close, and she needs to stay focused on her future with me." Josh glowered as he stepped forward and jabbed a finger in Leon's face. "Stay away from her."

"Josh, what are you doing here?" Susie appeared without warning, the building's back door slamming in her wake. "You said you were going to the hardware store."

"I could ask you the same question," Josh retorted. "You said you were going to the farmers market."

"I did go to the farmers market." She lifted the plastic grocery bag she held. "You didn't meet me in the parking lot, so I went looking for you. When I didn't find you at the hardware store, I thought maybe you came here to check on the chairs for me. Ben told me you two were out here." She set the bag on the ground and walked between them, holding up a hand to each of them as if to stop a fistfight. "Why are you arguing? Stop acting like *gegisch kinner!*"

"I'm sure you want to talk to Leon—alone. I'll be waiting for you at the buggy." Josh glowered and then marched toward the far end of the parking lot.

Susie's cheeks flushed bright pink as she looked up at Leon. "I'm sorry. I didn't know Josh planned to come here today. He said he needed to run a few errands, and I asked to go with him. I didn't know he only came to see you."

Leon balled his hands into fists as he looked to where Josh had disappeared around the corner of another store. His body shook with anger. Then he looked back at Susie. "Why are you with him? What do you see in him?"

Her eyes narrowed, reflecting the emotion he knew she'd seen in his eyes. "Do you really think that's any of your business?

Josh is a loyal—" She stopped, as though on some level she was giving up. On him? On Josh?

"Never mind, Leon," she said, controlled anger spiking every word. "You wouldn't understand. You don't know what it's like to stick with a relationship. But Josh does. He'd never give me up like you did."

Leon flinched as if she'd struck him, and then he stepped away from her as his own fury flared once again. "Well, now I really do know what you think of me."

With betrayal and anguish pressing down on him, he headed inside. "I'll see you when your chairs are ready," he tossed over his shoulder.

"Leon! Leon!" Susie called after him as regret crawled up her spine and dug its sharp claws into her shoulders. "Wait!" She rushed into the workroom and past his father's office to his workstation, where her grandfather's rocking chair lay on the floor. With his shoulders hunched, Leon stood staring at his workbench.

"Please look at me," she pleaded with her heart caught in her throat. "Leon, please." She took a step toward him and fingered the hem of her apron. "You have no right to be angry when you're the one who broke up with me!" Her words shook with the weight of her anger.

Leon spun around, and his dark eyes glistened as his face reddened. "I broke up with you?" He pointed a shaky finger at her. "You were the one who decided we should break up! You made it clear it was over between us when I said I wasn't ready to get married. I said we could be *freinden* instead because that's what I thought you wanted. Maybe you need to think about what really happened."

Leon took a step toward her and tripped over her grandfather's chair, shattering the spindles as he fell to the floor.

She quaked inside, clutching her hands as she took a step backward. Tears stung her eyes as she shook her head. "How could you?"

"I'm sorry, Susie! I didn't mean to break it." His face crumpled. "Please forgive me."

"You've ruined everything!" She hurried out of the shop through the back door, tears pouring down her burning cheeks. When her shoes hit the gravel lot, she ran as heaving sobs overtook her.

"Leon?" *Dat* stepped into the shop and walked to where Leon sat on the floor, staring at the broken treasure.

Leon covered his face with his hands and groaned as humiliation and despair became his burden. "I guess you heard everything."

"I did." Leon looked up to see *Dat* frowning as he sat down on Leon's stool.

"I really made a mess of things." Leon picked up a splintered piece of wood and shook his head. "Now she'll never talk to me again. And to make matters worse, I destroyed her *daadi*'s chair. These chairs mean everything to her, and they were my only link to her."

"I think we can fix the chair."

Leon raised an eyebrow. "This is an antique."

"I have some antique hickory to match it." *Dat* pointed to a few of the pieces. "And some of those are salvageable." Then he tilted his head. "Do you love Susie?"

"With all my heart." Leon blew out a deep sigh. "But she's going to marry someone else. I never should have let her go." He fingered another piece of wood as a suffocating dread clogged his throat.

"Do you still want her to know how you feel?"

"*Ya*. I do. Even if she's going to marry Josh, I need her to know."

"Then repair the chairs and take them to her." *Dat* stood. "Stand up. I'll help you cut the pieces of wood you'll need."

Hope ignited in Leon's soul as he stood and started assessing the damage. Maybe, just maybe, the chairs would be the legacy of love he needed to ask for her forgiveness and prove just how much he cared for her—even though Josh had won her heart.

Susie stared at the road in front of her as Josh guided his horse down the road toward their farms. After she left the furniture store, she rushed to his waiting buggy, but so far they hadn't spoken at all. The tense silence had hung over them like a thick, unforgiving fog, choking back her words. The only sounds came from the *clip-clop* of Josh's horse and the rumble of passing cars.

She glanced at him and took in his handsome profile. He sat rigid in the seat, gripping the reins with such force that his knuckles had turned white.

As she considered his set jaw and hard frown, a full realization took hold of her. *I'm not supposed to marry him. I don't love him, and I can't tie him down for the rest of his life. He deserves someone who loves him for who he is, not who I wish he was.*

Josh wasn't the one God had chosen for her. She was certain of it, and she could feel it to the very marrow of her bones. The notion shook her, and she took in a ragged breath as tears filled her eyes and fear squeezed her lungs.

Then as quickly as the shock of her realization had hit, a calm settled over her, replacing her anxiety. She had to tell Josh she wasn't going to marry him, and she had to do it now. She bit her lower lip and contemplated what words would be right as he guided the horse up her driveway and to her back porch.

When he halted the horse, he turned toward her with little expression in his voice or on his face. "I'm sorry I didn't tell you I was going to see Leon. You have every right to be angry with me."

"I'm not angry." Her voice was steady and even, and she felt calm, as if her heart was not about to break for Josh because of what she was about to say.

He gave a sarcastic snort. "You certainly seemed angry earlier."

"I was angry, but I'm not now." She fiddled with the door handle as she took a steadying breath, and then she looked into his eyes. "Josh, I've realized something, and I need to be honest with you."

"What is it?" He swallowed.

"I can't marry you. You're a *gut freind*, but I'm not in love with you. It's not fair for me to trap you in a loveless marriage."

His eyes narrowed. "This is about Leon, isn't it?"

"No, it's not." She reached for his hand, but he pulled it away. "This is about what I want and what you deserve. I want a marriage like my grandparents had, where they were deeply in love. They also teased each other and made each other laugh. I thought those feelings would grow between us over time, but I've realized that probably won't happen, and I can't make myself feel what I don't.

You deserve someone who will love you completely, and I'm sorry I can't be that person." She sniffed as tears streamed down her cheeks.

His expression was pained, and it splintered her heart. "What can I do to make this better?" he said.

"Nothing. I've prayed about it, and this is the answer I feel is coming from God. We don't belong together." She wiped away her tears and cleared her throat against a swelling tangle of emotion. "I'm sorry you've invested so much in our relationship. I hope someday you can forgive me." She leaned over to kiss his cheek, but he shifted away and faced the windshield.

"I need to go." His voice sounded strange to her, and he stared straight ahead. "Good-bye."

"I'm sorry," she whispered before picking up her grocery bag, climbing out of the buggy, and running up the porch steps and into the house. She found her mother and sister making supper in the kitchen.

"Susie!" Betty called when she turned and saw her face. "What happened?"

"Josh and I broke up." Susie set the bag on the table and dropped into the closest chair. She yanked a paper napkin from the holder in the center of the table and wiped her eyes and nose. Guilt twisted a heavy knot in her stomach.

Mamm sat down beside her and rubbed her shoulder. "I'm so sorry. I know this is painful for you."

Betty sat on the other side of her and touched her hand. "Can you talk about it?"

"It was terrible." Susie told them everything. "I know in my heart God doesn't want me to marry Josh. I prayed about it, and the answer came to me clearly today. But I still feel terrible for breaking his heart. The pain in his eyes nearly tore me in two." Susie's lip quivered. "Why does it hurt so much when I know I did the right thing?"

"Because you care about Josh." *Mamm* patted her arm. "I promise you the pain will subside over time."

"*Ach*, Susie. It will be okay," Betty said.

"I don't know if it will." She shook her head. "Josh built me a *haus*, and he planned his whole life around marrying me. What if he doesn't recover?"

"He will," *Dat* said.

Susie turned her head toward the doorway leading to the family room. "*Dat?* I didn't know you were standing there. How much did you hear?"

"Enough." Her father joined them at the table, sitting down across from her before taking her hands in his. "I know you're worried about Josh, but do you believe you're following God's path for you?"

"*Ya.*" Susie wiped at her eyes. "I'm sure of it. I had a sense of calm as soon as I made the decision to break up with him."

"Then trust God to take care of Josh. And you." *Dat* squeezed her hand. "He has the perfect plan for all of us."

Susie looked at her mother. "Do you think God could give me a marriage like *Mammi* and *Daadi* had, and like you and *Dat* have?"

Mamm's lips turned up in a watery smile. "*Ya*, I do. Have faith." As she pulled Susie in for a warm hug, Susie wanted to believe God would do that for her.

But as far as she could tell, God hadn't chosen Leon any more than He'd chosen Josh.

CHAPTER 9

T his is your best work."
     Leon spun toward his father as they both stood in the workshop. "I didn't know you were standing there."

"I'm sorry. I didn't mean to sneak up on you." *Dat* nodded toward Susie's rocking chairs, now fully restored. "You're one talented carpenter. You've surpassed both your *bruder* and me in skill."

"No, I'm not even close to you." Leon shook his head as he studied the chairs. He'd spent every free moment of the past month finishing the grandmother's chair and rebuilding the grandfather's chair. He'd poured his heart and soul into them, coming to work early in the morning and staying late into the evening. He prayed his effort would be enough to show Susie how much he cared for her, and he hoped she would forgive him for all the mistakes he'd made, both in the past and more recently.

"You taught me everything I know, *Dat*. I could never surpass you."

Ben appeared in the doorway. "I don't know. I think that's the best carpentry I've ever seen."

"That's exactly what I just said." *Dat* squeezed Leon's shoulder. "When are you going to deliver them to her?"

Leon rubbed the back of his head. "I suppose there's no time like the present. I just hope she'll talk to me. When she stormed out of here weeks ago, she was furious with me. What if she throws me off her porch and tells me to stay away from her?"

"I'm certain she'll talk to you," *Dat* said. "She'll have cooled off by now, and you two have known each other a long time."

"But will she forgive me?" Leon heard the thread of worry in his voice.

"She will." Ben jammed his thumb toward the front of the store. "I'll call our driver and then help you load the chairs."

"Susie," *Dat* called from the mudroom. "Someone is here to see you."

Susie set a platter of lunchmeat on the table and then turned toward her mother. "Are you expecting someone for lunch?"

Mamm shook her head. "No, I'm not."

Susie hurried to the mudroom, and her father smiled at her. "Who is it?"

"He's on the back porch." *Dat* touched her shoulder. "Hear him out. Don't close the door in his face."

She blinked, hoping it wasn't Josh. "Okay."

As *Dat* disappeared into the kitchen, she pulled on her coat and then pushed open the back door and stepped onto the porch.

Leon was standing behind her two rocking chairs. She cupped her hand to her mouth as sudden tears burned her eyes. The chairs looked brand new, and her grandfather's rocker looked as though it had never been broken. Leon must have spent hours and hours finishing them for her.

Did that mean he might still care about her? After the awful things she'd said to him?

Her chest tightened as she looked into his eyes.

"Hi." He gave her a sheepish smile.

"Hi," she managed as she took in his handsome face. An invisible force seemed to pull her to him. She'd spent the past month trying to clear all thoughts of Leon from her mind, but she still cared for him.

"I brought you your chairs." He gestured toward them as he took a step back. "*Mei dat* had antique wood that matched the spindles I destroyed, and I cut them to the right shape and sanded them before staining the chair. They were the right shade of hickory, so I don't think you'll notice any difference."

"Oh, Leon." She stepped closer and ran her finger over each chair. "They're perfect. They're better than perfect. They're exquisite." She looked up at him and smiled. "*Danki* so much. What do I owe you?"

"Nothing." He blanched and shook his head. "Actually, that's not true. You owe me one thing."

"What's that?"

"A few minutes of your time."

"Okay."

He gestured toward the chairs again. "Would you sit with me?"

"*Ya.*" She sank down into her *mammi*'s chair and shivered as the late-October breeze seeped through her sweater. She moved the chair back and forth, and it rocked in a smooth motion. The chair was definitely perfect.

Leon moved her *daadi*'s chair in front of her and sat down, folding his hands as if he were pleading with her to listen. "I want to say I'm sorry. I'm sorry for everything—for letting you go four years ago, for hurting you. You were my first and only love, and my biggest regret is not holding on to you. I know it's too late now, but I have to tell you how I feel."

His words hit square in her chest. "Leon, I'm not going to m—"

"Wait." He held up his hands. "Please let me finish. I've spent the past month evaluating what went wrong between us, and I realized you were right. I did give up on us, and I was wrong. If I could go back in time, I'd still tell you I wasn't ready to get married, but I'd also promise to marry you when the time was right." He paused. "I never would've let you give up on us, because I would've given you my all."

Her chin trembled as her heart swelled with a deep love for this man, and she had a feeling he could see that love in her eyes. Why hadn't she realized she loved him all along?

He looked confused as he searched her face. "I *am* too late, right?"

She shook her head and smiled.

"I'm not too late?"

"I'm not going to marry Josh."

"You're not?" His eyes sparkled.

"I broke up with him the afternoon you and I argued. I realized I didn't love him the way I should."

"What do you mean?"

She looked down at her lap, choosing her words carefully. "I'd had doubts for a while because there was, well, no spark between us. Josh is a *gut* man, but I'm not in love with him. It wasn't fair to hold on to him when he can find someone who'll love him the way a *fraa* should love her husband. I had prayed about it, and the answer came to me while I was riding in the buggy with him on the way home that day." She peeked up at Leon and found him watching her with an intensity that sent heat roaring through her veins.

"I told him I was sorry for letting him down, but I couldn't marry him. He was really upset. We haven't spoken much since that happened. He nods at me when I see him in church, but that's it. I know I hurt him, but I couldn't risk being stuck in a loveless marriage."

Leon seemed to be processing this news as he sank back against the rocking chair. She understood and elected to give him a few moments. Finally, he took a deep breath and gestured toward the two chairs. "While I was restoring these chairs, I realized something. These chairs are like me. They're flawed and imperfect, but they're sturdy and reliable, like my love for you. I will make mistakes, but I'll always be here if you'll have me."

He leaned forward and took her hands in his. "I hope you can find it in your heart to give me another chance. I believe God wants us together. I feel it to the very depths of my soul."

A strangled noise came from her throat as happy tears flowed, her heart swelling with both excitement and love as she looked into his chocolaty-brown eyes. *Am I dreaming? Is this really happening?*

Leon moved closer. "I can't let you slip through my fingers again, Suze. It's almost as if your grandparents helped to bring us together through these chairs. I want to build a life with you." His eyes shimmered with what looked like hope. "I'll do my best to take care of you, and I won't give up on us. I'll follow this through. I'll work hard and try to make you *froh*. I promise. Are you willing to give me that second chance?"

"*Ya.*" Her lungs seized as she fought back more tears. "*Ya,* I will."

She waited for him to take her in his arms, but he hesitated as though he wanted to say more. Was something wrong?

"I know I just asked for another chance, but to be honest, that's not enough for me. I don't want to wait to start a life with you. Will you marry me?"

Her heart felt as though it could burst from the exhilaration swelling inside of her. "*Ya, ya!* I would be honored to be your *fraa.*"

Leon pulled her to her feet, and when his lips brushed hers, liquid heat sizzled through her veins. She closed her eyes, savoring the feel of his mouth against hers. When he drew back, she smiled up at him as a calm settled over her. Leon was the man God wanted her to marry. This was the path He had chosen for her, and she was certain of it down to her very core.

"*Ich liebe dich*, Suze," he whispered in her ear, sending a shiver dancing up her spine.

"I love you too."

As Leon pulled her close for a hug, Susie rested her cheek on his shoulder. God had used her grandparents' chairs to return her one true love, and she couldn't be more grateful.

DISCUSSION QUESTIONS

1. When Leon attends his friend's funeral, he realizes life is fleeting and he wants to settle down and have a family. Have you ever been emotionally affected by an unexpected death or accident? What Bible verses would help?

2. When Susie is torn about her feelings for Josh, she turns to prayer for answers. Think of a time when you found strength through prayer and share your story.

3. What significance do the antique chairs have in the story? What role do they play in Susie and Leon's relationship?

4. Susie treasures the antique rocking chairs that belonged to her grandparents. Do you cherish a special family heirloom?

5. Which character can you identify with the most? Which character seems to carry the most emotional stake in the story? Is it Susie, Leon, Josh, or someone else?

6. While Susie struggles with her confusing feelings for Josh, she turns to her mother for advice. Does someone in your life help you through difficult times? How?

7. Susie is certain she's not supposed to marry Josh, but she feels guilty about hurting him. Have you ever felt torn between telling the truth and hurting someone's feelings? How did the situation turn out?

ACKNOWLEDGMENTS

As always, I'm grateful for my loving family, including my mother, Lola Goebelbecker; my husband, Joe; and my sons, Zac and Matt. I'm blessed to have such an awesome and amazing family that tolerates my moods when I'm stressed out on a book deadline.

Special thanks to my mother and my dear friend Becky Biddy, who graciously proofread the draft and corrected my hilarious typos. Becky, thank you also for your daily notes of encouragement. Your friendship is a blessing!

I'm also grateful for my special Amish friend who patiently answers my endless stream of questions. You're a blessing in my life.

Thank you to my wonderful church family at Morning Star Lutheran in Matthews, North Carolina, for your encouragement, prayers, love, and friendship. You all mean so much to my family and me.

Thank you to Zac Weikal and the fabulous members of my Bakery Bunch! I'm so grateful for your friendship and your excitement about my books. You all are awesome!

To my literary agent, Natasha Kern—I can't thank you enough for your guidance, advice, and friendship. You are a tremendous blessing in my life.

Thank you to my amazing editor, Becky Monds, for your friendship and guidance. I'm grateful to each and every person at HarperCollins Christian Publishing who helped make this book a reality.

I'm grateful to editor Jean Bloom, who helped me polish and refine the story. Jean, you are a master at connecting the dots and filling in the gaps. I'm so happy we can continue to work together!

Thank you most of all to God—for giving me the inspiration and the words to glorify You. I'm grateful and humbled You've chosen this path for me.

The Cedar Chest

BETH WISEMAN

To Leta Mae Beatty, my grandmother. I miss and love you. And I cherish the cedar chest that was once yours.

CHAPTER 1

Emma stared out the window and waited for Catherine to pull into the driveway. Something was wrong with her daughter, but Emma hadn't been able to get Catherine to talk about what was troubling her.

As Emma raised the green blinds higher, rays of sunshine soared through the glass pane and lit the way for tiny dust particles to float aimlessly across the room. No matter how much she cleaned, the old farmhouse collected and held on to dust like sand on wet feet.

Emma moved toward the front door when she saw Catherine's buggy approaching, and she silently prayed her daughter would open up to her today. They'd always been close, so Catherine's unwillingness to confide in her caused Emma's chest to tighten every time she considered things that might be wrong. *A health issue? Was Abram's job coming to an end?* Her son-in-law had been worried about his job at a local construction company and whether his position was stable. Or was Catherine's depressed state of mind because she and Abram hadn't yet conceived a child?

As Catherine tethered her horse, Emma stepped onto the porch and breathed in the flowery aroma of spring, then eyed the dewy mist glistening like fallen stars atop dark-green blades of grass.

"*Wie bischt, Mamm.*" Catherine kissed her mother on the cheek before she followed Emma into the house. "You've been baking." Her daughter sniffed the air. "Smells like peanut butter cookies."

Emma smiled as she pointed to a plastic container on the coffee table. "Those are for you and Abram. I know they're his favorite."

"*Danki.*" Catherine lifted the lid on the container and took out a cookie.

"*Ach*, Abram's slacks are in the bedroom. Be right back." Emma retreated to her room and picked up two pairs of pants she'd offered to mend for Catherine the last time she was at her daughter's house.

"*Mamm*, you really didn't have to do that," Catherine said with a mouthful of cookie when Emma returned.

"I know I didn't *have* to." She set the clothes next to the cookies. Catherine was a wonderful cook and she kept a fine house, but Emma's daughter despised any type of sewing, even simple mending projects.

"I need things to busy myself anyway. Now that Lloyd is off and married, I'm constantly looking for things to do." The last of her *kinner* had gotten married in November. Emma and Jonathan had planned to travel, to visit relatives in Ohio and Indiana, but somehow they'd settled into a quiet life with little mention of those plans.

"What about the books for the auction? Did you find them?" Catherine's cheeks were stuffed like a chipmunk's.

Emma put her hands on her hips and grinned. "I hope you don't always talk with a mouthful of food like that."

Catherine stuffed the rest of the cookie in her mouth and attempted to say, "Of course not."

Emma sighed and shook her head. "The books are in the basement. It's a heavy box, so it will probably take both of us to get it up the stairs. I didn't want to ask your father to help because of his back problems." She started toward the door that led to the basement, her heart a bit lighter today. Catherine was in better spirits this morning.

"I don't even remember the last time I've been down here. Since I moved the preserves to the kitchen cupboard, I don't have much need to be in the basement." Emma turned the doorknob, then felt around for the flashlight hanging on the wall to her right. She flicked it on and started down the stairs, Catherine on her heels.

Steadying herself with each step, Emma made a mental note to remind Jonathan to construct a handrail. She didn't think of herself as old, but in two years she'd be fifty, and she'd already had one frightening fall on the steep stairs.

At the bottom, she shone the light into the darkness, to the left, then to the right. "Hmm . . . I think the books are over there with your school memories." She'd kept two boxes for each of her children—crafts, first pair of shoes, baby blankets, and various keepsakes. "Let's see." She moved toward the corner and squatted down, illuminating the area. "That's Lloyd's school stuff," she said, pointing to the nearest box. "And there are yours and Benjamin's boxes."

Pausing, she stood up. "I know that box of old books is around here somewhere."

Catherine was across the room, having found another flashlight, and she was leaning over something flush against the far wall.

Emma spotted the books. "Here we go. It's this big box."

But her daughter didn't move, so Emma went to her.

"Whose is this?"

Emma shrugged as she pushed a cobweb from the piece of furniture. "I guess it's mine now. It was actually my great-grandmother's cedar chest, your great-great-grandmother."

"What's in it?" Catherine tried to lift the lid. "It's locked."

"*Ya*, I know. When your grandparents moved to the *daadi haus*, I asked your *mammi* if she wanted to take it with her, but she said to leave it here, that it was too heavy and awkward to get up the basement stairs. Of course, that was years ago, and I'd forgotten about it."

She edged closer. "The key is jammed in the lock. *Mammi* said it was broken off when her grandmother left it to her mother, and then her mother left it to your *mammi*."

Emma wondered if her grandmother had intentionally broken off the key in the lock to keep Emma's mother—or anyone else—from seeing the contents. All she had to go on regarding that theory was something her grandfather had said on his death bed. When Emma had questioned her grandmother about his comment, she'd waved it off as nonsense. Her mother had refused to open the chest, with little explanation, leaving Emma to assume that some things were better left alone.

Catherine shined her light to the ceiling, illuminating both their faces. Emma recognized her daughter's wheels spinning as Catherine tapped a finger to her chin. She had always been a curious child. Now, at twenty-four, she hadn't changed. "That means this cedar chest hasn't been opened in . . ." She raised an eyebrow. "How long?"

Emma took a few minutes to do the math in her head. "Uh, let's see." She closed her eyes to concentrate, and when she opened them, Catherine's anxious expression remained. "*Mei* great-grandmammi* Elizabeth would have been born in the early nineteen hundreds. She married *mei* great-*granddaadi* when she was nineteen, I think." She shook her head. "I'm not sure exactly how long."

Catherine's jaw dropped. "I can't believe three generations of women have left this cedar chest unopened—four if we count me and we don't open it. Whatever is in there was put in there by my great-great-grandmother." She let out a small gasp. "We have to open it."

Emma hadn't seen a glow in her daughter's eyes for a long while. Mostly Catherine was quiet and detached. She had a more playful air about her today, and as leery as Emma was to unlock the past, she'd do it to spend time with her only daughter. Maybe her grandfather's final words were just the rumblings of an old man who didn't remember things correctly, as her grandmother had said. But something inside Emma said otherwise.

Both women got down on their knees, Emma's popping an objection. They brushed away the dust and cobwebs from the top and sides, revealing a white sign on the front of the chest below the lock. *Lane Company Pattern No. 2244 Certified Moth-Killer*, followed by more verbiage.

Catherine chuckled. "Certified *moth*-killer?"

"It's cedar inside, and that helps keep moth larvae off clothes, supposedly." Emma pulled a pair of reading glasses from the pocket of her black apron and leaned closer.

"Just think of all the things that might be in there. Maybe quilts or knickknacks that have been hidden for nearly a hundred years."

Emma swiped her hand across the top again, sending another plume of dust into the air. "Or it might be empty."

Catherine stood and shone the flashlight on her apron as she brushed off the dust and cobwebs. "We're going to need more light."

Emma got to her feet and brushed off her clothes too. A tickle of dust caught in her throat and she coughed. "It's dusty, dark, and a bit chilly down here. Maybe we can carry it upstairs." Emma bent to try to lift one side of the chest, which was about four feet long. Catherine went to the other side. "Lift on three. One . . . two . . . three."

"It's not budging." Catherine sighed and placed her hands on her hips as she stared at it. "Since *Daed* can't help, maybe Benny or Lloyd can."

"Your *bruders* have their hands full running the furniture store." Emma stared at the chest. "Like I said, it might be empty, just a heavy piece of furniture with nothing in it." She lifted one shoulder and lowered it slowly. "It might not be worth the effort of hauling it upstairs."

"Only one way to find out. How can we get it open?"

Emma took a deep breath. Her daughter was determined, and once Catherine set her mind to something, she usually followed through. Emma glanced around the basement. Boxes were every-where. Two kitchen chairs, each missing a leg. A Ping-Pong table was folded up and leaning against the wall. Emma remembered all the Sunday singings they'd had down here when the *kinner* were younger, how she'd covered the table with a white cloth and put out snacks and a punch bowl.

"I don't see anything we can use to pry it open. Let's go out to your father's workshop and see what we can find."

Catherine led the way up the stairs as Emma began to speculate about what might be in the chest, if anything. Her grandfather's words swirled around in her mind like a tornado gathering strength.

CHAPTER 2

Catherine threw her weight into prying the chest open with the crowbar they'd found in her father's shop. She was rewarded when the lock busted and a shard of wood splintered and flew off. She and her mother lifted the lid easily, and Catherine breathed in the woody aroma of cedar, a fragrant smell that reminded her of pencil shavings. She lifted a folded quilt from the top, a double-circled print in blue, green, yellow, and pink pastels.

"A double wedding ring quilt," her mother said as they inspected the cotton fabric and quality of the work. "This type of quilt symbolizes a never-ending bond."

"I wonder if my great-great-grandmother made it." Catherine carefully placed the heirloom on the wood floor beside her. She reached back into the chest and took out two silver candleholders, tarnished from time, but heavy in her hands. "I bet these could be shined and used." She set them aside and waited as her mother lifted a tiny pair of black, high-topped baby shoes, both missing the laces.

Mamm smiled as she gingerly rolled the shoes over in her hands. "I bet these were *mei granddaadi*'s."

"What's this?" Catherine pulled out a small white box and opened it. "A ring? We don't wear rings."

Her mother leaned in for a better look. "A gold wedding band. Hmm . . . that's odd."

Catherine closed the small box and carefully tucked it back inside the larger chest. "Ew." She flicked a dead spider off several bundled handkerchiefs, then reached farther into the chest, pulling out a cardboard box. It was larger than a shoebox, but smaller than the breadbox on their kitchen counter. A blue ribbon was tied around it. She glanced at her mother, who shrugged. Catherine slipped off the ribbon and removed the lid, revealing dozens of yellowed envelopes. She gasped. "Look. Old letters."

Her mother took out one of the envelopes. "This one is addressed to Elizabeth Zook in Paradise, Pennsylvania." *Mamm* pointed to the scratchy penmanship. "Elizabeth Zook was my great-grandmother. She married into the Lapp family." She shined the light on the return address and smiled. "And the letter is from Isaac Lapp, my great-grandfather. The return address is in Texas." She stared at it for a while, grimacing a little. "I never heard much about him."

"How did Isaac Lapp end up here in Lancaster County? This was my great-great-grandparents' house, right?"

"I'm not sure how he ended up here, but *ya*, your *daed* and I are the fourth generation to occupy this house. Elizabeth and my great-grandfather Isaac were the first, then my grandparents, Jonah and Rose, and my parents, Mary and Amos." She sighed. "Then your father and I raised you and your *bruders* here."

Catherine heard the sadness in her mother's voice. It had only been seven months since *Mammi* passed, and *Mamm* still missed her mother. They all did. Catherine hadn't been back to the *daadi haus* on the back of the property since her grandmother died. For as long as she could remember, her grandparents had lived in the *daadi haus*. Then her grandfather died three years ago, so her *mammi* lived there alone until her death this past September. Someday Catherine's parents would likely move to the *daadi haus*, and Catherine and Abram would move here, the fifth generation with their own children. Assuming they had any children. They argued so much that making a baby had fallen off the agenda.

"Are we going to read it?" Catherine bit her bottom lip as she raised an eyebrow, hopeful her mother was curious about the contents too. She leaned closer. "Look, the postmark is dated May 12, 1928. But there isn't a zip code."

"I don't think they used zip codes that long ago." Frowning, her mother sighed. "This is personal correspondence between my great-grandparents. I don't know if we should read it."

Catherine touched her mother's hand. *"Ach, Mamm.* They won't know." She lifted the flashlight higher and locked eyes with her mother. "Maybe just one?" She shone the light inside the box as she gingerly ran a finger across the other envelopes. "Maybe they share a beautiful love story between my great-great-grandparents." She readjusted the light and pointed it to the letter in her hand.

Her mother twisted her mouth from one side to the other. "Maybe just one."

Catherine eased back the flap of the envelope and slowly slid out the letter, unfolding the yellowed paper carefully, hoping to find some words of wisdom from a great-great-grandfather she'd never known. She needed something to give her hope, a distraction from everything she had going on in her tormented mind. Things she wasn't ready to tell anyone. Even her mother.

Mamm leaned in closer, holding her flashlight on the letter. Then they read silently.

May 12, 1928

Dearest Elizabeth,

On the day of my eighteenth birthday, I slept beneath the branches of the large Cypress tree that forms a partial umbrella over the Tucket Creek bridge. My only food in three days has been an apple and a loaf of bread offered to me by a kindly old man I met when I stumbled upon his small home in the woods. I've also consumed as many dewberries as I've been able to find, leaving my hands a deep-purple reminder that my life has changed. I thirst for something more than the water from the creek, which tastes like the mud it shares space with.

If only you hadn't made that phone call we could be together now. But I shall stay on the run here in Texas until I am able to clear our names, or at the very least, to seek guidance from a trusted source, which I have yet to find.

Know that in this darkest of hours, my heart still longs to be with you, and my love for you has not diminished. Stay hidden with your Amish cousins. I pray you will be in my loving arms soon.

Dearly,

Isaac

Catherine dropped her flashlight, rummaged around on the floor until she lifted it again, then brought her free hand to her chest. "What does this mean?"

Mamm had her flashlight on the letter as well, casting a double glow of arcs, each one shadowing the other. "I don't know, but . . ." She shook her head. "I don't know," she repeated before she reached for the letter, folded it up, and put it in the envelope. She lifted herself from the floor and placed the letter back in its box. She put the top on, then Catherine's mother put all the items back in the cedar chest. "Now let's see if we can get that box of books you wanted up the stairs."

Catherine stayed seated on the cool concrete, the cedar chest still open, beckoning to them. "What? Don't you want to read more of the letters? What was *Granddaadi* Isaac running from? Why was he in Texas? I can't stand not to know. And it almost sounds like *Grandmammi* wasn't Amish." She let out a small gasp. "Maybe *Granddaadi* wasn't either."

Her mother sighed, raised her chin for a couple of seconds, then lowered the lid of the cedar chest. "We agreed to read one letter."

Catherine gaped at her mother. "*Mamm*, aren't you curious to know more?"

"*Mei maedel*, they are not our letters to read." Her voice was firm, and Catherine knew better than to argue. She had enough to worry about without creating a squabble with her mother.

But still, Catherine had finally found a distraction from her troubles, and she wasn't ready to leave the cedar chest or the story the letters told. "*Mamm*, someone left all these keepsakes— the tiny shoes, the candleholders, the quilt . . . and these letters. If they weren't meant to be read, then why are they here?"

Emma didn't have an answer for her daughter, and she was glad when they were back in the main house breathing in the aroma of the peanut butter cookies still cooling on the rack. Catherine made a hasty exit, not hiding her disappointment about leaving the rest of the letters unread. Emma feared they might bring forth more than either of them wanted—or needed—to know.

She squeezed her eyes closed and struggled to recall the conversation she'd had with her *granddaadi* Jonah on his dying bed when Emma was barely a teenager. They were alone in the room, and he'd mentioned something about his father having been on the run for a crime he'd committed. Later, when Emma asked her grandmother about it, she insisted it was all rubbish, that Emma's grandfather was talking out of his head. But Emma had always wondered if that was true. Her *mammi* had always been a proud woman, even though pride was frowned upon in their community. If anyone would have hidden family history that was less than perfect, it would have been her grandmother. Emma remembered several times throughout her childhood when her grandmother encouraged her to cover up details as opposed to revealing the truth. It wasn't exactly lying, but it wasn't being truthful either. Emma's mother had inherited the same tendency.

Once when Emma was a child, she'd taken Hannah Zook's new spinning top on purpose. She loved the toy and stuffed it in her backpack since her mother wouldn't get one for her. Her grandmother discovered the toy when she came to visit a few days later and told Emma's mother. The three of them went to the Zooks' house. But instead of having Emma apologize for what she'd done, both her mother and grandmother said Emma had accidently taken the toy home. There were plenty of other times when Emma's mother and grandmother twisted a situation to save face, but that particular incident stuck with Emma because she could still see Hannah's knowing expression.

Emma had tried to raise Catherine differently, relying on the truth whether or not it caused their family any embarrassment. She poured herself onto the couch, wishing the walls could talk. What stories they would tell. She leaned her head back, kicked her feet up on the coffee table, and closed her eyes. A cool breeze blew through the window screens, and Emma tried to envision what life might have been like for her great-grandfather, a young man living in Texas, a state Emma had never visited.

She couldn't help but share her daughter's curiosity about the letter they'd read and temptation tugged at her thoughts, but something deeper inside warned her to leave well enough alone.

CHAPTER 3

Elizabeth paced her cousin's cabin, nervous as hunted prey and expecting someone to burst through the door, grab her by the hair, and take her directly to jail. Or the nearest hanging tree, if such things still occurred.

"Quit your pacing now, child," Aunt Lavinia said as she crossed through the living room carrying a stack of folded towels. "The mail carrier ain't gonna get here any faster, whether you're pacing or sitting, so I suggest you go sit at the kitchen table and help Naomi peel vegetables so I can get the stew to simmering. Your uncle won't take kindly to supper being late."

Elizabeth nodded, then waited for her aunt to go out of view before she looked down at her baggy blue dress covered by a black apron. It was a homely looking getup, but it was the way women in an Amish community dressed. Naomi had loaned Elizabeth the traditional clothes to wear, and even though the dresses weren't flattering, they were comfortable. The loose garments hit below the knees and came in dark colors—blue, green, and maroon mostly. Women wore black aprons atop the dresses, a good idea since they cooked a lot. There was so much to take care of on an

Amish farm, and Elizabeth helped as best she could. All the women in their Amish community also wore prayer coverings on their heads, which they called *kapps*. When they were home, they often covered their heads with scarves, and Elizabeth had followed suit on that as well.

She was grateful to her aunt and uncle for taking her in, especially under the circumstances, but Elizabeth could tell her aunt wasn't comfortable about the situation. Aunt Lavinia always steered Elizabeth away from windows, discouraged her from collecting eggs with Naomi, and instructed her to keep the bedroom blinds upstairs drawn at all times so the sun wouldn't bleach the quilt on Elizabeth's bed. Her aunt also insisted that Elizabeth wear Naomi's clothes, even though she hadn't seen a soul since she'd arrived.

Most people had cars or pickup trucks in Pennsylvania, but Naomi's family got around in a buggy. So did their Amish friends. They all went barefoot a lot too, something Elizabeth had taken a liking to. The feel of the grass between her toes reminded her of her childhood, hot summers in Texas, and frolicking around barefoot before adult complications smacked her upside the head.

Elizabeth glanced out the window one last time before she made her way to the kitchen table. She had no way to send a letter to Isaac since she didn't have any idea where he was. So she picked up a potato, then a paring knife, and started peeling. Naomi was slicing an onion, her mouth awkwardly wide, clearly trying to breathe through it to keep her eyes from watering. That had never worked for Elizabeth.

After another minute or so, Naomi blew out a big breath of air, set down the onion, and scurried across the kitchen. She slammed her palms on the counter and squeezed her eyes closed.

"Blasted onions. Strongest ones I've ever cut into." Elizabeth's cousin blinked a few more times before she reached for a glass of water on the counter, gulping it down as if that might help somehow.

Elizabeth set aside the peeled potato and reached for another one, discarding the peel in the wastebasket to her left. With each mundane stroke of the knife, she tried to picture where Isaac might be. Was he still hungry? Had a stranger offered him more food and water? Were dewberries still plentiful where he was? Elizabeth hadn't seen any dewberries since she'd been in Lancaster County.

"I'm sure you'll be getting another letter from Isaac any day now." Naomi dabbed at her eyes with the hem of her black apron, leaned against the kitchen counter, and folded her hands in front of her. She was nineteen, two years older than Elizabeth, and engaged to be married in a few months. "Try not to worry so much."

Elizabeth swallowed the knot in her throat, afraid that if she said anything, tears would flow like a river down her face. She took a deep breath and picked up another potato.

"Maybe Isaac is on his way here now, and that's why you haven't heard from him since that first letter." Naomi offered a weak smile, and Elizabeth appreciated her hopefulness, but she and Isaac were in a mess of trouble, and even if Isaac did show up on the doorstep, there was no guarantee he and Elizabeth would be together the way they'd planned. All their dreams had gone up in a plume of smoke two months ago.

"I'm not sure how he'd ever find this house. There's not a soul nearby for miles." Elizabeth recalled the ride in her uncle's buggy from the train station to her current home. She'd ridden in a buggy when she was little, before most families owned a car, but this buggy was gray in color, smaller, and felt much bumpier than she remembered.

From the main highway, they'd turned onto gravel roads, and with each mile, the rock streets had narrowed down to not much more than a walking trail. Thick groves of trees canopied overhead in many places, giving it the feel of a tunnel, always with a light at the end of it, before they emerged into wide-open fields of tobacco, cotton, and various types of hay. But the last few miles to the house had dense forest on either side, the final turn barely even a road.

"Folks in town know we're here." Naomi paused, smiling a little. "They just don't know *you* are here."

Elizabeth sighed, not looking up from the potato she was peeling. Her uncle seemed okay that she was there, but Aunt Lavinia scowled a lot. Uncle John was Elizabeth's uncle by blood, her mother's brother. She'd heard the stories about her uncle falling in love with an Amish woman named Lavinia when he'd gone to Pennsylvania for his job, but up until now, she'd never really known her uncle and his family. Elizabeth wasn't blood kin to her aunt, so maybe that was why her aunt wasn't as willing to hide their "wanted" cousin. *Wanted for assault, maybe even murder.*

Elizabeth shivered every time the thought crossed her mind, and few minutes went by without her reliving the nightmare. She regretted them running off as much as she regretted what happened.

Where are you, my love?

Isaac kept an ear peeled to the radio nearby, trying to look like he was interested that a woman named Amelia Earhart would attempt to be the first woman to successfully cross the Atlantic Ocean. It was the least he could do for his generous hosts, who were hanging on every word coming through the booming box.

"It's just unbelievable that they're going to be taking a woman across the ocean." Ronald Dowdy shook his head. His wife, Leona, frowned.

"A woman can do anything a man can do," Leona huffed before she left her husband and Isaac alone in the living room.

"She might not always know her place, but I love that woman with all I am." Ronald turned off the radio when the story about the transatlantic flight was over. He smiled, motioning for Isaac to follow him to the porch, where they'd likely smoke a cigarette, and Isaac would briefly feel a sense of normalcy, even though he'd never smoked until he met Ronald Dowdy. The good reverend had assured Isaac that the Lord didn't disapprove of smoking, only drinking, calling alcohol the devil's cocktail. Isaac wasn't sure, but he'd nodded and enjoyed a smoke with Ronald the past four evenings.

They were quiet for a while, each puffing on a Lucky Strike from the comfort of the good reverend's cottage deep in west Texas. It was hundreds of miles away from his beloved Elizabeth, but when the reverend had stopped his truck to relieve himself at the banks of the Colorado River where Isaac was sleeping, the reverend had taken it as a sign to help a wayward soul.

For five hours Ronald—which he insisted on being called, as opposed to Reverend Dowdy—had told Isaac about the Lord and all the Deity had to offer, even for a lost soul such as Isaac. The man never questioned Isaac as to why he was sleeping by the river in clothes that hadn't been washed in weeks, nor did he pass judgment in any way throughout their journey. Ronald had stopped at a motel, paid for a room for a few hours, and waited at a nearby coffee shop while Isaac showered and dressed in the new clothes Ronald bought for him on the route back to his home.

"You said you have a good woman waiting for you in

Pennsylvania." Ronald blew a smoke ring, then smiled at his accomplishment. "Elizabeth, did you say?"

Isaac's chest tightened at the mention of her name, but he nodded as he took a drag off the cigarette, then coughed, hoping Ronald wouldn't ask Elizabeth's last name. Even a man of God couldn't be completely trusted right now.

"I expect she's a lovely woman, and youthful like yourself." Ronald turned to Isaac and lifted a bushy dark eyebrow. The man was easily old enough to be Isaac's father, his hair graying at the temples, fine lines feathering from each eye.

"Yes, sir. She is beautiful." He cleared his throat, hoping to clear the lump in it. "Elizabeth is seventeen."

Ronald nodded. "And you expect to make your way to her soon?" His eyebrow was still raised, his eyes staying on Isaac.

"I hope to, sir. Yes." Isaac held his breath.

"I see." Ronald faced forward again, gazing out into the sunset as birds soared toward home and an occasional frog's presence resounded from the wooded fields. A coyote howled in the far distance. "Tomorrow is the Lord's day, and I shall be leading the worship at our church in town." He slowly turned back toward Isaac, that eyebrow lifting again. "Will you be joining Leona and me for the service?"

Isaac swallowed hard, opened his mouth to speak, then took a deep breath.

"Or perhaps you still aren't rested and would enjoy a quiet day to yourself. I'm sure the Lord will hear your prayers from our humble abode as well as He will in town." Ronald smiled all knowingly at Isaac, and Isaac wondered what he would think if he knew he was housing a wanted man. Would he call the police or merely toss Isaac to the curb? And surely the reverend wouldn't leave a man like Isaac alone in his home, free to steal anything he wanted.

"I would enjoy a rest, sir." A wave of adrenaline shot through Isaac's body as he waited for the reverend to question him, but Ronald dubbed out his cigarette, stood up, and opened the screen door that led to the living room. He paused and looked over his shoulder.

"I do not know God's plan for my having stumbled upon you by the river, but I can be certain there always *is* a plan. Our Father sees to that. Whatever ails your soul, my son, I will pray that peace finds you. And that trouble doesn't."

Ronald continued into the house. Isaac hung his head as shame wrapped around him like a thick, wet blanket.

Trouble has already found me.

CHAPTER 4

Later that evening Catherine lowered her head in prayer when Abram did, and she prayed the same thing she'd been praying every day for weeks—that she and Abram would find a way to work through their problems, which seemed to be piling up on top of each other. She opened one eye, looked at her husband, and wondered if he was praying for the same guidance. A few moments later when she lifted her head, Abram smiled at her.

"The roast is *gut*."

She forced a smile back at him. *"Danki."*

"How was your day?" Her husband slathered butter on a slice of bread Catherine baked early that morning.

"It was fine." She picked at her roast, then shuffled the meat around with her sweet peas. They were reduced to small talk, both too afraid to confront the baby elephants in the room. None of the issues were huge. No one was dying or anything as awful as that, but all combined, their worries were overwhelming. Sometimes Catherine wanted to scream, to lash out at someone, but it wasn't their way.

"I went to see *mei mudder* this morning."

"*Ya*, I saw my pants on the bed. Thank her for mending them for me." Abram shoved another chunk of roast in his mouth.

Catherine's stomach was twisted with anxiety ninety percent of the time. For a little while this morning she'd been distracted by the contents of the cedar chest. She considered telling Abram about the letters so that maybe they could keep their problems in perspective. It sounded like Elizabeth and Isaac were in serious trouble. Maybe Catherine and Abram's marital woes shouldn't seem so bad.

"I could have mended your slacks," she said as she lifted one shoulder, then dropped it slowly. "But I guess *Mamm* is trying to find things to do. *Daed* stays busy in his workshop a lot."

"*Ya, ya.*" Abram consumed the rest of his meat, followed by a big swig of tea.

Catherine's stomach continued to churn, and her bottom lip started to tremble. Twisting the string on her *kapp*, she finally couldn't stand it anymore. "Are we ever going to talk about . . ." She wasn't sure where to start. "Things."

Abram laid his fork across his plate louder than necessary. "I'm tired. I worked all day, and I have enough to worry about right now." His eyebrow twitched the way it did when he was angry.

"And you don't think I worry?" She fought the tears building in the corners of her eyes. "Not talking about the things that are bothering us isn't going to help." She pushed her chair away from the table and walked away, deciding maybe she wasn't up for the conversation either.

Abram wanted to move to Ohio, they hadn't been able to conceive a child, and the tension between them was growing daily. Neither one of them represented the person the other had married. Catherine didn't like herself any better than she liked Abram lately. The bitterness that had subtly crept into their lives was now festering like an infection.

When she reached their bedroom, she slammed the door

behind her and ripped off her *kapp*. Then she threw it on the floor and let her long, brown hair tumble past her shoulders.

God wasn't hearing her prayers.

Emma and Jonathan finished their devotions for the evening, and Emma's husband settled back in his recliner with a book. Since they'd become empty-nesters, Jonathan had taken to reading whenever he wasn't working in his shop. Emma occasionally found reading enjoyable and relaxing, but it was hard for her to be nonproductive. She'd spent her life, up until the end of last year, taking care of others. Her children, her husband, and her mother. Tending to only Jonathan now left her with lots of free time on her hands. She'd taken up needlepoint, a task she hadn't enjoyed when she was younger, and after a couple of weeks, she realized she still didn't like it.

She picked up a book from the coffee table, one off a short stack Jonathan planned to read, he'd said. She read the foreword and flipped to the first chapter, but after a couple pages, she just wasn't retaining any of it. It wasn't the story. She couldn't keep her mind from drifting back to the box of letters in the cedar chest. Maybe she should reconsider her resistance to reading them. If she suggested they go through them, she'd have more time with Catherine and maybe find out what was troubling her.

"Catherine was here this morning." She paused, waiting to have her husband's attention.

Jonathan lowered his reading glasses and looked over them. "Did you find out what's wrong?"

Emma shook her head. "*Nee.* But she seemed in better spirits. She even laughed a little."

"Ach, well, that sounds hopeful."

Jonathan wanted to get back to his book, Emma thought, as he waited for her to go on. "She was here to pick up some books for the auction coming up." She strummed her fingers against the hardback cover. "But while we were in the basement, she noticed my great-grandmother Elizabeth's cedar chest."

"The one with the key broken off in the lock?"

Emma cocked her head to one side. "How did you know about that?"

"Your mother asked me if I could help her get it open one day. She was still living here." *So* Mamm *was tempted to see what was inside.* "But by the time I returned with the tools, she told me never mind."

Emma tapped a finger to her chin. "Hmm . . ." She waited for her thoughts to unscramble. "I feel like my grandmother didn't really want anyone to get into that chest."

Jonathan closed the book and took off his reading glasses. "Why do you say that?"

Emma told her husband about the letters and what her grandfather told her when she was a teenager, about a crime being committed.

"It seems to me that your mother or grandmother would have destroyed the letters if they didn't want anyone to read them," Jonathan responded.

Emma shrugged. "I don't know. But Catherine really wants to read them all, and it would give us time to spend together. Maybe she'd confide in me about whatever is bothering her. It's not like her not to come to me when she's upset about something."

"She's older now." Jonathan leaned forward. "Maybe she's just trying to work things out on her own."

"Maybe." Emma remembered when she'd quit telling her mother things because she didn't want to worry her. She hoped Catherine wasn't doing the same thing. Not yet anyway.

She picked up the book again, but after a few minutes, she put it back on the stack and went to her bedroom. She retrieved her cell phone from the bedside table. *Emergencies only.* Jonathan's words rang in her ears. He'd been opposed to getting a mobile phone, but when Emma's mother fell ill, Emma had insisted on it. She dialed Catherine's number.

Catherine kept her eyes closed as Abram got dressed in their bedroom. She'd woken up crying, and she was afraid if she had any conversation at all with her husband, she'd start up again. She waited until she heard his buggy heading down the driveway before she lifted herself out of bed. Lately she wanted to stay in bed all day and sleep so she didn't have to think about all the things bothering her. Possibly having to move, to leave her family and friends, and her husband's unwillingness to consider her feelings about it. Catherine touched her stomach, longing to feel life inside, but that blessing hadn't arrived either.

At least for today she had something to look forward to. Her mother had called to say she'd reconsidered reading the letters. The only downside to the anticipation of learning about her great-great-grandparents was the effort to keep a happy face around her mother. She thought she'd done so yesterday, but how long could she keep it up today?

She picked up her prayer covering from the rocking chair, where Abram must have put it this morning. Carrying it with her to the bathroom, she felt a tinge of guilt over throwing it to the ground, but with each day, her faith was floundering right along with her marriage.

After getting dressed, she ate a bowl of cereal. She hadn't been rising early to make Abram's breakfast, and she didn't know if he was eating a little something at home—no evidence he was—or stopping on the way to work for breakfast. Either way, childish as it was, she wasn't cooking breakfast for her husband until he agreed to talk.

By the time she pulled her buggy into her parents' driveway, it was pouring rain. Her mother met her at the door with a towel.

"Well, at least you took the covered buggy and not your spring buggy," *Mamm* said, handing her the towel.

"I didn't think it was supposed to rain today, but dark clouds were rolling in just as I was leaving. I decided not to take the chance." She dried herself as best she could, then followed her mother inside. "What made you change your mind about the letters?"

Mamm shrugged. "It's hard not to be curious." Grinning, she winked.

Catherine nodded and tried to smile. Maybe once they started reading the letters, she could slip into Elizabeth and Isaac's story and detach from her own thoughts.

Each toting a flashlight, they made their way downstairs to the basement. This time Catherine's mother brought a lantern along too. Once they were set up and had sufficient lighting, they lifted the lid on the cedar chest, and Catherine's pulse picked up. They decided to organize the letters by the postmark date.

"There are more from Isaac to Elizabeth than from her to him." Catherine looked at her mother. "Maybe we should just open the last letter first." She grinned, which felt good.

"*Nee!*" Her mother spoke in a loud whisper, which added an

air of excitement to their little adventure. "Let's read the one dated next, and let the story unfold. Here it is."

Catherine waited as her mother pulled the letter from its envelope, Catherine shining a flashlight on the words from her great-great grandfather.

June 22, 1928

Dearest Elizabeth,

I hope this letter finds you well. I'm sorry I haven't written sooner. A kind man of God and his wife have taken me in. I am a long way from where I started, though, many miles from my home here in Texas, and many miles from you in Pennsylvania. I had reason to worry as of late when a lawman came through the area. Elizabeth, he asked around about me, and although I have no idea how he might have tracked me to this small town, I have stayed quiet and hidden.

I don't understand why the people I'm staying with are not giving me up to the police. It seems odd. They are very trusting folks. I try to repay them for their kindnesses. I rebuilt their shed that was falling down, and I did some repairs to their fence. I collect the eggs for the woman each morning, and I tend to the cows and horses. I feel safe here. Their home is miles from town, and if a visitor does arrive, I retreat to my room. The reverend and his wife live well, better than I ever did. But they seem right with the Lord, so maybe that's why.

The reverend doesn't ask me any questions. Only thing he said was that when a kindness is done to a person, that person needs to carry it with him until he sees fit to double the kindness for someone in need. I'm not sure how I'll do that, but somehow I'll find a way.

I'm really sorry for what I said in my last letter to you. None of this is your fault. It's all mine. I reckon calling the police was the right thing for you to do, but I got spooked, Elizabeth. That's why I ran.

I'm going to have to leave this place and these nice people soon before I get found out. Elizabeth, I will never ever tell them about you, where to find you, or anything else. I will protect you forever. I will write again when I am able.

Loving you always,

Isaac

Catherine's heart pounded against her chest, and there was a sense of excitement and dread swirling in the pit of her stomach. "What in the world could they have done, *Mamm*?"

Her mother shook her head, staring at the letter. "I don't know."

Catherine took a deep, cleansing breath, hoping to slow her heart rate. Now it was she who wasn't sure if she wanted to know how this story ended.

She and *Mamm* stared at the next letter in the stack. *Mamm* reached for it and slowly opened the envelope. It was longer than the others, but there was a knock at the door upstairs.

"*Ach*, that is probably Mary Petersheim bringing me the money from our bake sale." *Mamm* handed Catherine the letter and rose to her feet. "Wait here. I won't be long."

Catherine tapped the folded letter against her leg for a couple minutes while her mother and Mary chatted upstairs. But when it sounded like the conversation wasn't going to end right away, Catherine unfolded the letter. It was dated only a few days later: June 26, 1928. She only meant to read the first page, but it was like a book she couldn't put down as her heart rate picked up again.

The more she read, the more her own problems didn't seem as bad.

When she heard her mother and Mary still talking, she lifted the rest of the envelopes into her lap, but as she thumbed through them, she realized that some of the letters didn't have a postmark on them. So they were written but never mailed. She kept reading.

Emma returned and Catherine looked like a deer caught in the headlights, her eyes round as she bit her bottom lip.

"I couldn't help it, *Mamm*. Some of these were never mailed, and I just kept reading. It sounds so tragic." She pushed several envelopes toward Emma. "Here, I'll wait while you catch up."

Emma took the letters, wishing Catherine had waited, but she read while Catherine went upstairs to the restroom and then out to collect the day's eggs.

Emma was just finishing the last of the letters when Catherine returned.

"Should we keep going?" Catherine sat down beside her mother.

"Let's wait. We've already read so many today." She was afraid Catherine would want to read them all in one sitting, and as curious as Emma was about the outcome, she also wanted to have more time with her daughter. "It gives us something to look forward to." She put the box of letters back in the cedar chest, then closed the lid.

"Isaac and Elizabeth must find their way back to each other, but it seems so heartbreaking." Catherine walked ahead of Emma, shining the flashlight at her feet, Emma doing the same.

When they were back in the living room, Emma said, "Sometimes even the largest obstacles can be overcome."

Please talk to me, Catherine.

But her daughter moved toward the front door. Before opening it, however, she turned around to face Emma. "Do you really believe that?"

"*Ya*, I do believe that."

Talk to me. Please talk to me. She tried to will Catherine to open up to her, but her daughter simply nodded. Pushing Catherine hadn't worked in the past, and it wouldn't work now, so Emma bit her tongue. "See you tomorrow?"

Catherine nodded, then strode down the porch steps. Emma could feel the load she carried on her shoulders as if it were her own, and she would do anything to carry it for her, if Catherine would just let her.

CHAPTER 5

Elizabeth and Naomi hung the clothes on the line in the late-morning light, and Elizabeth thought about the weather back home in Texas. July and August were the hottest months of the year, and usually by midafternoon it was so humid it was hard to breathe. The heat wasn't as bad in Lancaster County, but Elizabeth had still broken a sweat while hanging the clothes to dry.

They'd meant to get an earlier start, but Elizabeth's aunt needed help finishing some baking for the upcoming Sister's Day. It was a monthly event when all the Amish women in the district gathered to quilt, can fruits and vegetables, or sometimes deliver food to the elderly.

Naomi had opted not to go because it was at her fiancé's ex-girlfriend's house. Her excuse seemed petty to Elizabeth, but she chose to stay home too. *Home.* That's what it felt like now, after two months. She missed Isaac, but a new feeling had also latched on to her. *Anger.* And Elizabeth wasn't sure where to direct the emotion. She felt the need to blame someone for her and Isaac's situation. God was an easy target since He could have prevented the mess they were in.

It had been a month since she'd received two letters from Isaac in one week, and she'd been fearful that he'd been apprehended or that something worse had happened. She'd been praying, at Naomi's insistence, even though she didn't see how that was going to help Isaac.

Naomi's wedding was set for October, and planning for the event was in full swing. Thankfully Naomi and Aunt Lavinia included Elizabeth in the preparations, a welcome distraction. Her aunt had warmed up to her during the past month or so, but deciding that no one was looking for her niece, she had been insistent that Elizabeth go to church service with them.

Elizabeth was growing close to Naomi also. They shared a bedroom and often stayed up late in the evenings. Naomi had shared about her romance with Samuel. It was such a sweet story. Elizabeth told her how she and Isaac had met, how they'd fallen in love, and through her tears, she told Naomi how she and Isaac had been blamed for assaulting a young man, maybe even murdering him. But she wasn't sure what had happened to the young man—something that haunted her daily.

Even though Isaac had been the one to pick up the shovel, Elizabeth had stood by and watched. Self-defense or not, a man had been injured and there would likely be consequences. Naomi had heard bits and pieces of the story from her parents, and Elizabeth filled in some of the blanks for her but spared her cousin too many details. Naomi had cried, which touched Elizabeth. She didn't have any brothers or sisters, and Naomi was like a sister now.

"All done." Naomi bounced up on her toes after pinning the last sheet on the line. "Let's take the buggy to town and treat ourselves to a soda or shake." She pulled a tissue from her apron pocket and dabbed at the sweat gathering on her forehead.

Elizabeth hesitated. She'd been to church with Naomi and her family, but she mostly avoided activities outside the community where they lived.

"Come on." Naomi waved. "Let's get our shoes on and enjoy a change of scenery."

The ride to town was short and bouncy. After they'd turned onto the main road, Naomi guided the buggy and maneuvered alongside automobiles that seemed to pay them no mind. Not something Elizabeth would have seen back in Texas.

A bolt of adrenaline coursed through her when a car turned right in front of the buggy, causing the horse's front feet to come off the ground when Naomi pulled back on the reins. She had the horse under control within seconds, but Elizabeth kept a hand to her heart. It was the same rushing apprehension she felt when she thought about Isaac. Elizabeth silently prayed for God to keep him safe. She also asked God to stay by her side, to help her grow in her faith. Naomi said blaming the Lord wasn't the answer. Elizabeth wanted to believe that God would right this horrible situation. Despite her doubts, she chose to put her faith in Him.

Another buggy passed by them. A woman was driving, and she had four young children with her. One of the oldest was holding a baby on her lap. Elizabeth was amazed at the independence women here had attained. They not only took care of their husbands and children, but they also tended gardens and took care of yard work. Most families had seven or eight children. Naomi had explained that her parents weren't able to have more children— *kinner*, they called them. But Naomi wanted a dozen children. Elizabeth couldn't imagine feeding that many mouths.

"There's the soda shop." Naomi pointed to her left, then began to lead the horse that way until she pulled into a small area where two cars and a buggy were parked.

Naomi tethered the horse like she'd been doing it since she

was a child, which apparently she had, driving a buggy on her own since she was twelve.

Elizabeth's stomach roiled as they walked to the entrance, anxious for a soda treat, but also worried about being out in public, away from the comfort and protection of the Amish community.

"Don't be nervous," Naomi said, smiling just before she opened the door. A bell rang to signal that new patrons were entering, and all eyes drifted briefly to Elizabeth, but the men's gazes landed on Naomi and stayed there. Elizabeth's cousin was tall with perfect posture, and even in a dress that resembled a potato bag, her curves were where they should be. Naomi had big blue eyes, and she smiled a lot, something Elizabeth needed to do more of, if and when her situation was resolved. Wisps of hair the color of straw framed Naomi's face beneath her prayer covering. Elizabeth wasn't surprised Naomi was engaged to be married soon.

There were a lot more people inside than she would have guessed based on the cars and buggy parked outside. But in Paradise, there were a lot of businesses within walking distance of the soda shop.

They had just ordered a chocolate shake to share when a man swaggered up to them wearing a short-sleeve blue shirt, black slacks with suspenders, and a straw hat. It was what Amish men typically wore, and even though Elizabeth was promised to another man, she found this Amish fellow to be very handsome with his square jaw, boyish smile, and solid build. He was tall, like a towering spruce, and a broad chest protruded from beneath his shirt, filling the fabric.

Naomi and the man exchanged greetings.

"Eli, this is *mei* cousin Elizabeth from Texas." Naomi smiled at him as Elizabeth nodded in response.

"I've seen you at church service. Are you enjoying your visit here in Lancaster County?" Still smiling, he rubbed his clean-shaven chin, which by Amish standards meant he wasn't married.

"Yes, it's lovely here." The knot forming in Elizabeth's throat felt like a baseball. She swallowed hard and tried to smile again as guilt wrapped around her like a serpent squeezing her, reminding her that this handsome man was not to be ogled. She lowered her gaze and took another sip of the shake.

"If you haven't been given a proper tour, I'd be happy to pro-vide one. Are you free on Saturday?" He smiled, and for a few seconds, Elizabeth's mouth stayed open as she gaped at him.

"Uh . . ." *Tell him you are spoken for.* She glanced at Naomi, who just smiled, not making any attempt to deter Elizabeth from what appeared to be a handsome suitor asking her on a date. "Okay," she finally said, barely above a whisper.

"I'll come calling at nine in the morning. Is that *gut?*"

Elizabeth nodded and glanced at Naomi, who was grinning with satisfaction, even as Eli walked away.

They finished the chocolate shake, then left to head back home, enjoying a silent ride for the first half of their journey.

"I feel like you set that up, me meeting Eli." Elizabeth turned to face Naomi as she struggled to keep her hair beneath the prayer covering. She'd forgotten to use bobby pins like Naomi told her to do.

Naomi shrugged. "Would it be so bad if I did set it up?"

Elizabeth dropped her jaw, unsure whether to be mad or hurt. "Why did you do that? You know I am promised to Isaac."

Naomi flicked the reins to speed up her horse as they crossed Lincoln Highway, then once the animal had settled into a slow trot, she turned to Elizabeth. "Then why did you say yes?" She grinned a little.

"Well, I, uh . . . It put me on the spot." She kept her gaze straight ahead, her chin raised.

"Eli isn't just handsome. He's a *gut* man." Naomi coaxed the horse to pick up speed. "Don't you want to live a normal life? What if you are on the run forever? That's no way to live."

"But I love Isaac." Elizabeth didn't even hesitate to respond. She was angry about the entire situation, worried, and sometimes confused about the ways she seemed to be changing while living in Lancaster County, but she hadn't stopped loving Isaac. "I'm going to cancel with Eli." She shook her head. "It's not right for me to go with him."

Naomi grunted. "Don't do that. Let him show you around, then see how you feel."

Elizabeth considered the idea, fearful her attraction to Eli might be a problem if she didn't cancel the date, and that was another confusing matter. How could she be attracted to a man she didn't know? She'd always thought she judged a person's beauty from the inside out, not the other way around.

"It's Isaac's fault you are in this mess." Naomi's words were clipped and a bit louder than before. "It's just not fair."

Elizabeth opened her mouth to snap back at her cousin, accepting responsibility along with Isaac, but she stayed quiet and reminded herself that Naomi cared for her and was only looking out for her best interest.

"It was my fault too," she said softly, not even sure if Naomi heard her.

But gnawing away in her mind was the possibility that things might have turned out differently if Isaac hadn't lost his temper. Maybe they could have talked their way out of their predicament at the time. And why hadn't Isaac written to her recently?

By the time dusk settled around them, she'd lost her appetite, and after barely eating and struggling through the family devotions, she went upstairs for some time alone. Naomi was on the porch with Samuel.

Elizabeth lit the lantern and placed it on the bedside table between her and Naomi's bed. She took out a pen and some stationary Naomi had given her. Then she wrote Isaac a letter to the return address where he was staying with the Reverend Dowdy and his wife. Elizabeth didn't know if Isaac would receive her correspondence since he'd written that he would be moving on soon, but she was desperate to communicate with him.

July 24, 1928

My dear Isaac,

I hope this letter finds you well, especially since I haven't heard from you in almost a month of Sundays. I don't know if you have been caught or have forgotten about me. With each day my mind wanders in a hundred directions.

Naomi is very involved in her wedding preparations, and the family has included me in the planning, which makes me think woefully about all the plans you and I had to be married. I am wondering if that will ever happen. I don't see how.

Oh, dearest, how my heart aches for you, but I also find myself confused and longing for what could have been. All of our hopes and dreams extinguished like a bright light snubbed out without warning, leaving only smoke and stench. Why, Isaac? Why did this happen to us? I pray about it since Naomi and her family believe that God answers prayers, but I often wonder if I should go to the police. Although that didn't work out well for us the last time, and my actions put you in harm's way.

Perhaps the fellow's father has had time to think clearly after mourning his son, if the young man had in fact died. Maybe he would see now that you were only trying to protect us when you struck back at his boy. If his son is alive and tells the truth, you and I both would be free to carry on with our lives as we'd planned. This tragedy continues to grow and grow, and I find myself wanting to run away from the memories of that night. It is all so heavy on my heart.

I miss my mother. Since my father died years ago, it was just she and I—until you. I have not heard from her, and when I left, she was falling ill, thus the reason she reached out to my uncle. I feel our situation brought on my mother's illness, or made it worse. I've tried not to be a burden on my uncle's family, and I actually have grown to feel as one of them.

Isaac, my love, I need to hear from you.

Tender regards as I miss you
and love you,
Your Elizabeth

She sealed the letter with a kiss. Then she laid the envelope on the nightstand and snuggled beneath a single bed sheet, thankful for the cool breeze that drifted through the window screens. Crickets chirped as birds bedded down for the night, and the frogs croaked a peaceful tune.

But as she lay in the darkness, listening to Naomi and Samuel laughing in playful whispers from the front porch, Elizabeth made up her mind about Eli and Saturday.

CHAPTER 6

I saac snapped the lid closed on the small red suitcase Leona had given him. He counted the money Reverend Dowdy insisted he take, enough to get a train ticket and a few days lodging until he could make his way back home. Then he reread Elizabeth's letter, returning it to the envelope before he read his return letter to her.

The reverend's words echoed in his mind, reminding Isaac about his promise to double the kindness. The best thing Isaac could do for Elizabeth was to let her go, to give her the freedom to marry someone else and go on with her life. His hand shook, his eyes moist as he read.

July 29, 1928

Dearest Elizabeth,

I love you with all of my heart, and I am sure this will be the hardest letter I've ever written. But you will not be hearing from me again. You must marry another, my beloved, so that you can have the family you've always dreamed of.

In a desperate and lonely moment, I confided in Reverend Dowdy, unable to bear my secrets alone anymore. As a man of God, the reverend doesn't condone violence, but he understands that my actions were meant to protect you. I also told him about the corruptness surrounding the situation. He chose to put out some feelers, as such, to see what he could find out. He is a fine man, he and his wife, Leona. It appears that the authorities are still looking for me, but according to Reverend Dowdy's inquiries, they do not seem interested in finding you.

You are far away, in a place where no one will likely look for you, and with a new married name, you can live a normal life. I plan to let a few days go by, then I will turn myself in. I can't live with the guilt over what I have done. I will truthfully tell the police that you and I lost touch, and I will continue to tell them of your innocence. I will accept the findings of a jury and fulfill any such penance that should come my way, as I am ultimately the guilty party, not you. Don't write me back at this address. I will be gone by the time you receive this letter, and there is no need to continue putting the reverend and his wife in danger because of me.

Live well and stay strong, my dearest Elizabeth. I will love and miss you for all of my days.

Regretfully,

Isaac

He sealed the envelope, then picked up his suitcase filled with the few belongings and toiletries he'd collected while he was there. Then he took a deep breath and left the main house, crossing through the dogtrot and entering the kitchen. He put the letter to Elizabeth on the kitchen table for Leona to mail, as she'd done for him since he arrived.

As he sat down at the kitchen table for the last time, he felt the cross breeze wafting in through the window screens.

Isaac sniffed the air, the hint of bacon livening his nostrils, but he'd overslept and missed breakfast. He'd planned to leave much earlier, but he'd been awake most of the night worrying about his final letter to Elizabeth. He stared at his last correspondence to his beloved, then stood up and left the kitchen, a fierce wind in the dogtrot catching his hat and pulling it off his head. He scurried to catch it, and once he had hold of it, he continued on and found Reverend Dowdy and Leona on the porch of the main house.

"Here is a sandwich and some snacks for your travels." Leona handed him a brown paper sack, then gave him a motherly hug, followed by a kiss on the cheek. "Be well, Isaac," she said before she dabbed at her eyes with a handkerchief and hurried inside.

"We wish you well in your travels," the reverend said. "We will be praying for you, that you will see God's path clearly."

Isaac nodded. He'd already told Reverend Dowdy he would be turning himself in soon. And for the first time in a while, the Lord's path for Isaac was coming into view. It was a muddy vision, not clear in its entirety, but Isaac was sure that telling the truth, no matter the outcome, would help him see the Lord's path with clarity. He shook the reverend's hand and pulled him into a hug, thanking him for his and Leona's kindness. The older man nodded, and Isaac turned and headed down the porch steps so the reverend wouldn't see the tears forming in the corners of his eyes. He'd walk the half mile to the main road, then hitchhike as far as he could on the route back to his small hometown in Texas. Reverend Dowdy had offered to drive him anywhere he wanted to go, but Isaac needed to be alone, to count on God's divine guidance.

As dark clouds rolled in and a brisk wind picked up, lurching the branches on the trees nearby, he wondered if he should have accepted the reverend's offer. He glanced over his shoulder, tempted to turn back, but Reverend Dowdy and his wife had gone inside.

Isaac picked up the pace, fighting the wind that was trying to slow his stride toward a new future. A future behind bars, most likely, and even worse . . . a life without Elizabeth.

SEPTEMBER 14, 1928

Elizabeth barely made it to the outhouse before she vomited for the sixth morning in a row. Over the past couple of months she'd had bouts of nausea, but she thought it was just nerves. After almost a week of mornings like this, she also realized that she had missed her monthlies since her arrival. *How did I not notice that sooner?* She felt silly, but she'd missed her period before sometimes when she was upset, and her mind had been filled with worry about everything. *This explains the weight gain too.* Elizabeth didn't know a lot about babies, but she knew how they were made, and her and Isaac's one indiscretion had presumably created a life. A life that Isaac would never know about. She put a hand on her enlarged waist, thankful for the baggy dress that had hidden a secret she didn't know she had.

Elizabeth's letter to Isaac had been returned unopened. She assumed Isaac must have left the reverend's house before it arrived. Perhaps it was just as well since the letter Elizabeth received from Isaac a few days later told her to find someone else. She'd cried for days, and that was before she even knew she was pregnant.

Staggering, she fought her way up the porch steps, one hand across her stomach. Eli would be arriving soon to take her to worship service. The small community had started to recognize them as a couple over the past two months, and Elizabeth was planning to be baptized soon. But now the Amish community she'd grown to love would see that she wasn't worthy of such acceptance. *Pregnant and unmarried.*

Isaac had abandoned her, giving up on their love. She wondered how he would feel if he knew Elizabeth was carrying his child, a child they'd created in sin. Was Elizabeth's punishment to be ousted by her beloved? Was he even alive? Did the young man's father do something horrible to Isaac, revenge for attacking his son, whom he believed to be an innocent victim? *If only we hadn't run away after taking him to the hospital.* But Elizabeth wasn't sure things would have turned out any differently since corruption flowed through the town like a turbulent river with hidden undertows.

Soon she would be spurned by the community. There wouldn't be a formal shunning since she hadn't been baptized yet, but a slow detachment process would begin. Would her aunt and uncle follow suit, distancing themselves from her, allowing shame to dictate their decisions? She wondered where she would go if they threw her out. Naomi told her that would never happen after Elizabeth had shared her worries with her, but Elizabeth wasn't so sure.

Eli had already professed his love for her, and Elizabeth suspected he would propose soon. She didn't feel the same way about him, the way she did toward Isaac, no matter how handsome he was. Isaac's edginess was what had gotten him in trouble, but it was also his sense of adventure and his chivalrous nature that she loved. Eli was safe and normal to the point of almost boredom some days. He would make a good father, Elizabeth was sure. But would he be willing to raise another man's child? The timing would be tricky, but could she and Eli pass off the baby as his?

Would Eli even be willing to carry the burden of the lie? Elizabeth wasn't sure she could live with the deception, even for the sake of her reputation and the future of her unborn child.

As her thoughts skidded and collided, she wondered where Isaac was and what he was doing.

OCTOBER 22, 1928

Isaac had fought tears as the judge sentenced him to a year in jail. He'd tried to picture what his parents would think if they were still alive. Isaac had never been in trouble with the law. His parents were taken from him far too soon in a car accident, but he was sure they were frowning on him from heaven.

He was still a blessed man, having learned that Sean Cunningham hadn't died. Living with a man's death—especially someone the same age as Isaac—would have been a heavy burden to carry, even if Sean had been holding a gun to Elizabeth's head, threatening to do the unthinkable to her. In those few blurry moments, Sean had turned his head toward a rustling in the barn behind him, and Isaac had picked up the shovel and struck him against the head.

The Lord must have had His hand on the young man because Sean had survived against all odds, and after another surgery on the right side of his head, he would live a fairly normal life. Reverend Dowdy said God always has a plan. Maybe Sean would change his ways after this. Even though Isaac was sure he and Elizabeth would likely be dead if he hadn't lashed out.

But justice was considered served, the kind of justice that occurs when a father's grief influences his testimony, ultimately obscuring the facts. Isaac and Elizabeth had been scared and took off once they made sure Sean had gotten to a hospital. Running away was a stupid thing to do, and it had turned a clear case of self-defense into aggravated assault charges.

Isaac had turned himself in almost three months ago and confessed, but only after the prosecutor had agreed to immunity for Elizabeth. He wondered what Elizabeth had felt as she read his last correspondence. Was she hurt beyond words? Possibly relieved?

He'd instructed the good reverend to return any letters Elizabeth might send, even though he'd asked her not to write to him. If she did so anyway, eventually she would stop writing and get on with the life she deserved. It was the least Isaac could give her.

But as he sat in a cold jail cell, his head shaved, his spirit hijacked by circumstances, he wondered what the future held for him. Especially without Elizabeth.

Why, Lord? Should I have let the woman I love perish at the hands of Sean, when she'd done nothing more than show him kindness?

Elizabeth folded her hands across her stomach when the baby kicked. Her unborn child had taken a dislike to anything spicy. Elizabeth should have known better than to indulge herself on the day of Naomi and Samuel's wedding. This was the second Amish wedding she'd attended in October, the first having been an older couple whose spouses had both died. Now, as the bishop placed a holy kiss on Samuel's cheek and the bishop's wife did the same, kissing Naomi on the cheek, Elizabeth fought the knot forming in her throat.

She'd only mailed one letter to Isaac, and it had been returned unopened, but she continued writing to him even though no other letters made it to the mailbox. It was a diary of sorts, a way to work through her feelings. But even that felt like a betrayal to Eli. They weren't promised to each other in a marital way, but they spent a lot of time together, and Elizabeth was growing to love him, even if it was in a different way than she loved Isaac.

"They make a lovely couple, *ya?*" Aunt Lavinia whispered as she watched the bishop blessing Naomi and Samuel's commitment to each other.

Elizabeth nodded, allowing her gaze to drift across the room until she locked eyes with Eli. He knew she was pregnant with another man's baby, and though he'd been hurt by the confession, he hadn't shied away from her. He had encouraged her to be baptized into the community, something that would have to happen if they were to be married.

Following the wedding ceremony, there was a grand meal, and then Eli asked her to go for a ride with him to someplace special. She hesitated, wondering if she should stay nearby for Naomi, but her cousin and Samuel only had eyes for each other, and Elizabeth suspected her presence wouldn't be missed.

Summer had faded without much of a good-bye, and fall drifted in on a subtle breeze that felt more like winter in Texas than fall. Elizabeth missed Texas, but with each day that passed with no news from or about Isaac, she found herself retreating within herself, to a place she wasn't familiar with. It wasn't completely dark and lonely, but it also wasn't light and beckoning either. She'd prayed for God to guide her, but she felt like she was at a crossroads that didn't exist. She struggled to move forward, but was unclear if she was imagining the fork in the road. There seemed to be only one obvious path. And it was to Eli.

The creek near the covered bridge was Eli's favorite place, and as much as Elizabeth wanted it to be a favorite place of hers as well, she thought of Isaac on his birthday, sleeping beneath a bridge back in Texas not so long ago.

Eli finished tethering the horse to a tree nearby, then joined Elizabeth sitting on a rock near the water's edge. Ripples of spring-fed water moved over shiny rocks downstream, the sound of the water soothing.

"You know I love you," Eli said softly as he perched beside her. Gently he placed a palm on her stomach. Elizabeth smiled when the baby kicked at his touch. "And I will love this child as my own."

Elizabeth blinked back tears, then squeezed her eyes closed, pushing away thoughts of Isaac. One night had destined her and Isaac to be parents. Another night had destroyed their future. Wherever Isaac was, she wished him well, knowing she would always love him. But maybe it was best they were apart. Even though they'd reacted to a threat, being together might be a constant reminder that an eighteen-year-old young man had been seriously hurt. Elizabeth was afraid to find out Sean Cunningham's ultimate fate. She prayed daily that he'd lived, despite what he'd attempted to do to her.

"I want you to marry me, Elizabeth. I want to love you for the rest of my life." Eli's kind hazel eyes gazed into hers. The baby moved again. *Kicking in agreement, or is it resistance?*

Elizabeth had already spoken to the bishop about her predicament, and since she hadn't been baptized into the faith, the bishop had assured her that she would be cleansed of any wrongdoings through baptism.

"You are a *gut* man, Eli." Elizabeth smiled. She wasn't fluent in *Pennsylvania Deutsch*, but she had picked up a lot of the dialect during her time in Lancaster County. "And I do love you."

She waited for fireworks to burst in the sky, for her heart to beat wildly at this admission, or for the clouds to open up and the sun shine blessings on her and Eli, God's confirmation that Elizabeth was where she was meant to be.

But none of that happened.

"You will marry me, *ya?*" Eli reached up and cupped Elizabeth's cheek with one hand, still gazing into her eyes.

She smiled. "*Ya.* I will marry you."

CHAPTER 7

Catherine thought about Elizabeth and Isaac all the way home that afternoon, her emotions twisting and churning in a way that made sense but that she regarded almost as trickery, a way to make her see Abram's way of thinking. Sometimes a new start might feel like a detour, but is it possible to see destiny clearly—the journey God created especially for them? Catherine didn't think it was a coincidence that she was reading her great-great-grandparents' letters at this particular time in her life. *Gott is trying to tell me something. My problems aren't as bad as I think.*

She was still pondering any relevance Elizabeth and Isaac's story might have to her own situation, but as she pulled the buggy into her driveway, she was surprised to see Abram's buggy pulled up by the barn, his horse already stabled. He wasn't due home for hours, and right away, Catherine wondered if her husband had lost his job.

After tethering her horse, she pulled her sweater snug and hurried across the yard, taking the porch steps two at a time. She opened the front door. Abram was slouched into the couch, a hand across his forehead, which he removed just as Catherine entered the room.

"*Wie bietch?* What are you doing home?" She held her breath, hoping Abram wouldn't confirm her fears.

He ran his hand the length of his short beard as his dark eyebrows furrowed.

Catherine let go of the breath she was holding. "Did you lose your job?" Her bottom lip trembled. If Abram no longer had a job, it definitely would mean a move to Ohio. Abram already wanted to go live near his cousins, and the feuding had started when Catherine told him she wasn't leaving Lancaster County. Her family and friends were here. She wanted to raise her children here. But a year into her marriage, she was still not pregnant, a possible move loomed on the horizon, and her husband seemed as miserable and unhappy as she was. They'd even taken to throwing hurtful insults at each other.

Abram had gotten so mad at her recently that he'd mouthed off and said he should have married Hannah Hostetler, his first girlfriend. He'd tried to take it back, but Catherine hadn't been able to get past it. Things spiraled downhill from there. Had she always been Abram's second choice, the way Eli would have been Elizabeth's second choice had she married him?

"*Nee*, I didn't lose my job." He scratched his cheek, his eyebrows still narrowed into a frown. "I got a promotion."

Catherine wanted to jump for joy, but she stayed silent and waited for some sort of reaction from her husband.

"I've been promoted to manager." He slowly turned his eyes toward her. "And it's a lot more money, so we won't be moving anywhere." He flashed a thin-lipped half smile at her. "I know that will make you happy."

Catherine bit her bottom lip so hard she thought it might bleed. The news should have elated her. She wouldn't have to leave everyone and everything she loved. But right at that moment

Abram's happiness mattered to her, maybe more than her own. Or did she just feel this way because they weren't going to move? She slowly walked toward him and sat down on the couch.

"Abram . . ." She waited until he locked eyes with her. "I will be happy wherever you are, wherever we are together. If you believe that to be in Ohio, then that is where we should go." Truthful words, she told herself, even if now she would be the one settling for second best. Leaving Lancaster County, her parents, friends . . . it was almost too much to bear.

Her husband stared at her for a long while. "*Gut*. Then we'll move." He smiled again, the same type of artificial grin he'd flashed earlier in the conversation. He slowly stood up and shuffled across the living room toward the kitchen.

Catherine sat taller and didn't move as she fought to hold back the tears. She wanted to jump from the couch, tackle him to the ground, and tell him he was the most selfish man she'd ever known. But she stayed calm as she spoke. "Maybe you would prefer to take Hannah with you instead of me?" She cringed the moment she said it.

Abram stopped, his feet seemingly rooted to the wood floors, his hands clenched in fists. He didn't turn around, and a few seconds later he resumed his trek toward the kitchen.

Catherine left the living room, and once she made it to the front porch, she let the tears flow.

The next morning Emma was pulling a rhubarb pie from the oven when the front door closed and she heard footsteps in the living room. Catherine walked into the kitchen a few moments later.

"I saw *Daed* pulling out just now. I talked to him for a minute.

He said he was going to have coffee with two of the deacons." Catherine took off her black cape and hung it on a hook by the door. When she turned around, Emma almost dropped the pie she was holding.

"*Mei maedel* . . ." She clutched the pie tightly with both oven mitts, a primal, maternal instinct kicking into gear. "What in the world is the matter? Your eyes are as swollen as eggs." She edged backward to the kitchen counter, then set the pie on the cooling rack, but she didn't take her eyes from her daughter. Would Catherine finally tell her what was troubling her?

"Allergies." Catherine took off her bonnet and hung it by her cape. "It's a bit too warm for this." She pointed to the cape and hat. "But I thought it was going to rain, and I didn't want to be soaking wet again when I got here."

Emma studied her daughter, tempted to push her for answers, especially since Catherine had never had allergies.

"I thought about Elizabeth and Isaac all the way home yesterday." Catherine sighed. "Elizabeth is going to marry Eli, even though he is her second choice." She shook her head as she grunted a little. "She's making a mistake."

Emma leaned against the kitchen counter and folded her arms across her chest, surprised at the emotion behind her daughter's statement.

"And Isaac told Elizabeth he was turning himself in. She should have tried to stop him, or at least stood by him." Catherine frowned.

Emma tapped a finger to her chin. "I think he just wanted to give her the opportunity to live a better life than he thought he could provide." She sighed. "And writing the letters, even though she didn't plan to mail them, was her way of working through her emotions, I think."

"He abandoned her, and if it was really true love, he wouldn't have done that."

Emma tipped her head to one side, trying to figure out where all this bitterness was coming from. "We can stop reading the letters if they are upsetting you."

Catherine shook her head. "*Nee*. It's too late for that. I want to know what happens. I'm curious if Elizabeth and Eli will tell the members of their community that the baby isn't Eli's. Because if they lie about it, that's wrong too."

Emma shrugged. "*Ya*, I reckon it would be wrong, but you have to keep in mind the way things were back then. It was 1928. People held harsher opinions about things like that. Nowadays it isn't unheard of for one of our own to get pregnant before marriage." She held up a palm when Catherine looked like she was going to object. "I'm not saying that makes it right, just more common now."

Catherine marched toward the stairs that led to the basement. Emma followed, still wondering what was festering within her daughter's mind and heart.

A few minutes later they'd lit two lanterns, each held a flashlight, and Catherine had the letters they'd sorted chronologically.

Catherine shined the light on the envelope in her hand. "Look, this one just has a date written on the envelope. November 2, 1929. It's not addressed to anyone."

Emma waited as her daughter unfolded the letter.

"It's not a letter. It's an itinerary." She read for a few seconds. "Isaac is going to go visit Elizabeth!"

Emma was glad to hear an air of excitement returning to Catherine's voice.

Her daughter reached back into the envelope and pulled out a few other things. "There's all kinds of other stuff in here, train ticket stubs, a hotel receipt, some newspaper clippings. And there's another note in here that looks like Elizabeth's handwriting." She smiled at Emma. "It's like someone put all of this together in this envelope for safe keeping."

"Well, let's see what Isaac has planned and how things progressed."

They both read silently, studying the various ticket stubs and receipts, and when they had finished looking at everything, Catherine lowered the flashlight, covered her face with both hands, and cried. "This is so sad, *Mamm.*"

Emma put her arms around her daughter. She was sad, too, after reading about Isaac's failed attempt to see Elizabeth, but her tears were for her daughter.

CHAPTER 8

Isaac arrived in Paradise, Pennsylvania, on the coldest day of the year so far, according to the train conductor. He would have traveled by foot from Texas to Pennsylvania, in snow two feet deep, if that's what it took to find Elizabeth. Her mother had passed a year ago, and Isaac read the obituary while he was in jail. The article said she was survived by a daughter, Elizabeth, of Paradise, Pennsylvania. There wasn't a last name, and Isaac assumed that was erring on the side of caution, Elizabeth not knowing that Isaac had made sure her name was cleared before his incarceration. He wondered if she attended the funeral.

A year in jail was more than enough time to realize he'd made a terrible mistake by turning his back on Elizabeth. Part of Isaac's punishment while in jail was that he couldn't have contact with her. Otherwise he would have written to her, asked her to wait for him.

Had she married another? Would she welcome him with open arms, cling to him with the same true love Isaac still carried for her? Was it even possible for them to pick up where they left off? Isaac felt right with God after serving his time in jail. His struggle took time, though. He couldn't say he would have done anything differently.

He put on his black felt hat, buttoned his heavy coat, and braced for the blast of frigid air that would hit him when he stepped off the train. Texas didn't have these freezing temperatures, and Isaac wished he'd layered more clothes. The wind cut right through the fleece-lined coat, through his long-sleeve shirt, and chilled him to the bone. *It's all worth it to be with Elizabeth.*

He unfolded the piece of paper in his pocket with Naomi's address. He was ready for a life with Elizabeth, if she'd have him. The Lord forgave Isaac right when he'd asked, though Isaac took a lot longer to forgive himself. But now he was ready to live in God's light with Elizabeth.

His teeth chattering, he scanned the busy streets of Philadelphia for a taxi, but he was distracted by a shiny, two-tone green Hudson Roadster that sped by him. It reminded him of a gangster's car. He wondered if he would ever own a car like that.

As he passed by a newsstand, he considered buying a paper for the hour-long commute to Naomi's family farm, but there were three people in line, and the thought vanished when he spotted a taxi. He took off in a jog, toting his small red suitcase, and finally hailed a cab. *See you soon, my beloved.*

Elizabeth cradled Jonah, a blanket wrapped tightly around his small frame, and made her slog to the mailbox at the end of the long driveway. Her thoughts drifted to her aunt, who'd passed in May. Elizabeth had grown even closer to Aunt Lavinia after Naomi married Samuel and moved out, and Aunt Lavinia adored Elizabeth's baby.

Uncle John was in failing health, and it made sense for Elizabeth to stay on at the farm to care for him. Naomi visited often, but she was enjoying married life and expecting her first child. Uncle John's mind was deteriorating, along with his health, and it wasn't safe to leave Jonah alone with him. Elizabeth still missed her own mother, and she regretted not being able to attend the funeral. Aunt Lavinia had been ill at the time, and at her mother's insistence, Elizabeth hadn't traveled to Texas for the funeral when the time came. Her mother still worried that Elizabeth was a wanted woman. *Maybe I am.*

"Are you okay in there?" She peeked at her beautiful son, cocooned against her chest. She picked up her pace, grateful the sun was out and that it had stopped snowing. She missed Texas this time of year. But the holidays would be here soon, and she was excited about Jonah's first Christmas.

Putting a hand to her forehead to block the sun, she walked faster to reach the mailbox, then sighed when the box was empty. She wasn't expecting anything, but even sales flyers would give her something to occupy her time while Jonah and Uncle John napped. She'd gone through the Sears, Roebuck & Co. catalog a dozen times. Everyone received it right before the holidays, even though she doubted many Amish families shopped from it.

Elizabeth recalled times not so long ago when she could afford such pretty things. But as she joyfully recalled her baptism into the Amish faith, she thought about how much her life had changed. Even if she could afford beautiful dresses and shoes, she had no need or desire for such belongings. Fancy things no longer held her interest, and she'd slipped into the plain way of living easier than she could have predicted.

Eli had married in October. Elizabeth saw him and Mary at worship service every other week. Mary was a lovely woman, and

Elizabeth was happy for them. She'd finally had to tell Eli that her heart still belonged to Isaac, who was surely married himself by now, unless he was in a prison or jail somewhere. Either way, he'd kept his word about ending their communication. And maybe it was easier for both of them this way. Recollections of that dreadful night might always stand between them, even though Elizabeth was sure she and Isaac would have been the ones to perish if Isaac hadn't defended them. Shivering, she could still feel Sean's hands on her, the gun pointed at her, and the whirlwind of activity when Sean lost his focus for a split second, enough time for Isaac to charge him with a shovel.

She was still standing in the driveway, lost in her thoughts, when she saw a bright-yellow car coming up the dirt road.

"Jonah, why would a taxi cab be coming this way? No one else even lives close by." She bounced the baby on her hip, then took another peek at him beneath the blanket, which had now become a game. The baby giggled, making Elizabeth laugh too. "I know it's cold. Let's just see who this is, then we will hurry back to the warmth of the fire inside."

Fiercely bright sunlight gave an illusion it wasn't as cold as it was. She blocked the rays with her hand to her forehead as she waited for the car to draw near.

Isaac was sure his heart was going to beat out of his chest as he neared Naomi's family's farm. It had been a bumpy ride down dirt roads to find the place. In the distance, he could see an Amish woman checking the mail and a baby's head poking out from beneath a blanket. *Naomi, perhaps?*

He'd considered writing before his visit, to let them know

he was coming, but he wanted to see the look on Elizabeth's face when she saw him. He would know right away if she still harbored feelings for him. Isaac wanted to believe he had enough love for both of them.

He'd already pulled out money to give the taxi driver and had hold of the small suitcase. He would jump out of the car the moment it stopped and ask Naomi if Elizabeth had married. If she had, he would have to decide if he should continue to the house. How would Elizabeth feel—married or not—if he traveled all this way to see her, only to leave like a wounded animal?

The automobile was almost to a stop when the woman looked at him. She wore a black cape and bonnet, her hand against her forehead blocking the sun.

Isaac gulped in the shock that slammed his heart into overdrive. "Keep going. Don't stop!"

"But this is the address you—"

"Go, I said! Don't stop! You will get your money." Isaac couldn't pull his eyes away from her, from his Elizabeth. And her baby.

Hope washed away like water, leaving his throat dry but his eyes moist. Elizabeth had moved on without him, exactly like Isaac told her to do. Why hadn't he considered that she might also be a mother? The sting of that fact was twisting his insides into double knots.

He stared out into fields covered by a white blanket, patches of brown foliage poking through here and there as he tried to picture Elizabeth living an Amish life with her husband and child. She'd always been keen on pretty things, and her family had lived better than Isaac's. He loved things plain and simple, undecorated, unadorned. He supposed he would have adapted nicely to the Amish way of life.

He wondered if it was easy for Elizabeth to make such changes. If you're in love, anything is possible, Isaac had learned that one fateful night when he realized Elizabeth was in danger.

But as he directed the cab driver to take him to a motel, anger bubbled to the surface. Anger at himself for encouraging Elizabeth to go on with her life. And anger at her for doing so.

After he'd checked into the small inn, he opened his suitcase and found the small box with the ring inside, a simple gold band he'd bought secondhand. He was tempted to throw it out the window, watch it land in the street below, maybe roll for a while before it came to a stop. But he carefully put it back in the little white box the shopkeeper had been kind enough to give him.

He'd thought about this day for three hundred and sixty-five days, and Isaac should have expected this, or at least prepared for it.

He was going to rest tonight, then catch the first train back to Texas in the morning. *What a fool I've been.*

CHAPTER 9

Catherine arrived early at her parents' house the next morning. Her parents were finishing breakfast in the kitchen when she crossed through the living room. *Mamm* was refilling his coffee cup. The morning visits were routine now, and Catherine suspected she would keep coming even after they'd finished reading about Elizabeth and Isaac. Despite some of the subject matter in the letters, Catherine had enjoyed sharing the experience with her mother. Maybe they could take on a new project after this.

"Abram got a promotion," she announced right away. "He'll be a manager now." Catherine breathed in the smell of bacon and eggs, glancing at the plates on the table, but her stomach was too upset to consider food.

Daed's eyes widened as he smiled, nodding his head. "I knew that boy was smarter than he gave himself credit for. Hard to make a living just tending the land. It's *gut* he has a job outside of that."

Her mother must have caught her ogling the food. "Are you hungry, *mei maedel*?" *Mamm* wiped her hands on her black apron, then blew a strand of wayward hair from her face. Catherine stared at her, suddenly wondering why she'd never heard her mother and father's love story. Was there one? A perfectly laid out plan they had followed to be together? Or was it fraught with obstacles and second-guessing?

Daed eased his chair away from the table and pulled his straw hat from the rack by the kitchen door. "I'll let you ladies be." He kissed Catherine's mother on the cheek. "Let me know if you find my baseball and mitt down there somewhere."

"I didn't know you played baseball, *Daed*." Despite her nerves, Catherine reached for a slice of bacon and took a bite.

"Your father headed up an entire team back in his teenage years." *Mamm*'s eyes twinkled as she spoke. "I can still remember everyone shaving tree branches into baseball bats before all the players had saved enough money to purchase real bats." She pointed out the window to the north. "The Stoltzfus' hayfield used to be the baseball field. Bags of flour marked the bases, and on a pretty day, all the girls lined up on a long bench and watched."

Catherine's father chuckled. "Those were the days." He gave a wave over his shoulder as he left. Catherine smiled, trying to envision her mother cheering for her father as a teenager. After they'd finished learning about Elizabeth and Isaac, maybe she'd press her mother for details about *her* romance. She doubted any of her brothers ever had an interest, but it was important to Catherine these days.

After she helped her mother clean up the kitchen, they headed toward the basement.

"There better be a happy ending to this story," Catherine mumbled as they lit lanterns and pulled out the next letter. She stared at it for a while, then shook her head. "Elizabeth and Isaac obviously end up together. But I wonder when. And how."

"I guess there is only one way to find out." *Mamm*'s soft voice held a hint of worry in it, like she was also afraid the star-crossed lovers parted ways.

November 3, 1929

My dearest Elizabeth,

I have so many things to tell you, but first I must tell you that Sean is alive. He did not die, which I have thanked God for daily, and I will probably continue to do so for the rest of my life. That day, when I saw him with his hands on you and you were screaming, I lost my head when I struck him with the shovel. After my final letter to you, I turned myself in, as I'd said I would. I was able to truthfully tell the judge that I had lost touch with you, and after stressing your innocence, the law people kept their focus on me, and I was sentenced to one year in prison for attempted murder. It could have been much worse for me since Sean and his father made up their own version of the truth.

But all of that is behind me now, and I saw that it is behind you too. You have moved on. I saw you. I traveled to Lancaster County to find you, to see if there was hope for us. But time has a way of healing wounds, and while it should have made me happy to know that you are with another and started a family, the blow to my heart might be unrecoverable. You did exactly what I asked you to do, but I thought our love would somehow endure over time. The Lord, however, has seen fit to continue my penance, and who am I to question His wisdom?

I will travel back to Texas, leaving you to be with your husband and child. Eventually I pray time will allow me to get past the dreams of what could have been.

I will always love you.

Isaac

Emma took a deep breath, worried that this ill-fated tale was only going to drive her daughter further into the dark hole she seemed to be living in.

Catherine folded the letter, stuffed it back in the envelope, and reached for the last three envelopes. "We might as well get this over with." She flipped through them. "It looks like only one actual letter. One has '1929 Memories' written on it, and the other one says 'Elizabeth's 85th birthday.' Let's look at all of them."

Emma took the envelopes from her daughter and shook her head. "*Nee*, we've already been cheating by reading more than one per day. Let's wait on this one." She was afraid she was running out of time to find out what was wrong with Catherine. Once they'd read the last letter, Catherine might not come by as often. She leaned back against the cedar chest, the lanterns and flashlights casting rings of light around them. She stared at Catherine, whose eyes filled with tears.

"It's wonderful Abram got a promotion," she said, hoping to open a door to Catherine's heart, or at least a window. "That should take some of the pressure off you both."

Catherine shrugged as she leaned against the chest next to her mother. "But money isn't everything."

Emma chuckled. "*Ach*, well, it's certainly what we've all been taught to believe, but it is all right to admit that financial hardships add stress, so eliminating that worry isn't such a bad thing."

They were quiet for a few minutes as Catherine held her flashlight, slowly making circles on the far wall.

Emma saw her daughter's wheels spinning. "What is it, Catherine? What is going on with you?"

"You've never told me about yours and *Daed*'s courtship. I know you met here in Paradise, that you only dated a few months." She turned to her mother. "Like me and Abram . . . but that's all I really know."

Emma planned to tread lightly. A mother's child didn't need to know every detail of her parents' history. "What would you like to know?"

Catherine faced forward again. "You and *Daed* are so happy. Even when the boys and I were young, I don't remember ever seeing you fight. You were always happy, and you made a *gut* life for us. You both stepped onto the path God intended for you, and you've been blissfully happy ever since." She jerked her head in Emma's direction, her eyes watery but blazing. "I want to know how to make that happen."

Emma's jaw fell as she realized she was going to have to recant on her thoughts. "Is that really what you think?" Trying to smile, she cupped Catherine's cheek for a moment, staring hard into her daughter's eyes, realizing that maybe this was a time for truth, not fairy-tale images. "Marriage is a hard job, *mei maedel*."

"Not for you and *Daed* apparently. It looked perfect to me."

Emma cleared her throat. "I promise you, it wasn't. And it still isn't." She paused, sighing. "I love your father, and we have had a *gut* life. We've been blessed, and I'm grateful for that. But perfect?" She shook her head. *"Nee."*

"My marriage is a mess." Catherine swiped at her eyes. "I feel like Abram hates me most of the time. He's angry. He wants to move us to Ohio, where his cousins live, as if moving to a new place will heal our marriage." She openly wept. "And we haven't been able to make a baby."

Emma thought her heart might explode as tears formed in her own eyes, but she blinked them back. Catherine might be an adult, but she was a young adult with much to learn. It was still Emma's job to be strong, but she would need to be more forthcoming with her daughter than she'd intended.

"There is plenty of time for *kinner*. You haven't been married all that long." Emma held her breath as she tried to imagine Catherine being so far away. "Has he changed his mind about moving to Ohio?"

"I think he still wants to move, but I can tell he is struggling with it now that he got a promotion." Catherine hung her head. "We've been married almost a year, and I'm still not with child, but I don't think that's what is bothering Abram. He just seems angry all the time. And then I get mad. And then we don't get anywhere, and with each day, I feel like we are growing further and further apart."

Emma didn't want to air her own dirty laundry, but if it would help her daughter see that the journey is never easy, perhaps she should. "Your father left me one time."

Catherine gasped as her eyes widened. "*Nee*. When?"

"Benny was about a year old. You and Lloyd weren't born yet." Emma's heart hammered in her chest. It was a story she'd never told anyone. She'd even kept the incident from her parents at the time, giving them a partial version of the truth, that Jonathan was working in Harrisburg for a while. Just as she had the thought, she realized she was more like her mother and grandmother than she'd thought. She hid family secrets too.

"I was certain he didn't love me anymore, enough so that he was willing to leave his wife and child. And, as you well know, divorces are unheard of. I sank into a horrible depression, and I didn't tell anyone. Even your *grandmammi* and *granddaadi* thought he was just on a long-term construction job." She paused, unable to look at Catherine. It had been a long time since she'd recalled that awful time in her life. "There had been a horrible drought, crops were failing all over the state, times were hard for farmers, and that was our only income back then. There was a lot of pressure for your *daed* to provide."

Emma found her daughter's hand and held it, squeezing it tight for a few long moments before she locked eyes with Catherine. "Before I go on, I want you to know that I see nothing but love for you when I look into Abram's eyes, and it's hard for me to imagine that love isn't reflected in his heart. He doesn't hate you, *mei maedel*."

"He acts like it. And our marriage isn't the way I thought being married is supposed to be." Catherine sniffled. "Everyone makes it look so easy."

Emma smiled a little. "Oh, sweet child, the best things in our lives never come easily. And so many times we veer off onto paths that some might look at as mistakes, but there will always be forks in the road, and we won't always choose correctly. *Ya*, we have free will, but sometimes those determents are necessary for us to grow and appreciate the things that are important."

"How long was *Daed* gone?"

Emma pulled up her knees to her chest, her maroon dress at her ankles as she wrapped her arms around her legs, feeling like she was eighteen again. "Six months."

Catherine gasped again. "What? Six months? What did you do?"

"I cried a lot."

Her daughter hung her head. "Oh, *Mamm*. I'm so sorry. I never could have imagined *Daed* doing that, and it makes me so mad at him, and—"

"*Nee*," Emma said firmly. "It is not your place to be mad at your father. It was our journey, our worries to shoulder, and it was a long time ago. Back then, your father was angry, and at the time, I thought all that anger was leveled at me, but your *daed* was angry with himself, for things I didn't even understand back then. He felt inadequate, unable to take care of his family. He'd lost his faith, and I didn't find out until much later that he'd had a falling out with his *bruder*."

"What happened?" Catherine had stopped crying, and she was hanging on Emma's every word. Emma prayed silently for wisdom, for a way to convey to her daughter that the journey is as important as the destination.

"He came home." Emma forced a weak smile. "And we worked very hard to find a way for our independent paths to merge into the journey God had planned for us all along. But had we stayed on a perfect path from the beginning, I don't know that we would have ever appreciated the blessings God bestowed on us."

Catherine didn't say anything for a while, so Emma stayed quiet too. Finally, her daughter sighed.

"I feel like Abram is angry at me." She turned to Emma. "And when he acts like that, I react badly, and I get mad at him." Shaking her head she said, "It's just not how a proper Amish *fraa* should act."

Emma smiled. "Sweetheart, do you think that because we are Amish we are expected to be perfect? We all sin. We all make mistakes, no matter our religious beliefs. We're not immune to any of the things the outside world struggles with."

"What do I do, *Mamm*?"

Emma thought for a while, sighing again. "As women, we are nurturers. Men are expected to provide. It's unacceptable for them to cry. They are expected to carry their own burdens and those of their family. Think about what burdens Abram might be trying to carry, burdens that are yours? Then consider lifting them from his shoulders. Allow him to feel nurtured." She grinned. "Without letting him know you are nurturing him. It's tricky stuff."

Catherine smiled a little. "So you are encouraging me to manipulate my husband into being happy by being overly nice to him?"

Emma chuckled. "Well, when you put it like that it sounds terrible. What I'm trying to say is, allow him to feel his emotions, dig deep into his soul. What is it about Abram that first drew you to him? What are you most in love with about him? Bring those things to the forefront. By putting his needs in front of your own, he will learn to do the same thing, and there can be much joy in sacrificing for the sake of another, even if it feels like suffering at the time. Marriage is an ongoing education of another person's feelings."

Catherine nodded.

"And, *mei maedel*, stay close to God. He never leaves you, but it is our nature to leave Him when things are a mess."

"*Danki, Mamm.*" Catherine put her arms around her mother's neck and held on tightly. After she eased away, Emma cupped her daughter's cheek.

"Should we break our own rule again and read the last letter?" Emma silently prayed that the ending to Elizabeth and Isaac's story would be a happy one.

Catherine smiled a little. "*Ya*, let's do it. It's Elizabeth and Isaac's journey, however it ends up."

They opened the letter.

CHAPTER 10

Isaac folded the letter, put it in the addressed envelope, then repacked his few toiletries into his suitcase. He barely had enough money for a train ticket back to Texas. He had a few friends there, and he'd get a job when he returned, working as many hours as he could physically handle to keep his mind off Elizabeth. The sight of her and her baby at the mailbox would likely haunt him forever.

But at the last minute he took the letter and put it in his suitcase. Once again he decided the kindest and least selfish thing to do was not to mail it. Why stir up hurt and confusion for Elizabeth, knowing he traveled to see her?

He went to the front desk, asked someone to call him a taxi, then took a seat on the sofa in the lobby and watched the cars moving up and down Lincoln Highway, merging with buggies. He thought about Elizabeth as an Amish housewife and mother.

Elizabeth finished helping Uncle John eat, and after doing so, she put Jonah in his lap, at his request. His frail body could only hold the baby's weight for a short time, but it always brought a smile to her uncle's face. Elizabeth sat in a chair nearby and finished polishing two silver candleholders.

"You should be getting on with your life," Uncle John said as he attempted to bounce Jonah on his lap in the reclining chair. "You should have married Eli."

Elizabeth leaned closer and wiped the baby's mouth with her handkerchief. Her uncle liked to share his food with Jonah, but Elizabeth expected he just didn't have much of an appetite these days. "He wasn't right for me, Uncle John, and Eli is happily married now."

The older man shook his head, his gray beard almost to his waist. Jonah ran his tiny hands through it, smiling. "You will be an old maid if you don't find a young fellow to court you."

"I'm only nineteen. That hardly makes me an old maid." She raised one shoulder and lowered it slowly. "Besides, I'm happy taking care of you and Jonah."

Naomi had been by earlier. Elizabeth told her cousin repeatedly that she didn't have to visit every day, but Naomi was insistent. John was her father, and she was responsible for him. Elizabeth liked keeping busy tending to her uncle and Jonah. Her uncle was kind and wise, and Elizabeth loved listening to him tell stories. Jonah was a good baby, an easy baby. Elizabeth was content with her life, but sometimes her mind drifted and she imagined what it would be like to have someone take care of her. And she always wondered about Isaac.

After her uncle had his fill of love from Jonah, Elizabeth set the child on the floor while she retrieved the basket of wet laundry. "Let's get these clothes on the line," she said in a whisper as her uncle drifted to sleep in the chair.

Quietly she picked up her baby and they left the living room, making their way to the clothesline out back. Elizabeth held Jonah's tiny hand as they went down the porch steps, then she gave him the freedom to walk on his own. He still wasn't steady on his feet, especially bundled up in a heavy coat, boots, and a wool hat over his ears, but he had plenty of padding when he fell.

It was warm for November. The cold blast had come and gone, and while it was still necessary to dress in winter clothes, it wasn't going to freeze the clothes on the line, and the fresh air would do Jonah good for a short time.

Elizabeth was hanging up the last towel when a taxi turned onto their long driveway. She clipped the towel, then picked up the baby and waited.

A small man wearing a long overcoat that looked too big stepped out of the car.

"Good morning, ma'am." He took short, determined steps, stopping right in front of her. "What a handsome child."

Elizabeth nodded. *"Danki.* Can I help you?"

He removed the cap he wore, the same kind she'd seen other taxi drivers wear when she was in town. Then he scratched his head. "Well, I reckon I don't know. Yesterday a fellow asked to be dropped at this address, but then at the last second he changed his mind, and he asked me to take him to a local motel in Paradise. Then this morning I get a call from the innkeeper."

He stood taller, smiling. "I'm a favorite in that area because I am prompt and efficient. So I pick up that same nice fellow and take him to the train station. Then I realized he left something in the cab. I went back to the train station, but I couldn't find him. I called the inn to find out who the guy was, but he'd only left a first name, so he'd be rather hard to locate based on that. So you're the only contact I got to him. At the time it didn't make any sense, but now I suppose I understand."

He reached into the pocket of his trousers and pulled out a white box. "Poor fellow must have chickened out yesterday, or maybe he changed his mind. But either way, I reckon this was for you. Maybe you can get hold of him?"

Elizabeth opened the box and saw a gold wedding band. "It's lovely." She gazed at the small ring. "But I'm afraid this wasn't intended for me. I'm not involved in a courtship, and even if I was, we don't wear jewelry, and this looks like a wedding ring."

"Well, all right, ma'am." The cab driver glanced at the box. "A real shame. It isn't a fancy ring or anything, but I sensed the man was excited to present it to someone. He said this gal was the love of his life."

He smiled before he tipped his hat and was just turning around when he said, "The fellow said he came all the way from Texas."

Elizabeth gasped and almost lost her hold on Jonah. "Do you remember his name?"

The man tapped a finger to his chin. "Uh, I'm trying to remember. It started with an *I*, and—I might remember if I heard it."

Elizabeth set Jonah down and put a hand to her chest. "Isaac?"

"Yes! That was it."

"Where is he now? Where is this man?"

The cab driver shook his head. "I ain't seen him since the train station, like I told you. I reckon he is on a train somewhere by now."

Elizabeth bent at the waist, fighting tears.

"I'm sorry, ma'am. Are, um . . . are you the one he was looking for?"

She straightened, swallowing hard as she picked up her baby and nodded.

The man took a few steps toward her and opened his hand, the white box in his palm.

Elizabeth took it.

He gave her a half smile, tipped his hat again, and said, "Good luck, ma'am."

She straightened, holding Jonah as the yellow taxi pulled out of the driveway. She couldn't leave Uncle John alone, and Naomi had already been by for a visit. By the time she was able to find a way to the train station, Isaac would surely be gone.

Why hadn't he written? Why would he just show up, toting a ring, after all this time and no communication?

She walked slowly back toward the farmhouse, her feet heavy as lead.

Isaac purchased his train ticket, then found a seat along with other passengers waiting to board a train. His heart was so heavy, he just wanted to sleep, but there would be plenty of time for that while he was on the train to Texas. He distracted himself by speculating about the other people waiting.

An older couple to his right held hands, their expressions solemn. He wondered if they had come from a funeral. It was an awful thought, and he hoped that wasn't the case. A mother tried to quiet two young girls a few seats down, but Isaac wasn't able to speculate about them. The woman reminded him too much of Elizabeth with her long, brown hair and dark eyes. Then his gaze drifted to an Amish woman walking toward him, and he wanted to stand up, but he was fearful his legs might not hold his weight. He took a chance, slowly rising and somehow moving forward, stopping a foot in front of his Elizabeth. She was as beautiful as she'd ever been, although covered completely, a black bonnet on her head, and a child in her arms.

"Elizabeth," he breathed. It took every ounce of his being not to embrace her.

She smiled. "Isaac."

I'm dreaming.

They stared at each other for a few moments before she set the child down beside her, then wrapped her arms around him. They held each other tightly, but one of Elizabeth's arms had lowered to hold the hand of her young son.

Isaac feared he might weep openly, so he took a deep breath and eased her away. "You are Amish now," he said, never imagining those would be the first words he would speak when he saw his beloved. He glanced around, expecting her husband to join her at any moment. Why was she here? "How did you know I was here?"

Keeping her hand on the child, she reached into the pocket of her black cape and pulled out a white box as tears streamed down her cheeks. "You left this in the taxicab."

Isaac couldn't move. The ring was in her hand, the way he'd imagined a thousand times. Although, in his dreams, it was on her finger, a promise of his love and devotion to her for the rest of his life. She pushed the ring toward him, which might as well have been a knife slicing his insides open.

"Keep it," he whispered. Maybe she could sell it. Isaac never wanted to see it again.

"We don't wear jewelry." Her eyes stayed locked with his. "I . . . I would have been here sooner, but I had to wait for someone to come stay with my ailing uncle. I almost didn't come. I . . . I was afraid you'd be gone by the time I got here."

"Where is your husband?" He silently prayed his knees would keep him on his feet.

"I don't have a husband."

Isaac nodded at the little boy. "But . . . ?"

Elizabeth picked up the child, smiling. "This is Jonah." She kissed the child on the cheek. "Isn't he a handsome fellow?"

Isaac took in the boy's features, his big brown eyes, dimpled cheeks, and a fuzzy head of light-brown hair. "Very much so." He paused. "He's missing his shoelaces."

Elizabeth grinned. "He is a smart boy. He unlaces his shoes often. The laces are in my pocket." She smiled. "He's your son, Isaac."

He covered his eyes with one hand, forcing himself not to cry. *Could it be, Lord?*

When he finally looked at Elizabeth, her eyes welled with tears. "I didn't know if you were alive or dead."

"I'm sorry for the letter I sent, the one telling you I must cease all communication. After a year in jail, I knew I'd made a terrible mistake. You are all I thought of. My final correspondence to you . . . I shouldn't have sent that."

Elizabeth's eyes searched his. "I thought you'd abandoned me forever."

Shamefully he hung his head. "It was my intent to give you your life back, but after I found out Sean had lived, I thought maybe I could forgive myself for my actions and we could find our way back to each other."

"In my heart, I never left you," she said. "Sean lived?"

Isaac nodded, still on shaky legs and feeling the need to pinch himself. But this wasn't a dream. "I wasn't allowed to write to you from jail."

"You are limping." Elizabeth picked up the child. Isaac's son.

"An incident in jail." She didn't need to know the details.

They stared at each other, and the noisy train station grew silent like someone had turned down the volume on a radio, and it was just the three of them.

"You're Amish," he repeated.

"*Ya*, I am." Her eyes stayed fused with his. "I was baptized into the faith, and I've made a commitment to follow the *Ordnung*."

"You even sound Amish." Isaac swallowed back the knot in his throat. "What is an *Ordnung*?"

"It's the unwritten rules we live by. Most of us know it by heart." She lifted the baby up on her hip. "I love the Lord, Isaac, and staying near Him has changed me in many ways. All things are ultimately of His will, but I have choices to make on my journey as well."

Isaac thought about all the prayers he'd said over the months they'd spent apart. *God was listening.* "I think I'd like to know more about this Amish faith you've embraced."

Elizabeth smiled, put the little white box in her coat pocket, then reached for Isaac's hand. "I can teach you all you need to know."

CHAPTER 11

Catherine placed the last items of her grandparents' love story back in the small box, then let out a heavy sigh of relief. "Oh, *Mamm*, I'm so glad Isaac and Elizabeth found their way back to each other without going through any more grief than they already had."

"A story with a happy ending," her mother said, smiling as she put the letters back in the box. "One you will probably tell your own children and grandchildren someday."

"*Mamm* . . ." She touched her mother's arm. "Can I have *Grandmammi* Elizabeth's ring? Not to wear on my finger. I'd just like to wear it on a chain around my neck, underneath my dress, to keep her close to my heart for a while."

Her mother smiled. "I think that would be fine. Just keep it hidden. You know the bishop frowns on any type of jewelry."

Catherine nodded as she took a final look at the cedar chest, eyeing the contents before her mother closed the lid. "I'm glad we did this. I feel stronger and . . ." She paused, lowered her eyes. "And I feel closer to you."

Mamm lifted Catherine's chin. "It will never matter how old you are, I want us to always be close. As parents, we do our best to shelter our *kinner* from things that aren't pleasant, but I sensed you might benefit from knowing that no one's life is perfect. Not yours, your grandparents, or mine and your father's."

"I'm going to talk to Abram when he gets home this evening. And I'm going to do things differently tonight." She smiled, feeling hopeful about the future. "I guess I should get that box of books for the auction."

Her mother chuckled. "*Ya*, we kind of forgot about that when we became entranced with Elizabeth and Isaac's story."

They carried the heavy box of books carefully up the basement stairs, then all the way to Catherine's buggy. She hugged her mother and whispered, "Thank you."

Mamm squeezed tighter. "Thank you, for opening up to me."

Catherine set out for home, her load feeling a little bit lighter.

By the time Abram came home later that night, Catherine had prepared his favorite meal—chicken and rice with extra cheese on top, homemade bread slathered in garlic butter, and a salad with almonds. Her husband loved almonds, but she kept the nuts mostly for special occasions since they were costly. Catherine was considering tonight a special occasion, a time when she planned to put all of her husband's needs before her own.

"Something smells *gut*," Abram said when he walked in. His droopy lids were a sign of how tired he was, but he smiled a little when he saw everything spread out on the table. "What did I do to deserve this?" He lowered his gaze and sighed. "I *don't* deserve this."

Catherine pressed her hand against her chest, the feel of her great-great-grandmother's ring beneath the fabric. *Give me strength and wisdom, Mammi. And* Gott.

She walked to her husband, leaned up and kissed him on the cheek, and smiled. "I love you. My life would feel incomplete without you in it. We have a partnership, and I will be happy doing whatever makes you happy." She threw her arms around his neck and held on tightly, Elizabeth and Isaac fresh on her mind, hoping Abram would embrace her and their lives as fully as Catherine intended to do.

He eased her away and stared at her. He'd been so ugly and unhappy lately that Catherine prepared for the worst.

"We aren't going to Ohio." He took a deep breath. "I haven't been very *gut* to you, Catherine, and I'm sorry." Scratching his forehead, he stepped away from her and began to pace. "I've been so angry with myself, and I've taken it out on you."

Catherine remembered her mother's words about the time her father was angry at himself. "You're a wonderful husband, Abram. Why are you angry with yourself?"

"Because I haven't been able to give you a child." He looked at her, blinking his eyes as they became moist. "I feel . . . inadequate."

Catherine's jaw dropped, and she moved closer to him. She'd worried plenty of times about why she wasn't with child, but through all of their arguments, neither of them had said anything about it. Obviously Abram had been harboring worries of his own about having a family. "A baby will come when the Lord is ready to gift us with that blessing."

"I've felt like you are mad at me because of that, and I've lashed out because I'm mad at myself, mostly for the way I've reacted and treated you."

"Marriage is a learning process, and we will learn from each other." She wrapped her arms around him again, burying her face against his chest.

"I'm going to be *gut* to you for the rest of my days, Catherine."

She smiled. "And we will hurt each other along the way, make wrong turns, and stray from *Gott*. Our love will grow naturally. A *gut* marriage will take work."

Catherine was glad she'd shared her heartache with her mother. Hearing about her parents' struggles hadn't been easy, but she was going to focus on where they ended up. And after reading about Elizabeth and Isaac, Catherine was sure no marriage went without challenges, some worse than others.

Abram insisted on cleaning the kitchen after they finished supper. It wasn't a man's job, and he'd never done it before.

"I want to do something nice for you."

Catherine smiled as she silently prayed she and Abram would continue this new practice of putting each other's needs before their own.

She thought again about Isaac and Elizabeth's happy ending, with plans to add her own memories to the cedar chest.

Thank you, Gott, for my many blessings.

Emma took out her family Bible from the bedside table and spent a few quiet moments with God before she put the Bible back in its place. She had much to be thankful for.

"You've been smiling all afternoon," Jonathan said as he came into the bedroom wearing only a pair of slacks as he towel-dried his hair. "I'm glad you were able to get Catherine to talk to you. Those *kinner* will have to find their own way, just like we did."

She tapped a finger to her chin. "It seems like a lifetime ago, doesn't it, when we were apart for all those months?"

Jonathan stopped drying his hair and the towel went limp in his hands. Emma couldn't remember the last time either of them had mentioned that difficult time.

"*Ya,*" he finally said as he started drying his hair again, then his beard. "Did you tell Catherine about that?"

Emma nodded. "*Ya.*"

Her husband hung the towel on the back of the rocking chair, his cropped bangs half dried and pushed to one side. "Did you tell her *everything?*"

Emma cocked her head to one side and grinned. "*Ya.* I told her that taming you had taken all of my energy, and that it's an ongoing process." She playfully rolled her eyes.

Jonathan twisted the towel, pretending he was going to pop her with it.

"Don't you dare!" She laughed as he fell into the bed and pulled her into his arms.

"I think we should take a trip, the way we planned," he said before he kissed her. "We're not too old to have some fun."

"I'd like that."

Emma snuggled against her husband, and her last thoughts before she slept were of Elizabeth and Isaac.

They'd found their way back to each other. Just like she and Jonathan had all those years ago. Catherine and Abram would find their way as well. And with that thought, she thanked God for His many blessings and drifted off to sleep.

EPILOGUE

MARCH 3, 1996

Elizabeth finished a late-night piece of birthday cake, marking her eighty-five years on earth. Isaac snored in the bedroom as she recalled the blessings of the day. It had been joyous to celebrate her life with Jonah, his wife, Rose, and their *kinner*, Mary and Amos, and Elizabeth and Isaac's great-grandchild, Emma. *Such a joy.*

She gazed at the cedar chest her husband had given her that day. Next to it, she'd laid out items she wanted to place inside for safe keeping. She'd chosen her double wedding ring quilt. The blue, green, yellow, and pink pastels had faded over time, but she cherished it. She picked up two silver candleholders she and Isaac had received as a wedding gift, the gold ring Isaac had given her, and of course, the letters, notes, and memorabilia that detailed their story. Maybe her children, or their children, or someone further down the line might benefit from an old lady's box of letters.

Elizabeth lowered herself to the floor, and then she gingerly set the items inside the chest, holding Jonah's baby shoes to her heart for a moment before adding them to her treasures. It seemed like only yesterday her son was untying his shoes and giggling, a baby who had grown quickly into a man, in the blink of an eye it seemed.

She stood up, smiled, and closed the lid on the chest, thanking *Gott* for His blessings and the memories she was able to pass on.

Discussion Questions

1. Isaac and Elizabeth had to go through a lot to finally be together. But if things had happened any differently, they might not have appreciated their ultimate blessings. Related to your own life, can you look back at a challenging situation (in romance or otherwise) that needed to happen in order for you to appreciate the better things ahead?

2. Catherine and Abram were growing apart. What was the biggest contribution to the marriage having problems? Was it their inability to communicate about the issues bothering each of them? What other contributing factors caused them to temporarily lose sight of what's most important in a marriage? Do you think this is typical of all couples in the beginning?

3. If you were in Emma's shoes, would you have shared the story about Emma and Jonathan separating when they were young? Emma didn't want to at first, but she saw it as a way to express to her daughter that marriage takes work and no couple is perfect. Did Emma do the right thing?

4. Do you have a cedar chest filled with memories? If not, would you consider getting one to store memories and keepsakes for future generations to enjoy?

Acknowledgments

This was not an easy book to edit because of the parallel storylines that jumped back and forth in time. Much thanks to my editors on this project, Karli Jackson and Jodi Hughes, for going above and beyond.

I have an amazing publishing team at HarperCollins Christian Fiction, and it truly takes a team for a project to see fruition. Thank you all from the bottom of my heart.

I don't know what I'd do without Wiseman's Warriors, the greatest street team ever. You ladies rock! And Janet Murphy, everyone knows how I feel about you, lol—I'd be lost without you by my side on this incredible journey. I love and appreciate you!

To my agent, Natasha Kern, thank you for giving of yourself repeatedly, both professionally and in my personal life. You are always there for me, no matter what is going on in your own life. Love and hugs!

To my family and friends, the journey continues. I'm blessed to have your continued love and support.

The Treasured Book

KATHLEEN FULLER

To James. I love you.

Chapter 1

Lucy Fisher had never been so drenched in her entire life. Still, she managed a smile as her bus drove away. She pressed her hand against her chest, a small plastic bag enclosed in her fist. She'd left it in her seat, almost losing its contents forever. "Thank you, Lord," she whispered, barely noticing the water dripping from the strings of her white *kapp*, grateful she'd been able to retrieve the bag before the bus disappeared.

As she stood beneath the station's awning, her heartbeat slowed. *It will be okay. Everything will be okay.*

She set down her travel case on the only strip of dry pavement and slipped the plastic bag into her purse. She was so tired from traveling throughout the night. No wonder she'd almost left it behind.

"Lucy?"

She froze, recognizing the voice instantly. Surprised and confused, she turned to see Shane Broyles standing near the bus terminal's entrance, holding a navy-blue umbrella over his head. As he walked toward her, her mouth dropped open. He was the last person she'd expected to see anywhere near Birch Creek. "Shane?"

He frowned and closed his umbrella as he joined her under the awning, shaking out the excess water. "You're soaked. How long were you out in the rain?"

She clutched her purse and glanced down at her plum-colored dress, now a dark purple from the rain. Water dripped from the hem and sloshed in her black shoes, and she didn't need a mirror to know her *kapp* was drooping. But when she thought again about what she'd nearly lost, she knew getting soaked was worth it. "Not long." She decided not to mention chasing after the bus.

Suddenly she was caught up in Shane's one-armed hug. She gasped, not expecting to be greeted in such a personal way. But she wasn't about to complain. She smiled, his nearness warming her through.

"Where's your umbrella?" he said, his mouth close to her ear. "Isn't it your motto to always be prepared?"

"I thought that was the Boy Scouts' motto."

He chuckled as he set her away from him. "I recall telling you you'd make a good scout."

"Not that good of one, considering I left my umbrella at home." Then she saw the dark stain on the front of his red shirt. "Sorry. I got you wet."

He shrugged. "Doesn't bother me."

"What are you doing in Ohio?" The rain beat a steady cadence on the metal above them.

He smiled, his straight teeth gleaming through his dark-brown, trim beard and mustache. During the six months she'd worked with Shane back home in Iowa, first meeting him a year and a half ago, he'd had the same look. He spread out his free hand and gestured to the parking lot. "We'll get to that. Meanwhile, your chariot awaits."

"*You're* taking me to Cevilla Schlabach's?"

He leaned forward a little. "Yes, ma'am." He looked her over again. "I think I have a towel in the backseat of my car." He popped open the umbrella, and then he turned and rested his hand lightly on the small of her back. "Let's get you out of this cold rain."

A steady rain shower in the middle of June didn't exactly qualify as cold, even though the air was a little cool for summer. And she knew Shane was touching her only out of chivalry, despite her wishing he had another reason. But knowing all that didn't stop a slight shiver from traveling down her spine. She couldn't believe she was this close to him. She'd thought she'd never see him again.

"Wait." He dropped his hand and held out the umbrella. "Hold this." When she took it, he slipped off his jean jacket and put it over her shoulders. "Better?" he asked, taking back the umbrella.

Much better. At around five feet ten, Shane was taller and broader than she was, and his jacket nearly engulfed her. But as she felt the warmth of the denim fabric and breathed in the fresh scent of soap, she smiled. If nothing else good happened during her stay in Birch Creek, at least she'd had the chance to wear Shane Broyles's jacket. And since this was the closest she'd ever be to him again, doubting there'd be another hug or reason to keep her warm, she'd take it.

They walked briskly to a silver car with New York license plates, and she immediately assumed this was the vehicle he mentioned in Iowa. He had used a rental car there, but he seemed to miss his own—a Mercedes, she thought he'd called it.

Shane handed her the umbrella and opened the back passenger-side door, put her travel case inside, and pulled out a beach towel. "It's clean," he said, handing it to her before opening the passenger door in the front.

"Thanks."

When she was safely inside the car, he took the umbrella and ran to get into the driver's side. A crack of thunder sounded as he slammed the car door behind him, and the rain suddenly increased. "It's supposed to be like this all day," he said, running one hand through his wet hair.

Lucy let out a little sigh. He was so handsome, even if his hair was too short, in her opinion. She preferred the long hair Amish men wore. Still, Shane's hair didn't distract from his good looks. She was sure her face was red, and she dabbed at her wet face with the towel as Shane started the engine. When she began removing his jacket to give it back to him, he shook his head.

"Hang on to it. I'm going to have the air-conditioning on a little, and I don't want you to get cold." He put his right arm over the back of her seat as he backed out of the parking spot.

Lucy spread the beach towel over her lap. Although she was typically quiet, and sometimes downright shy, Shane had always made her feel comfortable. She leaned back in the seat and looked at him. "Now, what are you doing in Birch Creek? You must know Cevilla somehow."

"I'm visiting her nephew, Noah. We've been friends for several years." At her questioning look he added, "Before we get into all that, I guess I have some explaining to do about the house in Iowa."

She shook her head. "You don't owe me an explanation."

"I do." He rolled his palm back and forth on the steering wheel. "I should have told you I was selling it. You and your dad were just as much a part of renovating that old house as I was. I was determined to do most of the work myself, but let's face it. If it wasn't for you two, I would still be trying to figure out which end of a hammer to use."

"You weren't that bad. And you paid us well."

"And you, as usual, are too kind." He flipped on the turn signal.

She glanced out the window, remembering the day she saw the unexpected For Sale sign next door. She'd been confused, but also hurt and, yes, a little bit angry. But those feelings had disappeared as soon as she saw Shane.

He made a right turn. "How are the new neighbors?"

"We haven't had any."

His eyebrow lifted. "Really? The guy I sold it to said he was planning to rent it out ASAP."

"He hasn't so far."

Shane didn't say anything for a long moment.

"I really had planned to keep that home, Lucy," he said as they turned down a road. "But sometimes plans change."

"That's true." At least it was true for everyone except Lucy. Her life was at a standstill, and it had been for years. Working with Shane those six months had been a splash of excitement in her otherwise dull life. Not that she didn't have a good life. She helped her father with his woodworking business, which after a few rocky years was doing well. Before that, her mother had gone through ovarian cancer treatment. She'd spent most of her twenties devoted to her parents in one way or another, and she wouldn't have done anything differently.

But during those years her friends had married and started families. And while she enjoyed holding their babies and celebrating their happiness, she experienced lonely moments. Shane had overcome some of those moments with his humor, friendship, and yes, lack of building skills.

And now she was sitting in his fancy car. The interior was beautiful, the leather seats comfortable. She didn't know much about cars, but she knew this one was expensive. Just like the watch Shane was wearing on his wrist and the denim jacket she was snuggled in. Shane, like most of his family in New York—he'd mentioned a brother-in-law, two cousins, and an uncle—was a lawyer in his father's successful firm. They all had to be very well paid.

As would be his lawyer fiancée, another member of the firm. At least she was only his fiancée the last she knew. But though she didn't see a ring on Shane's finger, that didn't mean they weren't married by now. Not all English men wore wedding rings.

"Is Jordan with you?" she asked, making sure her tone was light. And why wouldn't it be? It wasn't as though Shane was, or ever would be, a viable romantic interest. He was English and he was taken—two insurmountable obstacles.

"No."

She lifted her brow as she looked at him. Even through his dark beard she could see the muscle jerking in his jaw. They had never talked about Jordan much, and Lucy met her only once, when the house was just about finished and about two weeks before Shane put it on the market. Jordan was tall, thin, pretty, and polite— exactly how Lucy would have expected a fancy, female New York lawyer to be. "She's not?"

"No." His tone was firm and unyielding.

Pressing her lips together, she dropped the subject. She didn't want to talk about Jordan anyway, but something was amiss. "How long have you been in Birch Creek?"

"Six weeks, believe it or not. I've more than overstayed my welcome at Noah's, but he and his wife, Ivy, won't let me stay anywhere else. When Noah mentioned you were the one visiting Cevilla for a few weeks, I offered to pick you up." He glanced at her. "He knew you and I had met in Iowa, but he'd forgotten you and Cevilla had a connection. He said you know her through your aunt?"

"*Ya.* She and my great-aunt Lois were friends when Cevilla

lived in Iowa. They've kept in touch all these years, and Cevilla always makes a point of seeing her when she visits Arbor Grove." She lifted the towel and ran her hand over the skirt of her still-damp dress. "Although I was surprised when Cevilla wrote to ask me to stay with her while she recuperated from spraining her ankle."

"Why?"

"Because she's lived in Birch Creek longer than I've known her, and I would have assumed someone here could help care for her."

"Plenty of people here would be happy to do that. But, as I'm sure you know, and as I've quickly learned, Cevilla Schlabach has her own way of doing things."

Lucy nodded. She'd turned Cevilla down, but then she'd promptly received another letter from her, insisting she come. "Don't let an old, decrepit woman suffer," she'd written, which had elicited an eye roll from Lucy. She'd met Cevilla several times over the years, and while the woman was in her early eighties, she acted neither old nor decrepit. Still, despite the heavy dose of attempted manipulation, Lucy was going to tell her once more that she couldn't come. Her father's business was growing, and Lucy was the only one who knew how to do the books. And even though her mother was clear of cancer, there was always a niggling thought in the back of her mind that she could get sick again. Her parents needed her.

So she was doubly surprised when her mother encouraged her to make the trip.

"We'll be fine," *Mamm* had insisted. "Don't worry about us."

Easier said than done.

"You're quiet all of a sudden," Shane said.

She touched her *kapp*. It was still damp too. "You know that's not unusual for me."

"I used to think that, especially when I first met you." He reached over and tapped her on the knee. "But I know you better than that. A wild woman lives underneath all that shy demeanor."

She laughed, hardly insulted by his insinuation. She was the furthest from wild a person could get. "I never should have told you about my crazy *rumspringa*," she said, playing along.

"You mean the time you—*gasp*—went to the mall wearing English clothes?"

"Hey, that was a big deal for me."

He paused, the smile slipping from his face. "I know. I didn't realize until now how much it was."

Her brow furrowed at the serious turn in the conversation. He was acting a little strange. Then again, she hadn't seen him for a year. Had something happened? Was that something about Jordan?

"You're going to like Birch Creek," he said, turning cheery again. "It's a great little community. I can see why Noah wanted to move here."

"So you two are friends?" She didn't know Noah very well. He was in his early thirties and she was twenty-nine, so he had always been one of the older boys in her school. He'd owned his own auctioneering business and had spent a lot of time away from Arbor Grove. She'd never paid much attention to him, except last year when she heard he had lost his hearing because of a disease, and then he moved to Birch Creek after marrying his wife, Ivy.

"We've known each other since we met at an auction in upstate New York. We've stayed in touch, getting together whenever he was nearby. When he learned I was looking for a house in the country, he told me about the one next door to you."

That tidbit of news surprised her. "I just assumed you'd found the property through a real estate agent."

"Nope. And while we were renovating, he was almost always traveling." He pulled into a gravel driveway, and then he stopped and put the car in park. "Stay there until I come around."

She slipped off his jacket as he opened her door, his umbrella closed. The rain had slowed to a drizzle, but from the gathering gray clouds in the distance she knew the lull wouldn't last.

"I'll get your bag," Shane said. "You can go on inside."

She got out, dodged a few small puddles, and ran to the front porch ahead of him. Her clothes and shoes were still damp, but she could feel the lingering warmth of Shane's jacket.

Lucy knocked on the door as Shane came up the porch steps behind her. She heard a thumping sound from inside, and soon the door opened. "Lucy," Cevilla said, a big smile on her face as she peeked outside. She opened the door wider. "I'm going to have to teach you the secret knock."

"Secret knock?"

She leaned forward and whispered, "Five times. Shane, you can use it too. Now, you two come on in."

Lucy walked in, Shane following her. "Where do you want this, Cevilla?" he said, holding up the small case.

"The spare bedroom upstairs." She touched Lucy's arm and then gestured for her to follow her farther into the living room. "Got to get off this foot," she said, leaning on her cane and limping over to a worn rocking chair.

As Lucy slipped off her wet shoes, she glanced down at the black boot encasing Cevilla's foot. She immediately felt guilty for initially refusing to visit her. "I thought you only sprained your ankle," she said.

"I did." Cevilla plopped down in the chair. "Doc said sometimes a sprain is worse than a break. He's right. Worst pain I've ever been through." She pointed to the boot with her cane. "I think this is a bit excessive, and I would be fine with a bandage, but both the doctor and Noah said I needed more protection because of *mei* delicate constitution." She sniffed. "They meant because I'm old. The things I do to appease *mei* favorite nephew."

"Can I get you anything?" Lucy asked. "Do you need lunch? I can make some tea or *kaffee*. Do you need to put *yer* leg up?" She was following Cevilla's lead in speaking *Dietsch* without Shane there.

The older woman chuckled. "I'm fine, dear. Why don't you relax a bit after *yer* long trip?"

Shane came downstairs. "I put the suitcase next to your bed, Lucy. Hope that's okay."

She nodded as Cevilla said, "Have either of you had lunch?"

Lucy and Shane both shook their heads. She hadn't realized how hungry she was until Cevilla mentioned food. Her stomach softly growled.

"Then get yourselves to the kitchen. There's some fresh bread and butter in the pantry, and some lunchmeat in the cooler."

"I'd like to change my dress first," Lucy said, turning to Shane. Her hunger could wait a few minutes longer. "Then I'll make your lunch."

"You don't have to go to the trouble," he said.

Lucy smiled. "It's no trouble. After all, you picked me up." She glanced at Cevilla before she went upstairs, and she could have sworn she saw the woman grin.

Shane walked around Cevilla's small kitchen as he waited for Lucy's return. He could make his own sandwich. Better yet, he could drive to nearby Langdon or Barton and hit any fast-food restaurant he wanted. But he hadn't eaten fast food since he'd arrived in Birch Creek, and he wasn't about to break that streak now. Besides, he knew firsthand that Lucy Fisher made the best sandwiches.

He stopped in front of the kitchen window and watched as the rain continued to fall, heavier now than when he'd picked her up. When Noah mentioned he had to arrange for a taxi to pick up Lucy Fisher from Arbor Grove, Iowa, Shane jumped at the chance to see her again. He didn't even stop to ask Noah why Lucy, of all people, would be the one Cevilla asked to help her. Cevilla's reasons didn't matter to him. He only cared that he would see Lucy again. He'd thought he never would.

He turned at the sound of her entering the kitchen, her footfalls soft but recognizable. They'd worked on his house with her father for six months straight, starting inside on a cold and snowy January day. He'd taken an extended leave from work, a plan his father hadn't been happy about. It wasn't the first time he'd disappointed him, and Shane knew it wouldn't be the last.

Lucy had replaced her head covering with a scarf and changed into a mint-green dress that accentuated her deep-set blue eyes. She was so pretty. Not in the glamorous way Jordan was, or even the sweet, fresh-faced way most Amish women were. No, Lucy had her own unique look about her, and when they first met after he bought that money pit of a renovation house, he'd had a hard time keeping his eyes off her.

But it wasn't long before he realized he was drawn to her not only because of her outward beauty. Unlike Jordan—and many of the women he'd known and associated with in his fast-paced New York life—she was calm and steady, with an inner strength and independence he admired. He'd quickly understood why her family depended on her so much, and she'd carried the weight without complaint.

All that attraction had led to a lot of guilt, considering he was engaged to Jordan at the time. *Not anymore.* Now he could be around Lucy and fully enjoy her company without feeling guilty or ashamed. But that didn't mean he was free to pursue her. Or that he even deserved her.

Is that why he hadn't just come out and told her he and Jordan weren't together anymore?

"Is something wrong?" She looked down at her dress, the skin beneath her abundant freckles turning a light pink. She had freckles all over her face, not just on her cheeks and nose. They matched the dark red of her hair, and he knew she was self-conscious about them. She shouldn't be, though. The combination of those freckles, those eyes, and her beautiful hair was irresistible.

Resist. Resist.

"No, you look fine." He spun from her and went to the sink to wash his hands, even though he'd washed them when he first entered the kitchen. When he finished he turned to see Lucy poking her head inside the pantry.

"Bread, butter, pickles, mustard." She gathered the items in her arms. "Oh, here's a bag of chocolate chip cookies." She gripped the top of the clear zippered bag between her teeth, went to the kitchen counter, and set everything on it.

Shane opened the small ice cooler, spotted a package of trail bologna, and smiled. Until he'd met Noah he'd never heard of trail bologna, or even the Amish. Now not only was the lunchmeat his favorite, but he was contemplating making the biggest change of his life—joining the faith he'd not only come to admire but to which he felt deeply drawn.

Yet he had to be sure before making that decision. He'd made more than one mistake in the past, and he couldn't be wrong about this.

He went back to the counter and put the bologna, along with a few slices of cheddar cheese he'd found, on the counter. He'd been to Cevilla's a few times over the past weeks and knew where she kept the dishes. And after all the delicious meals Noah's wife, Ivy, had prepared, he'd appointed himself the official dish washer, a chore he didn't mind. He'd grown up with a maid and a chef and hadn't had to wash a single dish until he was living on his own in college. He still had a lot of time to make up for.

Lucy made quick work of the sandwiches and took their plates to the table. Shane poured two glasses of iced tea, and then he sat down across from her. They both bowed their heads and prayed. While Shane asked God to bless the food, he also, as always, asked for wisdom in making the decision looming over him.

"I should make a sandwich for Cevilla," Lucy said as soon as Shane opened his eyes.

"Did she say she was hungry?"

"No. But she might be anyway." Lucy glanced at her plate. "It doesn't feel right to eat while she's sitting alone in the living room."

"Hang on a minute." Shane got up and crept to the living room. As he suspected, Cevilla was asleep in the chair. "Not even awake. She's fine," he said, sitting back down.

Lucy looked a little doubtful, but then she picked up her sandwich as Shane took a big bite of his. He knew this was just bread and cheese and meat, but for some reason, when Lucy made food, everything tasted better. "Delicious," he said around a mouthful.

"It's been awhile since I made you lunch." She smiled. "It's like old times."

"Not exactly. I don't see sawdust on my plate or musty old boards surrounding us."

She laughed. "You know what I mean."

He did, and he was also struck by how right it felt to be sitting here with her, eating a simple sandwich while the rain continued to fall outside. In fact, life felt more right at this moment than it had for a long time. "*Danki*," he said.

"It's not much of a lunch."

"I appreciate it anyway," he said in *Dietsch*.

Her light-red eyebrows lifted. "Have you been practicing?"

"A bit." A lot. When he contacted Noah and asked to visit for a few days, he hadn't expected to be here this long. But the moment he'd set foot in Birch Creek, he'd felt the familiar sweet peace that had drawn him to buying that house in Arbor Grove. That peace had only fueled his yearning to live among the Amish. No, not to just live among the Amish, but to *become* Amish. He'd confided as much to Noah, who insisted Shane stay with him and Ivy as long as he needed to.

Since then he'd immersed himself in the Amish way of life and community as much as possible. Today was the first day in almost a month he'd driven his car, and the jeans and short-sleeved polo shirt he wore felt strange to him. He longed to get back into the broadfall pants and homemade shirts Ivy's mother had kindly made for him. But he hadn't wanted to surprise Lucy too much—or worse, make her think he was mocking her faith by playing dress-up.

"I didn't know you wanted to learn our language," Lucy said. "Is there a reason why?"

Her open face and direct question didn't surprise him. Lucy wasn't one for beating around the bush. He appreciated that in her, especially since most of the people in his life had either avoided confrontation or been experts at passive-aggressive communication.

He guessed now was as good a time as any to tell her. "Because I'm thinking about joining."

"Joining?" she said, her eyebrows arching again.

He paused, but he made sure to keep eye contact with her. He wanted her to understand that he wasn't taking this decision lightly. "I think I want to join the Amish church."

Her eyes widened. "You do?"

"Yeah. I mean, *ya*." He grinned and finished off the last bite of the sandwich, noting the confusion in her eyes.

"I had no idea." She sat back in her chair. "I thought you sold the house because you were getting . . . married. That you'd changed your mind about owning a home in Iowa."

He didn't want to tell her the real reason he'd sold the house was that Jordan hated the idea of ever spending time in Iowa. Besides, his thoughts were centered on how attracted he was to Lucy, not on the beginning of the end with Jordan. And why had Lucy just hesitated before mentioning marriage? Had she not wanted him to be with Jordan?

He nearly shook his head. He had to remember his attraction to Lucy didn't mean she felt the same way—even though he knew a small part of his heart had always longed for her to. Even back when he couldn't do anything to encourage romance between them. He'd been committed to Jordan then, and to the life expected of him. "Marriage was the plan."

Her gaze flitted to his bare left hand. "And?"

He couldn't stop himself from leaning forward. "Plans change."

"Oh." She glanced at her lap, her long eyelashes hovering over the top of her freckled cheeks. "I see."

Shane waited for her to ask more questions. Instead, she picked at the crust of her sandwich. Her lack of curiosity—at least about his wanting to join the church—was a little disappointing. He realized he wanted to talk to her about this, but if she wasn't interested, he wasn't going to force it. Instead, he switched the conversation back to her, her family, and the community in Arbor Grove. They talked for another half hour, until Shane glanced at the clock.

"I should get going," he said, pushing back from the table. He'd been gone longer than he'd expected, but he'd enjoyed every minute with Lucy. "I told Noah I'd help him with inventory this afternoon."

"Inventory?"

"He and Ivy opened an antique store in Barton. It's a quick drive from Birch Creek." He stood. "I can take you there some-time if you want. They have some interesting items there."

She stood. "I'd like that. But my first priority is Cevilla. I wouldn't feel right leaving her here when she needs me."

He saw the determined set of her jaw. "Understood. Cevilla comes first." He started to look for his hat, but then he realized he didn't have one. Funny how quickly he'd become used to wearing a straw hat, when before he'd rarely worn even a baseball cap. "I'll see you later, then."

"Wait." She picked up the bag of cookies. "Here." She opened it and took out two of them. "For the road," she said, smiling.

Her smile was so pretty. Well, everything about her was pretty. He cleared his throat. "*Danki*," he said, giving her one last look before leaving the kitchen. He could spend all day with her, but she was right—Cevilla was the reason she was here. He shouldn't forget that.

He crept by Cevilla in the living room. She was still asleep in her rocking chair, her mouth slightly open. Slowly he opened the door and stepped outside, making sure to shut the door behind him quietly. The rain had stopped, and rays of sunlight peeked through the clouds. Maybe the forecast had been wrong and the skies would clear up after all.

He took a deep breath, breathing in the scent of wet earth and residual rain. He really did love it here. He glanced over his shoulder at Cevilla's house and smiled. He didn't think Birch Creek could be any better. But now that Lucy was here, it definitely was.

A moment later he realized he'd been so distracted he'd forgotten his role as official dish washer.

CHAPTER 2

S hane already left?" Cevilla said as she hobbled to the kitchen. Lucy was washing dishes.

"He had to get back to help Noah with inventory." Lucy would have been happy if he'd stayed longer, especially once the conversation shifted away from the marriage she'd thought would already be a reality. She'd been so confused that she hadn't even asked Shane more about why he thought he wanted to become Amish.

Then again, she'd meant it when she said Cevilla was her priority, and she needed to remember that. Any time Shane was around, she'd be distracted.

Lucy pulled the plug out of the sink, rinsed her hands, and then turned off the tap. She faced Cevilla. "Can I make you something to eat?"

The old woman shook her head. "I'm fine. Had a large breakfast."

"Then what would you like for me to do?" Lucy said, ready to fulfill her purpose for being here.

"Unpack, for starters." Cevilla sat down at the table and gripped the handle of her cane. "And this evening we can play a game of cards."

Cards? Lucy had been prepared to work, not play. "Are you sure I can't do something you need around here first? Clean the *haus*, or the barn?" She peeked through the kitchen window outside. "The rain has stopped. I can sweep the front porch. How about the laundry?"

Cevilla chuckled. "*Mei* laundry is all caught up, and the porch is clean as a whistle. As you can see, there's not much to do." She leaned her cane against one of the empty chairs. "Really, I'm fine here by myself."

Lucy frowned, confused. "Then why did you ask me to come help you?"

"Because I like the company." She sniffed. "That, and *mei* niece-in-law was insisting she come stay here until *mei* ankle healed. I wasn't about to allow that. Ivy and Noah are still newlyweds."

Suddenly Lucy thought of Shane. Which was ridiculous. Now that she'd had a moment to really to think about it, she was almost certain he was no longer engaged. But that didn't mean he and Jordan weren't still together, or wanted to be. But she couldn't deny the tiny flutter she'd felt in her chest when he'd told her he was considering joining the Amish. Did that mean Jordan was too? Lucy couldn't imagine Jordan Palmer trading her short, highlighted hair, bright-red lips, high heels, and more jewelry than Lucy had ever seen on one person in her life for plain dress. Then again, she'd never thought Shane would be considering joining the church. When they worked together on his house, he'd never said anything about it.

"Besides," Cevilla continued, looking Lucy directly in the eyes, "you needed to get away from home. You've spent far too much time caring for *yer* parents and not enough on building a life for *yerself.*"

Lucy was a direct person herself, but Cevilla's point-blank

words took her aback. "I . . . I have a life." She lifted her chin, suddenly feeling defensive. "I have *mei* friends, *mei* parents, *mei* job . . ." She paused. "And of course, *mei* faith."

Cevilla's eyes softened. "*Ya.* You do have that, which is the most important thing. But don't you want something more?"

Again, Shane came to mind. Lucy averted her gaze. "I don't know what you mean."

"I think you do." Cevilla grabbed her cane, stood, and hobbled over to Lucy. She set one gnarled hand on Lucy's shoulder. "I hope you'll find what you're looking for while you're here." She patted Lucy's arm. "Now, *geh* unpack *yer* things and meet me back here. I'll *geh* get the cards. Why not play now?"

"But—"

"*Nee* buts!" Cevilla left the kitchen.

Lucy put her hands on the back of a chair. *Find what I'm look-ing for in Birch Creek?* That didn't make any sense. She wasn't looking for anything. Her gaze moved to the empty doorway. What was Cevilla talking about? Lucy did have a good life back home, even though she was getting a little bored with bookkeep-ing and sanding wood blocks. That brought on more feelings of guilt. She should find satisfaction in hard work. But if she were honest with herself, she'd have to admit the idea of spending the rest of her life putting numbers in a ledger and sweeping sawdust off the floor didn't appeal.

Yet what choice did she have? Her parents needed her, and she wasn't about to abandon them because she didn't enjoy the type of work she did for her father. She loved her family more than that.

She turned from the chair, thinking about Shane again. It was so good to see him, and of course her old feelings for him had resurfaced. She didn't know how long she'd be in Birch Creek, and she didn't know how much longer he'd be here, but she had to make sure their paths didn't cross too often. There was no point in getting excited about something that was never going to happen. She and Shane weren't meant to be. They were too different. Besides, he and Jordan could still be together, even if they had some things to work out. Like Shane thinking about becoming Amish.

"Lucy?"

She jumped at Cevilla's voice coming from the living room. *"Ya?"* She went to her. "What can I do for you?"

Cevilla's smile was kind, even though Lucy could see the wrinkled corners of her mouth tugging down. She rested her hands on the arms of her wooden rocker. *What happened to getting the cards?* "Always eager to help someone else out. You're a sweet *maedel.*"

Lucy's gaze dropped to the floor. She wasn't used to such compliments. Her parents were appreciative. She knew that. But they weren't demonstrative, something Lucy had accepted. Still, it felt good to hear something nice and unexpected.

"And since you asked what you can do for me, that reminds me—I'd like to *geh* to Noah's store in Barton on Monday. I meant to mention that to you earlier, but it slipped *mei* mind. I haven't seen *mei* nephew and Ivy for a few days, and there's a yarn store next to their shop. It's also been awhile since I've seen Noelle, and I'd like to say hello."

"Noelle?"

"She's the English owner of the store. A very nice woman. You'll like her." Cevilla held out a small scrap of paper. "Here's the phone number for Max. He's *mei* usual taxi driver. The phone shanty is at the end of the driveway. You should probably arrange for a taxi right away."

Lucy nodded, and a few moments later she was dodging more raindrops as she ran to the shanty, the respite from the rain short-lived. Max answered right away, and he said he would be happy to pick them up Monday morning. Satisfied, she thanked him and then went back to the house.

Cevilla was still in the living room, now crocheting what looked like a baby blanket. "Everything set?" she asked.

"*Ya*. Max will be here on Monday."

"*Gut*. Now sit down and relax a bit."

"I should *geh* unpack."

Cevilla waved her hand. "That can wait. Let's visit for awhile."

Knowing it was useless to argue, and realizing that Cevilla could change her mind with lightning speed, Lucy sat down on the couch. Soon she was listening to stories about Cevilla's community here in Birch Creek. Cevilla was a good storyteller, and Lucy found herself fascinated by her tales. So much so that she forgot about Shane.

Later that night, after they'd eaten their light supper and Lucy had cleaned the kitchen, they played a quick game of Crazy Eights. Then after she'd seen to Cevilla's mare, she made sure her host was settled in bed.

"You don't have to hover over me," Cevilla said as Lucy straightened her covers.

"I'm here to take care of you."

"You're here to keep me company. I can take care of myself." Cevilla shooed her out of the room. "See you in the morning. Sweet dreams."

Lucy closed Cevilla's bedroom door and shook her head. This was going to be more difficult than she thought. But it was also a welcome change of pace. Cevilla was definitely a character.

She went through the first floor and ensured everything was

in order before going upstairs. Cevilla's house was small, but the spare bedroom was roomy. She glanced at her purse, which was lying on the bed. Shane had taken it upstairs for her with her suitcase. She sat down on the bed, opened her purse, and pulled out the small plastic bag she'd nearly lost. She smiled at the miniature book encased inside. It was a tiny Bible, so small it fit into the palm of her hand. She'd held it tight during the entire bus ride. She was prone to motion sickness on long trips, and she had prayed the entire journey that she wouldn't throw up. The Bible had given her comfort. It always had, ever since Shane had given it to her the day his house was completed.

"Isn't this a part of your collection?" she'd asked when she opened the plainly wrapped gift. Shane was a bibliophile, and he had mentioned his book collection several times. He had over two thousand books, along with a dozen or so miniature books like this one.

"Yep. It was the first book I collected. Open the cover."

She did, and in tiny print she could barely read, she saw the copyright date. "Eighteen seventy?"

"Miniature books were popular in the latter part of the nineteenth century," he explained. "They were easy to carry when traveling. I've always been fascinated by how small they are, yet they contain so much text. This is a New Testament."

"I can't take it," she said, holding it out to him. She was touched as well as confused that he would give her such a precious item. "This is too special."

He folded her hands over it. "I want you to have it. It's a small token of appreciation for helping me fix up this house over the past six months. You've been more than any employee; you've been a friend. I couldn't have done it without you."

She pulled the book out of the plastic bag as she thought about that day. He'd been so proud of the work they'd done on the house. To be honest, she'd been proud too. She'd accomplished some tasks she'd never tried before, like staining the floors and helping her father tape up drywall. It had been hard work, but it had also been satisfying.

From that day on, she kept the Bible on her nightstand, often reading a chapter or two before going to bed. The print was tiny and it was a bit of a strain to read it, but something about reading a book printed so long ago was thrilling. Who owned the book over all these years, before Shane bought it? Did they treasure it the way she did?

The tiny Bible also reminded her to pray, and not just for Shane. She prayed for her parents, for her community, and for her friends. When she decided to go to Cevilla's, she couldn't imagine leaving it behind, so she placed it in the small plastic bag to protect it. When she realized she'd left it on the bus, she panicked. Thank God she'd been able to retrieve it. It was her most precious possession.

She set the Bible on the bedside table. She was tired, but not sleepy. She went to the window and looked out. It was still raining, and although it was dark outside, she could see droplets of water sliding down the window pane. She followed one of them with her fingertip and thought about what Cevilla said earlier. Lucy didn't need to get away from home, although she had to admit she felt a little bit more relaxed. Playing cards with Cevilla had been fun. But she didn't want anyone pitying her, especially an older woman she knew only through her great-aunt.

But she also wondered if Cevilla was right. She'd felt dissatisfied and stuck lately, deep in her heart. But she was where God wanted her to be, right? "Honour thy father and thy mother" was a commandment, one she took seriously. And unlike her friends in the community, she didn't have siblings to share the care of her parents.

She leaned her forehead against the window pane. Did she dare hope for something more? For something different? Shouldn't she be content to care for her parents, whom she loved deeply?

Lucy straightened and took a deep breath. Yes, she should be content. Her life was fine. No, better than fine. She had her faith and her purpose—caring for her parents. That was enough. It had to be. She didn't see her future being anything else.

On the Monday morning after Shane picked up Lucy, the weather couldn't have been more different—not a cloud in the bright-blue sky, and the temperature was perfect. He started to put on his Amish clothes, but then remembered he and Noah were going to Middlefield today. Since Shane would be driving his car, he didn't want to add to any confusion by wearing Amish clothes. After he dressed, he went downstairs, where the scents of rich coffee, freshly baked biscuits, and sausage gravy greeted him. He'd put on a few pounds while staying with Noah and Ivy, but he didn't mind. The past several months of trying to figure out his future had robbed him of an appetite, so he could afford the extra weight. But not for long if he kept eating all this good Amish cooking.

"Smells *gut*," Shane said as he took a platter from Ivy's hand. He glanced down at the fluffy biscuits. "Again, are you sure I can't pay you?"

Ivy shook her head, a spark of annoyance in her eyes. "You ask that every morning and the answer will always be the same. All the work you've done on the store is payment enough. Not that we expected you to pay for anything," she added. "You're welcome to stay with us as long as you want. For *free*."

He sighed and took the platter to the table. That was the only thing that didn't feel right about being in Birch Creek—bumming off Ivy and Noah's kindness. While he knew hospitality was the Amish way, he could easily afford to pay them room and board. But neither of them would hear of it. Noah had given him the same answer yesterday. And the work he'd done on the store wasn't that much—painting the storage room, helping Noah hang a new sign in front that also advertised Ivy's new bookbinding business, working on some of the faulty wiring in the store, a skill he'd learned when he renovated the house in Iowa. He'd even helped Noelle, the woman who owned the yarn shop next door, with a few things, like unloading deliveries. None of that came close to earning his keep. And after spending his whole life being catered to and, yes, spoiled, he wanted to make his own way. But he couldn't do that while he was still living in this house.

Again, he sighed. He had to make a decision, and soon.

"Are you all right?" Ivy asked as she put a plate of scrambled eggs on the table.

He looked down at her. She was a petite woman, not even five feet tall, which made her and Noah a visually interesting couple, since he was more than a foot taller than she was. But they were also a perfect couple, clearly happy and in love. He couldn't imagine being at such peace with Jordan, one more reason they hadn't been suited for each other. He smiled. "I'm fine. Just a lot on my mind lately."

Ivy nodded, but she didn't pry. She wiped her forehead, her fingers brushing against the blond hair that peeked out from under her white *kapp*.

At that moment Noah walked in. "Morning," he said as he put

his hat on the corner of his chair back. After he washed his hands at the sink, he grabbed a mug and poured coffee from the percolator on the gas stove. "Smells delicious," he said, leaning slightly down to speak in *Dietsch* to his wife.

Shane was picking up more and more words and phrases each day, even though Noah and Ivy were kind enough to speak English with him most of the time. Still, he was starting to grasp the language, which pleased him.

As soon as they all sat down to eat, a knock sounded on the front door.

"Are you expecting company?" Ivy asked Noah as she got up from her chair. He shook his head, and she left the kitchen to see who'd come. Shane kept his hands in his lap, knowing they wouldn't eat until Ivy came back and they gave thanks for the meal.

A few minutes later she returned, and to Shane's surprise Cevilla and Lucy trailed behind her. "We've got a couple of guests for breakfast," Ivy said with a sweet smile.

But while Ivy might have been happy about their arrival, Lucy clearly wasn't. Her displeasure wasn't all that noticeable, but Shane knew her well enough to see the slight scowl on her face. He recognized the tension around her mouth, the slight frown at the corners. No, she wasn't happy at all.

Cevilla's cane plunked on the wood-planked floor as she hobbled to the table. "My goodness, this looks delicious. Doesn't it, Lucy?" She looked at Noah. "Hope you don't mind us dropping by," she said to him in a loud voice.

"Of course not," Noah said. "Also, you don't have to yell. I'm pretty *gut* at reading lips, you know. Plus, I still have some of *mei* hearing, and *mei* hearing aids work just fine."

"I know." She sat down at the table. "I just wanted to make sure you heard me."

Noah chuckled, and Shane had to marvel at the man. He occasionally called Noah on the cell phone his friend owned strictly for his business. Shane had learned the Amish didn't use their cell phones for idle chitchat, but he and Noah did discuss their latest auction and flea market finds. Especially Shane, who had always found great joy in reading and collecting old books.

Shane thought back to when he'd learned Noah had Meniere's disease, which caused hearing loss and ringing in the ear. When he started to lose his hearing and received the diagnosis, Noah had been devastated, knowing he'd have to give up his auctioneering business. But in a little over a year he had built a new life for himself and Ivy. He was the same smart, good-natured guy he'd always been.

Lucy glanced at Shane and mouthed the words, "I'm sorry."

"You two are just in time," Noah said. "We were about to start the prayer."

Lucy moved to sit down next to Cevilla, but before she could, Cevilla put her cane across the chair. Lucy stared at Cevilla, who seemed completely engrossed in examining the edge of her plate. Lucy had no choice but to take the seat beside Shane.

Shane didn't mind at all. This was turning out to be a pleasant morning. He pulled out the chair for Lucy, not missing the smirk on Noah's face.

"Shall we pray?" Ivy said, her lips twitching as she and Noah exchanged a look.

Shane almost laughed himself—until he glanced at Lucy. Her frown had deepened. Did that mean she didn't want to sit next to him? Nah, that was a stupid thought. Why would she care?

Everyone had already closed their eyes and was praying. Shane followed suit. He prayed for the food to be blessed, but he also prayed once more for wisdom. He was pretty sure God was tired of hearing the same prayer, but this wasn't a decision he could make on his own. Trouble was, he wasn't getting much direction lately.

When he opened his eyes, Lucy picked up the platter of biscuits and held it out to him. He leaned toward her as he took one. "You look like you lost your best friend," he said in a low voice.

She glanced down at the platter. "I'm afraid we're being a little rude, coming over here unannounced like this. It wasn't my idea."

"Of course not." He leaned closer, his lips almost touching her ear. "We all know who the true mastermind is."

Lucy giggled, which made Shane grin. She had a cute laugh, and he didn't like seeing her uncomfortable, especially when there was no reason to be. He put the biscuit on his plate and glanced up . . . only to see Ivy, Noah, and Cevilla looking at both him and Lucy with keen interest.

"What?" he said, trying to divert their attention from Lucy, who started to squirm beside him.

"*Nix*," Cevilla said.

"Nothing," Noah added.

"What brings you by this morning?" Ivy asked, turning to Cevilla.

Shane heard Lucy's sigh of relief. When he looked at her, she quickly buttered her biscuit and shoved it into her mouth.

"Nothing in particular. Except I wanted to ask Shane to show Lucy around Birch Creek."

Lucy started to choke. Shane handed her a glass of water. "Are you okay?"

She nodded, taking a long drink. "I'm sure Shane has better things to do than drive me around Birch Creek," she said, her voice cracking.

"Actually, I wouldn't mind being your tour guide." Shane

couldn't help but smile at Cevilla's sly grin. The woman was less than subtle. And while Shane didn't have any hope of her blatant matchmaking being successful, he still wanted to spend time with Lucy.

"See?" Cevilla looked at Lucy, her expression triumphant. "Great minds think alike, obviously."

"Shane, you really don't have to." Lucy lowered her voice. "I don't want you to go to any trouble."

"It's no trouble." But to make sure she didn't feel even more uncomfortable, he added, "After everything you and your father did for me, it's the least I can do. We just have to set up a time."

"What about today?" Cevilla said.

"Shane and I are going to an auction at the Middlefield fairgrounds this morning," Noah said.

Cevilla clasped her hands together. "I have a great idea. Lucy, why don't you go with them? You'll get a chance to see Middlefield. It's a lovely community, although it's been a while since I've been there."

"I'm supposed to be taking care . . . staying with you," Lucy said, a confused expression on her face.

"No worries. I'll be fine without you for a few hours." She patted Ivy's hand. "This will give Ivy and me a chance to catch up."

"I have to open the store this morning," Ivy said, looking uncertain for the first time since Cevilla and Lucy's arrival.

"Perfect. I'll go with you. I'd love to see what new antiques you and Noah have acquired since I was there last. After the auction, Shane and Lucy can pick me up in his car and bring us back here to get *mei* horse and buggy." She picked up her coffee mug. "There. I'm so glad we settled all that."

Lucy looked anything but settled, and Shane had to admit his head was spinning a bit. In the span of a few minutes Cevilla had managed to totally rearrange everyone's day. That took quite a bit of skill.

Shane saw the lines of tension around the corners of Lucy's mouth. Not a good sign.

Noah suddenly jerked. "Ow," he said, looking at his aunt, who was giving him a hard side eye. "Um, since the two of you are going to the auction, I think I'll, uh, go to the store and help Ivy?"

"An excellent idea." Cevilla nodded and turned to Ivy. "Don't you think so?"

"Sure." Ivy gave Noah a questioning look, which he returned by turning his palms face up and giving a slight shrug.

Shane was starting to feel uncomfortable too. Cevilla's antics were humorous, but it was clear Lucy didn't think so. He didn't like the idea of her feeling coerced into something she didn't want to do. "I can go to the auction by myself," he said, hoping to help her out. "I've been before, and I know what to look for."

"But it's far more fun to go with someone." Cevilla looked straight at Lucy. "Don't you agree?"

"*Ya.*" Her shoulders slumped a bit.

"Then it's settled." Cevilla pushed away her plate with its half-eaten biscuit. "Delicious as always, Ivy."

"You barely ate anything, *Aenti*," Noah said.

"Because she had breakfast before we came," Lucy muttered.

"You two better hurry up," Cevilla instructed. "You don't want to be late for the auction."

Shane and Lucy dutifully ate their breakfast. Shane offered to help with the dishes before leaving, but Ivy refused. "It won't take long to clean this up," she said. As Shane put his dishes in the sink, he overheard Ivy speaking to Lucy. They spoke *Dietsch*, so he couldn't make out all the words, but he caught the gist. It would be easier to go along with Cevilla than to fight her. Shane couldn't help but agree.

Noah went outside to put up Cevilla's horse and buggy. He and Ivy would be taking their usual taxi into Barton.

When Shane and Lucy were in his Mercedes and he started to turn his key, she said, "I'm sorry."

He turned to her. "About what?"

"Cevilla." She folded her hands in her lap and stared at them.

Shane had the urge to take her hand and reassure her everything was okay. Instead, he turned the key in the ignition and backed the car out of Noah's driveway. "Do you like to *geh* to auctions?" he asked in broken *Dietsch*.

"*Ya*, although I don't *geh* very often." She paused. "I tried talking her out of going to Noah and Ivy's this morning, but she wouldn't listen to me."

"I'm not surprised by any of that." He turned down the next street and headed for the freeway, the quickest route to Middlefield.

"I didn't realize she was so stubborn."

"But harmless," Shane added.

Lucy sighed. "I'm not so sure."

Shane started to slow the car and reverted to all English. "If you want me to take you back, I will. I can go to this auction by myself."

"No, it's okay. I really don't mind. I just don't like to impose on anyone."

He nodded, fully understanding. He also knew he had to reassure her or she would be on edge for the rest of the trip. "You're never an imposition to me, Lucy. Please believe that."

Chapter 3

Lucy had been mortified from the moment they'd arrived at Noah and Ivy's, and her embarrassment increased when she realized why they had gone over there. Cevilla was matchmaking her and Shane. She'd had no idea, although that grin she thought she saw when Cevilla sent her and Shane to the kitchen on their own the day of her arrival might have been a clue.

She had just sat down to eat the oatmeal she'd prepared for her breakfast—Cevilla having eaten well before dawn—when Cevilla announced they would be going to her great-nephew's home, not to his store in Barton.

"I don't think that's a *gut* idea." Lucy had forced out the words. She didn't want to offend Cevilla, but she had to speak her mind about this. And yesterday had been such a peaceful Sunday. There was no church, and she and Cevilla had relaxed and napped throughout the day. It was quite nice. Now things were back to being turned upside down.

"Nonsense," Cevilla replied. "My nephew is a hospitable *mann*. He and Ivy will be glad to see us. Now, cancel the taxi and get the buggy ready, or I'll do it myself."

Lucy would have preferred to eat her oatmeal there in the kitchen, but she recognized how stubborn Cevilla could be. She hadn't doubted that the woman would hitch up the buggy on her own, sprained ankle and all.

And now Lucy knew she'd have to stand her ground eventually, despite Cevilla's eccentricity. It was pointless to push her and Shane together after she got back from Middlemore. Or was it Middlefield? She was so flustered she'd forgotten where they were going.

She was also flustered by Shane's words, and the way he said them. His voice was low and kind. Almost tender. But she was sure she was reading more into that than was there. She had to remind herself this was Shane, and he was off-limits. But it was hard to do when he was right next to her and they would be spending the morning together.

"Lucy?"

Shane's voice pulled her out of her thoughts. "*Ya*," she said. Then realizing she hadn't acknowledged what he'd said about her never being an imposition, she added, "*Danki* for that. It does make me feel better." And it did. At least he wasn't upset with her.

"I mean it." He leaned back in the seat, his plain white T-shirt showing his strong biceps and forearms. He was in good shape, something she'd noticed when they were working on the house. She felt warm, and not because it was a sunny morning. She pulled her gaze away from him and looked at the passing landscape, trying to focus on enjoying the view outside the car—not the one inside.

Shane reached for the radio, only to pull back. "Sorry," he muttered. "Force of habit."

"It's okay. I'm not supposed to listen to the radio, but it's *yer* car. If you want to turn it on, that's fine."

"I need to get used to not having it. But I must admit it's hard. I really enjoy music."

"It's definitely easier not to miss something you never had. I don't know what it's like to drive a car, or have a radio, so I don't miss them. I imagine it would be hard for someone English to give up those things."

"But it shouldn't be." He glanced at her. "It's all superficial stuff. Unnecessary things, in light of what you get in return."

His words intrigued her. "What do you mean?"

"I've learned that a lot of what we think we need and can't live without is really just a distraction. Like my cell phone. I haven't turned it on since I got here."

"How are you keeping in touch with your family?"

He paused. "I'm not."

She shifted a little in the seat until she was angled toward him. "Don't they miss you? Aren't they worried about you?"

"They know where I am. Why I'm here." His hands gripped the steering wheel. "If they need me, they can find me. So far, they haven't." He shrugged. "But that's fine. It makes *mei* life easier in some ways. I don't have them trying to coerce me into coming back. I don't have that pressure to make a choice, at least not from them."

Despite his words, he didn't sound too happy. "So you still think you might want to become Amish?"

"I do. At least I think so. I haven't decided yet, which is why I've been staying in Birch Creek. I want to make the right decision."

She admired him for taking his time, and for taking her faith seriously. "What made you want to join our church?"

"A number of things. The focus on faith in everyday life. It's easy to forget about God when you're in the middle of the rat race. Then there's the community."

"I know they're not Amish, but doesn't New York City have communities?"

"It does, but the city is so big. And crowded. You'd be surprised how lonely you can be in a sea of people. Don't get me wrong. Plenty of people thrive in that environment. They can't imagine living anywhere else."

Lucy got the impression he was talking about Jordan. Was that why they ended their engagement? Did he want them to live in Iowa and she didn't? Was it just a matter of geography? That didn't seem an insurmountable hurdle to her.

"What made you decide to join the church?" Shane asked.

She paused. They'd never discussed that, despite having many talks over lunches and suppers when he was in Arbor Grove. Then again, at the time she thought he was renovating a vacation home he might visit once or twice a year once he returned to his practice. She hadn't known he was thinking deeply about the Amish faith. "It was never really a question for me," she said. "I wasn't like some of *mei* friends during *mei rumspringa*. I didn't feel the need to explore the English world. I felt peace in *mei* soul, and I knew it was because of *mei* faith and community. When the time came to join, I didn't hesitate."

"We're drawn to the same things, it seems," he said quietly.

"I guess we are."

They talked the rest of the way, with Shane mostly asking her questions about *Dietsch* and practicing his pronunciation. When they entered the city limits, their conversation shifted to places of interest in Middlefield.

"There's the cheese factory," he said, inclining his head toward a building on the left side of the road. "And there's the shop. It used to be called Middlefield Cheese, but they changed the name. It's now Rothenbuhler Cheese Chalet."

"Sounds fancy," Lucy said with a smile.

"It's a nice shop and deli. You can get great sandwiches there."

"How many times have you been to Middlefield?" she asked as they passed the shop. Lucy noticed the lovely flowering landscaping in front of the building.

"A couple. They hold this flea market and auction every Monday at the fairgrounds. It's usually not too crowded when the weather's bad. But today should bring out a lot of people."

After Shane paid for parking, they pulled into a large lot. As he predicted, a lot of people were milling about, walking through aisles with booths displaying a variety of both old and new merchandise and fruit, vegetable, and flower stands. "I usually stop in that building over there," Shane said as he nodded toward one of two structures on one side of the fairgrounds. "They sometimes have some interesting things in there. Would you like to see?"

She nodded, and they went inside. Tables filled with merchandise were set up in the middle and along the sides. At first glance she didn't see anything much different from what was being sold outside, with the exception of a homemade candy stand.

"Not much to see here today," Shane said.

"Are you looking for something specific?"

"I'm always looking for books." He scanned a table of tools in front of one of the booths. "Noah likes unusual items." He looked at her as they kept walking. "We should probably hit the auction. It's in the building at the back of the fairgrounds."

She followed his lead as he headed out the side door. The rest of the morning Lucy learned how the weekly Middlefield auction worked. Instead of an auctioneer standing at the front of the room, he walked along with the crowd, stopping at each booth, which was just a section of items on a few long tables. Once the items were auctioned off at a given booth, they moved on to the next one.

Shane bid on a couple of items—an old wrought-iron gate,

a collection of rag dolls, a camera he said was from the 1970s. He was outbid by everyone, but he didn't seem to mind. "I don't see anything here we have to have," he said. "Sometimes that happens."

The auction was almost over when they stopped at the last booth. Shane picked up an old leather Bible sitting in the middle of one table. "It's not old or unique, other than being a Bible," Shane said. "But I'd like to bid on it."

When the auctioneer started the bidding, Shane threw out a number. "Five dollars." When no one else countered, the auctioneer told Shane the Bible was his and Shane paid him.

When the auction was over, Lucy and Shane went back outside. The crowd had thinned out a lot. "It's lunchtime," he said. "The market closes at one, but people usually leave around noon. They like to visit the local restaurants." He turned to her. "Are you hungry?" When she nodded, he said, "Let me treat you to the best trail bologna you'll ever have."

When they reached the car, Shane opened the door for her. "Would you mind holding this?" he asked.

She took the Bible from him and slipped inside the car. When Shane climbed into the driver's seat, he said, "You can look through it if you want."

Lucy ran her hand over the top of the Bible. It was a regular-size book, and the cover was cracked and peeling. She thumbed through it and found a pressed flower. "A pretty petunia," she said, looking at the faded yellow-and-purple petals.

"I've found lots of interesting things in books," he said. "Hairpins, a few bookmarks, and of course pressed flowers are popular. I've also found old photographs. And I'm fascinated with the notes people write in the margins of their books, especially Bibles. I find them inspiring."

She'd never thought about that before. They had one family Bible in their house, and she would never dream of writing in it. But she knew English people had many Bibles, and some even colored on the pages. "What made you decide to collect books?"

"My mom's dad liked to go to estate sales in upstate New York. When I was old enough, he took me to a few of them, and I wandered off to find books. At first I would read them out of boredom—there's not much to interest a seven-year-old in an old house. But as I got older, I realized the history I could learn from old books. Not just from the contents, but from the little items I found in them." He turned into the Rothenbuhler Cheese Chalet parking lot. "To me, there's something comforting about an old book. Or any book, for that matter. I have good memories of my grandpa, of course. But I also enjoyed the unique stories I encountered over the years."

"I don't collect anything," Lucy said. She'd never been drawn to owning things, although she did appreciate the quilts handed down to her mother through several generations. But she had never considered them a collection, especially since they were still in use.

"No one in my family does either." He parked the car. "I've always been the oddball among them."

She detected a somber note in his voice, but he got out of the car quickly before she could question him further. She took that as a hint he didn't want to explain his remark.

They walked into the restaurant and at the counter ordered two bologna sandwiches, chips, and drinks. The place was busy, and the small eating area was full. "I know a park nearby," he said as they looked at the occupied tables. "We can have an impromptu picnic of sorts."

"Sounds like a good idea."

A short time later they were sitting on a park bench near a

playground. "How did you find this place?" she asked, opening her small bag of potato chips.

"Driving around and exploring." He took a bite of his sandwich. After he swallowed, he added, "I do some of my best thinking when I'm wandering. The first couple of weeks I was here, I wanted to check out the area. I went all around Ohio Amish country—Holmes County, Ashtabula, and Geauga. This state has some beautiful places."

She took a sip of her bottled water and watched as two small children—a boy and a younger girl—had fun on the playground equipment. Nearby was a woman she assumed was their mother because she was watching them carefully. The air had grown warmer, but not too hot, and the park was filled with large shade trees. She could hear the traffic from the road, but it wasn't intrusive. She focused on the birds singing, the breeze ruffling the leaves, the delighted laughter of children playing. She finished her sandwich, which *was* the best trail bologna she'd ever had, and enjoyed the peace. "It's nice, isn't it?"

"*Ya*," Shane said. "It is."

At the tender tone in his voice she turned and looked at him. The smoky look in his eyes as he gazed at her reached her toes. Her mouth suddenly went dry, and the butterflies in her stomach took flight as he ran his thumb along the corner of her mouth.

"You've got a bit of mustard there," he said and then handed her a napkin.

"Oh." She felt heat in her neck rise, along with feeling like a fool. He hadn't been looking at her with the longing she'd wanted to see. When she glanced at him again, he was polishing off his sandwich.

He crumpled up the paper bag and stood. "Ready to get back?" he asked.

"*Ya*," she said, rising from the bench. She looked back at the park. Even though her heart was foolish, she'd enjoyed sitting here with Shane. She'd enjoyed the entire morning with him. But that was no surprise. *Because friends are comfortable with each other.* Why did she have to continually remind herself he would never be more than a friend?

As she and Shane walked back to his car, another car whipped into the parking lot. Wow, it was moving fast. Then a little boy dashed in front of it in a flash. Terrified he was going to get hit, Lucy ran toward the oncoming car.

The scene in front of Shane seemed to play out in slow motion. He'd noticed the car as soon as it entered the parking lot. He also noticed it was going too fast. What he hadn't noticed was the child running in front of it—not until Lucy took off directly in the path of the speeding car.

"Lucy!" he shouted as the brakes squealed.

She swooped up the young boy as the car skidded to a stop in front of them. Lucy crouched on the ground, hugging the child to her chest as both Shane and a woman ran toward them.

"Spencer!" the woman cried as she carried a little girl. This was the mother and her children he'd noticed at the playground.

Shane knelt beside Lucy. Her eyes were closed tight as the little boy squirmed in her arms. "It's okay," he said, releasing him from Lucy's grip. "It's okay."

The child ran to his mother and grabbed her legs.

"Oh, wow. I'm so sorry."

Shane looked up to see the driver, a kid probably no more than seventeen or eighteen years old. He was wearing a fast-food uniform, had a cell phone in his hand, and his face was white, no doubt from shock.

Shane jumped up from the ground. "What do you think you're doing, racing into a parking lot like this?"

"I-I'm sorry." The kid took a step back. "I was texting my girlfriend and we were fighting—"

"You think that's an excuse? You almost ran over two people!" Anger burned inside him as he moved closer to the kid.

"Shane . . ."

Lucy's soft voice pulled him back from the brink. He turned to see her standing behind him, her small body shaking, but her expression strong. "We're okay," she said. "Don't be too hard on him."

"Too hard?" He clenched his fists. Lucy had no idea what hard could be. He couldn't sue the kid or have him arrested, but he could scare him with enough legalese that he would wish he'd never gotten out of bed that morning. As he turned to do just that, he spied the woman and her two children. They'd moved to the grass. She was crouched down, still holding her smaller daughter while hugging her son close. The boy looked at him, his eyes wide and fearful.

That cooled Shane's anger. He took in a deep breath and turned to the driver. His anger further cooled when he realized the kid was also shaking.

"I swear," the driver said, his voice trembling, "I'm really sorry."

Shane went to him, ashamed when he saw him flinch. He touched him on the arm. "It's okay, kid. Just don't ever text and drive again. You might not be so lucky next time."

"Yes, sir." He shoved the cell phone into the pocket of his pants and went back to his car.

Shane turned to see Lucy talking with the mother. As he walked over to them, he could hear the woman thanking Lucy.

"He got away from me," she said in a shaky voice. The boy was still clinging to her legs. "One minute he was beside me, and the next he was dashing into the parking lot. I don't know what I would have done if he'd been . . ."

"It's okay." Lucy's voice was low and gentle. "Everything is fine now."

"Thank you. Thank you so much." She reached out and hugged Lucy, who hugged the woman in return.

The mother took her son's hand and led him to her car, lecturing him about running into the parking lot. The boy nodded, still a little pale and clearly unsettled, if not outright scared.

Shane put his hand on Lucy's shoulder. "Are you okay?"

She turned, and for the first time he saw terror in her eyes. His mind flashed to seeing her in the direct path of the car, and a frisson of fear traveled down his spine. On impulse, he pulled her against him.

CHAPTER 4

The last few minutes had been a blur to Lucy. She was glad the boy was safe, but she also realized how close they'd both been to being hit by the car. The thought made her body shake. But that wasn't the only reason she was trembling. Shane was cradling her in his strong embrace, and even though she knew he was holding her only out of fear and to comfort her, she didn't want him to let go.

She leaned against his chest, hearing the thump of his heart. He smelled of soap and fresh air and the mustard he'd added to his trail bologna sandwich. When she pulled away, she realized he had a drop of the condiment on his shirt. Without thinking, she wiped at it with her hand.

He dropped his arms and stepped back. "Uh, sorry," he said, shoving his hands into the pockets of his jeans. "I . . . I just wanted to make sure you're okay."

"I am." She was a little breathless, and she clasped her hands behind her waist.

"I'd tell you not to put yourself in danger like that again, but I know you better than that."

"I couldn't let the child get hit," she said, a little dismayed that he was questioning her decision to save him.

"I know." His tone softened, and a soft smile formed on his lips. "You're amazing, you know that?"

She didn't feel amazing. Her trembling body was just starting to calm down. "Anyone would have done the same thing," she insisted.

He continued to stare at her. "I'm not so sure."

She averted her gaze, her cheeks heating as they always did when she received a compliment. That made her cognizant of her freckles. She had so many of them, living up to her childhood nickname of "Freckle Face," which wasn't too original. No one called her that anymore, but she was still self-conscious about them. Freckles weren't exactly attractive. "You're giving me too much credit," she said, squaring her shoulders and forcing a smile. "We should head to the antique store. I'm sure Cevilla is wondering what happened to us."

He nodded, his eyes still intense. Which unnerved and excited her at the same time. *Get it together already.*

Neither of them spoke much on the ride to Barton, which gave her the time she needed to settle her emotions. Once there, Shane pulled in front of a quaint two-story building and parallel parked. She looked up at the sign, reading the words "Schlabach's Antiques" in old-fashioned script. "And bookbinding" was written underneath the store name. "They do bookbinding too?" Lucy asked after she stepped out of the car.

"That's a recent development," Shane said. "Ivy and her sister, Karen, used to work for a couple who had a bookbinding business before they moved away from Birch Creek. People started bringing old books to the antique store, and Ivy offered to repair a few of them. Noah convinced her to start doing more of that, enhancing the business." He opened the door for Lucy and she walked inside, but not before she noticed a stack of old letters tied with a red ribbon on a stool in the middle of the front window display. A Not for Sale placard sat next to it.

Lucy glanced around at the merchandise. She saw a lot of old and antique items—lamps, chairs, pictures and old photographs, clocks, even a case of jewelry. Several quilts were displayed on quilt racks. Curious, she went over and looked at them. Even without reading the date on the tags, she could tell some were old. But a couple were new, and clearly handmade.

"Noelle started a quilting class," Ivy said, coming up behind Lucy.

"She owns the yarn shop next door, *ya?*"

Ivy nodded. "When she first opened her place, she sold only yarn goods, but she expanded and started selling fabric. She held her first class a few weeks ago, and these are two quilts its members made. Some others are in Noelle's shop, and the proceeds from all the sales go to charity."

Lucy smiled. The quilts were lovely. She wasn't great at sewing, but she had enjoyed the few quilting bees she'd attended before her mother became sick. Thinking of *Mamm* reminded her she should write a letter to her parents. Odd how she was so consumed with her parents' welfare when she was with them, but she hadn't thought or worried about them the entire day. A wave of guilt washed over her.

"Something wrong?" Ivy asked.

She shook her head. She wasn't going to admit she'd forgotten about her parents only two days after arriving in Birch Creek. What kind of daughter did that? "Where's Cevilla?"

"After we had some lunch in the back room, business was slow here, so she went next door to Noelle's. Even when Noelle doesn't have many customers, Cevilla likes to sit and crochet and talk to anyone who does come by. I'm sure she's talking to someone right now." She paused. "Did you get anything from the auction?"

"Shane bought a Bible, but I think it's for his collection." She saw him showing the book to Noah. After the men talked for a few minutes, he came over to Lucy and Ivy. "Ready to take Cevilla home?"

"Yes. I shouldn't have been gone so long, though."

"Why not?" Ivy said. "Cevilla's fine. She's getting along better than I would with a sprained ankle."

They walked next door, and just as Ivy predicted, Cevilla was talking to a customer. The younger Amish woman was holding several skeins of yarn against her chest with one arm. "Lovely color choices," Cevilla said to her from a rocking chair.

"Danki." The woman held out an open pattern book for Cevilla to see. "I'm going to try *mei* hand at these daisy granny squares."

"Those are fairly easy to do," Cevilla said. "If you get stuck, though, let me know. I can help you."

"I might take you up on *yer* offer. I just started crocheting. Now that the *kinner* are teenagers, I have a bit more time on *mei* hands."

"Just wait until you're *mei* age. You'll have more time than you'll know what to do with. Oh, Lucy and Shane. You're back already."

Cevilla introduced her and Shane to the woman, who then turned and went to the front counter. Lucy glanced over her shoulder at the woman behind the register. She figured she had to be Noelle. Lucy looked at Cevilla. "What do you mean—*already*? We've been gone most of the day."

"Time flies when you're having fun, doesn't it?" She winked and put her crochet into her bag. "You did have fun, didn't you?"

"Um, *ya*," Lucy sputtered. She couldn't very well lie, because she did have a good time—except for the near accident in the parking lot. At least that experience had a happy ending, thank the Lord. She glanced up at Shane, expecting him to be annoyed with Cevilla's matchmaking. It was starting to annoy Lucy.

Instead, he was grinning. "It's been an interesting day for sure," he said, winking at Lucy.

"Your chariot awaits," he said, holding his hand out to Cevilla.

"Oh, how fancy." Cevilla took his hand and stood. She picked up her cane and said, "Thanks for the company, Noelle."

"Any time, Cevilla." She smiled at Shane shyly. "Nice to see you again, Shane."

He nodded and smiled at Noelle in return, settling the fluttering his wink had elicited in Lucy's heart. Shane was friendly with everyone, and it was clear Noelle found him attractive. Honestly, who wouldn't? It made more sense for him to be interested in someone like Noelle, who was pretty, young, and English. *But he's thinking about joining the Amish, remember?*

Cevilla insisted on sitting in the backseat. "I'm more comfortable back there," she said.

"But there's more room up front," Lucy pointed out.

"These short legs don't need much room." She got into the backseat as Lucy got into the front. Shane drove them back to Noah and Ivy's house, and when he got out of the car, he opened the door for Cevilla and assisted her. *I should be the one doing that.* Lucy brushed past Shane and went to Cevilla's other side. As she chastised herself, she could see the weariness on the old woman's face.

"I'll get your horse and buggy hooked up for you," Shane said.

"I can do it." Lucy's voice was sharp, and she flinched at the sight of Shane's surprised look. But she had spent enough time indulging herself today.

"Let the boy do it," Cevilla said, motioning to the barn with her cane.

"But—"

"Lucy," Shane said. "Please listen to Cevilla." He started to walk away. "She's a wise woman."

"I knew I liked that *bu* for a reason," Cevilla said, speaking in *Dietsch*. "Well, more than one reason." She looked at Lucy. "I'm glad you had a *gut* time with him. You deserve it."

Surprisingly, Lucy's eyes stung. Cevilla's look was soft and tender, with none of the underlying machinations she expected to see.

Cevilla reached for Lucy's hand and gave it a squeeze. "It's okay to have some things for *yerself*. You're not being selfish or neglectful."

"I . . ." She wasn't sure how to respond to that since she'd been feeling both selfish and neglectful at different points of the day. "I didn't come here to spend time with Shane. I didn't even know he was here. I thought he was living in New York."

"But he *is* here." She squeezed Lucy's hand again before letting go. "And there's something special between you two. Isn't there?"

Lucy shook her head, but her heart felt different. Then she sighed. "It doesn't matter how I feel."

"Don't ever say that. *Yer* feelings are as important as anyone else's."

Lucy blinked at Cevilla's reprimand. She was wondering how to respond when Shane came back with the horse and buggy. He helped Cevilla into the passenger side, and Lucy went to the driver's side. She grabbed the reins as Shane walked around the horse.

Cevilla leaned over and looked at Shane. "Why don't you come over for supper tomorrow? Lucy is an excellent cook."

Shane grinned and met Lucy's eyes. "*Ya.* She definitely is."

"Be there at six sharp," Cevilla said, leaning back against the seat.

Lucy saw her close her eyes briefly and realized the woman was indeed tired. She needed to get her home. She gave Shane an absentminded wave and headed for the road. When she pulled onto it, she expected Cevilla to make another comment about her and Shane. But when Lucy looked over, she was already asleep.

On the way home Lucy thought about Shane, Cevilla's words, and the events of the day. She hadn't expected any of this when she agreed to help Cevilla. And she couldn't spend the next several weeks, or however long she would be here, confused and uptight. But what could she do about it? Tell Shane how she felt? If she did, he probably would never want to see her again. Which would break her heart, especially now that they had spent time together here in Ohio. He was different, but in a good way. And if possible, he was even more attractive than before.

She didn't need Cevilla to matchmake. She needed to act on her own behalf. But her palms grew damp and her stomach churned at the idea of telling Shane she had feelings for him. A pain squeezed her chest at the thought of his rejection, of not seeing him again, at least outside of church services. Telling him how she felt would jeopardize, and probably end, their friendship—especially if his relationship with Jordan wasn't over. But she couldn't continue her time in Birch Creek being wound up in knots. She had to come clean with Shane, no matter the risk to her heart. And no matter the risk that he'd decide not to join the church, perhaps the biggest risk of all.

The following day seemed to drag for Shane. He helped Noah catalog some new inventory in the morning, and then he took a drive on the back roads of Birch Creek. He slowed by a plot of land on an almost deserted road. Two houses stood at the end of the road, but otherwise the area was undeveloped. Shane was aware that this part of Ohio was rich with oil, and that many of the residents of the Amish community had sold their rights and were independently wealthy, although no one would know by the simple, modest ways they lived their lives. Birch Creek didn't just have the appearance of humility and simple living—its people walked and breathed it. He particularly admired the bishop, Freemont Yoder, a farmer who guided the community with a fair and just hand. His sermons were always on point too. At least Shane thought so. He'd learned more about growing closer to the Lord in the past few weeks than he had sporadically attending church his entire life.

He pulled over to the side and got out of his car. He'd been here before. The For Sale sign was still stuck in the tall grass, although it wasn't askew the last time he'd been here. He straightened it and then glanced at the undeveloped land. He could imagine a house here. A small one, but built with the intention of adding on as his family grew bigger. He also envisioned a barn, a garden, and a plot of land he could farm himself. He didn't know the first thing about farming, but he could learn. Or thanks to Lucy and her father, he could go into home renovation. He was tenacious enough to start a new business. That was one thing his father had complimented him on—his tenacity. *The only thing he ever complimented me on.*

Shane gave his head a firm shake. He wasn't here to think about his father. Nor his life back in New York. That life seemed more distant and unreal with each passing day. He was here to contemplate his future—a future he realized he wanted to share with Lucy. Maybe here, maybe in Iowa.

He smiled and tapped his foot against the ground, pressing down some of the tall blades of grass. He hadn't been able to get her off his mind since she'd arrived in Birch Creek. And last night it dawned on him that she might be another confirmation that joining the Amish was the right decision. Of course, she wasn't the only confirmation, and not even the most important one. But he'd been asking God for guidance, and then Lucy appeared. Was she the final push he needed?

If she was, then he needed to be honest with her. It was getting harder to keep his feelings to himself anyway. That had been difficult even when they were working together in Iowa. Only his commitment to Jordan had kept that desire in check. But now Jordan was out of his life permanently, and his heart was free. No, not free. It belonged to Lucy.

Doubts were creeping in, however. Not about his feelings for Lucy, or even about joining the Amish. The doubts were about Lucy's feelings. A few times yesterday he thought he'd seen something in her eyes, heard a softness in her voice directed at him. Or it was wishful thinking. Either way, he couldn't see spending time with her yet hiding how he felt. But if he told her, would that drive her away? She'd seemed quiet and a little withdrawn as they'd driven from Barton to Ivy and Noah's house. Had she been put off when he drew her into his arms at the park? Had he already pushed her away at that point?

He returned to the car. Life wasn't without risk. He'd lived safely within his family's boundaries his entire life, and he'd been smothered by them. Lost inside them. He was taking steps to follow God's path for him, and he felt deeply in his heart that telling Lucy the truth was one of those steps. He'd do it tonight, after supper at Cevilla's. He'd make sure she knew Jordan was no longer in his life.

Would she reject him? Probably. But she would also know how much he cared about her, and if there was even the slightest chance that she felt the same, it would be worth the potential heartache.

Shane drove to Noah's and parked his car in the driveway. Inside, he glanced at the living room clock and realized it was nearing suppertime. He went upstairs and into the bathroom, stopping to look at his reflection in the mirror. He touched the hair that covered his cheeks and upper lip. He'd had the beard and mustache since he was twenty. He'd grown it to spite his father, who said it looked unprofessional and sloppy. He'd intended to shave it off after law school, but by that time beards were back in style. Jordan also insisted he keep it, dictating the length and style. It had grown out some since he'd been here, even though he'd trimmed it a few times. He wasn't even sure why he was hanging on to it. If he was going to become Amish, he'd have to shave it off.

"No time like the present." He picked up his toiletry case, slipped off his shirt, and began to shave. By the time he was finished, he barely recognized himself in the mirror. He'd forgotten about the small scar on his chin from a water-skiing accident when he was ten, as well as the dimple near the left corner of his mouth, a genetic trait on his mother's side of the family. She'd been disappointed in him, too, when he left the law firm six weeks ago. He'd disappointed them all.

For the first time since he'd come to Birch Creek, a heaviness settled over him. He wished things were different between him and his parents. He wished they would understand that their dreams for him weren't his dreams. His brother-in-law, Blake, also a lawyer, was more like the son his parents had always wanted. At least he wasn't leaving them alone.

Shane blew out a breath and jumped into the shower for a quick rinse. He dressed in fresh Amish clothes—which were becoming more comfortable to him by the day—cleaned up the sink, and then went downstairs. Ivy was in the kitchen, stirring what smelled like chicken and dumplings, which was fast becoming one of his favorite meals.

"Don't set a place for me," he said.

"Wait." Ivy looked at him, her expression filled with surprise. "Your beard and mustache. They're gone."

"Yeah." He rubbed his bare chin. "Thought the time had come." He went into the mudroom to get his hat.

"Where are you off to?" Ivy asked.

He poked his head back into the kitchen. "Cevilla's. She invited me over for supper."

"What a surprise," Ivy said dryly.

Shane paused. "What do you mean by that?"

Ivy turned and smiled. "She's becoming the town matchmaker."

"So you think she's trying to get Lucy and me together too?"

"I know she is. That little trick with the cane this morning? She used that on me and Noah once, when we were at a restaurant in Barton. I think she can be too meddlesome sometimes."

"That just shows she cares." He gave her a small wave and headed out the door. "Don't wait up!"

He heard her laugh and say, "I won't."

Jordan honked her horn at the Amish buggy slowly moving in front of her. This was ridiculous. She maneuvered her rental car so she could peer around the obstruction. When she didn't see any traffic coming in the opposite direction, she whipped into the other lane and sped past the plodding horse.

Not for the first time, she questioned her decision to come

here. It wasn't as if Shane was the only handsome and wealthy attorney in New York City. But with wealth and looks often came ego and infidelity. Shane was one of the good guys, and she'd realized that too late. Maybe she shouldn't have insisted he get rid of that house in Iowa. But at least if they married—no, *when* they married—she wouldn't have to worry about him spending late nights at work with his secretary, the way her father had. Her mother had been able to turn a blind eye to her father's escapades, but Jordan hadn't. She'd vowed never to marry a man who would be unfaithful, which was why she wasn't about to let Shane go.

She checked the GPS on her watch and saw she was nearing the house where Shane's mother said he was staying with that Amish friend of his. Jordan thought she'd find an ally in the woman when she explained her plan to bring Shane back to New York.

"I don't think that's a good idea," his mother had said, adjusting the strand of cultured pearls she always wore around her neck.

"Why not? We all know he belongs here, not in some backward, backwoods town in Ohio."

"At one time I would have agreed with you," she said. She took a sip of her lemon water. "But now . . . I'm not so sure. He was unhappy. He's been unhappy for a long time."

Jordan gripped the steering wheel as she remembered his mother's words. The implication was clear—he'd been unhappy with Jordan. But she'd prove her, and him, wrong. She knew how to make Shane happy. How to make all men happy.

She pulled into the driveway of a plain house. When she got out of the car, she smelled the awful scent of manure and grass. She sneezed. Great, now her allergies were kicking up. She pulled a tissue out of her designer handbag and patted her nose before climbing the front porch steps and knocking on the door.

A diminutive woman about Jordan's age answered the door. "May I help you?" she asked.

"I'm looking for Shane."

A wary expression crossed the woman's round face. Why did all these Amish women look so plain and boring? "I'm sorry, but he's not here."

Her patience was already at the breaking point. "Where is he?" When the woman hesitated, she said, "I have an urgent message for him from his family. I need to see him right away."

Any more hesitation, and Jordan would have to amplify her lie. But the woman finally said, "He's at a friend's house."

As the woman gave her directions, Jordan hid a smile. It wouldn't take long to convince Shane to come home. She thought about the two plane tickets she'd already purchased. Yes, she would succeed. She wouldn't make the same mistake twice. She wasn't about to lose him to these simple people.

CHAPTER 5

Lucy couldn't keep her eyes off Shane. When he arrived right before supper, she didn't recognize him at first. Now that they were sitting across from each other at the table, she had to force herself not to stare. He'd been handsome with the beard and mustache. Without them, he was gorgeous. And this was the first time she'd seen him in Amish clothes—broadfall pants and a homemade, short-sleeved yellow shirt.

"Have some more bread," Cevilla said, passing the plate to Shane. "Lucy baked it fresh this morning."

"It's delicious," he said, looking at Lucy as he took the plate from Cevilla. "Everything is."

Lucy felt a shiver down her spine. Shane kept his eyes locked with hers as he put a slice of bread on his plate. Something was different about him, and not just his clean-shaven face. His eyes sparkled, and he seemed to have a smile playing on his lips, even when he wasn't grinning. She pulled her gaze from his and reached for the bowl of creamed cabbage, not realizing he was also reaching for it. Their hands touched, and another shiver made it all the way to her toes.

"Well, I'm full." Cevilla pushed away her plate. "That was a lovely meal."

Lucy glanced at her. She'd barely touched her meat loaf and mashed potatoes. But Lucy was learning Cevilla didn't have much of an appetite. It didn't seem to affect her, though. "I made cherry pie for dessert."

"I'll have some later. I think I'll go to *mei* room for a while." Cevilla pushed herself up from the table and reached for her cane. "Why don't you two sit on the front porch for a while after you're finished? It's a lovely night for it."

"Sounds like a *gut* idea." Shane looked at Lucy. "Don't you think so?"

"Um, *ya*." She'd spent the whole day calming her nerves, focusing on cleaning the house and making one of her favorite meals. She'd been fairly successful until Shane showed up. And now that Cevilla was hobbling toward the living room, leaving her alone with Shane, Lucy's nerves went into overdrive. She rose from the table. Shane was silent as she quickly put away the leftovers. "I'll cut the pie," she said.

Shane stood. "It can wait until later."

"All right. I'll wash the dishes, then."

"Later." He moved closer to her. "Let's sit on the front porch. We need to talk."

She couldn't believe he was giving her the opportunity she needed to tell him how she felt. She'd been talking herself into doing that all day. But now that the time had come, she was losing her courage. "It won't take me long."

"I'll help you with them . . . later." He took her hand. "Come sit with me, Lucy."

She glanced at her hand in his. Before she could say anything— or even question why he was holding her hand—he led her to the front porch. He let go of her hand as she sat down on the swing, and he lowered himself to sit next to her.

He pushed the swing into motion with the toe of his boot. They moved back and forth for a bit, the birds and insects the only sound in the air. She should be nervous, especially because of how close they were. But instead, she felt herself relax a bit against the back of the swing. "I'm surprised you walked over here tonight."

"The weather is perfect for it."

"*Ya*, it is."

She closed her eyes, allowing herself to enjoy the moment. "Beautiful."

She opened her eyes at Shane's voice. They were facing the field next to Cevilla's house, which had a certain wild appeal, but she wouldn't call it beautiful. Then she realized he wasn't looking at the field. He was looking at her.

"Does it bother you that I called you beautiful?"

It should. She wasn't supposed to be prideful or vain. But hearing him say that to her, knowing he thought it . . . "You think I'm beautiful?"

He grinned, and she saw a dimple appear on his cheek. "Of course I do. I always have."

Now she was confused. "You have?" She touched her cheek. "Even with all these freckles?"

He chuckled and brushed the back of his hand across her other cheek. "Especially the freckles." Then he took her hand again. "I have something to tell you." His expression turned serious. "I've been trying to think of the right words all evening, but to be honest, I'm not exactly thinking clearly right now." He angled his body so he was facing her.

His gaze was so intense in the growing dusk of the evening that she could barely breathe. Something inside her broke free, and the nerves she'd been dealing with all day disappeared, replaced by a deeper, more satisfying feeling. In this moment everything was right, and she felt happier than she'd ever had.

"Lucy, I . . . I—"

A car suddenly whipped into the driveway, spewing gravel and dirt into the air. Lucy and Shane broke apart, and Lucy jumped up from the swing and walked to the other side of the porch. Whoever that was, she didn't want them to see her and Shane together that way. Because even if she had the wrong idea, she didn't want anyone else to get the wrong idea.

The car pulled to a stop close to the front porch. The driver's door opened, and out stepped a tall, thin, smartly dressed woman. Lucy could smell the sweet perfume on her before she reached the porch. Her shoes—high heels with pointed toes—were a little unsteady on the gravel drive, but she maintained her grace. Dread filled Lucy's stomach as she realized who the woman was.

Shane got up from the swing and went to the porch railing. "Jordan?" He didn't give Lucy a second glance as he bounded down the steps. "What are you doing here?"

Jordan stared at Shane for a moment, and then she threw Lucy a triumphant look before focusing on him again. "I'm here to take you home."

Shane couldn't believe what was happening. One minute he was in heaven and about to tell Lucy what was on his heart. Cevilla had been right, the evening was perfect for sitting on the porch, and when he saw Lucy relax and close her eyes, he couldn't stop himself from saying the words waiting on his lips. She was absolutely gorgeous, and he decided at that moment that even if she didn't feel for him what he felt for her, he wasn't about to give up that easily. He'd take things slowly and show her how he felt.

But when he saw the way she was looking at him, how her hand fit so easily in his, he knew he'd been afraid for nothing. And before he spoke, he'd thanked God that very moment that Lucy was in his life.

And now one person had ruined all that. The last person he wanted to see. "Jordan, I don't know what you're talking about."

"Aren't you tired of playing this game?" Jordan moved closer to him. "You've had your little vacation. You've had your fun, wearing those silly clothes." She closed the gap between them. "It's time to get back to where you're supposed to be."

"I am where I'm supposed to be." He took a step back from her, the heel of his boot hitting the bottom porch step. "You're the one who doesn't belong here."

A flash of anger crossed her face. She looked around him, at the porch, and then back at Shane. "Let's go somewhere private and talk about this."

"There's nothing to talk about, and I'm not going anywhere with you."

Tears filled her eyes, but Shane was unmoved. He'd been down this road with her before. She could cry at the drop of a hat, and she'd told him one time in a rare show of vulnerability that she'd learned how when she was a kid and wanted something from her father. "He's a sucker for tears," she'd said without remorse. But the ice around Shane's heart didn't stay solid for long. Even though he knew she was probably faking it, he didn't want to see her cry. "Jordan, don't."

She touched his cheek. "You shaved." When he started to pull away, she locked her arms around his waist. "Come home with me, Shane. I love you. We never should have broken up, I know that now. We belong together."

He'd started to move her hands away when she quickly reached up and kissed him. He was shocked, but he still heard the front door slam shut. *Lucy.*

Shane ducked out of Jordan's embrace and wiped his mouth. "Stop it," he said, looking over his shoulder at the closed door. Lucy had seen Jordan kiss him, and he had to tell her it wasn't what she thought. He turned, dashed up the steps, and rushed inside the house. Cevilla was waiting in the living room, sitting in a chair near the front window.

"Where's Lucy?" he said, looking around the room. Her harsh glare informed him she knew what happened. He had no doubt she'd seen everything. Great. He'd have to explain it to her later, because right now he had to talk to Lucy.

"Upstairs." Cevilla glanced out the window. "Your fancy girlfriend is still waiting for you."

"She's not my girlfriend." He started to go upstairs, but then he turned back to Cevilla. "I have to talk to Lucy," he explained.

Cevilla paused and then nodded. He heard the old woman sigh as he ran up the stairs. Yes, he had a lot of explaining to do.

He stopped in front of Lucy's door. It was open a crack, and even though he knew he should knock, he couldn't keep from going inside. She was sitting on the edge of the bed, holding something in her open hand. He slowed down when he realized what it was. The tiny Bible he'd given her. She brought it with her? At the time he'd hesitated to give it to her. Not because the book wasn't special. It was the most special one in his collection. But he thought she might think he was weird for giving her a tiny Bible as a thank-you for helping him with his house. Yet once she'd looked at the book with wonder and respect, he knew he'd made the right decision. He'd never thought she'd keep it so close to her, though. "Lucy?"

She looked up at him with pain in her eyes, but not tears. "I'm sorry."

"You're sorry?" he said, dumbfounded. "You have nothing to be sorry for."

"I shouldn't have stayed on the porch so long." She looked at the Bible in her hand and then set it on the bedside table. "I shouldn't have intruded on a private moment."

Was she kidding? None of this was her fault. He sat down next to her, his heart pinching when she moved away. "I'm the one who's sorry. I had no idea Jordan was coming here. If I'd known she even wanted to, I would have told her to stay in New York."

"It's obvious she still loves you," Lucy said, not looking at him.

"No, she doesn't love me. She loves the *idea* of me."

Lucy looked at him, confused. "I don't understand."

"I've known Jordan since college. When we started dating, it was pretty casual. A lot of guys were interested in her, and she liked keeping her options open. We didn't get serious about each other until law school." He didn't like telling Lucy all this, but if they were going to move ahead with their relationship, she needed to know his past. "Jordan's smart. She's an excellent lawyer, but she sells herself short. She could have joined my father's law firm on her own merits, but she wanted to make sure she had an ace in the hole."

"Ace in the hole?"

"She wanted to be sure she'd be hired on at our family business. Once she got the job, she really didn't need me anymore."

"Is that why you two broke up?"

He shook his head. "We broke up because we want different things out of life. I wanted out of the law firm. I want simplicity, peace, and a closer relationship with God. She wants . . . other things." He took in a deep breath. "I'm not going to judge her decisions. Or her desires."

To his surprise, Lucy had a faint smile. "Sounds very Amish of you."

"I guess so." He looked at her again. "I broke up with Jordan, Lucy. I let everyone believe she dumped me, and I didn't mind. But I had to break it off with her. My place is with the Amish." Saying the words out loud only cemented what he truly believed. "Not only with the Amish . . . but with you."

Lucy fought to control her emotions. She'd been so thrown by seeing Jordan and Shane kissing that she had run away. Not because it was a private moment, but because she was a coward. Seeing them together made her realize any feelings she had for Shane, and any she'd hoped he had for her, couldn't be acted on. Not now, and possibly not ever. This had been a jolt of reality, one she needed.

She got up from the bed, crossed to the other side of the room, and then faced him. "Shane," she said, suddenly feeling calm. No, more than calm. She felt at peace. "You have a lot of decisions to make."

He got up and started toward her, but when she held out her palms in front of her, he stopped. She heard the pleading in his voice. "I've finally made up my mind. I'm going to become Amish. And after that we can seriously talk about our future."

"Our future?"

He nodded. "I like you, Lucy. No, it's more than like. I—"

"Stop." She shook her head. "Don't say anything else."

"Why? Because you don't want to hear the truth? Because then you'd have to admit your feelings for me?" He moved closer to her. "Because I know you like me too. Can you tell me that isn't true?"

She wouldn't lie to him. "I can't." At his satisfied look she added, "But my feelings don't matter right now."

Disbelief crossed his face. "How can you say that? Your feelings do matter."

"I'm starting to learn that." And she was, thanks to Cevilla and Shane. But that didn't matter right now. "You don't need my feelings, or your feelings about me, clouding your decision. Shane, you can't take joining the Amish lightly."

"You don't think I know that? I've been agonizing over this for a long time, way before I came to Birch Creek. I've known my life isn't in New York. My vocation isn't law. I can't just pay lip service to my faith when my conscience tells me to. I've always wanted something more meaningful. I've craved closeness with God, and I feel that closeness when I'm among the Amish."

"Then let that be your guide. Not your feelings for me."

"They're not."

"Then prove it. Not to me, but to yourself. We can't see each other anymore. Not until you're sure about your faith. Not until you know the only reason you're joining the Amish is because of God. Nothing else. Not until I'm sure too."

"Lucy—"

"If you don't leave, Shane, I will. I'll tell Cevilla I can't stay."

He took a step back, his handsome face stricken. "You don't have to do that," he said, his voice quiet. "I'll go." He turned to walk out of the room, only to stop and look at her bedside table. "You still have the Bible," he said.

She looked at it. It had meant everything to her from the moment he had given it to her. It wasn't just a token of his friendship and appreciation; it was special to her. When he gave it to her, she knew it had been special to him.

She went to the table and picked up the tiny book. Then she put it in the palm of his hand and folded his fingers over it. She also had to prove that she could let him go for a higher purpose. She let go of his hand and went to the window, keeping her back to him. She didn't move until she heard him going down the stairs. Only then did she let the tears fall.

CHAPTER 6

This is all *mei* fault."

Lucy reached out and patted Cevilla's hand. "*Nee*, it's not."

"Oh yes, it is." She glanced out the window for the third time. "I can't believe he left with her," she said.

Lucy stiffened. She'd come downstairs after the front door closed, wiping her eyes and trying to hide any trace of her feelings from Cevilla. They'd watched the car leave, and now she saw the scowl on Cevilla's face. She wasn't surprised Shane left with Jordan. Not only had Lucy sent him away, but he clearly had unfinished business with her. Maybe he would even realize he'd been about to make a huge mistake—in more ways than one.

Cevilla walked to her rocking chair and sat down. She looked at Lucy, and for the first time Lucy saw a lack of confidence in the woman's eyes. "I have a confession to make," she said. Then she reached down and unstrapped the boot on her foot. "*Mei* ankle is perfectly fine."

"What?"

"Oh, I did sprain it. But by the time you got here the swelling had gone down." She rolled her ankle around. "See? *Nee* pain."

Lucy didn't know whether to be shocked or angry. "But why didn't you tell me?"

"Because I thought I was helping you." She let out a sigh. "*Yer* great-aunt and I have been worried about you. Not just *yer* great-aunt. *Yer* parents too."

A stab of fear went through her. "What's wrong with *mei* parents?"

"*Nix*. And there's a prime example of *yer* problem. You instantly jumped to the conclusion there was. You're overly concerned about them, to *yer* detriment." She gave her a weak smile. "Such a wonderful quality, but it's also a double-edged sword. So when I sprained *mei* ankle, I mentioned I might have to have some help. *Yer* great-aunt volunteered you. When she told *yer mamm*, she agreed."

"Why didn't you just invite me for a visit?"

She peered at Lucy over her silver-rimmed glasses, making her feel like a chastised schoolgirl. "Would you have come? Would you have left *yer* parents behind for a vacation?"

Lucy sat back in the chair. Cevilla knew her well. "*Nee*. I wouldn't have."

"Which is why I didn't ask you to just visit." She looked at her lap, her gnarled fingers that had such skill with a crochet hook loosely clasped. "I also had an ulterior motive. Shane is here to consider joining the church, right? And I thought you two would make a *gut* couple. I still do. I'm rarely wrong about these things. But I should have realized the timing isn't right. He's still wrestling with the decision to join the Amish."

This woman was full of surprises. "I didn't realize you knew that."

"I know a lot of things, *yung* lady, but that's not the point. I shouldn't have tried to push this. Neither of you is in a good place for a relationship right now."

Lucy let out a sigh. Cevilla was right. "Do you think he'll go back to New York?"

"I don't know." She looked down at her hands. "That decision is such a personal one. I know from experience. When I was a *yung* woman, I had to decide whether to join the Amish after living in the English world when *mei* father and English stepmother married." At Lucy's surprised expression, she added, "Not many people who know about that are still around, by the way. Lois doesn't even know that about me, and I'd like to keep it that way."

She let out another sigh. "I'm sorry I've made things more complicated for you. It's just that when I saw you and Shane together when he brought you home from the bus station, I couldn't help myself. Once I saw you two together, I had this feeling, stronger than the one that made me get you here." She put her hand over her heart. "That feeling hasn't left, but I realize I need to let both *yer* futures take their course without *mei* meddling." She rolled her eyes. "It's not like God hasn't given me that message before. Noah and Ivy can attest to that."

Lucy had no idea what Cevilla was talking about, but she didn't press her. The woman looked like she felt terrible to begin with, which made Lucy want to comfort her. This wasn't her fault. Well, it was partly, because she had crossed the line a little bit. But Lucy could tell her intentions were coming from the right place. Cevilla was a special and unique woman. "*Danki*," she said, getting up and hugging her.

Cevilla let out a small gasp of surprise. "For what? Being a meddling old woman?"

"*Nee*. For caring enough about me to meddle." She kneeled in front of her. "I'm not sure how I'm going to let *geh* of this worry about *mei* parents. I can't remember a time when I didn't worry about them. In fact, it seems like I worry about a lot of things I shouldn't."

"'Be careful for nothing; but in every thing by prayer and supplication with thanksgiving let your requests be made known unto God,'" Cevilla quoted. She took Lucy's hands in both of hers. "Give *yer* worries to Him, dear girl. One prayer at a time, one day at a time. That's all any of us can do."

Later that night Lucy went upstairs to her room. She looked at the empty spot on her nightstand. She missed the tiny Bible. More than that, she missed Shane. As long as she had the Bible she'd had a connection to him, even when she thought they would be permanently apart. Now that connection was severed, and she wondered if it could ever be repaired. *Be careful for nothing . . .*

She knelt at the side of her bed and began to put Scripture into practice—just as she should have been doing all along.

Shane pulled his rental car into the circular driveway in front of his parents' East Hamptons house. This was their vacation home, one of three on the East Coast. They also owned a beach house in California, which Shane had been to exactly twice, both times at Jordan's request. He parked and looked at the manicured lawn, the fountain in the middle of the circular driveway, the brickwork on the arched entryway that cost more than a dozen Amish homes put together.

The last time he was here he'd looked at this display of wealth with dismay. That was also the day he left New York, for what he thought would be for good. Now he was back, ten days after he and Lucy parted, facing the home he grew up in. Well, at least on weekends. During the week the family stayed in their Manhattan brownstone.

He didn't think he would ever be back here, but he'd realized he had to return.

He went to the front door and rang the bell, which felt odd. Normally he would have walked in. He waited, and a few minutes later Mariska, their longtime housekeeper, answered the door.

"Shane," she said in her thick Russian accent. "You've come home."

The words were said so matter-of-factly and with such a lack of emotion that Shane almost laughed. "It's nice to see you too, Mariska." He went inside, and she closed the door behind him.

"I'll bring you a cocktail," she said, starting to move away.

"Just water, thank you."

She nodded and headed down the hall to the kitchen. *Nothing has changed here.* But everything had changed inside him.

"Shane?"

He turned to see his mother sweeping down the long staircase in front of him, her ever-present pearls around her neck. They'd been a tenth-anniversary present from his father, and she wore them with everything, even her most casual clothes. Mother was so elegant that the necklace never looked out of place. She stopped in front of him, studying his face. She gave him a tiny smile. "You look so different. It's been so long since I've seen you without a beard."

He'd forgotten all about his beard, already in the habit of shaving every morning. "*Ya.* I mean, yeah."

"It's good to see you. Your father and I are having drinks on the patio in a few minutes. Will you join us?"

He saw the hopefulness in her eyes. "Of course."

She led him out to the patio, which surrounded a large square pool that overlooked a semiprivate beach on the Atlantic Ocean.

The scent of salt air hit him. He'd always loved the smell of the ocean. The sand between his toes, the waves as they crashed against the shore. There were good things about New York. Lots of good things.

"You can sit here," she said, gesturing to one of the patio chairs. As he sat down, the French doors opened.

Shane turned to see his father coming toward them. His gait hitched ever so slightly, the only hint that he was surprised Shane was there. He stood and held out his hand. "Dad."

"Shane." His father shook his hand with businesslike precision and then sat down next to his mother. Mariska, as if on cue, brought out a tray of drinks. She set water with lemon in front of Shane, on the low table that separated him from his parents.

After Mariska left, the three of them sat in silence. Shane sipped his drink and listened to the ocean waves as he stared across the beach.

"I'm assuming since you're here you've come to your senses."

He turned at his father's voice, a calmness inside him. "You could say that."

"Did Jordan go out to see you?" Mother said, sipping her mimosa.

"She did."

"Then we have her to thank for your seeing the folly of your decision to leave the firm?" Dad said.

"No. She has nothing to do with why I'm here." He set down his drink and shifted his chair to face them more squarely. "I'm joining the Amish next week. I've been studying privately with the bishop in Birch Creek, and he's agreed to baptize me."

A muscle jerked in his father's cheek, signaling the reaction he'd expected. Shane tensed up for an argument from them both.

"Good."

Both Shane and his father stared at his mother. "Sharon, what do you mean by that?" his father said.

"If joining the Amish is what our son wants to do, then I support his decision."

"I certainly don't." Dad slammed his drink down and glared at Shane. "I thought you were here to beg for your job back."

Shane shook his head. "I came to tell you about my decision. I didn't think it was fair or right for me not to, or not to do it in person." He turned to his mother. "Thank you," he said softly. "Your support means a lot to me."

"I can't believe this." His father jumped up from his chair. "You're going to give up everything, all of this"—he held out his hands and gestured to the private beach and expensive swimming pool—"to live in a shack?"

"It's not going to be a shack," Shane said. "I plan to build a nice house, on my farm."

"A farmer. You're going to be a farmer." His father ran his hand through his salt-and-pepper hair. "All that money and time in law school, not to mention sending you to Harvard and before that to the best private high school in the country, all so you could become a farmer."

"I appreciate everything you've done for me, Dad, but I never asked for any of it." Shane rose from his chair, feeling his anger rise. But he took a deep breath and let it subside. "I'm not here to fight. I'm here to tell you about my decision. It's my life, and I have to live it the way God wants me to."

"For crying out loud, I'm not listening to any more of your nonsense." Dad spun around and went inside the house.

"I'm sorry," Shane said, his voice breaking.

"Give him some time." His mother came up beside him and put her hand on his shoulder. "He'll understand, eventually."

Shane turned to her. "Do you think so?"

"We can hope for it." Tears swam in her eyes. "I've always known you were unhappy. That your father was forcing his dreams and ideals on you. I wish I would have tried to do something to stop it."

"I'm sorry for disappointing you."

"How can I be disappointed? You're choosing to follow faith. I'm not sure how you ended up with such strong convictions. Your father and I haven't been shining examples in that department."

"I can tell you, if you want to hear."

The tears spilled freely down her cheeks. "Yes, Shane. I want to hear about God."

Lucy wiped the kitchen table clean as her mother put on her bonnet. "I'm headed over to Frances's for a quilting bee," she said. "Would you like to come?"

Lucy shook her head. "I'll stay here to help *Daed*."

Her mother lifted an eyebrow. "He has Jacob for that, remember?"

Lucy nodded. When she'd returned to Iowa a month ago, she learned her father had hired Jacob Miller, a young man in the district, to work with him in the workshop. Her parents had also sat her down and told her they wanted her to start living her own life. "We didn't realize how hard we were leaning on you until Cevilla and *Aenti* Lois pointed it out," *Mamm* had said.

"It's high time I hired someone for the shop anyway. Jacob's a *gut yung mann* and eager to learn. He'll be a fine apprentice."

But Lucy had thought *she* was her father's apprentice. And her mother's support. "Neither of you needs me?"

"We need you to be our *dochder*. Not our employee or our maid. We also need you to be happy."

But going to quilting bees didn't make her happy. "I'm fine staying here," she told *Mamm*.

"All right. But come on out if you change *yer* mind."

After *Mamm* left, Lucy washed and dried the dishes. She stared out the kitchen window and sighed. Her parents were moving on, and they wanted her to move on too, but all she could think about was Shane. The last time she saw him he'd left with Jordan, and she hadn't heard from him since. Noah and Ivy said he'd thanked them for their hospitality and left that same day, but he didn't say where he was going. Even though Cevilla had revealed her ankle was fine, Lucy stayed for another week, meeting the residents of Birch Creek and spending some time with Ivy, her sister, Karen, and their extended families. It was fun, and the constant activity had kept her mind off Shane. Cevilla had even taught her how to crochet, along with Ivy, who'd been learning for the past year. Upstairs in her room she had a small purse she was working on, but she didn't feel like getting it out.

She was restless, and she had been ever since Shane left.

She wondered where he was, what he was doing, what he had ultimately decided about his faith. Since she hadn't heard anything about him joining the Amish church, she assumed he'd decided not to. Maybe he and Jordan had worked things out. It wouldn't surprise her if they had. The pull of the world, especially the one Shane grew up in, would be almost impossible to resist.

She decided to take a walk, and she was partly down the road when she heard a vehicle pull up behind her. She was about to turn around when she heard someone shout her name. She did turn around and then froze.

"Wait up." Shane jogged toward her as a taxi made a U-turn and headed the opposite direction.

"What are you doing here?" was all she could think to ask. She looked him up and down, He had on a straw hat and Amish clothes. But why?

"It's nice to see you too." He put his hands on his hips, looking a little disappointed.

"I'm sorry." She held out her hands. "I'm just . . . surprised to see you."

"I imagine so." His half smile faded. "I have some explaining to do." He let out a small laugh. "I seem to be saying that to you a lot lately."

She waited for him to speak, her heart thrumming at the sight of him. But she forced herself to stay calm. Not because she didn't want him to know how she felt, or even because she was still denying how she felt. The important thing was whether he'd made a decision to join the Amish, and for the right reasons.

"Lucy . . . I joined the church."

Her heart made a tiny leap. "You did?" She clasped her hands together with joy. "When?"

"A couple of weeks ago. I asked Cevilla not to tell you, although she was chomping at the bit to write you a letter."

"But I thought you went back to New York with Jordan."

"It's true I went to New York, but not with her." A car slowly passed by them. He suddenly took her hand. "Come with me," he said.

"Where are we going?"

"You'll see."

She followed him, expecting him to drop her hand once he realized she was. But he held on to it. When they reached her house, she started up the driveway. *"Nee,"* he said, tugging her hand gently. "I have another destination in mind."

He took her to the house next door, the one she and her father had helped him renovate. The one he'd sold a year ago. The one no one had occupied since then. He led her up the driveway to the swing he'd installed on the front porch right before he sold it. "We can talk here," he said, sitting down on the swing.

"We're trespassing," she said, not moving. "As a lawyer, you'd know that. At least I would think so."

He grinned, the dimple in his cheek deepening. "It's not trespassing if the owner gives permission." He patted the empty seat next to him.

"The owner knows you're here?"

"Ya." He patted the seat again. "Please, Lucy. Sit down and I'll explain everything."

She sat, but she also made sure to keep her distance, even though being this physically close to him made her heart thump harder.

"When Jordan came to Cevilla's in Birch Creek and then you asked me to leave, I insisted she and I go to a coffee shop in Barton." He gave her a little smile. "I had to convince her she could be seen in public with a man wearing Amish clothes, but . . . well, we had a long talk." He looked down at the front porch floor, the one she'd helped him seal and weatherproof so long ago. "I'm sorry about what happened when she showed up out of the blue. I had no idea she was going to . . ."

"Kiss you?"

"That"—a pink tint spread across his clean-shaven face—"and show up without warning. She said everything she could think of to convince me to get back together with her, and trust me, she's persuasive. She's an excellent lawyer."

Lucy didn't really want to hear him compliment Jordan, but she held her tongue. She didn't need to be petty.

"But everything she said cemented what I already knew," he continued. "I don't love her. I don't think I ever did. For a long time, though, I tried to convince myself I did, just like I'd done my whole life—talking myself into fitting into someone else's idea of what my life should be." He turned and looked at her. "But God has another plan. One that's better than anything I could ever imagine."

She was caught up in his passion. "What is it?"

"That's the exciting part. I have no idea what He has in store for me. But I trust Him. I trust Him with my life. And I feel more peace than I ever have."

"That's wonderful." She smiled, her heart swelling for him.

"When I said good-bye to Noah and Ivy that day, I found another place to stay in Barton. Over the next week I talked privately several times with Freemont Yoder. He helped me figure out that I did want to join the church—and for the right reasons. Then I went to New York to tell my family, and when I returned to Birch Creek, I was baptized." He gestured to the house. "Now I've returned to the beginning. I bought this place back, and from here I intend to build my new life."

So much had happened in such a short amount of time. "How did you get the house back?"

"I contacted the owner. He'd bought it as a rental property, but he'd never been able to find a responsible renter. When I offered to buy it back for more than he paid for it, he jumped at the opportunity." Shane held out his hand. "Hi, neighbor."

She chuckled and shook his hand. When she started to remove it, he held on.

"We have some unfinished business, don't you think?"

She swallowed at the hazy look in his eyes. He was right. They did have unfinished business. And she suddenly realized what was keeping her from moving on. She couldn't take a step forward until she told him how she felt, and nothing stood in the way of her doing that. "Shane, I . . ." Her mouth went dry and the words flew out of her head. Why was she becoming shy with him again?

He waited for her as he ran the tip of his finger over the top of her cheeks, where she knew her freckles were so thick they clumped together. The love she saw in his eyes calmed her heart. "I love you."

He leaned forward and kissed her lightly on the mouth. "I love you too."

She put her arms around his neck and hugged him tightly, closing her eyes. When they separated, he took her hand. "I came to tell you I love you and I want to marry you," he said. Then he reached into his pocket. "And to return this to its rightful owner." He placed the tiny Bible in her hand.

She closed her fingers over it and gripped it tightly. "Thank you," she said.

"You mean *danki*," he said. "Maybe you can give me some private language lessons later, *ya?*"

"*Ya.*" She laughed and leaned her head against his shoulder, and at that moment she felt peace. Shane loved her, and she loved him. She held on to the Bible as they talked about their future, and silently thanked God for the treasures in her life—a tiny book and a wonderful, godly man.

Discussion Questions

1. The heirloom Bible is very special to Lucy. Do you have an heirloom or an object that is special to you?
2. Shane says, "You'd be surprised how lonely you can be in a sea of people." Have you ever felt that way?
3. Shane believes life isn't without risk. Was there a time in your life when you had to take a risk? How did God help or influence you?
4. Do you think Lucy does the right thing when she lets Shane go? Why or why not?

ACKNOWLEDGMENTS

A huge thank-you to my wonderful family for their support (and willingness to eat a lot of takeout) during the writing of this book. Especially to my husband James, who is always there with encouragement and chocolate, when necessary. Thank you, Becky Monds and Jean Bloom, my wonderful editors who make every story I write shine. And thank you, Dear Reader, for reading Lucy and Shane's sweet story. I always appreciate you!

The Midwife's Dream

KELLY IRVIN

To my daughter, Erin, whose dream was always to be a mother. You're doing a great job, sweetie! Love always.

Wait for the LORD;
Be strong and take heart
And wait for the LORD.

PSALM 27:14 NIV

Featured Jamesport Families

Cyrus and Josephina Beachy (Deacon)
Iris

Joseph

Rueben

Samuel

Carl

Louella

Abigail

Jeremy and Bertha Kurtz
Nathanael

John

Avery

William

Salome

Mahon

Jason

Mary

Mark

Bartholomew and Rachel Shrock
Liam

Annie

Micah

Aidan and Bess Graber
Joshua

Chapter 1

The baby boy slid into Iris Beachy's hands so fast a person might think he was late for supper. He opened his mouth wide and declared his dislike of his new surroundings with a loud wail.

"Hello to you too, sweet one." Her best friend's new son weighed at least ten pounds. He arrived with a full head of dark hair that stood up in wet spikes around his red, wrinkled face. Iris chuckled and held him up for Rachel and Bartholomew Shrock to see. "He's a full-grown man. Better set him to work chopping wood."

"He's here. Our boy's here, *fraa*." Bartholomew left his wife's side to take a closer look. His big grin split his face over his long brown beard. "He's a giant."

"Built like his *daed* for sure." Iris suctioned fluid from the baby's nose and mouth with a syringe. He didn't like that at all. The wail turned to an aggravated howl. "Hush, hush, you're fine. It's a good thing you've done this before, Rachel. He had plenty of room to squeeze out without any tearing."

Twice before. Fortunately, Rachel's mother had taken little Annie and Liam to her house at the beginning of the six hours of labor that started on a cloudy February afternoon in which the

Missouri sky spit ice and snow at passersby as if to taunt them for daring to venture outdoors.

Iris wiped the baby off and looked him over from top to bottom. His skin was pink, his toes and fingers perfectly formed, his legs and arms strong. She laid him in the old blanket Rachel had placed in the cradle by the bed. They would save the tumbling block crib quilt Iris made for later when he was dressed. She placed a clip on the cord and cut it.

"Your *suh* has a healthy set of lungs."

She handed the squalling baby to Rachel, who sank back onto the pillows and tucked her new baby into the crook of her arm. His cries subsided seconds later. "He's built like Bart, but he looks like me. Don't you think?"

"He looks like my *groossdaadi*. No teeth, all hair." Bartholomew leaned over Rachel and tickled his son's cheek with one huge, callused index finger. "Micah. We'll name him Micah."

Rachel smiled up at them. Bartholomew's hand moved from his baby to his wife's cheek. She held it there with her free hand. The look her friends exchanged brought a lump to Iris's throat. She ducked her head and dealt with the afterbirth.

Be thankful for Rachel and Bartholomew's blessing. Be joyful. Be thankful. Be content.

Iris reminded herself, as she always did, of God's blessing in giving her this role in the Jamesport community. She'd delivered six babies on her own since Laura Kauffman retired as the *Gmay* midwife. Many more under Laura's tutelage. To be able to bring her friends' babies into the world was a gift. God allowed her to be present when a new life bounded into her arms and began this journey in the world.

Thank you, Gott.

Even if He hadn't fulfilled her one and only dream. That

of her own family. A husband and her own babies. Not yet, she amended. On His time, not hers.OnO She gathered up the bloody towels and sheets. She refused to lose faith. Not when her friends married and had their babies. Not when her twenty-third birthday passed.

Plenty of time, her mother kept saying. Plenty of time.

"It's dark out already. I better do my chores." Bartholomew headed for the door. "I'll let you women do what you do. Iris, I'll hitch up the buggy and bring it around front so it'll be ready when you are."

Iris cleared her throat of that annoying lump. "I won't be long. The road will be bad and getting worse."

Fortunately, the Beachy farm was only a stone's throw from the Shrocks'. Perfect for visiting back and forth. Perfect for watching Annie and Liam grow and change. Now Micah. The annoying lump returned. Iris made a pile of the bloody towels and stood. "Micah is a fine name."

"I told Bartholomew we couldn't pick Ephraim because I know you want that name for one of your boys." Her tone airy, Rachel smoothed Micah's blanket. "It would be too confusing when they get together to play."

Leave it to Rachel to hop over all the parts in between. Finding that special friend. Courting. Marrying. "You can use the name for your next one."

"You'll need it. Don't you worry." Rachel patted the bed in a sit-with-me motion. "You have lots of time. Look at it this way, when you get married, you'll be too busy having your own *boplin* to deliver other people's. You'll miss it."

Rachel was a good friend. She'd just given birth and she chose to focus on how that made Iris feel. She always knew what Iris was thinking. All the way back to when her *daed* became the deacon and he started taking care of *Gmay* business. Then *rumspringa* and the singings. And Aidan. Iris settled onto the bed and began to re-braid Rachel's hair. "You're a mess."

"Don't change the subject."

"No point in talking about it. *Gott*'s will is *Gott*'s will."

Rachel kissed Micah's forehead. His eyelids fluttered. He went back to sleep, lips puckering as if he were sucking. "You are the kindest, nicest, sweetest person I know, Iris Beachy. And no man would say you're hard on the eyes. Your turn will come. I promise you that."

"You're sweet, but you can't promise me anything."

"Mahon Kurtz likes you."

"He has a funny way of showing it."

"He knows you're still in love with Aidan. He's waiting until you're ready."

"Am not."

"Are too."

"Don't be silly." Iris tugged at Rachel's chestnut hair. "Aidan asked me to marry him. I said no. Not the other way around."

"Ouch. Not so hard." Rachel pushed Iris's hands away from her head. Even with her skin blotchy, hair sweaty, and nightgown stained and wrinkled, Rachel was the pretty one. At sixteen, Bartholomew asked her to ride home with him after their first singing. They never looked back, marrying two days after her nineteenth birthday. "Because you're wise beyond your years. Aidan loves Bess, and you knew it before he was willing to admit it. Mahon is waiting for you to give him a sign you're ready."

"You see what you want to see."

"What does Salome say?"

Salome was the other still-single woman in the gaggle of girls who'd once been inseparable. She taught school and waited for her special friend. She was also Mahon's sister. "She thinks her brother is short a few tools in his toolbox. He's busy working the farm with his *bruders* now that his *daed* is retiring. And when he's not, he draws pictures and looks at the stars."

Rachel giggled. "So draw him a picture."

"Don't laugh. It's not like our paths don't cross at church and at every frolic and every school picnic."

"You like him. You know you do."

She did like him. In a warm, content, he'll-always-be-around sort of way. She'd simply never thought of him in that light. He was Salome's goofy brother who wore glasses and knew the names of all the constellations in the sky before he learned his multiplication tables.

"He needs to know you're interested back." Rachel smoothed Micah's wild hair. He sighed, the sweetest, most tender sound imaginable. "Most men do."

"If he's not interested enough to approach me first, then I reckon it's not meant to be."

"Admit it." Rachel scooted up on the pillow. Her face had that same fierce expression it did when she accused her little brother of eating her lunch at school. "You won't do it because you're mad at *Gott*."

"Am not."

"Are too."

"I think we've had this conversation already."

Rachel laughed. Micah frowned and sputtered. She shushed him. "Go home, *freind*."

"Do you want something to eat first?"

"I'll get it in a while. Help yourself if you're hungry." Rachel pulled the quilt up so it covered both her and Micah. "I'm going to enjoy lying here with no little ones tugging on my skirt or asking me for a cookie or needing a diaper changed for a while longer. Bart will be hungry after he finishes the chores. We'll eat together."

Rachel would be back on her feet making breakfast in the morning, and Iris would get a good night's sleep before doing her own chores. She glanced out the bedroom window. The icy panes reflected the kerosene lamp back at her. The days were short this time of year. "*Mudder* will have left a plate warming on the back of the stove for me. She'll be sitting by the fire, waiting."

"That's where you get your sweetness—your *mudder*." Rachel grinned. "Definitely not from your *daed*."

"*Daed*'s different at home." Rachel was teasing, but Iris couldn't help but defend her father. "His bark is worse than his bite, always has been."

To others, Cyrus Beachy might be a stern deacon who taught baptism classes. But at home, he was still a big, overgrown teddy bear to her. The man she'd climbed all over as a little girl, the man who tickled her until she shrieked on cold winter nights after she beat him three times in a row in checkers. The man who read stories to his children every night before presiding over their prayers.

She wanted a husband who would be a father like that. Aidan would've been that kind of husband. She gritted her teeth and administered a silent scolding as she always did when these thoughts wiggled their way into her brain. Aidan belonged to someone else now. "I better get going."

"Talk to you soon."

Rachel's sleepy voice trailed after Iris as she tugged on her wool coat, mittens, scarf, and bonnet. Her satchel in one hand, she trudged out into a biting wind that took her breath away. Icy snow-flakes pelted her cheeks as she slipped and slid down the porch steps and slogged toward the buggy Bartholomew had retrieved as promised. Sable snorted, whinnied, and stamped her feet as if to say *hurry up*. Iris ducked her head and grabbed her bonnet to keep it from flying away.

Minutes later she turned the buggy onto the highway and headed for home. Her hands and feet were frozen and her nose numb. It had been a long day. The urge to doze overwhelmed her. Her stomach rumbled. She snapped the reins, and Sable picked up speed. Home, a grilled-cheese sandwich, a hot cup of tea, and bed, in that order. The buggy's wooden wheels skidded under her. "Whoa, whoa. Take it easy, girl."

Only a mile more. One more mile. The wind whipped through her coat as if she wore nothing. An engine revved behind her. Who else was silly enough to be out on the road in this weather? She eased toward the shoulder. A horn blared. She swerved still closer to the edge, afraid to go too far for fear of landing in a ditch she couldn't see under the heavy blanket of snow.

The horn honked again and again in an irritating refrain. She twisted in her seat. Headlights blinded her. "*Ach*, okay, okay." She pulled over a little more, halted, and threw her hand up in the air to wave them on.

Instead of passing, the *car*—or was it a truck—pulled in behind her and stopped. The engine idled in a weak *put-put-put*.

She strained to see the black form behind the lights. A pickup truck maybe.

A door opened. Words were exchanged. English. The door slammed.

Sudden heat rushing through her, Iris gripped the reins. She couldn't outrun a car in her buggy. She heaved a breath and licked chapped lips. Her whole mouth was dry. "Who is it? What do you want?"

The headlights illuminated a form that moved toward her. Her heart hammering in her chest, she squinted.

A man strode toward her.

CHAPTER 2

Iris couldn't see his face. He wore a dark hat. A dark coat, black pants, black boots. A Plain man? Why would a Plain man be in a car that pursued her on an empty country road on this icy cold night? Her heart whipped itself into a frenzy of off-kilter beating. The taste of metal in her mouth made her gag. She swallowed against the acid taste. "Who is it? Speak up."

"It's me. Mahon."

Her heartbeats fought to resume their normal rhythm. The *whoosh* of adrenaline leaving her body left her weak. Her lungs ached with the effort to breathe. A rush of anger followed, warming Iris from head to toe. She hopped from the buggy and trudged toward him. Her rubber boots, a size too big, sank into the snow, halting her forward progress, which served to aggravate her more. "What are you doing following me in a car? Are you driving? Why did you honk at me?"

She paused for air. Plain women did not talk to Plain men this way. Even if it was Salome's little brother. Iris's breath puffed white in the dark night. The rush of cold air burned her lungs. Her heart beat in her ears like a huge drum.

"You're needed."

Mahon let the words hang in the air as if they made perfect

sense, as if they answered every question. He offered no apology for scaring the living daylights out of her. Iris blinked. Had he said he needed her? Or had she imagined that?

"Turn off the headlights. I can't see."

"There's no time. You're needed." He jabbed one thumb over his shoulder. He wore no gloves. Some days men weren't the brightest of animals. "We were headed to your house. What are you doing out here in this weather?"

"Delivering Rachel's baby . . . Why am I answering your questions? What are you—"

"Hurry up! We're freezing." Salome's sharp schoolteacher voice pierced the darkness. The headlights disappeared, leaving them in the darkness of a country road with no lighting. "The heater in this thing only works part of the time. I think Jessica's water broke just now."

Iris closed her eyes and opened them, hoping they would adjust to the dark. "Salome?" Not only was Mahon in this English car, but so was his sister. And who was Jessica? Iris could see the vehicle now, a light-colored van. Tan or brown. A man sat behind the wheel. A stranger. "Get out here and tell me what's going on."

"*Ach.* It's too cold." Salome hung out the passenger door window. She pulled the scarf wrapped around her neck up over her bonnet with one hand. "We've got a lady in here who's expecting. We'll explain the rest at your house, I promise, but we need to get there before this baby comes. Jessica thinks it's coming soon."

A baby. Why hadn't Mahon said that? "I'll meet you there. Go on ahead. *Mudder* will help until I get there."

Her father wouldn't be happy about Salome and Mahon bringing strangers to his door, but Cyrus Beachy would never turn away a person in need. Iris plunged through the snow as fast as her boots would allow, hoisted herself into the buggy, and waited for the van to pass. The engine rumbled and whined before settling into a hit-and-miss putter. The wind blew the nasty smell of gas fumes and burning oil in her face. They would arrive long before she did, but her mother would know what to do. No longer tired or hungry, Iris urged Sable into a canter. Fifteen minutes later she pulled in next to the van, which blocked the hitching post in front of her house. Sable was a patient horse. He would wait for one of her brothers to stable him—if she didn't wait too long to ask.

She ran up the steps, skidded across the icy porch, and tugged open the door.

Two English teenagers sat on the couch by the fireplace, a tattered blue gym bag on the floor at their feet. Mahon sat across from them in the straight-backed chair wiping condensation from his black-rimmed glasses. It had been years since she'd seen him without his glasses. He glanced up at her entrance. His eyes, normally a brilliant blue behind the lenses, looked softer and warmer. He and Salome could be twins. He nodded and stood. "This is Quinn and Jessica from Iowa."

The girl was rail thin except for her swollen belly. She wore a wool navy peacoat not large enough to button across her stomach. Someone—probably *Mudder*—had placed a blanket over her shoulders. Her porcelain skin, huge blue eyes, and curly blond hair that hung to her waist gave her the look of dolls Iris had seen in the toy store windows in St. Louis. She wore no makeup. Tiny earrings like purple jeweled flowers adorned her ears and one side of her nose. The boy had wispy brown hair on his lip and chin that didn't match the darker hair cut close to his head. A single diamond stud flashed on his right earlobe. His eyes were bloodshot. He tucked a cell phone into his jeans pocket and put an arm around Jessica in a protective gesture.

"I'm Iris."

"I know." Quinn's tone stopped short of belligerent. "They said you could help Jess. Are you a nurse?"

"A lay midwife. I deliver babies."

"We don't have much money." Jessica offered this fact in a high, tight voice. "We don't have insurance."

"I wouldn't take your money—"

"I'm more worried about whether you know what you're doing," Quinn broke in. "Did you go to medical school?"

"I apprenticed—"

"She knows." This time Mahon interrupted her. He plopped his glasses on his nose. "That's why we brought you to her. We could always go into town."

"No."

They both spoke at once. Quinn's tone definitive, Jessica's less certain.

Iris glanced at Mahon. He shrugged. "Your *mudder* is getting a room ready. Salome is in the kitchen making hot cocoa with your *schweschders*."

"I thought she was about to deliver."

"Your *mudder* says no." His tone was apologetic. His face, with its chipmunk cheeks, was red. He stood and walked past her, his stride swift as if he couldn't wait to escape. No Plain man wanted to discuss these things with a woman not his *fraa*. "I didn't ask for details. I'll put up your horse and the buggy."

She caught his woodsy scent as he passed. "Bundle up."

What a silly thing to say. Of course he would bundle up. They'd known each other since they were old enough to catch tadpoles in the pond and make mud pies for pretend frolics. It had never been awkward between them, never been a boy-girl thing. More of a brother-sister thing. Until her friends planted the seed. Had his done the same? This wasn't the time or the place to find out. Iris waited until the door closed behind him. Then she went to Jessica and knelt in front of her. "Can I touch you?"

The girl nodded. Iris placed her hand on the girl's black-and-red plaid flannel shirt pulled tight over her belly. A minute ticked by. Another. And then another. "When are you due?"

"Not for three more weeks." Jessica glanced at Quinn as if seeking permission to speak. He shrugged. "That's why we thought we had time to get to Texas. I was gonna find a doctor there. I even have my bag packed and ready."

She motioned to the gym bag on the floor. The knob of her delicate wrist stuck out under the frayed sleeve of her shirt. "I brought a nightgown for the hospital and diapers and formula and some bottles and a pacifier—even an outfit to put her in."

Formula and bottles. "You don't want to nurse your baby?"

Jessica wrinkled her nose. "I know it's good for her, but I still have to finish school, and I probably have to get a job for after school, and I can't be carting her around with me everywhere."

Who would care for the baby while Jessica went on with her life? That was none of Iris's business. "It's a girl?"

"That's what the doctor said. We saw her in the sonogram and everything. She was mostly a blob, though."

"What else did he tell you the last time you went to see him?"

"*She* said Jess needed to eat more. She wasn't gaining enough weight." Quinn snorted. "She eats like a horse."

"Do not."

Iris smiled at the girl. "You're eating for two."

Jessica nodded and leaned back. Iris waited. Quinn smelled of cigarette smoke. Jessica's scent was flowery, like lilacs. Quinn sat rigid and unmoving, while Jessica's face grew whiter. Her lips trembled. Finally, muscle contracted under Iris's fingers.

"Oh no. Not again." The girl gasped. She grabbed Quinn's

free hand and gripped so tight her knuckles turned white. She sat up straight. Her mouth gaped open. "Ow, ow, ow."

"Breathe, breathe through it." Iris kept her voice gentle. She stroked the girl's other arm. "Relax into it."

The contraction subsided. Jessica sank back into her chair. "See, it's getting close. My baby's coming."

"It's not time yet."

"That's what the other lady said." Quinn snorted. "I thought when the water came out, it was time for the baby to come."

"The contractions are still far apart."

"But they hurt so much." Jessica sniffed and wiped at her face with the back of her coat sleeve. "It feels like it's killing me. I can't do it. What if I can't do it?"

Iris had seen this before with other first-time mothers, but never this young. She wanted to ask Jessica how old she was, but she bit back the question. That also was none of her business. "You can. I promise. Women do this all the time. All over the world since the beginning of time. We'll get some cocoa to warm you up. If you want to walk around for a little bit, that might help move things along."

"Walk around?" Quinn tightened his arm around Jessica, his look suspicious. "Aren't you supposed to get in bed?"

"No. Unless you're tired and want to rest for a while."

"She hasn't been sleeping good."

"You wouldn't either if you had a watermelon sitting on your bladder and had to pee every five seconds." Jessica's voice crept higher with each word. "You wouldn't sleep if your back felt like you'd been lifting fifty-pound bags of potatoes all day."

"It'll all be over in a few hours." Quinn swung his gaze toward Iris as if seeking reinforcement. "You'll be fine."

"It might be a little longer than that."

"We have to get on the road."

"There's no rushing a baby." Iris stood. "I'll see about the cocoa."

She grabbed her satchel and fled to the kitchen where she found her little sisters, Louella and Abigail, vying for Salome's attention while she poured cocoa into mugs and added miniature marshmallows.

"Iris! Iris, an *Englisch* lady is in the front room." Louella, who was eight, beat six-year-old Abigail by a hair's breadth in their mad dash across the room. "She's having a *bopli*."

"I know." Iris took turns kissing each girl on the top of their *kapps*. "Where's *Daed*?"

"Isaac Borntrager died." Louella held out a sticky hand full of crushed marshmallows. "Want some?"

"*Nee*, but it is nice of you to offer." *Daed* would help Bishop Freeman Borntrager prepare for his father's funeral. The man had lived to the great age of eighty-nine, but recently he'd taken to bed with a terrible cough. Her little sister was matter-of-fact about the situation.

"Can you sit at the table and drink your cocoa while I talk to Salome?"

They could, so she took their mugs to the table and settled them in. Then she turned to Salome. "Tell me everything."

"He had pneumonia."

"I know, bless his heart. He lived a *gut* life. Tell me about our visitors."

"They ran away from home. That's what I think." Salome sipped her cocoa and winced. "Hot."

"Stop drinking hot chocolate and spill the beans. How did you end up in their van?"

Salome leaned on the counter and wrapped her hands around

the mug. "Mahon walked out to help *Daed* with the chores and saw them sitting in the van with the engine running. He asked if they needed something. Quinn said he needed help for his wife."

"I don't think she's his wife."

"Me neither, but he said they're driving to Texas. He has a job there and a place to live. He said so and she just kept nodding."

"Why didn't Mahon give them directions to the medical center in Chillicothe?"

"He tried. Quinn said there was no time."

"Her contractions are still ten minutes apart, even now."

"I know that now." Salome shrugged. "I reckon they've never had a baby before."

"I hope not." Iris poured more water into a pot on the stove and turned up the flame. Then she opened her satchel and pulled out the tools of her trade that needed washing. "They don't seem prepared to be parents at all."

"What did *Mudder* say?"

"She hugged the girl and asked Quinn if he wanted some venison stew."

That was *Mudder*. Unflappable.

"He said he wasn't hungry."

Iris turned. Her mother stood in the doorway, a pile of sheets in her arms. "The girl looks like she could use a meal, but he said no before she got a chance." *Mudder* frowned at the memory. Her first instinct was always to feed people. Especially if they needed fattening up. "I put fresh sheets on your bed and covered it with the plastic one. I don't reckon you'll be sleeping tonight."

"*Gut*. It'll probably be awhile before she delivers, but it's nice to be ready."

Mudder deposited her load on a chair by the table, then trotted over to the stove. She stuck her hands above it. "It's cold in there, but she'll warm up once she gets going. She's walking around in circles now in the front room. She said you told her to do it. Her friend asked me why he can't get on Facebook out here."

Iris's chuckle mixed with Salome's. Mother surely had no idea what Facebook was. "Did you tell him we have no Internet access?"

"Stop laughing. I know what Facebook is."

Both Iris and Salome knew from *rumspringa* experience that a cell phone signal could in fact be had on the farm. Quinn could likely make a phone call if he needed to or send a text, but there was no Internet service. Of course, *Daed* wouldn't like him chatting on the phone in the house.

"I hope this isn't causing you too much trouble." Salome set her mug on the counter and went to stand by the woman she sometimes called *aenti*, other times *Mudder*-number-two. "We didn't know what else to do."

"I don't consider it trouble, helping strangers in need." *Mudder* patted Salome's arm. "It's what Jesus did. It's what the good Samaritan did."

"Do you think *Daed* will feel the same? *Englischers* having a baby in his house?" Iris watched the expression change on *Mudder*'s face as she rubbed her wrinkled hands together to warm them. "Will everyone feel that way?"

She didn't have to specify. They knew she meant Freeman.

"I'm going there in a few minutes. I'll tell him myself."

"In this weather?" Iris shook her head. "You shouldn't be out there. You have a cough already."

"I'll be fine. Rueben will take me. They'll need help with the preparations."

Death notices. Food. Cleaning. The viewing. Building the coffin. It wouldn't have to be big. Freeman's *daed* had shriveled in his old age, a wizened little man with big ears, sparse hair on his head, and a beard that reached his waist. He wouldn't take up much space. The cold, hard earth in the cemetery would be difficult to pierce. Iris shivered. "Take care."

"You too." *Mudder* slid her coat from the hook by the back door and shrugged it on. "That girl is small and she's scared and she has no idea what she's in for. It'll be a long night."

"The baby will be here by midnight, I reckon."

"Babies come on their own time."

CHAPTER 3

Mothers are always right. Iris glanced at the wooden clock shaped like a log cabin hanging on her bedroom wall. Midnight had come and gone. The hands crept toward one. Jessica sat on the side of the bed, her hands gripping the rumpled sheets on either side of her body. Her toes, with nails painted bubblegum pink, curled into the piece rug on the floor. Sweat soaked her tangled hair, her eyes were red-rimmed from crying, and snot ran from her nose. Her shoulders heaved as she sobbed. Quinn had collapsed on the floor across from her, his back to the wall, long legs sprawled in front of him. He clutched his phone as if somehow he could wring help from it.

Her back to Jessica, Iris slipped over to his side and squatted.

"Try rubbing her back and shoulders."

"No way." He shot a panicked look at Jessica. "She doesn't want me messing with her. You heard her. She bit my head off. She blames me for all this. Like she wasn't even there."

"It'll help if she relaxes. We're on the homestretch. She needs you."

"Oh no, oh no, oh no."

Iris pivoted. Her face contorted, Jessica plopped sideways on the bed and curled up in a ball. "I can't take this anymore. I can't take it."

"Yes, you can." Iris straightened and moved to the bed. She took a washrag from a basin of water sitting next to the kerosene lamp, wrung it out, and wiped Jessica's face with gentle strokes. She handed her a tissue. "You're almost there. You're doing great."

The girl's ragged sob said she didn't agree. She rolled to her other side and rubbed her belly. "Have you ever had a baby?"

"No, but I've delivered plenty." Iris eased onto the mattress and massaged the girl's thin shoulders. She worked her way down Jessica's knotty spine. "Babies mostly come on their own. They just need a little help."

"Did the mother ever die?"

"Not one. No babies either."

Laura had prepared Iris for that. It happened rarely, but it happened for reasons only God understood. So far she'd been spared the anguish. Iris worked her way back up the spine and across the shoulders. Jessica uncurled a little. Her head lolled forward. "That feels good. I'm so tired."

"I know you are. Tell me about yourself. How old are you?"

"I turned sixteen on Christmas Eve."

Sixteen. The age Plain girls and boys began their *rumspringa*, a time of courting and seeking a special friend. The time before making the decision to be baptized. She glanced at Quinn. His head lowered, he used his thumbs to tap out something on the screen. Texting. She'd like to pluck the phone from his hands and toss it in the snow outside the window.

"How long have you and Quinn been together?"

"Since seventh grade."

"A long time."

"He's my soulmate. I knew it the first time he kissed me after our basketball team won state and he made thirty points."

"Where's your school?"

"I'll do that." Quinn stood next to her. His hand brushed hers away. He put both hands on Jessica's shoulders and squeezed. "I texted my cousin. He says he's got room for us. We just have to get there."

"It hurts. Oh, it hurts." Jessica's voice rose. She screamed. "I hate this. I hate you. I hate your cousin."

Quinn stumbled back. "Do something for her! You're supposed to help her."

"I'm sorry! I didn't mean it. I love you, Quinn. I love you." Jessica sobbed. "Help me, help me."

"You'll be okay, babe, I promise." He glared at Iris. He had tears in his eyes. His Adam's apple bobbed. "Do something."

"It's okay. Jessica, you're doing fine. You're almost there." Iris moved to the foot of the bed. She patted Jessica's knee and lifted the sheets. She took another peek. "It's time to push. Quinn, you can help."

He looked as if he wanted to be anywhere in the world except in that bedroom. "You don't need me. You're the midwife."

"Quinn, help your wife deliver your baby girl. Now."

"She's not my wife."

"But this is your baby, isn't it?"

He wiped at his face with the back of his hand. "Yah, it is." He gripped Jessica's shoulder. "I didn't mean that in a bad way, babe. What do I do?"

"Get behind her. Encourage her."

He did as he was told. Iris moved into position. "You can do this, Jessica. Give it all you have. Just think, in a few minutes you'll see your baby."

Jessica screamed again and again, but she pushed. For a skinny girl, she had great lungs and plenty of muscle. The contractions ripped through one after another now. Four pushes and the baby's head crowned. Iris gently rotated her shoulders. "Give another big push. A big push now."

The shoulders slid out. Then the rest of the body. Jessica and Quinn had an itty, bitty baby girl. Her eyes were closed. Her mouth gaped, but no sound came out.

Iris cleared her nose and throat. "Come on, sweet thing, come on."

Seconds ticked by. "Come on, sweetie." She rubbed the baby's belly and patted her back.

"She's not crying." Jessica sat up. "Why isn't she crying?"

The baby's arms flailed. Tiny fingers rolled into fists. Her eyes opened. Finally, she wailed.

Quinn tottered one step in Iris's direction. Shaking his head, he stared down at the baby. His mouth dropped open, and he bawled almost as loud as his new daughter.

CHAPTER 4

Iris shifted the dirty sheets into one arm and closed her bedroom door with a shove of her elbow. She stood in the dark hallway for a few seconds, enjoying the silence. *Thank you,* Gott, *thank you.* She leaned her head against the door. The wood was solid and cool against her warm forehead. *Thank you.* She never doubted for a second God was good, but some days—and nights—were hard. These English kids, barely able to navigate life, were now responsible for a baby. Iris had cleaned up the little mite, watched while Jessica diapered her, and convinced her to try nursing. That didn't last long. Both nodded off to sleep after a few minutes. Quinn mostly stared out the window, even though it was dark and he could see nothing. She left him with a quiet good night he barely acknowledged. She wanted the responsibility he so obviously feared, but it had been denied her for reasons she couldn't fathom. She took a deep breath of cold air and straightened.

She would not ask the question. She simply would not.

Why, Gott?

Shaking her head at her own prideful audacity, she strode through the hall to the stairs. God must be so disappointed in her inability to trust in His plan for her. If she never married, never had children, she would accept it as part of a bigger plan she couldn't see but would come to know. She was not, as Rachel put it, mad at God. She was certain that was not allowed in her *Gmay*.

She might not like it, but she would be an obedient believer. A cheerful believer. She started down the stairs, repeating the words in her head, ignoring their grubby tarnish after forty-eight hours straight of delivering babies. "I just need to sleep."

"Who are you talking to?"

Iris lurched to a stop. She grabbed the bannister with her free hand. Mahon sat at her father's desk against the wall under the bannister. His hat lay on the desk next to a pad of paper, the one her *mudder* used to write to her pen pals. His big hands covered the top sheet. He stared up at her, looking much like a child caught stealing a still-warm apple pie from the windowsill.

"What are you doing here still? I told you to go home." She glanced around the front room. A fire blazed in the fireplace. "Is Salome here too?"

"*Nee.* Your *bruder* took her home." Mahon tore the top sheet from the pad, wadded it up in a tight ball, and tossed it in the wastebasket next to the desk. He stood and stretched his head from side to side. He rubbed his neck. He had thick, curly brown hair. "The *bopli* is *gut*?"

"In this weather?" Mahon had nice hair. She shouldn't be thinking about Mahon's hair. It was just that she hardly ever saw it. "Which *bruder*?"

Mahon smiled, a slightly lopsided smile that made him look less like Salome and more like his father. "Joseph. Rueben went with your *mudder*. Samuel and Carl went to bed when your *schweschders* did."

Mahon could be counted on to keep track of everyone. To keep little ones safe and bigger ones in line. She tromped down the remaining stairs and headed for the kitchen and the laundry room. "*Jah*, the *bopli* is *gut*. Small, but she has all her fingers and toes and a healthy cry. The *mudder* is fine too. Giddy with relief. The *daed* almost fainted."

"They'll get the hang of it." The tread of his boots told her Mahon followed. "It stopped snowing a couple hours ago, but I figured I should stay around. It didn't seem right to leave you alone here with strangers I brought into your house."

Joseph took Salome home. Did that mean they were courting? Salome hadn't said a word. Joseph often disappeared in the evenings, but a sister didn't ask questions. If something was going on, neither would want to make Iris feel bad in the wake of Aidan and Bess's marriage. She didn't feel bad. She was thrilled for her friend. Joseph was a hard worker, faithful, kind, and the joker of the family. He and Salome might be well suited to each other.

The rest of Mahon's statement registered. "I'm not alone." As the oldest of seven children, Iris didn't remember a time when she'd ever been alone. "Didn't Reuben come back from taking *Mudder* to Freeman's?"

"He did, but he went to sleep."

Mahon's yawn echoed in the laundry room.

Laughing, Iris dumped the sheets next to a pile of shirts and dresses. Nine people in one house made for a long laundry day on Mondays. "Sounds like you should do the same." She turned in time to catch him with his glasses in one hand and rubbing his eyes with the other. He looked up at her. He did have nice blue eyes. Right now, they were sleepy eyes. "You'll have chores to do in a few hours."

"I'll sleep when you do." The words hung in the air for a few seconds. Red scurried across his clean-shaven face, coloring chipmunk cheeks. "I mean . . . I didn't mean . . . You'll sleep here and I'll go home and sleep. I mean—"

"I knew what you meant." Iris grinned at him. "You're the one who's addled from lack of sleep. Do you want some hot tea before you go?"

"That just might hit the spot."

Iris brushed past him and went to the kitchen. She made tea while he sat at the table and watched. He didn't seem to need conversation. Or maybe he was afraid of what might come out of his mouth after that last gaffe. Inhaling the aroma of cinnamon and spice and everything nice, she smiled as she set the mug on the table. She pushed the teddy bear plastic bottle of honey toward him. He smiled back and squeezed a generous dollop into his tea and then another and another.

"Would you like a little tea with your honey?"

"*Mudder* says my sweet tooth is part of why I'm so sweet." His face colored all over again. "I should just shut up."

His *mudder* was right about him being sweet. Even though he was the younger brother, he'd kept watch over Salome growing up when they went to the pond to swim or fish. He shared his cookies with them and carried Iris to the house the time she sprained her ankle falling out of the pony wagon the day after her tenth birthday. He never told on them when he saw them coming back from a party at the Rankins' farm during their *rumspringa*. "How's your *daed*? I haven't talked to Salome in a while."

He stirred his tea, his expression somber. "He and *Mudder* will move into the *dawdy haus* this spring."

"Nathanael and his *fraa* will take the big house?"

"And run the farm with my other *bruders*."

"You're not happy about it?" Iris sipped her tea. The aroma of cinnamon reminded her of the tea her *mudder* made when Iris had a cold. All she lacked was the scent of fresh lemon. "You and John get along like puppies from the same litter. You always have."

"It's not that." He cupped the mug in his hands and blew on the hot liquid. "There's John and Nathanael and Avery and William."

"You do have a bunch of older brothers." At twenty-three, Mahon was number five of the Kurtz boys. Only Jason and Mark were younger. He and Salome had one other sister, Mary, who was sixteen. "But Avery has the harness shop."

"He found himself a decent living." Mahon nodded, but his gaze wandered to the kitchen windows. "Me, I don't like being inside."

"Which is *gut*, since you're a farmer."

"I like farming." He yawned so wide his jaw popped. "It's just tough to making a living these days, especially with my *bruders'* families depending on the income."

She couldn't hide her smile at his attempt to cover another yawn. "Do you want to do something different?"

"I would like to make some of my own decisions about how to do it, that's all. To do it better."

"There's a lot of that going around." Iris had listened to plenty of similar discussions among her brothers and her father at the supper table. "My *bruders* and *daed* don't always agree either."

"*Daed* says it's pie in the sky, like the stars I'm always looking at. He says I should get my head out of the clouds and pay attention to what has always worked. It's not like I want to run off and buy a tractor or hook up electricity." His voice deepened, became gruffer. "But we do the same thing, generation after generation. It's what we do. How we stay who we are. Keeping the world at arm's length."

He stopped and drew a breath. His Adam's apple bobbed.

"You only want to provide for your family better."

He nodded. "Now land is hard to come by and there are too many of us. I want to make a decent living on my own so I can . . ."

"Can what?"

"Pie in the sky, that's all." He ducked his head, then raised it so his gaze met hers. He shook his head. "That's a discussion for another day."

He wasn't talking about farming anymore.

A spiral of heat drifted through Iris, warming her cheeks and her hands. The kind she hadn't felt in a long time. "You better get home. Dawn will be here before you know it."

"You should be the tired one."

"I'm always wide-awake after I deliver a baby." She dabbed at a drop of honey on the table with her finger. "It never stops being a mystery. It never stops being a gift."

"*Gott* is *gut*."

She lifted her gaze to his. "He is."

He smiled. She smiled back. Nothing goofy about that smile. He had full lips and even, white teeth. Why was she thinking about his lips? The heat intensified. She grabbed her mug and lifted it to her lips. Liquid slopped over the edge and burned her fingers. "Ouch."

"You're getting punchy." He stood. "I better go."

She didn't want him to go. The thought startled her. "It's so cold and dark. Be careful."

"Worried about me?"

She hesitated.

"Don't answer that. Joseph said I could borrow a horse." He paused next to her chair. His hand brushed her arm for a split second, a move so swift and so soft she might have imagined it. "I'll try to get it back here sometime tomorrow. I want to check on you anyway."

She touched the place where his fingers had been, then followed him to the front room. "Why?"

He stuck his arm in the sleeve of his wool coat. "I told you, I feel responsible for them. I brought them here."

"I'm the midwife. Where else would you take them?"

"Into town, I guess. Will your *daed* say it was a good choice?"

"He will." She was sure of it. She knew her *daed*. "We don't turn people in need away from our door."

He buttoned his coat. "We'll see." His gaze remained fixed on her face as he tugged open the door. An icy blast of winter air blew through Iris. It did nothing to cool her. She must be coming down with something. "We'll see about many things, I hope."

The door closed. Iris remained in the middle of the room, staring at it, debating whether she shared the sentiments his eyes suggested.

CHAPTER 5

The feathers tickled. Iris wiggled under the weight of the blankets and quilts on Abigail and Louella's bed. She didn't want to open her eyes. Not yet. Her eyelids were too heavy.

Tickle. Tickle. She wrinkled her nose and slipped her hand out into the frigid morning air to scratch it. Too cold. Icy cold. She rolled on her side and curled up. To her delight, she didn't encounter the warm, space-hogging body of either sister. For little girls, they certainly took up more than their share of the bed. If they were up, it surely meant dawn had broken. Time to roll out of bed. On the other hand, a few more minutes wouldn't hurt. *Mudder* would understand. She always got breakfast when Iris had a late night.

Tickle. Tickle.

"Stop it."

"The baby's crying."

"What?" She forced her eyes open. Morning sunlight coming through the bedroom window made her squint. A short, blurry figure stood by the bed, silhouetted in the light. "Huh?"

Tickle, tickle.

Iris's sight adjusted. Abigail crawled onto the bed. The

mattress creaked. The little girl's pudgy fingers trailed down Iris's nose and across her cheek. Her middle, lower teeth were missing so she tended to lisp when she talked. She smelled like peanut butter and looked as perturbed as a six-year-old with freckles and auburn hair could look. "The *bopli* is crying."

Iris propped herself up on one elbow. She had to think a minute. Rachel's baby? No. Jessica's baby. She probably *was* crying. Newborn babies did. "Why are you telling me?"

"There's nobody else to tell. *Mudder* and *Daed* are still at Freeman's."

"Where are Jessica and Quinn?"

"I don't know. I asked Samuel. He says he hasn't seen them." The little girl shrugged. "I ate a peanut butter cookie, but I'm hungry. Can you make pancakes? Louella is trying, but I think she put too much milk in the batter."

"Coming."

Iris struggled into her dress. She would deal with her hair later. She raced down the hall to her bedroom. The wails were loud and insistent. The baby was hungry. She rapped hard on the door. "Jessica? Quinn? Time to get up. Can't you hear the baby crying?"

No answer. The cries wound themselves around Iris's heart and squeezed. How could anyone hear a baby cry and not want to hold her and hush her and rock her? She turned the knob and shoved the door open. "Jessica? Quinn? Your baby—"

The room was empty. Except for the baby, who had been laid in the wooden cradle Iris had positioned by the bed before leaving them to sleep. Iris rushed to its side. The baby was wrapped in a faded, nine-patch crib quilt with purple, pink, and lilac squares. The quilting was beautiful, intricate, and hand-stitched. The white cotton batting on the backside had yellowed with age and had a ragged stain that looked like coffee or tea. She scooped up the baby and tucked her in her arms. "You poor thing. Are you feeling neglected?" She sank onto the bed and rocked back and forth. "You're fine. I've got you. I've got you."

The baby's face turned a deep reddish-purple from exertion. She beat her tiny fists against the air and demanded satisfaction. "I know, I know," Iris crooned. "You poor thing. Where is your *mudder?*"

She examined the room, searching the corners with her gaze as if Jessica or Quinn might be hiding in the shadows. The scruffy gym bag still sat next to the cradle. It was open, the sides flopping down, revealing an array of plastic baby bottles, cans of formula, disposable diapers, baby wipes, and a few outfits—frilly dresses not warm enough for a winter day. Iris tucked the screaming baby against her shoulder and patted. "Oh my, oh my, you sweet thing. You need a diaper change and a good feeding."

A folded piece of notebook paper had been attached to the bag strap with a safety pin. Iris struggled to unpin it with one hand. Finally, she gave up and ripped it off, tearing one corner. She managed to unfold it and smooth it out on top of the heap of sheets and quilts.

Dear Iris,

Her name is Lilly Marie. Grandma was right. We can't keep her. We thought we could, but now that she's here, Quinn and me know it's not gonna work. Quinn says we can come back for her after we get settled and get jobs and I finish high school. You know a lot about babies. I'm not afraid to leave her with you. You'll take good care of her. I'll come get her as soon as I can. I promise.

Keep track of how much you spend on diapers and

formula. I'll pay you back. I promise. Quinn says this note can be like an IOU.

Talk to you soon.

Promise.

Jess

Iris continued to rock. Her throat ached. She rocked harder, but Lilly kept crying. Maybe she knew her mother and father were gone. Maybe she missed the scent of her mother and the warmth of her womb. *IOU one baby.* "I'm so sorry. I'm so sorry," she whispered. "She'll be back. She says she'll be back."

They'd entrusted Iris with this baby. Whatever possessed them to do that? What circumstances or sequence of events led to abandoning a baby in the home of strangers? Inhaling the scent of baby spit-up and wet diaper, she tilted Lilly back and examined her face. A few curly wisps of blonde hair graced her soft scalp. Her eyes hadn't decided yet what color they would be. The shape of her face and her rosebud lips made her look like her momma. Not much of Quinn and his dark, brooding looks in her. "Hello, Lilly. It's nice to meet you—again."

Lilly wailed.

"I know, I know." Iris laid her on the bed and unwrapped the beautiful crib quilt. Someone had stitched it with love many years earlier. She made quick work of changing the diaper. "We'll find you some warmer clothes, little one, and cloth diapers. *Mudder* may have some tucked away in her chest or we can borrow from Rachel. She'll have saved Annie's clothes in case she has another girl."

Iris had prayed for a family of her own, but not like this. Not the abandoned baby of another woman. Still, who was she to argue with God's plan? And wasn't Lilly better off with someone like Iris who knew about babies and who had family to help? Or was that her own pride and desire talking?

Maybe this was simply Quinn and Jessica's plan. God surely frowned on abandoning babies. They were gifts from Him.

"*Ach*, Lilly, what am I to do?"

Gott, what do I do? Show me the way.

"What is all this caterwauling?"

Iris started. "*Daed*. You're here."

"I am. I came to take care of chores." He strode into the room in the bowlegged walk he'd passed on to his boys. "Where are these *Englischers* who spent the night in my house?"

"They're gone." She held out the note, pleased that her hand didn't shake. "They'll be back, though. Jessica promises."

Daed adjusted his wire-rimmed spectacles, the frown over his gray beard deepening as he read. The wrinkles in his forehead pinched at that spot over the bridge of his nose between bushy, matching eyebrows. His gaze met hers, his blue eyes piercing. "They're two teenagers who most likely ran away from home. They left a baby only a few hours old in the hands of strangers. You believe that promise?"

"I know if I were her *mudder*—"

"You're not."

Iris swallowed hard against the bitter bile in the back of her throat. She picked up Lilly and hugged her to her chest. *Daed* didn't mean to be cruel. He didn't have a cruel bone in his hefty body. "I know, but I've watched many *mudders* with their newborn *boplin*—"

"And not one of them has run off and left that *bopli*, has she?"

"Nee."

"We need to find them. We can't be responsible for their child."

"Mahon and Salome will help." She grabbed the gym bag and handed it to *Daed*. "She needs to eat."

He took the bag and followed her out the door to the stairs. "They certainly will. They meant well, but bringing these people into our house wasn't a good idea."

"You would turn them away in the snow and ice? She was having a *bopli*."

"Are they *mann* and *fraa*?"

She couldn't lie. *"Nee."*

"What kind of example does that set for your *schweschders* and *bruders*?"

"She was having a baby."

"I know." His growl softened to a low rumble. "And now we have a baby. If they can't be found, we'll have to get the *Englisch* authorities involved."

"Daed—"

"How will she be fed?"

"They left formula and bottles. The *mudder* provided for her."

"The *Englisch* way." With a snort, he clomped down the stairs. "Formula costs a lot. Feed her and then go into town for more. We don't want the poor thing starving in the meantime."

His bark was worse than his bite. But his tone left no doubt. He was serious. What English "authorities" would be involved with an abandoned baby? Was it really abandonment if Jessica and Quinn left the baby with someone like Iris? If they told someone at the sheriff's office, Jessica might never get her baby back.

"We'll figure it out." She held Lilly closer. "I promise."

CHAPTER 6

Sweet, sweet silence. Iris tiptoed from the cradle nestled between the table and the wood-burning stove across the kitchen to where her mother washed breakfast dishes at the sink. Fed, burped, and freshly diapered, Lilly had succumbed to sleep after a few lingering, halfhearted sobs. *Daed* left the house to go back to Freeman's. Likely he would share the latest news with the bishop. Freeman would offer counsel. He might think it best to call the sheriff's office. In the meantime, Iris planned to take good care of this newcomer, as she would any other guest in their home.

Mudder glanced up from the cast-iron skillet in her hands and smiled. "Finally—"

"Shhh!" Iris put her index finger to her lips. "You'll wake her."

"She'll get used to sleeping through anything around here." *Mudder* chuckled and handed the skillet to Iris. "No point in baby-ing the *bopli*."

"Very funny." Iris kept her voice low all the same. She picked up a towel and dried the skillet. "I need to go to Salome's. Do you think you can take care of her for a few hours?"

"I think I can handle it." *Mudder* made quick work of a pot and laid it in a plastic drain on the counter. "Do you really think you can catch up with them? I reckon they've gotten pretty far down the road, and you don't even know what direction."

"Quinn said they were headed to Texas, but they would have to stop in town for some supplies for Jessica." Heat toasted Iris's cheeks. Even talking to *Mudder* about these things was awkward. "We don't know what time they left either."

"Samuel said the truck was gone when he went to feed the animals." *Mudder* dried her hands and went to the table. She picked up a rumpled piece of paper. "What do you know about this?"

Iris peered over her shoulder. It was a drawing in pencil. The artist had a delicate touch. The details were fine, the wrinkles in her dress, the stains on her apron, the tendrils of hair that had escaped her *kapp*, her long chin. Iris didn't own a mirror, but she'd seen herself in mirrors many times. Her mind replayed the previous evening. Mahon at the desk, his hands over the tablet. The swift move to crumple the top sheet and toss it in the wastebasket. "That's me, isn't it?"

"Any idea how this got in our wastebasket?"

"Mahon was sitting at the desk last night."

"Why would he draw a picture of you?"

Why indeed? Heat curled its way up her neck and across her cheeks. "Did *Daed* see it?"

"*Nee*, I was cleaning the front room, and I emptied the basket." *Mudder* crumpled the sheet. She marched to the stove, opened the door, and tossed it in. Flames consumed it in an instant. "I knew he sketched. His *mudder* mentioned it."

"Nothing wrong with that."

"Animals, landscapes, and the like, *nee*." *Mudder* bent over the cradle and adjusted the quilt around Lilly's chin. "Leaving portraits of you lying about is another thing. We don't abide by pictures of ourselves. It's vain and leads to idolatry."

A sermon Iris had heard many times. During *rumspringa*, she and Salome took their pictures in a booth in town. Black-and-white strips of half a dozen silly poses, arms around each other, tongues sticking out, laughing so hard, their mouths hung open. *Mudder* found the strip. The lecture lasted twenty minutes and the photos disappeared into the fire, the paper curling and crackling in the flames. "He threw it away."

"But he drew it." *Mudder* went back to her dirty dishes. "What's done is done, I reckon. As long as you understand why I burned it."

"I'm not one to think highly of myself." Her tone was far too sharp for a daughter addressing her mother. She softened it. "I'm sorry. I'm tired."

"And worried, I suspect. Worrying helps nothing."

"*Daed* wants Quinn and Jessica found or Lilly turned over to the authorities. I don't even know what authorities it would be."

"Your *daed* will figure that out with Freeman. He wants what's best for the *bopli*." *Mudder* made quick work of another pot and laid it on the counter. "So do you, I reckon."

"Jessica is so young. I'm not sure she can be a *gut mudder*."

"But you can?"

"You don't think I can?"

"I know you *will* be. When the time comes. But this isn't your time."

"If it ever comes." The words were out before she could corral them. "I mean—"

"I know you're impatient. You're uncertain." *Mudder* examined a plate, then dunked it in the tub that held rinse water. "I can understand that, but there's no hurrying *Gott*'s plan. His timing is different from our own."

"Maybe it's not a matter of hurrying the plan. Maybe the plan doesn't include me being a *mudder*."

"You talk about being a *mudder*, but you don't mention being a *fraa*."

That would require a *mann*. She dried the pot and returned it to its spot in the cabinet. How could she explain the vacant space in her heart? She no longer ached for Aidan. Knowing he loved another had closed that door forever. "I feel as if I'm waiting for something. I've been waiting forever."

"Or someone?" *Mudder* scooped up silverware from the bottom of the tub and began to scrub. "Like someone who draws pretty pictures of you."

"Mudder!" Mahon had been bored, nothing more. Iris cast about for another topic. "I know it's been a few years, but do you have any cloth diapers stored away? Or any of Abigail's baby clothes?"

"I have a few things tucked away." *Mudder* tugged the towel from Iris's hands. She patted her fingers dry, a faraway look on her lined face. Iris knew what she would look like when she reached middle age. Fine wrinkles framed her *mudder*'s blue eyes. Gray had overtaken her blonde hair. Her figure grew rounder with each child and each passing year. "The baby's crib quilt is very pretty, for sure."

Iris followed her mother's gaze to the cradle. "It's old. The colors have faded, and there's a stain on the back."

"It's strange . . ." *Mudder*'s voice faded away. She dropped the towel on the counter. "I have something to show you."

After a last peek at Lilly, who slumbered with one fist against her tiny mouth, the other hidden under the quilt, Iris scurried to catch up with her mother, who headed for the back hallway and the bedroom she shared with *Daed*. There, she flipped up the clasps on a massive trunk at the foot of the bed. Iris had never seen it open. She used to ask as a child, but *Mudder* never let her look inside.

"What is all that?"

"Originally this was my hope chest. Now it's mostly full of quilts and keepsakes. A few things my *mudder* gave me." *Mudder*'s voice had an odd tremor in it that Iris had never heard before. She smoothed her hands across a baby's lilac nightgown, then held it up. "This was your sister Molly's."

"I don't have—"

Iris stopped, compelled to silence by the pain etched on her mother's face. She looked much older for a split second. She looked like *Groossmammi* Plank before she passed.

Mudder laid the nightgown back in the chest with the care reserved for something precious and irreplaceable. "Molly was our first *bopli*. Your older *schweschder*. She only lived a few hours."

She plopped onto the bed and picked up an envelope yellowed with age. Her head bent, she turned it over and over. Finally, she lifted the flap and showed Iris the contents. A single, small lock of wispy, auburn hair. Her fingertips, callused from years of gardening, laundry, and sewing, caressed the tendrils and then returned them to the envelope.

"I didn't know." Iris eased onto the bed next to her mother. "You never talked about her."

"Some of *Gott*'s gifts are fleeting." *Mudder* shrugged. "My pea brain isn't big enough to understand them all. She was here. Then she wasn't. No point in dwelling on it. You came along a year later."

She patted Iris's hand. Her fingers were warm and sturdy. "I'm glad you stayed around."

It was as close as her mother ever came to expressing affection through words. Iris cleared her throat. "Me too."

She had had a big sister. Her life would've been so different with an older sister to share a room, to share secrets, impart wisdom, make mistakes with, and learn from them together. They might have teased their brothers together, gone to singings together. Molly would've known what to do about Aidan. Big sisters knew these things. They might have bickered over which side of the bed to sleep on or whether to have the window open or closed on a fall evening or who would wash and who would dry the dishes. Life would've been different. "No one knows? There's no marker at the cemetery."

"We were visiting your *aenti* Esther in Haven." *Mudder's* voice cracked. She reached for a tissue from the box on the table next to the bed. "I was sick after the birth. We stayed almost a month. We buried her there. It was a long time ago."

"But it still hurts."

"*Boplin* are *Gott's* gifts. Their days with us are in His province. Still, my prayer for you is that you never have to know how much."

Mudder placed the envelope back in the chest, nestled in the folds of the nightgown. She bent over and lifted a pile of quilts. "Here it is." She laid a crib quilt in Iris's lap. "A nine-patch quilt."

The same pattern as the one Jessica left for Lilly. The colors were different. Black blocks framed the outside. The inner blocks were purple, a pale lavender, and black. It was old as well, but someone had cared for it better. "Where did this come from?"

"It's been handed down, *mudder* to *mudder*, for generations on my family's side." *Mudder* patted the quilt. "I intended to give it to you when you had your first baby. That's the way we've always done it."

"So *Groossmammi* gave it to you when you were expecting Molly."

"Jah."

"It would've gone to her?"

"It would have, but instead it'll go to you."

Iris ran her hand over the pieced cotton blocks. The quilting, done by hand, was perfectly stitched. She held it out to *Mudder*. "It's not time. Keep it until it's time."

"I wanted you to know I have faith. It's more than a quilt that warms a baby on a winter night. It reminds us that behind our faith and community, family is most important to us."

"I know."

"Don't lose faith because of what happened with Aidan."

It was the closest her mother had come to speaking of her courtship with Aidan. "I loved him for a long time."

"But you knew in your heart that he was meant for another. When we marry, we are yoked for life. You don't want to give that gift to the wrong person." *Mudder* wrapped her arms around the quilt and held it to her chest as if wrapping it in a hug. "You were wrapped in this quilt on your first day on earth. It kept you warm. It let you know you were loved. You are still loved. And one day you will find your mate."

Iris managed a smile. "If I don't marry, there's always Louella."

"Wait upon the Lord." *Mudder* cleared her throat and smiled back. "In the meantime, I think I have a small stack of Abigail's clothes in here somewhere." She pulled back a folded full-size quilt to reveal more nightgowns. "I guess I wasn't quite ready to let go of them. Just in case."

In case Abigail wasn't the last. There would always be room

in the Beachy house for one more and in a mother's heart. "I'll take them to the laundry room."

Mudder laid the crib quilt back in the trunk. "It'll be here when you're ready."

Iris nodded. No need to tell *Mudder* she'd been ready for years now.

CHAPTER 7

Gott had a way of providing. Iris studied the two drawings. Others in the *Gmay* might not think much of Mahon's skill as an artist, but it was a God-given gift. Perfect likenesses of Quinn and Jessica stared back at her. When Mahon heard that the couple had left their newborn daughter at the Beachy home and disappeared before dawn, he had agreed to help. It took him less than five minutes to sketch the two pictures with Iris peering over his shoulder at the table in the Kurtzs' toasty warm kitchen that smelled of baking cinnamon rolls and simmering beef stew. He caught Quinn's dark, handsome features and Jessica's elfin quality in the shape of her chin, upturned nose, and large eyes.

"You draw well." Her mind's eye pictured the rumpled sketch *Mudder* had tossed in the stove earlier in the day. Iris picked up the drawing of Quinn. The tuft of brown whiskers under his bottom lip spoke of the desire to look older. The beard wouldn't grow no matter how hard he tried. "It's not just how he looks, but how he is."

Mahon glanced at his mother, who stooped to pull the cinnamon rolls from the oven. He shrugged and laid his pencil next to a thick, rectangular sketch pad. "It's just something I do in my spare time. Anything to help you find them."

A *harrumph* from the vicinity of the stove told Iris that Bertha Kurtz was listening. Iris slid into the chair across from Mahon. She flattened her hands on the rough pine to keep from reaching for the sketch pad. Curiosity killed the cat. "It's raining now and the snow has turned to slush. Not much to do in the way of chores."

"I know. I was waiting to return the horse until it lightened up." He picked up the pencil and stuck it behind his ear. "It's a mess out there. I should drive you into town. We can talk to a few folks, see if anyone saw them or talked to them."

"Maybe they told someone where in Texas they're headed."

"Sounds like something Salome should do with Iris." Bertha turned from the stove, potholder mitts still on her hands. Her wrinkled cheeks were rosy from the heat. "I reckon your *daed* will need help with something before the afternoon is over."

"Salome won't be home from teaching until late." Mahon's tone was respectful, but firm. "Cyrus wants this taken care of. He has concerns."

Iris waited. Her heart did a crazy one-two-one-two beat that made her catch her breath. Because of the baby, not because of the prospect of spending an afternoon with Mahon. Their conversation the previous evening had replayed in her head, keeping her awake for more than an hour after his departure, despite her exhaustion. That touch. Had she imagined it? Rachel had planted the seed. It was the power of suggestion, nothing more. The power of suggestion made her warm despite icy temperatures outside. That was all.

"He's right about that." Bertha frowned. She wouldn't disagree with the deacon. No member of the community would. "See to it that you're back in time for evening chores. Your *daed*'s back is out of whack again."

"We'll take your buggy since it's already hitched." Mahon

stood, sketches in hand, and headed for the door. "You can drop me off on the way back."

"We should take this." Iris picked up the sketchbook and scooted away from the table. "In case you need to draw something."

It sounded lame in her ears. Because it was lame. Mahon grabbed his coat from the hook by the back door. The look of discomfort on his face said he thought so too, but he shrugged and nodded. He put on his coat and held out his hand. "I'll take it."

"I can carry it. You'll be driving."

His anxious gaze fixed on the sketchbook, he chewed on his lower lip for a second. "I'll be back before supper, *Mudder*."

Bertha sniffed. "Don't track mud in the house when you do get here."

A few minutes later they were on the road to Jamesport under a gloomy, gray sky that threatened to open up and drench them. Iris held the sketchbook in her lap with both hands. It was important to Mahon, which made it seem heavy and substantial to the touch. She studied the fields as they rolled by, searching for a topic of conversation. Patches of snow shone white against the muddy earth spattered with rain. The weather? The baby? She couldn't stand it anymore. "Can I look at your drawings?"

She opened the book before he could reply. The first few sketches were landscapes. Missouri in spring. A horse pulling a buggy on a road that wound past an open field, a red barn in the distance. Roses on a trellis outside a front door, complete with a welcome mat on the porch. An oak tree and an unoccupied tire swing. The strokes were fine and sure. The drawings contained as much detail as a black-and-white photograph, like memories caught and suspended in time.

"I wish you wouldn't."

"Why? They're beautiful."

Iris turned the page and found her own likeness staring up at her. She sat in a lawn chair, a glass of something in her hand. Her head was thrown back as if she were laughing. She looked up at someone who stood just beyond the page. She glanced at Mahon. He scowled straight ahead. A pulse beat in his jaw.

"I'm sorry." She shut the sketchbook. The *clip-clop* of horse's hooves in the muck filled the silence for several seconds. Half a dozen thoughts whirled through her head. He'd captured her image at a singing or a picnic. A happy, carefree moment. Such moments seemed long ago. For him, too, perhaps. But he'd never approached her at a singing. She always left with Aidan. Mahon's presence barely registered in those days. "Why do you draw me?"

"I draw other people."

"Other women?"

He didn't answer. The squeak of the wooden wheels as they spun in the muck punctuated the question. The wind whistled through the bare branches of the sycamore and elm trees that lined the road. It cut through her wool coat. She shivered. "I didn't mean to pry."

"My *daed* says drawing doesn't serve a purpose. He says it's like daydreaming, filling up time with doodles." He cleared his throat. "He's never mean about it. He only wants me to understand. It's not like making furniture, which is useful and can be beautiful too. Or the crib quilts you make for the babies. The quilts keep them warm, but they're pretty too."

He'd noticed her crib quilts. She set that observation aside to study later. It sounded as if he'd heard this lecture many times. "But you still draw."

"It doesn't interfere with my chores." Mahon's glance sideswiped hers. His face turned a deeper hue of scarlet than the cold warranted. He snapped the reins as if to hurry along this never-ending ride. "I think while I do it. I puzzle things out. I record memories. It doesn't hurt anything."

He stumbled over the words as if searching for the right ones to explain something he feared she would never understand. But she did. While she pieced and quilted the crib blankets she, too, puzzled over life's strange twists and turns. She imagined the lives the babies would have, what they would look like, the world they would inherit in years to come. She, too, tried to understand that which couldn't be understood. What did farmers think about during those long afternoons when they tilled the fields? What did *Mudder* think about as she toiled over load after load of laundry or pulled weeds in the morning sun on a spring day? Was it any different? *Daed*—and the bishop and the minister—would argue the end results were. Food from the fields and the garden, clean clothes, quilts, useful products unlike these sketches that served no other purpose than to memorialize a moment in life. "*Gott* made beautiful flowers. It doesn't seem they serve much purpose other than to make us smile and tell us spring is here."

"I'm sure they serve other purposes." His expression softened and he smiled. "They provide food to the bees."

"I'll give you that one."

The silence was more companionable then.

She longed to open the sketchbook again. Is that what her mother meant by pride? What Freeman talked about in his messages on Sundays—personal vanity, idolatry. The sin of worshipping one's self. All that in an innocent sketch of her laughing. Or maybe it was the call of the forbidden, like the keggers during her *rumspringa*. She'd been so anxious to gulp down that red cup of beer. Then, when Salome wasn't looking, she'd spat it out and rushed in search of water to drown the nasty taste. The English farm boys had scoffed at her queasiness.

"Why don't you want me to look at the sketches?"

"My whole life I've been told not to get carried away with it. To drop the pencil and go do something worthwhile."

"I used to get that when I read books instead of darning."

"But you didn't feel . . . compelled to read."

"*Nee*, I just like it." She grinned, thinking of her early foray into Nancy Drew mysteries, eventually replaced by Miss Marple and Hercule Poirot. Lives so different from hers and worlds apart. Vocabulary too. "I keep a book in my room and go to bed early."

His chuckle sounded rueful. "I share my room."

"You didn't answer my question."

"I don't draw other women."

"Why do you draw me?"

He snapped the reins. "Giddy-up." As if he couldn't wait to reach Jamesport. "It passes the time."

"The time until what?"

"Until you're ready."

Maybe she should ask him to draw *her* a picture. "Ready for what?"

"I don't remember you asking so many questions." He glared at her. "Me."

One syllable could be worth a hundred drawings, if it was the right syllable.

She wasn't cold anymore. In fact, she considered removing her mittens and her coat.

"You asked." He growled deep in his throat, like an old barnyard dog awakened from a nap. "I'm waiting for you to get over Aidan Graber, come to your senses, and see we're meant to be together."

CHAPTER 8

Come to my senses? Heat scorched Iris's ears. The burning on her cheeks had nothing to do with the icy-cold wind. She inhaled and counted to ten. Three times.

"You asked." Mahon sounded as aggravated as she felt. "More than once."

How dare he? *Get over Aidan.* "What are you talking about?"

"You forget I live in the same house as Salome. I spent as much time with you as her when we were *kinner*. I watched you leave with him after the singings. I watched your face when you watched him at Caleb's funeral. I saw your face when he married Bess. All this time I've waited for you to see what's on my face."

He'd found the words after all.

"Well, well . . . I don't . . ." Iris sputtered. "You never . . ."

"You did ask."

Iris laid the sketchbook between them. His words hung in the air. Rachel was right about everything. Mahon's feelings came as no surprise, truly, so why was she so stunned? The depth and breadth astounded her. He'd held his peace for a long time. Now the words rushed out like a torrential river that bowled her over. "I don't know what to say."

"Don't say anything. Do me that favor."

To say nothing would be unkind. Yet his declaration put him far ahead of her on this path. He couldn't expect her to race to meet him at the end. "It's not fair."

"What's not fair?"

"You could've tried." As if she would've had eyes for anyone other than Aidan in those days. Now she wasn't being fair. No other words came that would help her explain the tumult in her heart and head. "You could've said something."

"Your heart was—*is*—with someone else."

"No. It's not. Not anymore. Granted, it was at one time, but I've made my peace. I turned him down."

"He asked you to marry him and you said no."

She turned her face toward the fields. Shame coursed through her. Did everyone know of her heartbreak? What passed between her and Aidan was private. Like having a leg amputated and experiencing phantom leg pain. "How do you know this?"

"Salome and Mary talk when they do their sewing at night. They forget I'm around."

The sound of the rain-engorged creek gurgling past her on the cool spring evening on which Aidan had proposed assailed Iris's ears. The way the rocks had smacked the water when she made them skip better than he did. Frogs croaked. A mockingbird trilled. Her heart beat in a ragged, painful tribute to what she knew was coming. "I had to say no. He didn't *lieb* me."

"Another woman might have said *jah*, thinking he would grow to *lieb* her."

"In three years, he never kissed me." She bent her head and stared at her hands, her voice a whisper. Mortified, she cringed and put her hands to her burning cheeks. Had she said those words aloud? "You don't want to hear this."

"I'm glad."

Her hands dropped. She swiveled and glared at him. "Why?"

The childish, chipmunk face disappeared, replaced with a man's fierce stare. His blue eyes were warm and liquid. His cheeks were red from the cold and emotion. He transferred the reins to one hand. His free hand landed on hers and squeezed, his grip hard, nothing like the soft brush of the previous evening. "It means your first kiss is reserved for the man who loves you." He let go and returned to the business of driving. "Me."

Her mouth gaped. Unable to think of a single word of response, she closed it.

They made the rest of the drive to the Jamesport Grocery Store in silence. Mahon pulled into one of the spots in front of the hitching post and tethered the horse. "They might have stopped here for supplies before heading out of town."

She owed him a response. The connection between her brain and her mouth was tied in a million knots. She nodded. He hopped from the buggy and looked back. "Are you coming?"

She nodded again. Shaking his head, he strode around the buggy to her side. He glanced around at the nearly empty street and then up at her. "Don't worry about it."

"I'm not worried." Her voice sounded breathless in her own ears. Her gaze fastened on his mouth. The power of suggestion? She had waited forever for that first kiss from Aidan. It never came. Mahon was right. It should be reserved for a man who loved her, whom she loved just as much. "Don't *you* worry."

"I've been waiting quite awhile. I'm used to it. I'm not going anywhere."

She studied him. He looked nothing like Aidan, who was tall and blond and had an angular face. But Mahon did have that same sense of loyalty. Aidan's love for a friend had kept him from courting the woman he loved. When Caleb died, Aidan had the opportunity to finally seek her out. Instead, he asked Iris to marry him because he felt an obligation after years of courting. Knowing his true heart, she'd sent him to Bess with her blessing. Mahon was waiting for her and only her. The thought was like needle and thread darning the rips in her heart. Still, no words presented themselves.

He smiled, a soft, tentative, knowing smile. "Except into the store."

She climbed down and followed him inside, where they found Kathy Myers behind the register. Snapping a wad of gum the size of her thumb, the teenager scratched the end of her pimpled nose and laid aside her cell phone. She took her time looking at the sketches. "Yep, I've seen him." She pointed to Quinn. "Right after I unlocked the doors this morning. He was waiting outside in a van. Parked right next to Mrs. Lumpkins's station wagon and Cheryl Reiner's pickup truck. They like to do their shopping early to beat the rush hour. Like we got a rush hour in Jamesport on a Thursday morning."

"Did he say anything? Like where he was headed?"

"Nope, and I never got a chance to ask." The bells over the glass double doors dinged. Kathy waved at Tillie Matthews, who waved back and headed toward the bread aisle. "You should show these to Dan Rogers."

"The sheriff's deputy?" An uneasy feeling churned in Iris's belly. "Why? Is he in town for something?"

"Mike called him." Mike was Mike Turner, owner of the grocery store. Kathy tapped Quinn's sketch with a fingernail painted neon purple. "After I called Mike to tell him this guy walked out of the store without paying for anything."

"He shoplifted. Are you sure?"

"He was carrying one of those green camouflage army

backpacks." Kathy pointed at the overhead mirrors. "I watched him pick up a package of sanitary napkins, some chocolate donuts. A bottle of aspirin. Some OJ. Next thing I know, I'm ringing up Mrs. Lumpkins and I hear the bell. I look up and he's out the door. I ran around the counter and sprinted after him. He took off like a bat out of hell in a brown van that sounded like it was on its last leg."

Mahon turned around and leaned on the counter between the gum and mints rack and the rack of sales flyers. He scooted down to let Tillie pay for her bread and milk. "Is Deputy Rogers coming to town?"

"He's already here." Kathy waved Tillie's twenty-dollar bill in the general direction of the street. "He was on his way to the Purple Martin Café for a piece of Zeke's chocolate cream and meringue pie before he headed back to Gallatin."

Iris whirled, tugged a cart from the row by the doors, and headed for the baby food aisle. How could Quinn do such a thing? Desperation? He only needed to ask. They would've helped. How could he do this to Lilly? How could he do this to Jessica?

A father who could leave his baby girl behind could also steal, it seemed. He'd left Iris with the responsibility of feeding his child. She picked up a can of powdered formula. The cost of one small can made her mouth drop. At this rate her small savings from selling crib quilts at the craft sales would be quickly depleted. No matter. She would earn more this spring. She grabbed two big cans and set them in the basket, followed by three gallons of distilled water.

"You don't want to tell him, do you?" Mahon halted near the long rows of baby food in jars of every color. He picked up a jar of purple plums, then placed it back in its spot, the label turned out. "You're worried about what it means for the baby."

"If we tell him about Quinn and Jessica, we'll have to tell him about Lilly."

"We have to tell him." Mahon took over the cart for her and headed toward the counter. "A man broke the law and we know something about him."

"We don't even know his last name." Iris tugged her wallet from her canvas bag. She counted the bills inside it, once, then again. "We can't help them find Quinn and arrest him. He's Lilly's *daed*."

"He's also a shoplifter."

"Would Freeman want us to get involved?"

"We're already involved." They waited for Mr. and Mrs. Haag to finishing paying for their groceries. A lot of frozen meals. Sugar-free cookies. Banana pudding. And prune juice. "Not to mention, your *daed* wanted us to find them. A sheriff's deputy can do that easier than we can."

"And put them in jail."

"Just Quinn. Which would force Jessica to go home to her parents and take her baby with her."

Her expression puzzled, Kathy shoved a lock of bleached blonde hair from her eyes. "I didn't know you two were married, let alone had a baby."

"We don't."

"We're not." Iris's words collided with Mahon's.

Kathy's dark, finely plucked eyebrows rose and fell. "Okay, whatever you say."

Mahon parked the cart. "I'm going to the Purple Martin. Are you coming or not?"

A baby should have a mother and a father.

A series of bad choices had brought them here. That's what her father would say.

Iris followed Mahon down the street to the Purple Martin Café, home of the best chicken fried steak in town. The aroma of bacon frying mingled with the scent of freshly baked apple pie greeted her when she pushed through the glass double doors. Her stomach rumbled. Owner Ezekiel Miller hustled toward them with his usual enthusiastic wave. If he found it odd they had walked in together, he didn't show it. "Table or booth?"

Mahon shook his head. Iris followed his gaze. Deputy Rogers sat at the counter polishing off a huge piece of chocolate cream pie crowned with golden, brown-tipped, puffy meringue.

About fifteen seconds into Mahon's recitation, Rogers laid down his fork. Thirty seconds in, he tugged a slim notebook from his shirt pocket and began to take notes. He asked a few questions about the van, Quinn's and Jessica's descriptions, where they were from and where they were going, all of which Mahon answered. Rogers sat in silence for a few seconds after Mahon finished.

"Can I keep these?" He pointed to the sketches.

Mahon nodded. Iris tried to read the deputy's expression. A word from her Agatha Christie novels came to mind. *Inscrutable.*

He leaned forward on his stool, looking past Mahon to Iris. "They didn't specify where in Texas?"

Iris shook her head.

"Neither one of them offered a last name or said where they came from?"

"They told Mahon they were from Iowa. That's all I know."

"And they left their newborn baby with you?"

"*Jah.* Yes."

Frowning, Deputy Rogers scratched his forehead with his index finger. "A shoplifting baby abandoner. This day just gets better and better."

"Are you going to take the baby?" To her chagrin, Iris's voice squeaked. Her *daed* would not want her inserting herself into a sheriff's investigation of two *Englischers*.

Deputy Rogers shoved his empty plate back and picked up his coffee cup. "That wouldn't be for me to say. I'll talk to the children's division and the juvenile office." He shook his head. "Either way, a judge has to make the order. Unless a kid is in imminent danger. Then we can put them in temporary protective custody until the judge reviews the case and makes a ruling."

Iris breathed.

"Are your parents willing to be responsible for the baby—at least for now?"

Iris nodded. She would take care of Lilly, but it was her parents' house.

Deputy Rogers dropped a dollar tip on the counter. He scooped up his bill and the two sketches. "I've known your parents for a long time. I reckon that baby is in good hands—better than she would be with those kids. They qualify as temporary protective custody in my way of thinking. Before anything regarding permanent custody of the baby can be decided, we have to find the parents."

Lilly would be in good hands—her hands. "How do you find people when you don't even have last names?"

"The sketches will help. We'll put out a BOLO—that's a "be on the lookout"—and send the sketches to other law enforcement agencies. We'll use social media. Believe me, we have our ways." He stood and headed for the cash register at the end of the counter. "I'll go by and talk to your parents before I head back to Gallatin. I want a look at the baby and the bag they left. If you think of anything else, let me know."

Iris nodded once again, but her mind repeated the two most important words he'd said. *Permanent custody.*

CHAPTER 9

Sleep. Sweet, elusive sleep. Maybe the sponge bath would relax Lilly enough to make her nod off. Iris rubbed her burning eyes and picked up the towel. Avoiding the spot where her belly button would one day be, she patted the baby dry. She'd been careful not to get it wet. So many things to think about with a newborn. Especially this tiny one who was a decent eater but seemed to have her days and nights mixed up. Cry and eat at night. Nap, cry, and eat all day.

"You're nice and clean after your first bath." Iris dressed her in a lilac nightgown she plucked from the bag of hand-me-downs Rachel had given her when she went over to check on the new mom and baby Micah. Both were doing well. Micah slept a lot. Lucky Rachel. "See how sweet you look in your nightie. And you know what that means? That means it's time to sleep. Can you do that for me?"

Lilly cooed and then burped, a loud, brash sound much too big for such a small baby. A stream of white, stinky formula spit-up followed. Iris sighed. "Just be that way, Lilly Marie."

Thank goodness for hand-me-downs. The next nightie was a soft blue cotton. Her arms heavy with fatigue, Iris redressed Lilly and wrapped her in the nine-patch quilt Jessica had left behind. Something from her real mother. It took more than blankets or blood to make a true mother. A true mother rocked her baby in the middle of the night. She patted her back when she had a tummy ache and nursed her when she was hungry. She didn't run to Texas while others slept. "Do you have a tummy ache, my sweet? Am I giving you too much formula?"

She didn't know anyone who bottle-fed so she had no one else to ask. Lilly didn't answer. She didn't wail either, which was a good sign. Iris settled into the rocking chair she'd moved into her bedroom, along with the cradle. "You're fed. You're clean. You have a fresh diaper." She began to rock. "Now you sleep. It's night. We sleep at night. Now close your eyes and sleep."

Lilly's head bobbed, but her eyes were wide open. She'd slept through Deputy Rogers's visit the previous afternoon, according to *Mudder*, who said *Daed* did all the talking. Yes, they would take care of the baby. No, they didn't know where the parents had gone. The deputy went through the gym bag and scoured the bedroom where they had slept, with hardly a word before telling them the same thing he'd told Iris and Mahon. If they thought of anything else, let him know.

"What else could there be?"

Lilly wrinkled her tiny nose and sighed at Iris's entirely rhetorical question, but her eyes remained open.

"*Ach*, *bopli*, *Aenti* Iris needs to sleep."

Aenti *Iris*. Would she ever be more than an aunt? Mahon's words spoken in the buggy reverberated in her mind. *Waiting for you to be ready.* Mahon didn't think of her as someone's aunt. He drew sketches of her. Beautiful sketches. Despite the cool air in her bedroom, a wave of heat engulfed her. The trip home from Jamesport as the dusk began to gather had been spent rehashing everything Deputy Rogers said at the restaurant. Neither had broached the subject of the sketches or Mahon's declaration. He hopped from the buggy at his house with a promise to return *Daed*'s horse as soon as he could and a backward wave. Just like that.

She closed her eyes for a second, remembering his smell of burnt wood and the way he bit his lip as he worked on the sketches. The way he cocked his head to one side and then the other as he studied his work, his dark eyes intent and critical. The sound of his voice when he said he was waiting for her. As if he couldn't quite catch his breath.

Why hadn't she said anything? It had been cowardly to leave him hanging. She didn't know what to say. To acknowledge his feelings was to make room for the possibility that she might also have feelings for him. That those feelings might grow. That she might have to explore again the path that left her wide open to pain and anguish.

"I'm not mad, *Gott*. I'm not." She spoke aloud, letting her voice drift toward the rafters. He already knew what she thought, what she felt, how she hurt, how she feared. God knew it all. So why didn't He do something? "Sorry, *Gott*. Sorry."

She'd spent her whole life learning the lessons of *gelassenheit*. Yielding to *Gott*'s will.

No one talked about not liking it. What did a person do with those feelings?

I'm waiting for you.

Mahon was waiting for her. How long would he wait? He said he was used to waiting. That he wasn't going anywhere. She could trust those words. She could trust him, couldn't she? The memory of his hand on her arm, the feel of his warm fingers—farmer's fingers that wielded a pencil with a deft touch. Touching her. She closed her eyes. To open herself up to Mahon, to trust him, was to trust God.

God was waiting for her too.

To yield to His plan. She was tired of going it alone.

"Is that how you feel, *bopli*?" She snuggled the baby closer. "You look tired. Like me. We both need to sleep."

"Sleep, baby, sleep." She sang, first in German, then in English, trying to blot the sound of Mahon's voice from her head. It was a deep voice, deeper than Aidan's, even though Aidan was a bigger man. Mahon was solid, barrel-chested, compact. A farmer who liked to draw. A farmer who read the stars the way she read books. He intrigued her. She'd known him all her life, and now it turned out she didn't know him at all. *"Grandpa tends the sheep, Grandma brings in the skinny cows."*

Lilly gurgled.

"Jah, it's a funny song. I don't know why they're skinny cows." She shook her head. All these thoughts spun round and round in her head. They had no place to go. She could tell no one. Not Rachel with her three little ones and her happy life. Not Salome. Mahon was her brother. She might tease him, but she loved her brother. "It doesn't matter. You need to sleep. I need to sleep."

Lack of sleep explained her silly thoughts. Not cracks in her good-girl façade. She held what she most wanted in her arms, but this baby did not belong to her.

Lilly babbled and swung her tiny fists. "You are a sweet thing, *jah*, you are."

The baby's mouth opened wide, closed, and formed what looked like a smile. "You smiled at me, didn't you? You smiled!"

Everyone said newborn babies didn't smile. *Mudder* would say it was gas. Iris knew differently. Babies often smiled at her after she delivered them. She was the first person to greet them in this strange, new world with its cold and dark shadows. She shared a special bond with every child she delivered. Iris touched Lilly's soft check and snuggled her closer to her chest. "You are loved, my sweet, you are cherished."

All babies should know that and feel it. Iris rocked a little harder. Her eyelids felt heavy, her arms limp. She didn't dare fall asleep before the baby did. She swallowed the lump in her throat. "How about 'Jesus Loves Me'?" Lilly might not understand about Jesus' love now, but one day she would. Did Jessica believe in Jesus? Iris didn't allow her voice to falter at the thought. Lilly's eyelids dropped. Her hands stilled.

Thank you, Jesus. Iris softened her voice to a low whisper. Lilly's eyes closed. *Thank you, Jesus.* She held Lilly's warm body, limp in sleep, close to her chest and inhaled the sweet scent of her hair, the scent of hope, of possibility, of dreams that can come true. "Sweet, sweet *bopli.*"

"Hey, there you are."

Iris jumped at the sound of Salome's voice. "Hush, hush," she whispered. "I just got her to sleep."

"Sorry." Shoulders hunched, Salome moved into the room in an exaggerated tiptoe. "Put her down so we can talk."

Mudder was right, as usual. Lilly would learn to sleep through anything in this house. "I'm tired." Iris eased from the chair. Holding her breath, she lowered Lilly into the cradle and stepped back. "I thought I would go to bed too."

"It's early." Salome shivered. "I'm cold. Let's go in the kitchen and make some hot tea."

Early for someone who was getting uninterrupted sleep. "One cup and then I'm going to bed."

Salome grinned and led the way down the stairs and through the front room. *Mudder* wrote letters at the desk, her head bent over the paper. She didn't look up. Their giggles boisterous, the girls played checkers with Carl. *Daed* sat in the rocker by the fireplace, *The Budget* newspaper in his lap. His glasses were tucked into the sparse hair on his head. Ethan Shrock, Bartholomew's brother, sat in the chair across from him. Both men smiled as Iris passed on Salome's heels. Ethan raised his hand and waved. Neither said a word.

"What are you doing out so late on a cold night?" Iris paused halfway through the room. Salome continued her beeline for the kitchen with barely a glance toward the other visitor. "Is everything all right with your family?"

"*Gut, gut.*" Ethan's gaze—which could only be described as hopeful—meandered toward Salome's back disappearing into the kitchen. "We—I needed to talk to your *daed*."

Daed simply nodded. He wore his deacon face. His lips would be sealed unless Ethan let the cat out of the bag. Which he obviously didn't intend to do.

"What is Ethan doing here? Do you know?" She followed Salome into the kitchen where she filled the kettle with water and placed it on the stove. Her mind was fuzzier than an old blanket. "I haven't been getting much sleep."

"We'll get to that. You looked tuckered out." Salome busied herself setting out mugs and teabags. "Motherhood is hard."

"I'm not the *bopli*'s mother."

"I hope you remember that."

"What are you talking about?"

Salome turned and faced Iris. "It would be easy to get attached to such a sweet little thing."

"She's a baby who needs loving. It's not her fault her parents took off."

"No word from Deputy Rogers?"

"Not yet. It's barely been twenty-four hours." Iris plopped into a chair at the table. She kept waiting for him to show up at the door to take Lilly away. Which made every moment she was responsible for this small, fragile life more bittersweet. "I'm sure it's like hunting for a needle in a haystack."

"Lots of nooks and crannies between here and the Mexican border." Salome opened a plastic container and selected a large chocolate chip cookie from its contents. "What will they do if they don't find them? They don't even have a last name to try to find other relatives."

"I'm not exactly sure. Something about a children's division and a judge." Iris rubbed a spot behind her right ear. Her head ached. "He said something about permanent custody."

"Ethan asked me to marry him."

It took a second for the abrupt change of subjects to register. "Ethan?" This explained his presence in the Beachy living room. "When?"

"Last night." Her nose crinkled, eyebrows lifted, and forehead creased, Salome laid a cookie on a napkin. She held it out to Iris from an arm's length away. Was she expecting a sudden explosion? "We told your *daed* tonight. He said he'll talk to Freeman tomorrow after the funeral. The announcement will be made Sunday."

"That's *wunderbarr.*" Despite her best effort to ward it off, a new ache spread down Iris's throat into her chest. She swallowed against it, stood, and held out her arms. Salome walked into the hug. "You never said a word."

"It's silly, I know." Salome's arms tightened around Iris. Her voice dropped to a tearful whisper. "I wanted to tell you before it was announced."

"I thought it might be you and Joseph."

"Silly you! Joseph? That would be like kissing my *bruder*."

Like kissing Mahon. The thought did cartwheels in Iris's head. *Stop it. Concentrate.* This was Salome's moment. "Joseph took you home the other night. The thought crossed my mind, that's all. Why didn't you talk to me about Ethan before?" Iris took a step back and peered into her friend's face. "You knew I'd be happy for you, right?"

"I knew you would be because you're that kind of friend, that kind of person. It's just that you and I are the last ones, and I know how hurt—"

"It doesn't matter." Iris forced a smile. The last ones in their group to marry. "Ethan is like Bartholomew. A *gut* man. You will be a *gut fraa* to him. I'm happy for you. I can't believe you kept it a secret."

Salome swiped at her face with her sleeve. "It really started about the time you broke it off with Aidan. I didn't want to add salt to the wound. Besides, courting is private."

"Except between friends." More than a year had passed. Aidan married Bess. Salome never said a word. Neither did Rachel. She had to know about her brother-in-law. How tender they must think her feelings. How fragile they must see her. Had she moped around that much? Friends and family should feel free to share their happiness. "I'm fine. Perfectly fine. I promise. I assume Rachel knows."

"*Jah.* I want the two of you to be my witnesses."

Iris hugged her a second time. "It would be an honor." Watching her friend marry would be a special day she would never forget. "Where will you live?"

"With his parents until he can build our house on a piece of Bartholomew's property. Just on the other side of Rachel's house."

Just down the road from the Beachy homestead. She would watch Salome's babies grow and play with Rachel's. They would bake and do laundry and cook together. They would piece the crib quilts and quilt them together. Just as they did now. God willing, there would be babies. Iris would deliver them. "And teaching? Who'll take over at the school?"

"It's for the *Gmay* to decide." Sadness crept into Salome's face. "I will miss it. I *lieb* teaching and my scholars. I think one of the Schultz sisters would make a *gut* teacher."

She took the tea kettle from the stove and poured steaming water into the two mugs. The calming scent of chamomile filled the air. Iris closed her eyes for a second, inhaled, and sighed.

"There's that sigh." Salome carried the mugs to the table, only slopping a tiny bit. "*Ach*, hot, hot. The sigh that says you're sad."

"It says I'm tired." And puzzled over God's plan for her.

"So, you went into town with Mahon." Salome set a mug in front of Iris and settled in a chair across from her. "What did you talk about?"

"Nothing in particular."

"Then how come he was so grumpy when he got home? He went out and chopped wood for two hours."

"You needed the wood, I reckon."

"Spill it, Iris."

"He draws pictures of me."

Salome paused, cup halfway to her lips. She lowered it to the table. "Like portraits?"

"Like black-and-white photographs." Iris nodded. "They're beautiful."

"*Daed* wouldn't like it."

"Mine either."

"Still, it says something about his feelings for you. You know it does."

Iris sipped her tea. It was scalding hot. Maybe that would pass as an explanation for the red that surely ran rampant across her cheeks. "He told me he's waiting for me."

Salome's face lit up in a grin. Mahon's grin. "I knew it. I knew it. He told you when you went into town."

"He said he would wait until I'm ready."

"My *bruder* finally stepped up." Salome hooted. "He finally grew up and admitted he likes you. And you like him back, don't you?"

"Courting is private."

"Which means you're courting." Salome clapped her hands. "I knew it. *Gott* is *gut.*"

One conversation and a touch on the arm did not courting make. Iris took the cup to the counter. "The funeral is tomorrow. *Mudder* and *Daed* are helping, so I'll have to take the girls. The boys will get there on their own. I really need to get some sleep now."

Ethan stood in the doorway, a silly grin stretched across his face. He towered over her, the spitting image of Bartholomew. He would be good for Salome, a sturdy place for the butterfly to land after swooping from one flower to the next. "I just came to see if everything is all right."

"For sure." Iris managed another smile. "I'm happy for you. Treat her right or I'll lock you in the outhouse."

He shifted from one boot to the other and ducked his head. "For sure."

"It's a true blessing. I mean it."

"We'll look forward to your day as well."

Ethan and Mahon had worked many frolics together. They hunted and fished together. What did he know? "I'm going to bed."

Salome's and Ethan's mingled laughter followed her out the door and up the stairs.

CHAPTER 10

A heart can be lifted at a funeral, even one held in a March wind that whipped bare tree branches, bending them to the ground. Iris tucked the quilt around Lilly's face and trudged toward the Borntrager home. The folded playpen hoisted between them, Louella and Abigail followed, their high-pitched chatter like birdsong. Isaac Borntrager had lived a long and full life. He would rest easy now. No tears were shed at the cemetery. None would be shed now as guests from across states gathered to eat and fellowship in his memory. Iris dropped a quick kiss on the sleeping baby's forehead. They didn't have many assurances, but the circle of life was one.

"Let me get the door for you."

Cold that had nothing to do with the wind swept through Iris. She forced her gaze up. Aidan pushed the screen door open and smiled down at her. "I saw you from the window. You have your hands full."

Their paths had crossed plenty of times in the last year. She saw him at church, at frolics, at weddings, including his own.

But they never talked, not just the two of them. He looked good, as always. Tall, lean, broad-shouldered. Sandy-brown hair and blue eyes that could pierce to the bone or drown a person with their unexpected flood of emotion. She shifted the bag on her shoulder. Traveling with a bottle-fed baby meant a full bag, but not more than she could handle.

"How are you?" Before he could answer, she squeezed past him, careful not to brush against his bulky winter coat. "I hope it's warmer in here than it is out there."

"I'll help the girls with the playpen."

A few minutes later he was setting up the pen in a bedroom. The girls had abandoned Iris for ham sandwiches and brownies. "I heard about the *Englischers*." He straightened and studied his handiwork. The pen had seen better days. All seven Beachy children had used it. "Any word on their whereabouts?"

"*Nee.*" She settled her bag on the floor and laid Lilly on the bed to unwrap her blankets. Her eyelids fluttered and then closed. She should be tired. She'd been up half the night alternately feeding and fussing. "I reckon they're some place in Texas by now."

"And left you holding the bag, so to speak."

"The *bopli, jah*." She tucked the quilt around the sleeping baby and faced him. "She's a sweet baby. The *mudder*'s note said she would be back for her."

"But you're hoping she doesn't come back."

"That's a terrible thing to say, Aidan Graber."

"I didn't mean it that way." He edged toward the door. "I just meant you *lieb* your *boplin* and you won't see one of them neglected or abused. It's one of the things I . . . like . . . respect about you."

"Most people wouldn't want to see that."

"Except one who leaves her with strangers."

"She thought it was best for this baby. That I might do better than she could. She had Lilly's best interest at heart."

Sometimes best wasn't easiest. Often it wasn't.

"You will be a *gut mudder*."

Their gazes met. The silence stretched. He tilted his head and gave a small shrug.

"*Gott* willing." She managed a quick nod. "I know."

"There you are." Bess stuck her head through the doorway. She held her son, Joshua, on her hip. The chunky two-year-old, with his almond-brown eyes and hair, was the spitting image of his father, Caleb. What a precious gift of remembrance from Bess's first marriage. "Henry and Timothy are looking for you, Aidan. Something about going hunting Saturday."

"Sounds like a *gut* idea to me."

Aidan strode toward the door. Joshua held up his pudgy arms. *"Daed, Daed."*

A grin spread across Aidan's face. He took Joshua from Bess, held him high until the boy giggled, then wrapped an arm around his waist so he faced outward on Aidan's hip. Aidan and Bess exchanged a look that made Iris duck her head and study the nine-patch quilt. A family heirloom from a family Lilly might never know. Someone had quilted every piece with loving stitches, thinking of the baby it would warm as she did. Who was she? Lilly's great-grandmother? A great-aunt? The ache in Iris's heart had nothing to do with Aidan. Not Aidan the man. It had to do with what he represented. Her dream of stitching a crib quilt for her own baby. To be a *fraa* and a *mudder*.

Aidan was no longer the man to fulfill those dreams. Her heart had let him go. She took a breath and released it, delighting in the sense of relief that flooded her. Time had healed that wound. Her head and heart were now together in knowing she had been right to let him go. Lilly's eyelids fluttered again. This time they stayed open. She stared up at Iris and batted her tiny fists.

"Sweet thing, you're awake." Iris scooped her up. "Did you have a nice nap?"

Mudder and the other women were serving food. She should help. Lilly would like the kitchen and its toasty warmth. So would Iris. She turned. Aidan was gone, but Bess still stood in the doorway, half in, half out of the bedroom. Her expression was equally uncertain.

"I wanted to ask you something."

"Here I am." Iris picked up her bag. "I was headed to the kitchen to help with the food."

"Me too."

Bess didn't move. She was a sweet, loving woman who made Aidan happy. He deserved to be happy. So did Bess, who'd lost her first husband in a buggy-truck accident after only a year of marriage. "What was your question?"

Bess stepped into the room. Her normally rosy face was wan. She put her hand to her mouth and cleared her throat. She smoothed her hands over her apron as if smoothing nonexistent wrinkles. "She's a tiny thing. What's her name?"

"Lilly Marie . . . something. I don't know her last name. She came early. She usually sleeps all day and fusses all night."

Bess trudged to the bed and sat. She blew out air so hard the tendrils of hair that had escaped her *kapp* fluttered. "Joshua did that for the first few months. I thought I would never sleep again. He had reflux—you know, he spit up all the time and it irritated his throat. And he had food allergies. I had to be careful what I ate."

"This one is bottle-fed. I wonder if that has something to do with it. Maybe the formula doesn't suit her." Iris rocked Lilly in her arms. It was apparent Bess didn't come to talk about reflux and spitting up. "Are you all right? You look peaked."

Bess wiggled. Her fingers plucked at the cotton material. "If you don't want to do this, I understand. It seems strange to ask you, but it would be strange not to ask you."

"Do what?"

"Deliver our baby." She put her hand to her mouth for a second, then let it drop. "I'm in a family way."

Plain folks didn't usually talk about being pregnant. Iris didn't pretend not to understand why Bess felt it necessary to bring it up now. "I'm happy for you. Really. This is *gut*."

"I wanted to tell you before it became obvious. To give you fair warning."

"That wasn't necessary." Iris wiped spit-up from Lilly's chin and stared into eyes that were leaning toward blue now. The baby gurgled and hiccupped. "You don't have to be concerned about my feelings. I'm fine. Really, I am. I promise."

She was as surprised as Bess, surely, to find this was true.

"I'm glad." Bess patted the spot next to her on the bed. "Sit down. You look tired. You look like a new *mudder*."

Iris took her suggestion.

"Can I hold her?"

Iris nodded. Her arms were tired, yet they didn't seem to want to comply. Bess slid her hands under the baby and tugged. Iris forced herself to let go.

"Do you look like your *mudder*?" Bess tickled the baby's face. "You're so tiny. I don't remember Joshua ever being this tiny."

Lilly wailed.

Bess rocked and cooed and soothed. Lilly's cries grew louder. Shaking her head, Bess handed her back. "She wants you."

The thought shouldn't warm Iris's heart, but it did. She bent her head, hoping Bess didn't read her face. "Shhh, shhh, baby. Shhh."

Lilly's wails subsided.

"She's attached to you, poor thing." Bess stretched. Her hand went to her mouth. She sighed. "I don't remember so much morning sickness with Joshua either."

"*Jah*, I will deliver the *bopli*." Iris would be there at this special moment in Bess and Aidan's life, the birth of their first child together. The thought didn't rankle as it would have once. Instead, she felt joy on their behalf. She touched Lilly's cheek. They were blessed to have each other and to be a family. Lilly should have that too. If not with her own parents, then with Iris's family. "We'll talk in a few weeks."

"*Gut*. That's settled." Relief spread across Bess's face. "Aidan always talks about how kind you are."

"Aidan talks about me to you?"

"You gave him a gift. He'll never forget that. He wants you to be happy." Bess got to her feet, hand still on her stomach. "I'll never forget it. I know how short life is. I hope you find your special friend soon."

Iris didn't answer. Mahon's face as he said, *I'm waiting for you* floated in her mind's eye. Courting was private.

CHAPTER 11

Maroon, navy, lilac, beige. The colors pleased Iris. Her head bent close to the kerosene lamp despite its heat, Iris laid out her diamonds, dark material cut on sixty-degree angles, along with triangles in the beige, that would create the blocks for her tumbling block crib quilt. This would be Bess and Aidan's gift upon the birth of their first child. She hummed "Trust and Obey" as she picked up her threaded needle and sewed together the first set. She would use another shade of blue for the border.

The wood in the fireplace snapped. The smell mingled with that of the kerosene. Tree branches, tossed by a fierce March wind, scraped the side of the house. March had come in like a lion, as usual. She loved night sounds. Everyone slept. Finally. Even Lilly slumbered in the second cradle *Daed* had lugged up from the basement. She smiled at the memory of his gruff willingness to perform these small tasks for the baby. Even Freeman had stopped to tickle her cheek after church. A gesture that released the floodgates. Everyone wanted to have a look at the *Englisch* baby.

The days had taken on a rhythm. Lilly slept better at night. She didn't spit up so much. Iris helped more with the chores. *Mudder* cared for the baby while she made her rounds to a few expectant mothers. Rachel's Micah continued to flourish. The Plank twins were putting on weight. Hannah Yoder would deliver any day now. Visiting with "her" mothers kept Iris busy, and her own mother loved having Lilly to herself. Louella and Abigail bickered over who would hold her and who would feed her. A nice problem to have.

No one talked about what would happen next. She glanced over at the cradle. Lilly had her fist tucked against her mouth, sucking on her fingers in her sleep. She had such a look of peace on her face. Such trust to sleep knowing someone looked after her.

What would she think when that day came and Iris tried to explain she wasn't her real mother? What her real mother had done. How could she break a child's heart like that? Maybe she could simply be her mother. After all, wasn't loving a child ninety percent of parenting? Providing food, clothing, and a roof over her head meant little to a child who wasn't loved.

Love wove together family and home, no matter the circumstances.

A soft knock broke the silence. She stilled her needle and listened. Maybe it was the wind. A more insistent knock. Her fingers went to the hollow of her throat. Her pulse pounded. Jessica and Quinn? So be it. She marched to the door and swung it open.

Mahon stood in the doorway. Rain dripped from the brim of his hat. His coat was wet. Mud caked his boots. "It's raining."

Iris looked beyond him. "So it is."

"It wasn't when I left the house. Spring has sprung, it seems."

"Took you by surprise."

"*Jah.* From the look on your face, you too."

He took her by surprise. His unwavering interest. His solid presence.

"Can I come in?"

She stumbled back. "I was sewing."

"I was hoping you were up reading." He glanced around. "And the others weren't."

"They're not much for reading."

He unbuttoned his soggy coat and slid out his sketch book. He laid it on the table without mentioning it. "I know we can't take a buggy ride, but I thought we could talk."

A buggy ride. Her mouth went dry. She licked her lips. "Would you like some hot cocoa?"

"How's Lilly?"

"Growing. She smiled at me the other night."

He grinned. "Can I see her?"

Iris pointed to the cradle, close but not too close to the fireplace. "She's sleeping."

He trod as lightly as a muscle-bound, hardworking farmer could toward the cradle. "She has Jessica's look."

"I'll make the hot chocolate. You dry off."

Her heart did jumping jacks as she heated the milk in the pan and added cocoa, sugar, and vanilla. She scrounged around in the cabinet until she found the last few marshmallows the girls had left. With hands that shook, she carried the mugs to the front room. Mahon sat in the rocking chair. He had the sketch pad in his lap and his pencil in his hand. He didn't look up.

She set the mugs on the table and went to look over his shoulder. His strokes were quick and sure. The soft line of her cheek. The tiny tuffs of blonde hair. The long lashes. Rosebud lips. The nine-patch quilt. "You've caught that peaceful look on her face. I'll remember that when she's awake and fussing."

He tugged the sheet from the pad and held it out. "For when they take her home."

Writers used the phrase "heavy heart" for a reason. Hers

suddenly weighed twenty pounds. Her throat ached as if she'd acquired a cold in the last few minutes. "You think they will?"

"I think you shouldn't get too attached." He took back the sketch and laid it aside with the pad. "I'm aware such advice comes too late. I know how hard it will be to let her go."

"No one could hold her and not become attached." Iris picked up the sketch and touched Lilly's face with one finger. "Who holds any baby and doesn't become attached?"

"Someone with a very cold heart or someone who is herself a child?"

"Young girls raise babies every day."

"Maybe she was unduly influenced by the father."

"What if they don't come for her? What then?"

"Decisions will have to be made."

By her *daed* and Freeman and the *Gmay*. By a judge. By everyone but Iris. She wanted to pick up Lilly, keep her safe, even if that meant running away with her. That would only make Iris like her parents. Runaways. She would never do that.

No matter how much she wanted to keep this baby safe forever.

Iris laid down the sketch and turned to the fireplace. She warmed her hands over the flames and tried to arrange her face in some semblance of a woman who could accept whatever fate God planned. She heard and then felt Mahon's presence next to her. His hand slid across her palm until his fingers fit between hers. He lifted her hand to his mouth and kissed it. Her muscles trembled as if each one played its own sweet note. "What are you doing?"

He dropped her hand and touched her jaw so she would turn to face him. His eyes were the color of sky and happiness and ocean. She'd never seen the ocean. Until now. The waves lapped, faster and faster. He inclined his head. His lips touched hers for a second, then withdrew. She started to protest, but his lips returned and covered hers. This time she put her hands to his chest in hopes he wouldn't move.

He tasted sweet and perfect.

His was the kiss she'd always wanted. She simply hadn't known it.

It had been worth waiting for all these years. From a friend who could be trusted with her heart.

He stepped back. "You were worth waiting for." His voice was a hoarse whisper. "I hope you know that."

Their timing was in perfect sync.

Lilly chose that moment to screech. They both jumped. Iris smacked her hand to her chest. Her heart beat against her rib-cage in an uneven *thump-thump*. "She's probably hungry." Her voice sounded high and breathless in her ears. "I need to fix her a bottle."

"I'll hold her while you do it. We don't want her waking everyone in the house."

Indeed, they didn't. Her father and mother slept down the hall. Only a few yards from where Iris had received that long-awaited gift of her first kiss. All those nights when she'd stood on the porch watching Aidan drive away, aching, disappointed, uncertain, ago-nizing over why that first kiss never came. God knew. God had a plan for her. For Aidan. For Mahon. At the doorway, Iris turned back to look at him. He held Lilly in his arms. He crinkled his nose, clucked, and then made *chirp-chirp* sounds. Lilly's cries subsided. Mahon eased into the rocking chair and looked up.

The words came easily. "You're worth waiting for too."

His smile widened. "It's *gut* you think so." His Adam's apple bobbed. "And you're right about not being able to hold a *bopli* and not get attached."

"You'll be a *gut daed*." Their gazes held. Lilly began to fuss again. "I better get the bottle."

"No rush. We'll be right here."

Her heart no longer felt so heavy. In fact, she felt so light she looked down to make sure her sneakers still touched the floor.

CHAPTER 12

The weather had turned unexpectedly warm for Salome and Ethan's wedding. Nearly limp with exhaustion, Iris wiggled in the backseat of the buggy and tried to stay awake. A whirlwind two weeks of preparations and now it was over. She and Rachel had served as Salome's witnesses. Mahon and Joseph had been Ethan's. She couldn't help but glance at Mahon. He winked at her, his face crinkled in a smile. That wink. It was all she could think about through the rest of the ceremony and the festivities. No time to talk to him. They both had their duties, making sure his sister and her best friend had a beautiful, special day. Iris smiled at the thought. She couldn't wait to talk to Salome in the next few weeks to get her impressions of the daylong event. After the dust settled. She straightened, then tickled Abigail's neck. The girl was nodding off against Louella's shoulder.

"Stop." Abigail whined and shifted so she leaned against the other side. "Leave me alone."

Iris chuckled and leaned back, her arm around Lilly's basket. Lilly had been passed around and loved on by many of the guests. She should sleep well. Home would feel good for both of them tonight. Maybe tonight Mahon, who'd been busy helping with the preparations, would make another visit.

Another kiss.

Her cheeks and neck warmed. Thinking about kissing Mahon in a buggy full of family wasn't a good idea. She couldn't help it. Between mulling over Lilly's fate—so intertwined with her own—and thinking about the possibility of a future with Mahon, she couldn't think straight.

"We have company."

Daed's gruff voice held surprise. In farmer time, it was late. Past their bedtime. Dusk had long come and gone.

Mudder sighed.

"Who is it?" Iris leaned forward and peered into the dark night. An unfamiliar green truck with Iowa plates sat parked at an odd angle—as if turned off in a rush—in front of the house.

Iris's happiness disappeared into a sudden knowing. She gripped the handle of Lilly's basket with both hands as if it might fly out of the buggy. The joy of seeing her best friend married slipped away, replaced by a sense of impeding anguish that must be faced and then accepted. His face twisted in a deep frown, *Daed* swiveled on the buggy's front seat to look back at her. "I knew it would come to this."

"We don't know what it's come to yet." *Mudder* patted *Daed*'s thigh with her gloved hand. "Let's just see who it is."

Daed pulled in next to the car. "I'll do the talking."

A gray-haired woman in baggy black pants and a short green coat eased from the car, using a cane to pull herself upright. She put one hand on her hip and stretched. "Hello there. I was getting worried you might not come home tonight. I've been sitting out here for hours."

Hours. For something important.

Iris hoisted herself from the buggy and turned to lower the basket.

"Is that her? Is that Jessica's baby?" The woman limped on rubber-soled rain boots toward Iris. An anxious smile bloomed on her face. She had dimpled cheeks and bright-blue eyes behind dark-rimmed glasses. Her hands fluttered. One came to rest on her ample bosom. "It's her, isn't it? The girl at the grocery store—Kathy Myer—said you have Jessica's baby."

His expression all deacon, *Daed* stepped between Iris and the woman. "Who are you?"

"I'm Jessica's grandma. Sherri Turner." The woman's voice trembled. She sniffed and wiped at her nose with a crumpled tissue. "That makes the baby in that basket my first great-grandchild. Could I see her? Please."

Iris stumbled back a step. "How do we know you are who you say you are?"

"Why would I lie?"

"We're sorry you had to wait so long. We've been at a wedding." *Mudder*'s smile encompassed them all. It landed on *Daed* last. "It's getting chilly. Let's go inside. I'll make some coffee. You can tell us your story."

"I'll come in and restart the fire before I tend to the horses." *Daed* tied the reins to the hitching post and nodded at the girls. "Abigail, Louella, go on upstairs and get ready for bed. We'll be up for prayers in a bit."

Eyes wide with interest, the girls went in first, taking their time, not wanting to be left out of whatever excitement was about to happen. *Mudder* shooed them through the door and held it for their guest.

A strange buzzing in her ears, Iris trudged up the steps and into the house where she set Lilly's basket on the front room table and removed her coat. She couldn't think. Sounds reverberated. Time stood still and sped up at the same time. As if that were possible. This was it. The baby who'd come into her life in the middle of a snowstorm would now leave just as abruptly.

Sherri edged toward the basket. "Could I see her?"

"Please sit down." *Mudder* pointed to the rocking chair situated by the fireplace where *Daed* was restarting the fire. "Have you come a long way?"

"From Des Moines. I drove straight through after I heard about the Facebook post."

"Facebook." Iris hung her coat on the hook by the door. Every muscle in her body wanted to grab the basket and run, run far, far away. But then she would be like Jessica and Quinn, who couldn't face what life offered them, and instead, dodged their responsibilities. "You heard about Lilly on Facebook?"

"It would be best if you start at the beginning." *Daed* stoked the fire with the poker, then stood. "The sheriff's office gave us temporary custody of the baby until something permanent could be worked out. We'll have to let them know if family has come for her."

"After Jessica and Quinn took off and I realized they weren't coming back, I started looking for them. I tried all their friends, everyone I could think of. I didn't think they would go far." Her gaze still on the basket, Sherri removed her glasses and blotted tears on her wrinkled cheeks. "Weeks passed and nobody knew anything. Then yesterday I got a call from my great-niece Tanya. She's on social media night and day. She said a friend of a friend had seen a post on Facebook that had been shared so many times it got to a friend of Tanya's. A girl named Kathy Myer from Jamesport had posted a picture of two sketches. She said the kids were wanted by the Daviess County Missouri Sheriff's Office for questioning in a theft at the grocery store where she works. Tanya said they looked just like Jessica and Quinn. She printed it for me."

Sherri delved into her gargantuan, black patent leather pocket-book and produced a ragged manila envelope. It held dozens of photographs. Jessica in a red cheerleading outfit. Jessica eating a slice of watermelon. Jessica blowing out candles on a birthday cake. Jessica in short denim cut-offs with frayed hems and a halter top leaning against the green truck now parked in the Beachy's front yard. Behind the smaller snapshots was a larger one, an eight-by-ten. A photograph of Mahon's sketches.

Iris forced herself to look from the sketch of Jessica to her grandmother. The resemblance was slight. The eyes. The shape of her face. It was hard to say with a woman now in her late sixties and a sixteen-year-old girl.

"Iris."

She started at the sound of her father's voice. She glanced at him. He nodded toward the basket. Swallowing a lump the size of a ten-pound sack of potatoes, Iris stood. She leaned over the basket and slid her hands under the quilt that kept Lilly warm. The baby's eyes opened. After a lazy yawn, she stretched and gave Iris a sleepy stare. With a heart this heavy, how would Iris manage to pick up this tiny baby and hand her over to a great-grandmother who hadn't wanted her?

"Iris."

This time her father's voice held a warning. She turned and moved toward Sherri. Every step seemed to cover too much territory, bringing her closer and closer to a precipice from which she would leap and there would be no return. She gritted her teeth, adjusted the quilt, and held Lilly out.

Tears rolled down Sherri's face. She accepted the bundled baby with no notice, no acknowledgment, of Iris or her pain. "My baby quilt."

Iris tried to follow her train of thought. "Your quilt?"

"I have chores to do," Daed interrupted. "I'll leave you two to talk."

His sharp tone told Iris what his expectations were. She nodded. His gaze softened and he smiled. "Be sure to give your guest something to eat. She's had a long drive."

Iris waited until the front door closed. She turned back to Sherri. "What were you saying about your quilt?"

"My mother gave it to me when Melissa was born." Sherri shook her head, her voice breaking. She used her free hand to shuffle through the photos. "Look. Jessica when she was a newborn."

A photo of a baby wrapped in the same nine-patch crib quilt with purple, pink, and lilac squares. "Your mother made it?"

"No. My grandmother. When she was pregnant with my mother. It's a family heirloom."

Like the one in *Mudder*'s chest down the hallway. A different pattern, but the same tradition of family and love and celebration of new birth. English or Plain. Family traditions created bonds between generations. Lilly belonged to that tradition, just as Iris belonged to hers. She swallowed her pain and cleared her throat. "I'm glad it didn't get lost in all the turmoil. Did you give it to Jessica?"

"I didn't intend for her to keep it. I wanted her to see that when the time was right, she would have a baby and we would do all this the right way. We had an argument. I told her after she finished school and got married and was ready to have a family, I would give it to her. It would be waiting for her." Sherri's voice quivered at the memory. "She looked at me like I was a monster. She snatched it up and ran out of the room before I could stop her."

Iris's shoes were cemented to the floor. She should back away, but she couldn't. If she did, she would never get Lilly back. "Jessica said you wanted to give her baby away. How could you?"

"I watched her get bigger and bigger. She looked more and more like her mother. It broke my heart to think of what the future held for her, for the baby, for me." Sherri tore her gaze from Lilly. "I've been through this before. With Jessica's mother."

"Where is she? Why doesn't she help?"

"She's dead."

"I'm sorry."

"Melissa was a wild thing. I was divorced. A single, working mom. I didn't have the time or the energy to corral her. In high school she went crazy. She got pregnant. I took care of Jessica so Melissa could finish school, make something of herself. Instead, she sank deeper into the life she'd chosen. Then she died of a drug overdose, leaving me with another little girl. Jessica. I raised her. I raised her the best I could."

She bowed her head and closed her eyes as if praying. Maybe she was praying—for forgiveness, for discernment, for her dead daughter and her missing granddaughter, for this new life in her arms. She opened her eyes and stared at Iris. "I didn't think I had the strength to do it again. I'm old and tired, and I have arthritis and bad back trouble. I told Jessica I couldn't do it. I'm too old. I wanted her to put the baby up for adoption. I'd already looked into it. That's why she ran away."

"Then she ended up giving the baby to me." Iris stifled the urge to shout. None of it made sense. Plain people didn't do these things. They grew up, they married, they had children, they raised them, they died. An orderly existence. "How is that different?"

"It was the one single selfless act Jessica has ever performed." Sherri smiled the saddest smile Iris had ever seen. "I've never been so proud. I'm not sure I'll be able to do the same, now that I've held this precious baby in my arms."

"How is it selfless to throw away a baby?"

"No one is throwing away a baby." Her voice grew fierce. "There's a couple in Des Moines who are desperate for a baby. They can't have one of their own. My granddaughter left her baby with you because she realized I was right. She's too immature to take care of a baby. Giving her to you was a selfless act of love. Giving this baby to that couple would also be an act of love."

Iris fought to control her own voice. She breathed. In and out. In and out. Shame assailed her. "You're right. Jessica wanted to do the right thing. So do you."

"Now there's a slight problem."

A slight problem. Hysterical laughter burbled up in Iris's throat. "Only now?"

"Now that I've held her, there's no way I can give her up. She's my flesh and blood. As long as I have breath in my body, I'll care for her. I need to tell Jessica this. I need for her to come home. Together, between the two of us, we can raise this baby."

"What about Quinn?"

"He's another child I'll have to raise, I imagine . . ."

Her voice trailed off. The pain on her face spoke to Iris. It told her a story of love, regret, pain, and uncertainty. While Iris took care of Lilly, this grandmother had suffered the agony of not knowing where her grandchild was. "They'll come home. In her note, Jessica said they would come back here. When they do, we'll send them home to you."

"You're a dear, sweet girl. I can see why Jessica took to you so quickly."

Lilly fussed. Iris gripped her hands behind her back to keep from reaching for her. Sherri laid her on her shoulder and patted her back. The cries grew in volume. *"Hush, hush, little baby, don't you cry,"* Sherri began to sing. *"Momma's gonna buy you a rocking horse . . ."*

The cries turned to screams. Iris's hands flew to her ears. Swallowing tears that couldn't be allowed to fall, she forced them down. Sherri shook her head and tutted. "She wants you."

"She's probably hungry. I'll fix her a bottle." Iris had to get out of the room. If she didn't, she would snatch Lilly back and never let her go. She inched backward. "She'll like you when she gets to know you. She's a friendly baby."

"You're the only mother she's ever known."

It seemed an awful thing to do to a baby. With God's grace, perhaps she wouldn't remember. Abandoned twice. "She'll adjust."

Iris turned and fled to the kitchen.

Her mother sat at the table, sipping her tea. "You and *Daed* abandoned me."

The irony of those words chilled Iris. She caught the sob in her throat before it escaped.

"You did a good thing, child."

Then why did her heart and her throat throb with pain and her eyes burn? She turned her back and picked up a bottle from the counter. She swallowed hard against the lump in her throat. "I feel heartbroken."

"You specialize in selfless acts of love."

Bottle still in her hand, she faced her mother. "You were listening."

"I know what you've done. You let Aidan go because you knew he belonged with someone else. It's what you're made of."

"You knew about that?"

"*Mudders* know everything."

"You took care of Lilly to give her mother time to grow up. You've fed and rocked and burped and diapered her for the first six weeks of her life. You've given her a fighting chance. It's time for Lilly to go home, and it's time for you to get on with your life."

Delivering other people's babies. Holding them when they come into the world and then handing them over to another woman to love? She stared at the bottle in her hand. What she did gave joy to others, which brought joy to her. Was it enough? Should it be enough? "What do you mean?"

"I mean don't keep Mahon waiting any longer. There's a crib quilt in that chest down the hall waiting for you."

Iris didn't bother to ask how *Mudder* knew. *Mudders* knew everything.

Her throat tight with unshed tears, Iris fixed the bottle and returned to the living room where Sherri cooed to her fussy great-grandchild. "It's late, and there are no hotels nearby. Do you want to spend the night? You can have my bed."

"The bed where this baby was born?"

"Yes."

"I couldn't do that to you."

"It's okay. I'm not tired."

She wouldn't sleep, not with her heart in pieces and Lilly no longer hers. It would be a long night.

CHAPTER 13

The half-moon and thousands of stars lit up the inky April
night sky. Iris welcomed their company. Feet bare, she eased
into a rocking chair on the porch. Still, it squeaked, the noise loud
in the stillness. She winced and sat unmoving for a few seconds.
Nothing stirred. Everyone slept, oblivious to the frogs croaking,
the crickets chirping, and the occasional questioning hoot of an
owl. Lilly slept in her crib next to the bed Sherri had taken in Iris's
bedroom. No cries emanated from the room. Surely the fact that
Lilly was sleeping through the night meant the baby felt safe and
secure next to her great-granny. Iris leaned her head back and
closed her eyes. For the first time in weeks, she had no responsibilities heavy on her shoulders like a wool winter cloak. No bottles
to fix. No diapers to change. No need to keep one ear awake while
the rest of her slept. Her duties had ended with an abruptness that
left a void where mothering had been.

Tears pricked her eyes. She swallowed the knot in her throat.
Gott knew best. Always. *Thy will be done. Thy will be done. What
would you have me do now?*

The *clip-clop* of horse hooves in the distance, interspersed
with the clatter of buggy wheels, brought her straight up from

the chair. She sped to the railing and peered into the darkness. Headlights appeared in the distance. Her heart banged. Mahon. It had to be Mahon. He had known somehow that she couldn't sleep. Maybe he couldn't sleep for thinking of her. What a prideful thought. She pried it from her mind and tossed it in a heap with all those prideful thoughts of how she would be the best mother for Lilly.

The buggy drew closer. She couldn't see the driver behind the brilliant lights. She padded down the steps and let her feet sink into the cold grass. Finally, the buggy pulled into the yard. Mahon. It was Mahon. Her fingers entwined themselves in the strings of her *kapp*.

"Iris. Iris, I'm here. It's me, Jessica. I'm back."

Jessica's high voice trembled.

Iris froze.

Jessica had come back for her baby.

Mahon halted the buggy and hopped from the seat. "She came to the door and asked for me. She wanted to come directly here."

"Why did you go to Mahon?" Life began to move forward again. *Gott*'s plan pulled her along with it. With Him. She held out her hand. Jessica took it and jumped down from the buggy. Her T-shirt was stained and her jeans dirty. She smelled of stale cheeseburger and pickle juice. "How did you get to Mahon's?"

"Is that Nana's truck? It is. It's Nana's truck." Jessica wrapped Iris in a quick, fierce hug. "It's her truck. Is she here?"

"Yes, she's here. She was looking for you."

"I was in Dallas with Quinn, but I couldn't do it. I couldn't stand being away from my baby."

"Where's Quinn?" Iris looked over Jessica's shoulder at Mahon. He shrugged, then cocked his head toward the house. Iris nodded. "Let's go inside. You can tell me the whole story."

"Where's my baby?"

"Sleeping. With your grandmother. She got here a few hours ago."

"I had to get my baby back." Jessica's voice broke. "Quinn wouldn't bring me back so I hitchhiked."

The idea of a young girl accepting rides from strangers all the way from Texas to Missouri made Iris's stomach twist. She put her arm around Jessica and led her up the steps to the house. Mahon followed. "I'm so glad you made it safely."

"The truckers were mostly nice. One dropped me off on the highway right by the turnoff to Mahon's house. I walked the rest of the way. Mahon's was closer, and I knew since he's your boyfriend—"

"Let's go inside." Iris held the screen. "Are you hungry? I'll fix you something to eat."

"I just want to hold my baby and tell her how sorry I am. I want to tell Nana how sorry I am."

The tears came in buckets. Iris hugged her again. "You'll scare Lilly and your nana. Dry your tears first, okay?"

Jessica nodded. She hiccupped one more sob, then wiped her face with her sleeve.

"Don't mind me." Mahon sank into the nearest chair and heaved a sigh. "I'll wait here."

Together, Iris and Jessica walked down the hall to the bedroom. Iris held up the kerosene lamp and opened the door. Jessica tiptoed across the room to the cradle. "Baby, my baby," she murmured. "I've missed you, baby."

She scooped up Lilly and wrapped her in her arms, tight against her chest. Iris opened her mouth to protest. The baby had never slept this long uninterrupted. She closed her mouth. Her job had ended. Soon they would say good-bye and go about their business as if they'd never met. As if she'd never mothered this baby as if she were her own.

"You're so beautiful. I'm so sorry. I'm so sorry," Jessica crooned. "I'm here now, baby, I'm here. I'll never leave you again. I promise."

"Jessie, is that you?" Sherri sat up in bed. "Are you really here? Where have you been, girl?"

"Nana, I'm so sorry." Jessica didn't move. "I've missed you so much. Forgive me?"

"I'm just so glad you're safe. I was afraid you were dead." Relief mingled with tears filled Sherri's voice. "Get over here so I can hug your neck."

Sobbing, Jessica rushed to the bed where more crying ensued. Lilly wailed.

"Oh, you poor thing, we woke you." Sherri patted the baby's cheek. "You're okay. Your mommy's here now."

Mommy's here now.

Lilly's wails turned to screams.

Both women looked at Iris. She tightened her grip on the lantern and her emotions. "She's always cranky when she wakes up. She's probably hungry. I'll get her a bottle."

"No, you've done enough. I have to figure out how to do this." Jessica rocked Lilly back and forth, then lifted her to her shoulder and began to pat her back. The wails subsided to a low roar.

"Thank you so much for taking care of my baby." Jessica's voice wobbled. "It was so wrong of me to dump her on you like that. I'm not a bad person. I just got confused for a little bit. I promise I'll take good care of her from now on."

"I believe you." Iris took a deep breath and let it out. Her time with Lilly had ended. "You're her mother. You'll do fine."

"We'll go into the sheriff's office tomorrow." Sherri patted the spot next to her on the bed, and Jessica slid under the blankets next to her. "We'll face the music and make this right, whatever it takes. Me and Jessie together."

They had a long road ahead of them. The legal system was a mystery to Iris. "I'll pray for you, all of you."

She would pray for God's will and God's grace and for Lilly's safe journey through this world. And for Quinn. Babies needed both their moms and their dads.

"Thank you, Iris." Sherri nodded, her wrinkled face streaked with tears. "You're a good girl. You'll be a good mother to your babies."

In God's time.

"We'll send you pictures," Jessica added. "Lots of pictures. You'll be like an aunt. She can come visit and learn about farm animals. You can teach her to make baby quilts."

Aenti Iris.

"I would like that."

Iris backed out of the room and shut the door. She let her hands drop and stood there, in the middle of the hall, trying to identify the feelings that tumbled around in her brain.

Lilly had her mother. Her true mother. And her nana.

Every baby should have a nana to tuck her in for an afternoon nap, tell her stories, teach her songs, and hear her prayers.

The ache in Iris's throat was the preamble to acceptance and peace. A kind of contentment that all was as it should be. She whirled and trotted to the living room. Mahon rose from the chair. He held out his arms. She walked into them and leaned her head against his chest. His heart beat in a comforting *thump-thump*. His hands rubbed her back in a soothing circular pattern. "Who is Nana?"

"Jessica's *groossmammi*. She raised her. She is willing to help raise Lilly too."

"Then *Gott*'s will be done."

Iris snuggled closer. "That's what I keep telling myself, but sometimes it's impossible to know, isn't it?"

"Come outside with me." He stepped back, grabbed her hand, and tugged her toward the door. "I want to show you something."

Outside, she scurried to keep up as he tromped down the steps and strode across the yard. He stopped at the corral fence. "Have a seat." He patted the railing, then put both hands on her waist and lifted her so she sat on the fence. "Hang on."

Her mind still grappling with the feeling of his hands on her hips, she managed to do as she was told.

He settled next to her and inhaled a deep breath, then exhaled in a noisy sigh. "It's a beautiful night."

"It is."

"*Mudder* and *bopli* are together again."

"As they should be."

"Yet you have regrets."

"Not exactly regrets. It's been a strange time in my life, but a special time. An uncertain time." She struggled for words that could describe the bittersweet feelings that engulfed her. "I'm happy I had this time with Lilly. I'll always love her, but I know this is what's best for her."

"There is something you don't have to be uncertain about."

"What's that?"

His big hand covered hers on the fence railing. His fingers tightened. "Me."

She felt his smile as much as saw it in the moonlight. She felt it in the warmth of that single syllable. "You?"

"Do you ever look at the stars?"

375

"Sometimes, but mostly the moon."

"The light of the moon is only a reflection of the sun's light. It has no light of its own. I like the stars better. They make their own light. And there are so many. All made by *Gott*. I don't feel alone when I look at them."

She let her gaze follow his finger pointing at the sky. "They're beautiful."

His words penetrated. In his huge, overflowing family, he'd been lonely. She inched closer to him. "You don't have to sketch pictures of me anymore. I'm right here."

"It's still hard for me to believe. I waited a long time." His voice was low, barely a hoarse whisper. He took her hand and pointed her finger toward the sky. "Do you see the Little Dipper? At the tip of the handle is the North Star. Polaris. Some people think it is the brightest star, but it's not. Sirius is the brightest star."

"Why do the stars interest you so much?" She leaned against his shoulder and stared at the Milky Way, trying to see what he saw. "Your feet are on the ground, but your head is in the sky."

"*Gott* made the heavens and the earth. I'm awestruck by His power." Mahon's hand brushed against her cheek. He leaned in, and his warm breath touched her face. He smelled of peppermint. "He made man and then He made woman to keep man company."

The pounding of her heart increased. The cool night air turned warm as if spring had turned to summer. "I reckon He had a *gut* plan."

"I reckon He's happy you think so." Mahon chuckled, a husky, sweet sound. The air warmed even more. Summer in the midst of spring. "Like He needed our approval."

"*Nee*, I just meant life would be sad and empty if we didn't have that one person we were meant to share it with."

"You thought that person was Aidan."

"But I was wrong." She sought Mahon's hand and held it tight. "We hear over and over in sermons from the time we're old enough to understand that *Gott* has a plan. That we can't fathom it. We can only trust and obey. Everything that has happened to me over the last few years tells me the truth of the matter. *Gott* had a plan for me. Not the one I asked for. The one He has, the one that is best for me. And it is *gut*."

"This plan. It includes me?"

"Jah."

"*Gut*." He slid from the fence and faced her. "I *lieb* you. I have always known that we were meant to be together. You haven't known as long, so I won't rush you, but I want you to know I plan to marry you someday soon."

"That's *gut*." Iris hopped down and stepped into his space. "That's *gut* because someday I plan to marry you right back."

He laughed as he bent down. His lips sought hers. The kiss, long and sweet and sure, sealed the promise. She reveled in the taste and feel of his mouth, the way his huge, callused hands cupped her face with a gentle touch.

She reached up and tugged his glasses from his face. His eyelids fluttered open. He ducked his head. "Why'd you do that?"

"I like seeing your eyes. Without the glasses, I can see all the way to your heart."

He shrugged, his expression pensive. "They don't work well. I can't see a thing without the glasses."

She gently returned them to their place on his nose. "That's okay. I don't want other people to see what I see." She leaned into him, inhaling his scent of man, and smiled. "*Mudder* has a crib quilt her *mudder* gave to her. It's been passed down for generations. One day it'll be mine."

Mahon's arms tightened around Iris. His Adam's apple bobbed. He cleared his throat. "And one day you'll give it to our daughter."

Together, they turned and stared at the sky, endless in its beauty and possibilities. Together, they would forge a life that would fulfill her dream of being a wife and a mother. She would have babies of her own to love. Her dream and God's plan, bright as the evening stars, were one and the same.

DISCUSSION QUESTIONS

1. Most Amish don't believe in having their photos taken. Their objection is based in scripture regarding "graven images." They also believe it's a form of idolatry that grows from vanity. This extends to Mahon's hand-drawn portraits of Iris. In the mainstream world, we've become handy with phone "selfies" and most people think nothing of regular posting of these photos on social media. Do you see any harm in this easy, instant access to photos and their online use? Why or why not? Does it have an impact on our sense of who we are and how "important" we are in the eyes of others? What impact do you think it has on children growing up in a "selfie" world?

2. Iris can't understand how Jessica can leave her newborn baby with a stranger. She says an Amish mother would never abandon or give up a baby, considered a gift from God under any circumstance. Jessica's grandma has found a couple who cannot have a baby who want to adopt her great-grandchild. They could provide a better home for the baby. Who do you think is right? Why? Is there room for both views in this complicated world we live in?

3. Cyrus is uncomfortable that Iris has brought a young unwed couple and their baby into his home. He's concerned for the example they set for his young children who live in the household. Do you believe children should be exposed to circumstances in which others have not lived up to God's commands or should they be taught these lessons in less obvious ways? Have you ever been influenced to do something you know is wrong because you spent time with friends who aren't Christians? What did you learn from that experience?

4. Iris spent three years courting with Aidan and waiting for him to propose to her. She prayed for God's plan to be revealed to her. In the meantime, Mahon was waiting for her to notice his feelings for her. Have you ever been certain you know God's plan for you, only to discover you were on the wrong path all along? How did you deal with it? What are some ways we can try to discern God's plan for us?

5. Do you think Jessica and her grandmother are making the right choice when they decide to keep Lilly?

ACKNOWLEDGMENTS

I am thankful for so many blessings that it's hard to order my thoughts when it comes to acknowledgments. My thanks to God for richly rewarding me with these opportunities to write these stories. My thanks to HarperCollins Christian Publishing for allowing me to be a part of this novella collection. I'm so thankful for every HCCP staff member who had a hand in bringing this particular story to fruition, but especially editors Becky Monds and Jodi Hughes. Their attention to detail and love of a good story inspire me. I couldn't keep writing if it weren't for my husband Tim's support and love. He cooks, buys groceries, does laundry, takes out the trash, and cleans the cat box. That is true love. I'm thankful for readers who spend their hard-earned funds to buy books. I pray that this story blesses each one of you. I look forward to sharing many more stories with you in the future. God bless!

Read more in these collections from our beloved authors!

AVAILABLE JUNE 2018

AVAILABLE JULY 2018

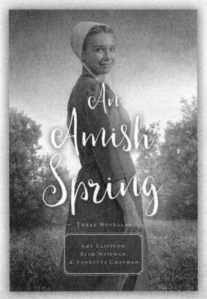

AVAILABLE IN PRINT AND E-BOOK

ABOUT THE AUTHORS

AMY CLIPSTON

Amy Clipston is the award-winning and bestselling author of the Amish Heirloom series and the Kauffman Amish Bakery series. She has sold more than one million books. Her novels have hit multiple bestseller lists including CBD, CBA, and ECPA. Amy holds a degree in communications from Virginia Wesleyan College and works full-time for the City of Charlotte, NC. Amy lives in North Carolina with her husband, mom, two sons, and three spoiled-rotten cats.

Visit her online at amyclipston.com
Facebook: AmyClipstonBooks
Twitter: @AmyClipston
Instagram: amy_clipston

BETH WISEMAN

Beth Wiseman is the award-winning and bestselling author of the Daughters of the Promise, Land of Canaan, and Amish Secrets series. While she is best known for her Amish novels, Beth has also written contemporary novels including *Need You Now*, *The House That Love Built*, and *The Promise*.

KATHLEEN FULLER

Kathleen Fuller is the author of several bestselling novels, including *A Man of His Word* and *Treasuring Emma*, as well as a middle-grade Amish series, the Mysteries of Middlefield.

Visit her online at www.kathleenfuller.com
Twitter: @TheKatJam
Facebook: Kathleen Fuller

KELLY IRVIN

Kelly Irvin is the author of several Amish series including the Bliss Creek Amish series, the New Hope Amish series, and the Amish of Bee County series. She has also penned two romantic suspense novels, *A Deadly Wilderness* and *No Child of Mine*. The Kansas native is a graduate of the University of Kansas School of Journalism. She has been writing nonfiction professionally for more than thirty years, including ten years as a newspaper reporter, mostly in Texas-Mexico border towns. A retired public relations professional, Kelly has been married to photographer Tim Irvin for twenty-nine years. They have two children, two grandchildren, and two cats. In her spare time, she likes to write short stories and read books by her favorite authors.